S A N T I A G O   R A G

FOR HONNAH
JM Gowan
may 2015

Published by
Access Press
80 Orchard St.
Cambridge, Massachusetts
02140

Library of Congress Cataloging-in-Publication Data:

Gowan, Al, 1934-
Santiago rag / Al Gowan. -1st ed.
1. Adventure- History- Cuba- Fiction
2. Military- America- Cuba- Fiction

ISBN 0-9663894-0-9
1.Title

Design and Photographs by the Author
Manufactured in the United States of America

June 1998

10 9 8 7 6 5 4 3 2 1

II

PROLOGUE

A RAG is a worthless piece of cloth. To rag someone is to scold or to ridicule. Then there is the musical form of ragtime, the music so popular in 1898.

Santiago Rag began with my grandfather's sword and with a puzzling word I first encountered in Santiago de Cuba.

Grandfather claimed the saber was a gift from the nephew of Robert E. Lee whom he served under in the Spanish-American War. As a boy of ten, I didn't much believe him, for the tinted Army photograph with his hat brim turned up made him look more like a Boy Scout than a real soldier. After all, World War II was on and I was more impressed with John Wayne as he crawled through the ground fog at Bataan to lob a grenade at the Japanese.

But in 1989 I finally stood on San Juan Hill. The plaques under the bronze sculpture of a resolute *Yanqui* had been torn off. Yet one statue of a somewhat ragged soldier had letters anchored in granite praising the bravery of the Cuban *Mambi*. That mysterious word triggered my imagination and I began to read everything I could find on what the Cubans call *La Guerra Hispano-Cubano-Norte Americano,* an event many Americans still trivialize as "that splendid little war."

The characters, places and events in this work of fiction are based on the written accounts of the participants themselves. But since I chose art, not scholarship, to tell my story, it has been necessary to invent some characters and a few events.

As I have since learned, Grandfather volunteered a month after the fighting in Cuba was over. But he did serve in the occupation of Havana with the Missouri Sixth Infantry, under Fitzhugh Lee, the nephew of Robert E. Lee.

Somewhere between my grandfather's sword and that provocative word first encountered on San Juan Hill lies the truth. That is where I have tried to place my story.

Al Gowan
Cambridge, Massachusetts
1998

Fictional characters:

Gabriel Scriven, *Roosevelt's trumpeter*
Marcus Hammer, *Gabriel's antagonist*
Touch-the-Cloud, *son of a Sioux Chief*
Snake, *a cowboy trooper*
Aura de Bretteville, *the girl back home*
Thelma Scriven, *Gabriel's mother*
Judge Marcus Hammer, Sr.
Colonel Raúl García, *of the Cuban
     Insurrectionsts*
Sergeant Eli Biddle, *U.S. Tenth Cavalry*
Prayerful Jones, *preacher-soldier*

Historical characters:

Theodore Roosevelt
Colonel Leonard Wood
General "Fightin' Joe" Wheeler,
     Commander of the U.S. Cavalry
Lieutenant Tom Hall, *Rough Rider Adjutant*
Clara Barton, *Founder, American Red Cross*
Edith Roosevelt, *wife of Theodore*
Lieutenant John J. Pershing,
     U.S. Tenth Cavalry

Correspondents:

Richard Harding Davis
Sylvester Scovel
Stephen Crane
Edward Marshall
Winston Churchill
Publisher William Randolph Hearst

IV

Rough Riders:

Captain Allyn Capron, Jr.
Lieutenant Richard Day
Captain Bucky O'Neill
Captain Maximillian Luna
Sergeant Hamilton Fish
Sergeant William Tiffany
Private Tom Isbell, *Pawnee scout*
Lieutenant James Church, *Surgeon*

Various General Officers:

Major General William Rufus Shafter,
  Commanding General, U.S. Fifth Corps
Major General Calixto García Iníguez,
  Commanding General of Cuban
  Insurrectionists, Oriente Province
General Jesús Rabí, *Cuban Insurrectionist*
Major General José Toral, *Commanding*
  General, Spanish Peninsular Army
General Joaquín Vara del Rey,
  Spanish Peninsular Army
Generals Hawkins, Kent, Lawton, Miles,
  Sumner, and Young, *U.S. Army*

Admiral William Sampson, *U.S. Navy*
Admiral Winfield Scott Schley, *U.S. Navy*

V

In memory of James Weinstein

With special thanks to:

Susan Hunziker
Gladys Gowan
Mary Orcutt
Ann Collette
Patricia Buddenhagen
Sarah Fresco
Jerry Howard
John Swenson
Sebastian Stuart
César Leál Jimínez
Miguel Uría
José A. Adan
Jórge Oramas
Larry Daley
Jeff Gowan
Ron Ziel
Johanna Branson
Thomas E. McNary
Herb Fuller
Steve Rose
Stephen Peckich
Jan Kubasiewicz
Dori Miller
Helen Hunt
Morton Baker
Eugene Gowan

SANTIAGO RAG

Al Gowan

PART I *A Gathering Storm*

June 30, 1897
Fort Chambers, South Dakota

THE RISING SUN sun chewed at the pale prairie as the steam engine chuffed past. Gabriel Scriven had always taken joy in the daily train— had thrilled at the music of its whistle. But this morning, sitting beside the sheriff in his buckboard, Gabriel stared down at his torn trousers. From the cab, the engineer tipped his cap as the engine hissed along the track that ran down the main street of Fort Chambers, shooting sparks into the air. He pulled six cars of freight and one of sleepy strangers toward the brightening east, where Gabriel believed everything was happening. But this morning, the train had no reason to stop. When the engineer blew a brief blast of the steam whistle, Gabriel had to fight an involuntary sob. He didn't want to cry in front of the lawman that had so often been a guest at his mother's table.

The caboose wound behind a bluff, Sheriff Markum snapped the reins, and they soon pulled up in front of the low, brick building that served as the sheriff's office and jail. Markum stepped down, tied the reins to the hitching post and waited. Gabriel didn't want to go in. His face felt numb and his limbs ached. He was still trying to wake up from the nightmare that had started the night before. Almost blindly, he stepped down into the street.

Once inside the jail, Markum hesitated. "Gabriel," he said, chewing his jaw, "I don't like this any more than you do. But when you hurt the Judge's boy, you made us both plenty of trouble. Judge insists I lock you up.

But maybe in a few days, we can get you out."

"Yessir," Gabriel murmured. When he moved his lips he felt the blood caked in his nostrils.

Then Markum led him past the main cell where three drunks lay like sour wood, and unlocked the last cell. Beside the double bunk a tall Indian straightened his bow tie with the help of a tin mirror. Markum swung the cell door open. Gabriel stepped in and waited for the clang behind him. But the sheriff closed it gently.

For Gabriel Scriven, whose mother had named him after the archangel, the lock rang like an anvil.

He sobbed once as he sank onto the wooden slats of the bunk. Ashamed, he glanced at the Indian, whose silk-backed vest caught the one ray of sunlight that wedged through the barred window. If the Indian heard him, he made no sign.

Gabriel closed his eyes, hoping he would awake in his feather bed in the rooms he and Thelma Scriven had above the school house. But now his nose was beginning to throb and the stale air in the jail was sawed by drunken snoring.

When he finally opened his eyes, Gabriel stared at his hands. It was hard to believe that Aura de Bretteville had held them just hours before, reading the patterns of white flecks beneath his fingernails. Had she really turned her serious gray eyes up to him and declared he would one day be a hero?

His finger nails were packed with Marcus B. Hammer's blood.

It had all started last night at the Grange Hall. The happiest event in Fort Chambers, the annual Commencement Dance, had started out fine, even if Aura de Bretteville had turned him down as her escort. She preferred to go unaccompanied, she'd explained. But Marcus B. Hammer, the Judge's son, had been quick to ask for the first dance and nobody afterward had the nerve to cut in. Marcus, a broad-shouldered bully whose boyish smile could quickly turn to a sneer, had them all buffaloed. Gabriel decided to make Aura jealous by dancing with every girl he could and that was not difficult, for he was a good dancer. As President of the Latin Colloquium, Glee Club member, and coronet player in the band, Gabriel was popular. He had learned to compensate for his tea-colored. He had even invented a few dance steps to the new ragtime music.

Marcus Hammer was quick despite his size. But on the dance floor, he was clumsy and willful. He kept stepping on Aura's toes. At first, she was patient, and she tried to guide his big frame along with hers.

As Gabriel swept one partner after another past the struggling couple, he burned as he saw Marcus holding Aura as if Doctor de Bretteville's daughter was his rightful property. Gabriel caught Aura watching as he spun a lively Swedish girl across the waxed floor.

And then the band struck up "There'll Be A Hot Time in the Old Town Tonight."

Marcus was baffled and nothing Aura could do could move him. Gabriel spun his partner away and bowed. He quickly stepped to Aura's side. "May I have this dance?"

Marcus's smile faded. "No," he blurted. Aura rolled her eyes but made no move, and Gabriel again bowed. "Later then," he said, meeting Marcus's stare.

Some moments later, as Gabriel watched the couple, he heard Aura shriek. He dashed to her, and before Marcus could protest, cupped his fingers against the small of her back. He felt Aura lean toward him and he deftly danced her away.

Marcus B. Hammer, scion of Fort Chambers, stood abandoned in the middle of the floor.

He swore under his breath. That teacher's boy had no business dancing with any white girl, much less his girl. And what made this unbearable to Marcus was that this was his last night with Aura. The next morning, as she very well knew, he would be on the train for New York. The Columbia football squad wanted him to report early.

Marcus watched with rising fury as Gabriel flung his heels and danced Aura to the far side of the floor. And she matched his steps and smiled with pleasure! With alarm, he saw Scriven lead Aura through the open doors onto the porch.

He barged through the dancers, then waited as long as he could before leaping through the door to see that they were holding hands! There was no decision, no thought. Marcus lunged toward them and tore Aura's hand away. He called Scriven everything he could think of, ending with what everybody in Fort Chambers whispered, but nobody until now had the nerve to say. "You're nothin' but a *Nigger!*"

To Gabriel Scriven, Marcus' words was a new whip on old wounds. Torn between Aura's shock and trying to defend himself, he was speechless. Then he drew himself up. "And you, Marcus Hammer, are a rude lummox."

Marcus spat on his fists.

Gabriel was able to duck the first swing. Then, as he saw his mother Thelma rushing toward them, lightning struck his face. Through a darkening haze, he heard her far-away voice. ""Stop this at once," she shrieked.

But Marcus's blow had unleashed a rage in Gabriel that could not be stopped. A cry he did not recognize rose in his throat as he flung himself at Marcus with such force that they both fell. As Thelma admonished them and school mates shouted encouragement, Marcus pummeled Gabriel's face and ribs with short, vicious punches. Gabriel was wiry, but he was no match for the larger boy's strength. He was about to pass out, when he saw, an inch from his destroyed nose, Marcus B. Hammer's ear.

Marcus screamed and jumped up. Blood shot between his fingers as he clasped the place where his ear lobe had been. "See, everybody he's a damned savage!"

Gabriel spat out the bloody ear. Then he saw Aura de Bretteville's eyes as she backed away. His classmates were struck dumb.

Marcus pointed at him and sneered. "You can't hide it anymore. Everyone knows now!"

Gabriel turned and leaped off the porch. He hit the ground hard, scrambled to his feet and ran. He thought his lungs would burst as he sucked moths into his mouth, felt branches tear at his arms and legs. Finally, in a thicket of young cottonwoods, he fell to the ground and listened for the sound of pursuit. But it was as if they had forgotten him. There was nothing he could hear but the rasp of crickets.

It was then that Gabriel realized he had done an unmanly thing. He spat again and again but the taste of Marcus's blood was rank and accusing. He should have stayed and fought, even if Marcus B. Hammer killed him.

Then, from a distance that seemed a world away, Gabriel heard the band striking up Strauss. His classmates were waltzing as though nothing had happened!

Gabriel found a thick branch and after several tries, broke it over his knee. He hoped Marcus would follow him, but as the music continued he began to sob. A Nigger? He lay there a long time, trying to think. His mother Thelma had shown him the scholarship award letter from Oberlin. She had urged him to get away from Fort Chambers and the taunting he had always endured. Her eyes had shown brightly as she handed him money saved for his train trip. She was proud that Marcus Hammer would not be the only Fort Chambers boy going East to college.

Finally, Gabriel walked out of the trees and towards the river. Once he heard its lapping current, he followed the bend, avoiding the Grange Hall, until he made his way to the three-story school building.

He noticed a buckboard hitched outside. And he saw light in the two rooms they occupied on the third floor.

Inside, Thelma waited at the kitchen table with Sheriff Markum. When she saw her son she embraced him. They held each other and when she let him go Gabriel saw that the sheriff had already stepped outside.

Thelma heated water and cleaned Gabriel's face. She had the same determined look she wore on examination day. When she was finished, she smoothed her dress. "What Marcus called you was both mean and dead wrong," she said.

Gabriel searched his mother's face as though seeing it for the first time. Her skin was fair, her hair black and curly. He had always believed she could never lie to him, but now he was not so sure.

Thelma Scriven pressed his hands to her cheek, fighting back her tears. Then she put on her brave face again and walked to the mantle. She held the gold framed daguerreotype of Gabriel's father, the long dead cavalry officer.

"There is something I must tell you, Gabriel." Her voice was unsteady now. She stared again at the photograph and smiled. "Yes. His name was indeed Paul Scriven and he died, as I told you many times. But Paul was not my husband. He was my brother."

Gabriel felt sick.

Thelma's face was pale and he could see that she had been waiting a long time to tell him this. "Your father, your real father, was a soldier. Paul was, in fact, his commanding officer. He was a good man, and he didn't intend for—well, not this way anyway. "

Thelma seemed suddenly like a stranger. He wanted to run again, out of this room, out of this town. But he could not. Too much had happened in a few hours.

She smiled, then said. "His name was Samuel."

He needed details like he needed breath. His voice was, he knew, hard and disbelieving. "Samuel what?"

"Scriven. Samuel Scriven."

Before he could protest, she stopped him. "You see, Samuel was a buffalo soldier. He never liked the name he'd been given from the days when his father was a slave. As he lay dying, he asked Paul if he could borrow his name—I think to give you one." She waited, and when she felt his hands tighten on her own, she continued. "You see, Paul's troop was sent to Wyoming, before I knew I was, well, with child—carrying you, Gabriel. But Samuel must have guessed it might be so. And Paul must have told him. He recorded your father's death in his regimental report as Samuel Scriven."

Gabriel was trying to call up an image, any likeness of his father. Thelma must have known he was struggling for she finally said, "He was not very dark and some thought he had Indian blood. I never told you because I wanted you to have a normal life. That's the way Samuel would have wanted it. Out here there are many that are of mixed blood. Indian and Negro mixed, white and Indian, and we are all God's creatures. None better than the next. I've always taught you that, son."

She didn't call him 'son' often, and Gabriel was strangely moved by it now. But he still felt hurt and betrayed by the woman who had been mother, father, and teacher. He could have handled the truth long before now and he resented not being told.

A soldier began to take shape in Gabriel's mind. The uniform was easy, for he had seen the Tenth Cavalry ride through Fort Chambers. And it was true; some of the men could have been white, tanned as they were from months under the prairie sun. Now he saw features under the wide brim of a Stetson. The trooper sat his saddle easily, lightly holding the reins. His hand was the color of strong tea.

Gabriel stared at Thelma with her creamy skin and tried to imagine the mix of blood that had made him whatever he was now.

Well, there it was. Marcus Hammer had been mostly right.

"The Sheriff has to lock you up, Gabriel," Thelma said. "For your own protection. A lot of people have turned mean over this." She handed him his scholarship letter. "You can start anew at the Conservatory."

Now, sitting on his jail bunk, Gabriel Scriven wished he were dead. Even his name was not really his own. He had been named after the archangel, but he was caged. Aura would never speak to him again. He felt like everyone in Fort Chambers had abandoned him.

*

That same afternoon
The lawn of the White House
Washington, D.C.

Standing on the manicured grass, President William McKinley patted his ample stomach. He beamed over the picnic celebrating his fifth month in office. Having just completed all of his appointments, he had had invited his cabinet, their wives, and guests. Earlier in the day it had threatened to rain, but now the clouds were gone and he was optimistic. This was a hale, well-met company. He had chosen well.

But at this moment, all eyes, including the President's, were fixed on the finish of a spirited croquet match. Assistant Secretary of the Navy Theodore Roosevelt had just shot. He polished his prince nez while Captain Leonard Wood, McKinley's personal physician, took a turn. In the center of the lawn, the tanned Captain gripped the handle of his croquet mallet. He tapped his ball and it rolled and just touched Roosevelt's. Then, setting his riding boot on his own ball, Wood bent in concentration. A bright medal dangled from a ribbon at his throat and caught the sun. The Captain paused, unbuttoned his breast pocket and tucked the medal inside.

When his mallet struck, Captain Wood's blow sent Roosevelt's ball ten feet to one side, where it stopped at an impossible angle.

The company was silent. Only the chirping of sparrows broke the tension. Captain Leonard Wood planted his feet again. With one sharp knock, he fired his ball through the final set of hoops where it glanced off a multi-striped stake. Everyone applauded. Even Roosevelt flashed a toothy grin.

"Bravo," shouted the portly President McKinley. "A precise operation, Leonard." The assembled men and their wives tittered at the President's pun, for Doctor Leonard Wood was more than McKinley's physicianhe had been Assistant Surgeon General for two years. The medal the Captain had pocketed so nonchalantly was his recently awarded Medal of Honor. Everyone, including Theodore Roosevelt, knew Wood had been given it for capturing Geronimo and his band of Apaches in the Sierra Madre Mountains.

Roosevelt eagerly pumped Wood's hand.

When a servant offered them whiskeyed punch from a silver tray, both men deferred. Instead, each ladled the other a tumbler of lemonade from a large cut-glass bowl in which rose petals floated. They also refused cigars, while the other men, including the President, cut and lit their own.

Roosevelt was a robust thirty-nine years old. As he talked to Wood, he stood on the balls of his feet, bringing himself to the Captain's height. Lifting his chin, he fired his words sharply in a high, ebullient voice. "I understand, Captain Wood, that you are a Harvard man."

"I am indeed, Mr. Secretary."

"It is strange that we've never before met." Then Roosevelt gave a smile that seemed full of too many teeth. "But I believe I graduated a few years before you, sir."

Captain Wood nodded. "I understand, Mr. Secretary, that you have a cattle ranch in the Dakota Territories."

Roosevelt laughed and put his hand on Wood's arm. "Let's walk, shall we? I do miss the strenuous life. And please, call me Theodore."

Wood gave a discreet smile. "Only if will call me Leonard."

Theodore clapped Wood on the back. "Done."

When they had reached the White House fence and were turning to go back, Roosevelt paused. "And do you believe, Leonard," he asked softly, "that there will be a war with Spain?"

Wood nodded gravely. "At the Inauguration, I heard President Cleveland warn President McKinley of it "

Roosevelt seemed to be all ears. "And?"

"Cleveland said he regretted passing McKinley a war with Spain," Wood, said. "a certainty within two years, he avowed."

Theodore Roosevelt grunted. "You've no doubt been following the papers. General Valeriano Weyler has rounded up thousands of Cubans and put them into concentration camps. And he's sliced Cuba into three sections with his confounded deforesting. Can you imagine? Two swatches of devastation across the island, each a half mile wide—every tree cut, not a bush in sight. And strung with barbed wire. Why, he has turned the island into an armed camp."

"A military strategy," Wood said. "Weyler is trying to contain Calixto García's rebels in Oriente and General Gómez's insurrectionists in Camagüey. If he can isolate García from Gomez, they will be unable to make a combined assault on Havana."

"But," Roosevelt complained, "The Cubans cannot win alone. No matter how many munitions we send. They lack fighting ability. We've got to go in and do it ourselves."

"No," Colonel Wood said, "According to Secretary Alger, we'll put a reconnaissance force of ten thousand ashore for a couple of days—long enough to supply García so that they can do the actual fighting. Then we are to withdraw."

Roosevelt struck his palm with his fist. "No, by God. We shall fight the Spaniard and drive him from Cuban soil. And I shall be the first to volunteer!"

Captain Wood looked surprised. "I didn't know you were a soldier."

Roosevelt raised his heels. "I have served briefly in the National Guard. And furthermore, as New York Commissioner of Police, I've led men against characters every bit as unsavory as Valeriano Weyler." He turned and stared down the lawn toward the White House. "I've been thinking of raising a regiment of volunteers."

Captain Wood thought for a moment. "Perhaps you'd like to join me for my morning run. Five miles every day along the Potomac."

Roosevelt's hand clasped the Captain's shoulder. "Why, thank you, yes. I romp a bit myself."

For the rest of the afternoon, the two men barely acknowledged their wives, much less the President they had both sworn to serve.

Compared to Roosevelt's, Wood's revelations were modest. The Doctor's hawk-like eyes, set under a heavy brow, seemed to emphasize each word, indeed every silence. Roosevelt decided Wood's large head indicated intellect, however taciturn the man's speech. After all, Wood had already won his country's highest honor. This West Pointer with poker posture and sincere countenance was very different from himself. Reticence could be a virtue,

Roosevelt realized. It was a quality he himself lacked. And Wood's heroism he both admired and envied. But this stoic soldier was sure to be ground to bits in the maw of Washington politics. Without a friend and advisor like himself, that is.

For his part, Captain Leonard Wood was relieved to find his distinguished opponent had taken his drubbing with good humor. He had heard of the boisterous Roosevelt and envied his easy intercourse with the guests. During their long runs together, Wood could imagine Roosevelt pacing him, forcing him to run harder. But, of course, a yard or so behind.

Despite their immediate attraction to each other, neither Roosevelt nor Wood revealed their real ambitions that afternoon. Roosevelt, already impatient with the incompetence he saw in Washington, had quietly resolved to one day run for President. And Captain Wood, whose physician father insisted he join his practice on Cape Cod had to prove the military, was a worthy career. Toward this end, he dreamed of becoming Commanding General of the entire Army.

CHAPTER 2

The new prisoner's chest rose and fell in sleep. Standing over the bunk, the son of Touch-the-Cloud guessed him to be about his own age—eighteen or so. He examined the young man's shoes. His feet were big for someone of normal height. Though caked with mud, the shoes were of soft, expensive leather. Like first-worn moccasins, imprints of his toes had rubbed shiny ovals in the nap of the leather.

The young man's hair was kinky, and something about the wide nostrils and the full lips hinted at Negro blood. He had been in a fight, with perhaps the wrong person, and the Indian guessed that would explain why the sheriff had acted so strangely.

Church bells broke the silence and the Indian straightened. He took out his pocket watch, shook it, then held it to his ear. Despite the cracked crystal, it still ticked. He set the minute hand, wound it not quite tight, and then tucked the watch away. Breakfast was late and his stomach growled. After ten days in jail, he was ashamed that he had been conditioned to punctual feeding like an animal. He hoisted himself onto the upper bunk, for he knew the deputy would not bring his food unless he was flat on his back. The Indian opened a leather pouch.

He took out what looked like a very small book, opened the hinged cover and stared. It was a good thing the deputy had not broken this or he would be dead by now. The face in the photo stared back at him.

When he heard the street door open, he slipped the daguerreotype back in the pouch. He leaned over the edge of the bunk and saw that his cell-mate's copper colored eyes were open. "Breakfast," he coaxed, but the boy's eyes shut again.

As the sheriff watched, his nervous deputy set a pan of biscuits on the floor. Then, glancing up at the Indian, he sloshed steaming coffee into two tin cups. Some of it missed and ran along the stone like a black river.

Sheriff Markum tapped Gabriel's shoes with his knuckle. "Wake up, son. You've got visitors."

This confirmed the Indian's guess. This was no ordinary prisoner.

*

In the Sheriff's office, Thelma Scriven looked small and somehow older. Gabriel saw, with a sinking heart, that she had brought Doctor de Bretteville, and he avoided the Doctor's eyes as he probed the throbbing lump of Gabriel's nose, then began to clean it with cotton dipped in alcohol.

Thelma bit her lip. She glanced through the window to where Markum waited, smoking with his deputy.

Gabriel thought of her as mother, but she had always wanted him to call her Thelma. The citizens of Fort Chambers must have passed this off as the progressive method of their eccentric but most effective schoolteacher. Now Gabriel realized she had long been uneasy with her lie.

Doctor de Bretteville finished and closed his bag. "Pedigree," he said, "is not everything."

Gabriel Scriven felt his face burn.

Doctor de Bretteville stared at him and said, "Remember, Marcus will soon be gone."

The Doctor knew he had been Gabriel's champion up to now. He had written a letter of good character for the music scholarship. To be truthful, the Doctor was relieved. Last night's fight had been a convenient catharsis. He had watched the growing closeness between this talented boy and his willful daughter with growing uneasiness. Of course, he was not prejudiced. Why, he'd been a staunch Abolitionist. But the thought of *café au lait* grandchildren was unsettling.

Doctor de Bretteville knew that Marcus B. Hammer would not be going to Columbia without Judge Hammer's intervention. As an alumnus of the Columbia Law School, the Judge had applied considerable pressure. Of course, young Marcus had a disarming manner, but he depended on that and so had never had to truly test his mettle. Had it not been for their need for a bulky footballer, even the Judge would have failed to get Marcus into Columbia.

*

When Gabriel returned to his cell, the Indian was sitting cross-legged on his bunk. He pushed the plate of biscuits across and, as Gabriel ate, the Indian began to speak. His words had long pauses between them and he nodded after he had spoken; though remembering the contents of a dream.

"I floated down from Pine Ridge in a skiff," he said. "I was tired and had a little whiskey. There was a barn near the riverbank and I went to sleep. I didn't know a poster had been issued for horse thieves—that one was supposed to be a red man." He gave a tight-lipped, bitter smile and nodded several times. "When I woke up, I was handcuffed, and that deputy was trying his best to break my ribs with his rifle butt."

The Indian's onyx eyes sparkled under a deep brow. His formal clothing and manner made him seem older. Partly to clear away his own puzzlement, Gabriel told what had happened last night.

His cellmate listened attentively. When Gabriel had finished, the Indian regarded him carefully. "You matriculated then."

"Yes."

Again the Indian grimaced. "They expelled me." He waited, then said, "For singing the national anthem."

Gabriel was puzzled. "They expelled you for that?"

The Indian smiled broadly now, for the first time revealing white teeth set in dark gums. "I sang it in Lakota." Then he grew serious and watched Gabriel's reaction as he said. "The Indian Schools are run by whites. They will not let us speak Lakota or use our real names." His hand passed over his vest. "And we have to dress like Christian gentlemen. The Headmaster gave me the name of Seymour Raines. It was his interpretation of Touch-the-Cloud, my father's name, because he was tall. The Lakotas give their names to their oldest son when he comes of age."

"So what do you want to be called? Surely not Seymour."

"T. T. Cloud will do."

Gabriel Scriven liked this young Lakota and he quickly offered his hand. "You can call me Gabe."

T. T. Cloud cocked his head. "That your real name?"

Gabriel forced a grin. "Not exactly," he said, "but 'Gabriel' is getting powerful hard to live up to."

*

A few days later, Judge Hammer ordered a porter to hoist his son's trunk onto the train. Marcus was in a cocky mood—had set his derby at an angle, nearly hiding his bandage. Nobody had been able to find his ear lobe, and he had started the rumor that Scriven had swallowed it. Marcus had added cannibalism to Gabriel Scriven's list of sins.

The Judge had already calculated how his son's sudden deformity would become an advantage. Marcus had listened and been convinced those New Yorkers were both fascinated and naive about the frontier. Marcus would tell his professors and classmates that his ear had been lost in a fight with a cougar. One that had carried off a child. Never mind there were no cougars near Fort Chambers. Easterners devoured the tabloids, the Judge had told him. They would happily imagine him, Marcus B. Hammer, swaggering from the gate of a wood-staked fort, trading his buckskins for the clothes of an eastern dandy. And Marcus could already imagine pulling on his sky-blue jersey to crack Yale's line for Columbia.

Marcus smiled at Aura de Bretteville, who clutched her father's arm further down the platform. To Marcus, her presence was indication enough that she was his. He convinced himself she would be waiting when he returned at Christmas.

But Aura was there only because her father urged it. What would it look like, he had told her, for us not see the boy off to college? Fort Chambers was a town of a hundred families. There was decorum to be followed.

Aura thought of Gabriel still in jail. Although she could not summon the courage to visit him, she felt that showing up for Marcus's departure was a betrayal. She had imagined it otherwise. She had thought both boys would be leaving on the same train. That would have been better. And their rivalry for her would have been stilled for awhile. She enjoyed their attentions for different reasons. And because of that horrible fight, the graduation dance had been ruined and everything had become sour and tangled. So she had come, and that was all that was expected. Aura de Bretteville had learned, even at the age of seventeen, to do the expected. She even managed a smile and a nod as Marcus mounted the train. When he saw it, he momentarily forgot the bandage, and tipped his derby.

As the whistle blew and the train jerked, Marcus waved. He was enjoying his celebrity. Leaving gave him a rush of excitement.

After the train had turned the bend, and blew its whistle a last time, he made his way toward the club car. The car was nearly empty except for a slim soldier who sat reading a newspaper. Marcus sat down, pulled his derby tighter over his ear and nervously removed a cigar from his breast pocket. Although he had been sneaking cigarettes for a long time, he was unsure of the etiquette of the club car. His father had dominated every social act. But he saw that the soldier had lowered his newspaper and was staring at him.

"Do you need a cutter?" the soldier asked.

Marcus, who realized this must be an officer, did not know what to say. But before he could gather his wits, the officer produced a cigar cutter, like the one Marcus had seen his father use.

"Why, thank you sir," Marcus replied. "I seem to have misplaced my own." Afraid his inexperience might show and aware his bandage had attracted the officer's attention, Marcus took a second cigar from his pocket and offered it. Then they introduced themselves.

"Glad to make your acquaintance, Master Hammer. My name's John Pershing. And I thank you for the cigar. It is certainly finer than those I usually smoke."

Pershing put his cigar into the loop of the cutter and squeezed it shut. Then he clipped the other in a similar manner and handed it back to Marcus. He struck a long match and lit Marcus's cigar, then his own. They puffed for a few moments, as the car filled with pungent, blue smoke. Marcus was trying hard not to cough.

The officer again lifted his newspaper and Marcus could read the masthead through the smoke. There was an illustration of a young girl behind prison bars.

The door opened and a porter came in carrying a newspaper. He paused before Marcus and bowed. "Would the young gentleman like a *New York Journal?* We took on a few at Pierre and I got one left."

Flattered with the attention, Marcus took the paper. Then he called the porter back. "How about a brandy for myself and the gentlemen?"

The porter's smile froze as he glanced at Pershing.

"None for me," the officer said.

Marcus stabbed his finger at the headline, CUBAN JOAN OF ARC IMPRISONED BY WEYLER. A few days before, his father had told him about the Spanish tyrants. Had called them garlics. "No doubt about it," Marcus said with as much authority as he could muster. "We'll have to kick those garlics out of Cuba."

Lieutenant Pershing, who had been enjoying his cigar, paused in mid-puff. "Garlics? I don't believe I've heard the Spanish referred to as such."

Marcus leaned forward. "Do you know they actually eat the stuff? Like popcorn."

"I use it myself," Pershing replied.

"But we've got to teach them a thing or two."

The Lieutenant regarded him with interest. "I see. And you intend to help do it, do you?"

The boy sucked at his cigar and rattled the newspaper. "Well, right now, I'm off to college. But if there's a war, Uncle Sam can count on me. I'll jump right in."

As Marcus had been speaking, Pershing lay his unfinished cigar on the smoking stand. "Yes. You and a great many others. But it will take experienced soldiers to beat the Spanish."

The boy realized, however dimly, that he was being rebuffed. And from a man who had been offered a drink and had already accepted one of his father's coronas! Marcus pretended to read his article, as though Pershing's slight had gone unnoticed. Under the illustration, a caption blared that Evangelina Cisneros, but sixteen years of age, had been arrested as a spy.

When the porter started back through the car empty-handed, Marcus stopped him. "Say, where's my brandy?"

The porter raised his white eyebrows at Pershing. He did not even look at Marcus. "We're run out. And can't get any more, 'cause South Dakota don't sell no liquor on Sunday."

"Ah, of course," Marcus bluffed. But as soon as the porter had left, he sneered through a puff of smoke, "Probably drank it all himself. You can't trust them, you know."

Pershing studied his half-smoked cigar, then slowly ground it out in the brass ash stand. "That, my young sir, has not been my experience. I command a troop of the United States Tenth Cavalry."

When Marcus showed no response, Pershing explained, "except for the officers, the regiment is made up entirely of Negroes. And I assure you, they are excellent troopers."

Marcus sank behind his paper. A Negro army? For an instant, he considered trying to redeem himself with his mountain lion story, then lost his nerve. The cigar had turned bitter and strong, and smoking it too fast and the swaying car was making him dizzy. Smacking his lips in feigned enjoyment, he said good-bye to the Lieutenant, who did not acknowledge his exit.

*

During their time in the cell, T. T. Cloud told how he wanted to hire on at a cattle ranch. He'd intended to float the Missouri to the mouth of the Niobara, where there was better grass. With the buffalo gone, T. T. Cloud explained, the Lakota Sioux would have to adapt. Maybe learn the cattle trade. In a year or two, he planned to return to the reservation with a seed herd.

The more T. T. Cloud talked with that hungry look in his eyes, the more Gabriel thought about postponing his scholarship. One night had turned his life upside down. He had to right it again and going off to music school did not seem to be the way. That would seem like hiding out. On a ranch he could learn manly pursuits. He would learn to ride as well as he could now follow notes. Going with T. T. Cloud seemed to be an opportunity to change his life.

*

The next day, Markum sent his deputy on an errand to Buffalo County, and then released them both.

Gabriel asked T. T. Cloud to wait at the river, while he told his mother that he was leaving. When Thelma had heard him out, she offered no argument. She wrapped fried chicken into a parcel. Then, as he packed a few essentials, she handed him his coronet. "Keep up your music," she implored. "At least do that."

Gabriel guessed that on a ranch, a coronet would be an embarrassment. "I'll take the mouth piece. I can still practice with that. Will you give this to Aura?" He handed her the letter, kissed her quickly, and before either of them could cry, Gabriel ran down the stairs.

*

Later that evening, Aura opened Gabriel's letter.

Dear Aura,

Did you really mean it when you said I would be a hero someday? I've left Fort Chambers. I shall miss you, and intend to write. But I will understand if you choose not to reply.
But I will think of you and that last Stephen Foster piece we worked on, wherever I am.

Respectfully,
Gabriel

*

Aura de Bretteville had already began to destroy his note when something stopped her. She realized that she would miss the afternoons they had spent practicing. Gabriel had been considerate and listened to her complaints about Marcus. Suddenly, despite the warm evening, she felt cold and she hugged herself. Although Marcus's attentions had been too rough and unwanted at times, she had now lost them both.

She opened a thin volume of poetry, a best seller her mother had given her- *When Hearts Are Trumps*. She leafed through it until she found a poem entitled "The Last Dance". Although the title seemed appropriate for the way she felt, the content was not. In author Tom Hall's poem, a heartless young officer seduces an unsuspecting debutante. But there was certainly nothing heartless about Gabriel Scriven, no matter what had happened. She began to blame herself. Perhaps the whole tragedy had been her fault. Aura marked the page with Gabriel's note and lay the book on her pillow.

She dried her eyes, stepped quietly into the parlor and sat down at her piano. She began to play but the melody was hollow. She missed Gabriel's horn, its warm caress blowing across her bare shoulder.

CHAPTER 3

November, 1897

In the last quarter of the homecoming game between Columbia and Princeton, his team behind by one touchdown, Marcus Hammer balanced forward on his knuckles. He dug his toes into the mud and waited for the Princeton center to snap the nearly round ball.

Although the only freshman on the field, "Wildcat" Hammer knew he was Columbia's most feared lineman. All afternoon, he had butted his leather helmet into the orange-jerseyed Princeton men, knocking the wind and courage out of them, muscling them back in the cold mud. But Princeton's quarterback, Simon Gimbel, had been a little too quick for a sacking. Just as Marcus was about to grab him, Gimbel would toss a lateral pass to one of his halfbacks, and Princeton would pick up another first down.

Marcus breathed hard. His legs were heavy with fatigue. But he knew Gimbel would make one mistake. Just one. He gritted his teeth. If Columbia had any chance of winning, the Jew would have to go down hard. And stay down. He hated the arrogance in Gimbel's eyes. Catch me if you can, those eyes taunted.

The ragged breathing of the exhausted linemen came to him—but over it, those infuriating, nasal calls of Gimbel—"TEN, ah- FOURteen, TWO, eLEVen..." His calls were as devious a loan shark's numbers.

Marcus waited. Every muscle in his body, his whole concentration, was set like a bear trap.

"SIX..." Gimbel called, then, "HIKE!"

Marcus lunged, his helmet glancing off the center's unprotected ribs—and there, trapped in a ring of blue jerseys, alone with that weasel frown, was Gimbel. He faked a few steps to the left and Marcus saw those hands close around the ball. Marcus feinted, then at the last minute, twisted right, grabbing Gimbel's thigh. But he fell with a muddy splash and the referee's whistle blew the play dead.

Through the tangle of bodies, Marcus saw Gimbel's sarcastic grin and that agonizingly clean jersey. The unscathed Princeton quarterback smiled up into the pulsating orange pompoms in the visitor's stands.

Damn! Another first down, on Columbia's twenty-yard line. Marcus got up slowly, remembering that one brief touch of stringy, kosher thigh. Wildcat Hammer was getting close. And, he had learned one thing. On that play, Gimbel's face had lost confidence. Wildcat Hammer knew he had seen— delicious, bloody fear! He licked his dry lips.

On the next snap, Wildcat screamed and lunged straight between the Princeton tackles. Gimbel froze, cradling his precious ball. As Marcus blindsided the quarterback with his full hundred and ninety pounds, he heard a satisfying pop—like a dry branch breaking.

The coaches and officials ran over to Gimbel. The Princeton trainer ran onto the field, dropped to his knees and swore. Gimbel lay in the mud, his face twisted in agony. His white, bloody femur protruded through the padded trousers.

*

Coach Webster was furious. It was bad enough that Princeton had beaten Columbia at Homecoming. But he had been hired to remind the sons of New York Knickerbockers in the art of fair play. The Ivy League was a gentleman's league, and Coach Webster was a gentleman's coach.

The muddy tackle before him had seriously injured the son of a New York retail magnate. In any other situation, this could be explained as the by-product of a hard-fought game between two old rivals. But why had Hammer been the only player on the field who didn't obey the offside whistle? Webster had clearly heard it over the roar of the crowd and so must everyone in the stadium. Had that cougar taken more than Hammer's ear? Had his best lineman lost his hearing as well? Or maybe, considering Hammer's low marks, some brain tissue?

Nobody would believe Hammer had not heard a whistle blown five feet away. And neither did Webster.

There was no need to ask. Of course, Hammer would deny it. He had denied inviting a chippie to his room, also. Even though the Proctor had caught the two of them *en coitus flagrante*.

Webster had to do something. Perhaps because Hammer was a freshman, the coach could blame the infraction on first year zeal. But no. He had stuck his neck out in starting Hammer. A coach takes full responsibility for any man he puts on the field. Aware that it might cost him a win in the upcoming game against Yale, Webster decided to remove Marcus B. Hammer for the rest of the season. His grades would be a legitimate excuse. There need be no admission of foul play. Besides, with another year to develop finesse, this lad might learn to control himself. He had the potential to be the best in the Ivy League.

But how could Webster keep the boy's back strong while building his character? Perhaps he could put Hammer in the charge of Hamilton Fish, Jr. Hamilton had played football before becoming captain of the rowing team. He was taller than Hammer and nearly as muscular. Uncommonly mature for a twenty-one old. Once "Wildcat" Hammer climbed into the heavy eighties racing sculls, Fish would make him row in stroke.

The Coach knew Hammer was a namedropper. He would be impressed that Fish's grandfather had been Ulysses Grant's Secretary of State. And that there always seemed to be a Fish in Congress.

Now Coach Webster smiled.

Marcus B. Hammer shifted his weight and gave a sheepish grin. As usual, he thought the coach's smile was just for him.

CHAPTER 4

February 15, 1898

It was nearly midnight and it was snowing heavily when a courier from the Naval War College pressed the electric bell at Theodore Roosevelt's brownstone residence. After some moments, the Assistant Secretary of the Navy swung the carved door wide, pulling his robe tight against the cold.

He had not been able to sleep for two nights, for Valentine's Day had horrible memories for him. As the young man's boots dripped on the vestibule tiles, Roosevelt screwed up the gas in the low hanging Tiffany lamp. He squinted at the note he had been handed. Suddenly, Roosevelt, normally not a man of profanity, shouted. "Damn!"

Seeing he had startled his shivering messenger, Roosevelt quickly composed himself. "Tell Secretary Long that, of course, I shall come at once. But on your way, stop at Captain Leonard Wood's residence." Roosevelt turned the note over and scribbled a few words. "And give him this."

A scant twenty minutes later, Roosevelt's carriage galloped down Pennsylvania Avenue. As he passed the White House, he saw that every window blazed with light—an almost merry sight. Although sobered by the deaths and heinous burns that must have resulted from the explosion of the *Maine*, Roosevelt believed the Spaniards, by blowing up an American battleship, had guaranteed war! He rubbed his muscular hands, as much in anticipation as from the cold.

Tomorrow he would contact his friend, General Francis Greene. Surely, after all the favors Roosevelt had rendered him while New York Police Commissioner, Greene could find him a place in the New York Militia. Before coming to Washington, had Roosevelt not served as a reserve captain for two years? True, his soldiering had been limited to parades, the main activity of the spit-and-polish New York Seventy-First, but by God he had worn the uniform.

Roosevelt knew Edith would protest. She was a strong-willed woman and after all, there were six children who were not to be left fatherless. And Edith had just recovered from an operation for a small stomach ulcer. But Roosevelt had an old score to settle. His own father, whom he had loved and respected, had not served in the Union Army during the Civil War. And why? At the pleading of his wife, a southern belle whose brothers would be fighting against him on the Confederate side. And so, he did what many wealthy men did—hired someone to fight in his place. Although this was common practice and not the least bit illegal, Roosevelt knew his father had never gotten over it. He made young Theodore promise that if the need ever arose to fight for his country, he would not be swayed by a wife's pleas for prudence and safety.

But Theodore Roosevelt's insomnia had been due to something more. For a moment, as the clopping hooves seemed to distort time, Roosevelt imagined Edith dying, leaving him as his first wife Alice, had, fourteen years ago, almost to the day. On that grim Valentine's day, in a matter of hours, his mother had died too. Roosevelt had drawn a large cross in his diary. How bitter and hopeless he had felt.

He had almost fled New York for the west. His ranch and the ruined hills of the Dakotas had made him whole. And now this stupefying Washington life would be the death of him unless he got into the fray! He had made no secret to Edith that he intended to serve. She would just have to be resigned to his decision. They had been friends long before they were husband and wife, and at this point she should not be surprised.

Edith was on the mend. Roosevelt knew this on the authority of the very best doctors. But with the *Maine* sunk, his nation was not!

*

At two in the morning, Captain Wood sat at his desk composing a letter. He was often too blunt for his own good, so he decided to begin with his boyhood on Cape Cod, his ties to Massachusetts. Several state militias would have to be activated to supplement the woefully small standing army. And his friend Nelson Alger, Secretary of War, had told Wood that the Massachusetts militia was certain to get the call.

But Wood soon breathed an exasperated sigh and slammed his pen down. He could not elaborate; had never been any good at beating around the bush.

He resolved to skip the flowery language for which he had neither the patience nor the aptitude. Instead, in short sentences, Wood informed the Honorable governor of Massachusetts that he would immediately resign his Captaincy in the Army Medical Corps to accept lesser rank in the Massachusetts Militia, for he preferred to serve with men from his native state. Furthermore, in a tropical war, the Governor should know that more men would die from fever than from wounds. As a doctor with military experience, he would be able to prevent an epidemic by enforcing strict sanitation and hygiene.

Wood was committed, he stated, as one who had already served as a regular, to assure that any new fighting force got supplies. He had seen millions of dollars and too many men squandered in the pursuit of Geronimo. In the end, when Geronimo had finally agreed to surrender, it was because his people were promised blankets, food, and shelter. Without adequate supplies, no army could win a sustained engagement, much less a war.

By the time he had finished, Wood was full of energy. Confident his letter would bring the desired results; he signed it and sealed it into an envelope. Then he pressed his West Point ring into the red sealing wax.

*

Daylight was breaking over the new fallen snow as Roosevelt returned from his frustrating night with Secretary Long. The Secretary had urged caution, despite Roosevelt's protests. Long insisted on setting up a Naval Board of Inquiry. There had to be undeniable proof of sabotage, he had insisted to the agitated Roosevelt. Divers would be sent to Havana to inspect the wreckage of the *Maine*.

They had wasted valuable hours waiting for a second cable from Havana; details about the number of dead and wounded and if there had been any communication with the Spanish authorities. These were details Long knew he needed for his breakfast briefing with the President. But a second cable never came.

Roosevelt swore under his breath. Once again, bureaucrats were missing the chance to act quickly. If he had gauged the American mood correctly—and he was confident he had—the country was ready to make any sacrifice to kick the Spaniards out of Cuba. The concentration camps and suffering of the Cuban people was intolerable. He could imagine the Hearst compositors already setting their huge headline. He hoped an enraged America would awake to newspapers screaming of the sinking of the mighty battleship.

As his carriage approached the White House, Roosevelt ordered the driver to stop. There on the avenue, a small, grim-faced crowd waited in the snow. Several were clutching special editions of the *Washington Post*. Across the avenue, the White House guard raised the Stars and Stripes. When the flag had fully unfurled against the gray sky, the color guard saluted. He swallowed hard as he watched them lower the flag to half-mast and tie off the halyard.

Roosevelt knew that in ten days Secretary Long would travel to New York. For that one day, Roosevelt would be in charge of the Department of the Navy.

He began to compose a telegram to Admiral Dewey. Long would be livid, but there were but few opportunities in life to seize the hour. And Roosevelt would seize his.

By the time the carriage had stopped in front of his residence, Roosevelt knew what he would command Admiral Dewey's pacific flotilla to do. It would be difficult to wait ten days to send his cable, but he would do so, and he was fully prepared to take the consequences.

*

Their Lazy A foreman had one eye and one method. If a cowboy worked hard, he got Sundays off. But if he thought a man might be shirking, that cowboy would work seven days, from two hours before sun-up until an hour after dark. If the foreman took a dislike to a man, as he did one of the Mexicans, that man cleaned stables and washed dishes and was kept from what he loved most—the saddle.

Gabriel and T. T. Cloud had been working at the Lazy A for, as the Indian liked to put it, seven long moons. There was nothing lazy about the Lazy A. The owner, who they had never seen, lived in Kansas City. The Lazy A supplied beef to the Army. Gabriel could see there were few steps required turning the stringy cows into jerky.

Cloud had taught Gabriel to ride well. Both of them avoided the lice-infested bunkhouse as much as possible. He and Cloud looked for any excuse to sleep outdoors, even on the coldest nights. T. T. knew how to heat stones in a fire and make a snug shelter from hides. The two men volunteered for herd duty and the foreman showed his appreciation by giving them Sundays off.

The ranch was a place where men with worn out luck survived on burned beans, fatty bacon, and meager pay. But it had been hard to find work since the Panic of '94. With the Indian wars won, the Army was at an all-time low, and the market for this poor brand of beef was diminishing.

Cloud looked awkward on the stunted bay the foreman had first sold him against wages. Gabriel's mount, a cranky sorrel, was not much better. Most of mounts were of more certain origin than their owners.

Under T. T.'s teaching, Gabriel had learned tricks that could make an ornery horse take notice. When neither knees, reins, nor spurs would get the horse's attention, Cloud had shown him how to lean forward along the horse's neck and grip the mane. The sorrel would instinctively jerk his head toward the pain and in doing so, would turn.

Cloud, who had learned to ride bareback, soon made his bay into an obedient mount. The foreman, a big chew of tobacco in his jaw, watched this with interest and gave them broncos to break. Gabriel had been thrown and stepped on, but had helped T. T. break a dozen ponies.

After the second month on the ranch, Gabriel wrote Thelma. He asked her to send him two pairs of wool longjohns, one for T. T. Cloud, and a Spanish-English dictionary.

Every night, López, a thin cowboy with a long scar across his cheek, played his battered guitar. His strumming style interested Gabriel, who began to learn a few chords. Gabriel's mouthpiece made a duck-like sound, and the Mexicans laughed. It became a source of *chistas verdes*—dirty jokes. To the guffaws of the Mexicans, López told Gabriel he sounded like a torpedo. It would be days before Gabriel learned that this was slang for a loud, musical fart.

Gabriel felt frustrated when the Mexicans started to sing along with López, for he could not follow the words. Now and again, when a word was rooted in the Latin, he caught the meaning. But then, the next few would be chewed in the wind or in the song and would be lost.

But once the dictionary came, Gabriel began to learn Spanish. By the spring thaw, in what T. T. Cloud called the month when ponies shed, Gabriel was writing letters in Spanish for the illiterate cowboys.

Rope, rawhide, and riding had toughened Gabriel's body and his resolve. Here at the ranch, a man's motives were obvious as a dog's. If a cowboy bothered you, you punched him—right then and there. And hard enough, Gabriel learned that he would not quickly get up. Grudges not solved in this manner would sometimes end in deadly fights. Even the good-natured López had to be calmed by Gabriel more than once. Most of the men were missing teeth and were likely to lose a few more every payday. Their four dollars a month would only buy a few twists of tobacco and a couple of quarts of whiskey.

Gabriel calculated he would have to work a year to pay off his pony. So he earned his tobacco and whiskey money writing letters. He could even compose little poems for the lonely cowboys to send. Soon, he learned to enjoy the sharp taste of chewing tobacco.

One Sunday, Gabriel awoke to find his silver mouthpiece missing. He announced at breakfast that whoever took it had till the next morning to put it back, for it was a gift from his mother. Gabriel had never seen the rough cowboys exhibit such hurt, innocent looking faces. When he lay down on his saddle blanket that night, he discovered a lump. His mouthpiece had been returned. But the next morning, López had gone.

Gabriel had noticed the leather pouch Cloud wore on a thong around his neck. It was bulkier than the medicine bags Gabriel had seen other Indians wear.

A few days later, as he and T. T. Cloud warmed themselves over their fire, he asked. Since they were alone, Cloud opened the drawstring and produced the daguerreotype. Once opened, a glass plate photograph caught the amber light of the fire. The Indian handed it over. "Twist it back and forth in the light," he instructed.

Gabriel could see the black parts turn silver and what had been silver go black. The Indian in the photograph had a nasty scar near his nose, nearly covered by two jagged streaks of white war paint. He wore a single braid, wrapped in fur. The other side of the Indian's face was plain—no paint, just long, loose hair. A feather, silver in the daguerreotype, was pinned across the top of his head.

T. T. Cloud's gaze returned to the steers as they drank from the shallow creek. "*Tashunca Uitco.*"

Gabriel did not understand.

"Ta SHUN-ca UIT-co, he repeated.

Gabriel tried the name and managed to get it right.

Touch-the-Cloud nodded his approval. "Crazy Horse."

Gabriel stared with wonder at the young Sioux face. Then Gabriel remembered. "But Crazy Horse was one of the Chiefs that never allowed himself to be photographed."

T. T. nodded.

"Then," Gabriel said, "how can...?"

Cloud knelt beside him. "Look at the eyes."

Gabriel twisted the glass back and forth. The image of the Indian seemed slightly astonished. His mouth was slightly open.

T. T. Cloud stood up. "This was taken after Crazy Horse died."

"What?"

The Indian's eyes flashed, anger Gabriel had not yet seen. He took the daguerreotype and replaced it in the pouch. An ember from the dying fire exploded.

After a long silence Cloud continued. "Worm, the father of Crazy Horse, and my father, who then bore my name, were allowed to stay in the jail that last night. After Crazy Horse died, the two friends knew the Army would want proof he was dead." He leveled his eyes at Gabriel. "We," he almost whispered, "are the only men alive to know this."

Gabriel felt a tingling at the back of his neck. The call of a coyote cut the silence.

"The Captain sent for a photographer. And while they waited, my father and Worm started to paint Crazy Horse's face, and to unbraid his hair. The Captain came back and was angry, but thought they had not finished."

T. T. Cloud smiled, almost to himself. "But this was not so. My father and Worm knew no Lakota brave would wear one braid."

Gabriel nodded.

T. T. Cloud grunted with satisfaction. "Yes. The photographer took this picture. But any Lakota who saw it would not believe it was Crazy Horse." He poked the fire and it crackled to life.

A long time later, when the embers had begun to coat with gray ash, Cloud looked up into the night sky. "For some of us, " he said, "*Tashunca Uitco* has never died."

CHAPTER 5

April, 1898

For two weeks, since the Board of Inquiry had determined that the *Maine* had probably been sunk by a Spanish mine, the United States and Spain had officially been at war. Yet, both Roosevelt and Wood had been denied commissions in the fighting forces that would liberate Cuba. Because of an abundance of men who were seeking commissions, even Roosevelt's influence seemed worthless. Even if none but the qualified were given commissions, the War Department explained, each regiment would still have more officers than men.

But Roosevelt and Wood had conjured one last chance to see combat. Now they sat in the packed Senate gallery, during the reading of President McKinley's request to fund three new cavalry regiments with "special qualifications." The measure had already been approved by a substantial margin in the House. Now the senators were being asked to vote. Roosevelt squirmed, trying to appear as merely an advisor who, along with Captain Wood, had pushed hard for this measure. Secretary Alger, who had drafted the request to recruit experienced horsemen and marksmen from Arizona,

New Mexico, and the Indian Territories, watched from a doorway.

The Senate leader acknowledged Joseph Wheeler of Alabama. The spry step of the white haired congressmen belied his age of sixty-one as he nearly jumped to the podium.

"I believe he is on Ways and Means, " Roosevelt whispered to Wood. "I hope to God he does not intend to kill this request."

As the chamber grew quiet, Senator Wheeler began in a gentle voice—a curious mixture of soft, southern Rs and the occasional New England phrase. "Mistuh Speaker, fellow Senators," he began. "As you know, up until this moment I have been in full support of the measures and appropriations required to mount a war with Spain."

The little Senator waited, acknowledging the murmurs of assent in the chamber.

"A few of you know of my past endeavors to stop General Sherman's march across Georgia." He waited for the polite laughter to subside. "Had we been as well supplied and supported as our Yankee brethren," he said, fingering his white goatee, "this assembly would be meeting in Charleston instead of Washington." This drew a round of applause from the Senators.

"Well," he continued, "we all serve one bannuh now. And I am right proud to do so." His fist came down like a hickory knot on the walnut podium. "Gentlemen, we cannot win this crusade without able cavalry. And at the moment, we have few squadrons with combat experience. In short, we are unprepared. It follows then, that we must not shirk our duty today." His nostrils flared as he took a deep breath. "When there is the question of the honah and glory of our country on one side and a few dollahs and cents on the other our path is clear. God forbid that the growing generation should be money-changers rather than brave soldiers, fighting, and if need be, dyin' in the front rank of battle. I do fully support this measure, and urge you to vote its passage at once."

The Senators roared then broke into applause. Within minutes the measure had been gaveled into law.

Barely masking his elation, Roosevelt led Wood out of the gallery and down the wide, curved stairway. Below, in the lobby, Secretary Alger waited with Senator Wheeler. To the observer, this was a formality—a polite congratulation for yet another vote for military preparedness. But Wood and

Roosevelt approached the two lawmakers, fully rehearsed for a very special encounter.

After shaking hands with Wood and Roosevelt, Alger cleared his throat. "Gentlemen, meet General Wheeler."

Roosevelt was taken off guard as Wheeler bowed. There was a mischievous twinkle in the former Confederate's eyes as Alger said, "General Wheeler has offered his services as General of the combined Cavalry." And before they could recover Alger quipped, "don't worry, he's half Yankee, since he spent much of his youth in Connecticut."

"And Theodore," Alger continued, "we'd like you to consider the Colonelcy of the Volunteer Cavalry. There is yet much to do—paperwork, requests, equipping, logistics." But Alger saw that Roosevelt was already shaking his head no.

"I am indeed honored, Mister Secretary," Roosevelt said gravely. "Although I have led men, it has never been in battle." He looked at Wheeler, as though for support. "It would take me at least a month to gain the necessary competence. And, sir, we do not have a month. As you say, we must begin tomorrow!"

Roosevelt turned to Wood, who seemed to have taken a sudden interest in the mosaic pattern in the polished floor.

"Of course I shall help with the paperwork and requests", Roosevelt continued, " but for the command of the First Volunteer Cavalry, there could be no better choice for the Colonelcy than Leonard Wood.

Captain Wood tried to look surprised, but he was no actor.

Secretary Alger hesitated. Then he saw Wheeler's white beard crinkle into a smile.

"But of course, Mister Secretary, General Wheeler," Roosevelt continued, "if you wish, I shall be honored to serve as Colonel Wood's second in command."

Within the hour, Roosevelt was at his desk at the Department of the Navy. Secretary of the Navy Long had gone to New York. Finally, Roosevelt was in charge. He had barely removed his coat, when he began to furiously pen a sparse but powerful message. The telegram would be sent and received before the foot-dragging Secretary could do anything about it.

Secret and Confidential
Dewey, Hong Kong

Order the Squadron to Hong Kong. Keep full coal. In the event of declaration of war with Spain, your duty will be to see that the Spanish squadron does not leave the Asiatic coast.
Then begin offensive operations in the Philippine Islands.
Keep the cruiser Olympia as your flagship until further orders.

Roosevelt, Washington

There was both purpose and strategy in his message. The British territory of Hong Kong would have to be neutral. Roosevelt knew that once hostilities were declared, the American squadron would not be allowed to leave Hong Kong for an attack against the Spanish, for that would make the British *de facto* participants. However, if Commodore Dewey supplied his ships with coal now, he could stand by off Hong Kong and steam toward Manila Bay with dispatch. If Dewey could surprise the Spanish and inflict enough damage, history would be made. America would at last have a base in Asia!

CHAPTER 6

April 25, 1898

Behind the carved oak doors of his study, Theodore Roosevelt lit the cigar of his new commanding officer, Colonel Leonard Wood. The two men had barely controlled their elation during the quiet dinner for four their wives had arranged. Theodore had wanted the children around the table, as usual. Their merriment and distraction would ease the tense meal with wives so clearly reluctant to send their husbands off to war. But Edith, a woman of resolve, insisted on dinner for four. Theodore had decided to go; yet she hoped he would stick to his forte—logistics. He should leave the actual fighting to Leonard Wood. Toward this end, this dinner was to persuade him.

It had been a quiet meal. As Theodore and Leonard finally begged their leave for cigars, Edith fired Theodore one of her sharp looks. Then she sighed and rang for Julius to clear the table.

Safely away from his wife, Leonard Wood's reserve vanished. "Theodore," he smiled, "I could do with a glass of port."

The preparations for their special cavalry regiment had already begun. From the beginning, Roosevelt insisted that it represent a cross section of America. Yet Republicans were certainly preferred over Democrats. The undecided, or politically naive, Roosevelt avowed, would in time be persuaded. But Doctor Leonard Wood was more concerned about a recruit's body than his politics. Every man would have strong lung capacity and be able to adapt to military discipline. They would have to be as tough and obedient as regulars.

For over a month now, broadsides had been displayed in post offices from New York to Arizona.

But rumor spread like wildfire.

Within three days of the time Congress approved the new regiment, Roosevelt had already received twenty-seven sacks of applications—some twenty-three thousand men. There had been telephone calls and personal visits from old colleagues. Despite their lack of military experience, most hinted at captaincies for themselves and places in the ranks for their sons.

Meanwhile, Colonel Wood had a few ideas of his own. He asked West Pointer Allyn Capron Jr. to recruit men from Oklahoma. When he heard of this, Roosevelt insisted. Capron include at least a few Indians.

And Roosevelt's New Yorkers were hardly ignored. Woodbury Kane would head up the a New York contingent, which included policemen, champion rowers, a polo player, and not a few boxers—athletic gentlemen all who had won Roosevelt's respect.

William "Bucky" O'Neill, Mayor of Prescott, Arizona, publisher and former sheriff, had been instructed to assemble Troop A.

Maximillian Luna, an insurance salesman Roosevelt and Wood's age from Santa Fe offered to raise a troop. The athletic, bi-lingual Luna had been educated in Washington while his father served in the Congress. The Luna family descended directly from the Spanish explorers and had lived on the Rio Grande since the 1600s. Maximillian had served in the New Mexico Territorial Legislature.

Of course any man might apply. But the odds were better for men who had sparred with Roosevelt in Manhattan, or who had fought the Indian campaigns with Leonard Wood.

Roosevelt poured two small glasses of port. As Leonard raised his glass, he proposed an old Army toast, usually reserved for the night before battle. "To us," he said. "May the war last long enough for us to be either wounded, promoted, or killed." The two men downed their drinks in one swallow.

Leonard wanted to show Roosevelt that he had a bit of dash too. Theodore was a man who rushed at destiny and Wood was normally cautious. Leonard Wood had his doubts about Roosevelt's discipline in combat. But there was little doubt that the first special regiment ever authorized by Congress, the only one that would not be crippled by Army seniority nor fettered by a governor, had been the creation of Theodore Roosevelt. Tonight, Leonard Wood decided, was no time for doubt. In fact, he felt a wave of euphoria. Although he had fought Indians in the west, this was his first declaration of war. For the first time in years, Wood accepted a second glass of port.

*

The willows bent low in the flooded river as Gabriel and Cloud herded their steers toward the railhead. With war declared, Army purveyors were buying any steer that could walk, even the Lazy A herd.

Gabriel had grown a mustache and his slightly kinky hair had grown to his shoulders. He was sure that if he showed up in Fort Chambers, only his mother would recognize him.

Talk around the chuck wagon had turned to the cowboy regiment. The posters claimed that if a man could ride and shoot, he might make it. If accepted, he'd get a uniform, three square meals a day, and thirteen dollars a month! That was a fortune to the underpaid Lazy A wranglers.

But the Cloud hated the idea of joining the army. Blue coats had killed too many of his people. He even held Indian scouts in contempt; convinced they had traded honor for food and shelter.

But Gabriel finally persuaded Cloud that as cowboys, it would take them five years to earn enough money to buy a seed herd of their own. Gabriel's music scholarship was a pale dream by now. He couldn't imagine going to classes with bluestocking girls and practicing piano.

There was something in the air that they all felt. Although Gabriel did not fully understand it, he felt swept up by this war with Spain. Although he had been sobered to the realities of life, he could not imagine dying.

Cloud worried that he would be rejected. Just twenty-two summers ago, his father led a band of warriors at The Little BigHorn.

Gabriel argued they both would gain status in this new war. Hadn't Cloud seen how the old Civil War veterans were given land grants, easy bank loans, and respectful treatment? The cowboy regiment was their chance to turn the bad luck they were still running from.

And the war would be surely be over quickly.

Lately, Gabriel had begun to study the white flecks under his fingernails. Maybe Aura had been right. Perhaps their pattern predicted that he'd really be a hero.

The two friends vowed that if the cowboy regiment didn't take them both, they'd head west to the silver mines.

Cloud had won a lever-action Winchester carbine in a crapshoot and he could already hit a whiskey bottle at full gallop. Gabriel's skill at letter writing earned a Colt Peacemaker revolver as payment. If he lay the barrel across his bridle arm, he could sometimes hit a post, but never a bottle.

During the weeks on the trail, the weakest steers had dropped from exhaustion. But now, what was left of the herd came over a low rise. Below lay dusty corrals and one street of pine board shacks. Beside the cattle pens, a long freight train sat on gleaming rails that stretched to both horizons.

As they later drove their herd through town, the hungry steers jerked their heads toward wagons laden with new hay. It was all the weary cowboys could do to keep them in line.

*

Over a plank Post Office, a new flag with forty-five stars fluttered in the dusty air. Under it, a line of men waited. Blue-shirted soldiers worked the line, eliminating some men outright—one for gray hair, another for missing teeth, anyone short a finger or a toe.

As they joined the end of the line, Gabriel wondered if they would be cut before they got to its head. He hoped he and Cloud could both pass as Indians. The recruits were sunburned outdoorsmen and it would be hard to tell a man's race until he had to take off his clothes.

Finally, the line moved into the Post Office. There, a sergeant with one empty sleeve full of yellow stripes looked up from his desk. "Jaysus," he cried out, "look at this one, would you! How tall are you, son?"

"Approximately six feet, four inches," Cloud replied.

The sergeant pursed his lips in a silent whistle. "Your name and place of residence?"

"T. T. Cloud, Indian Territory."

The sergeant licked the point of his pencil, then printed the name on his list.

Gabriel had already decided to use a false name so the Army could not trace him back to Fort Chambers. Judge Hammer might quash his enlistment. But a false name would have a price. The one-armed sergeant made him realize that he might die after all. And if he used a false name, neither Aura nor his mother would ever know. He did not want to be an anonymous hero. So Gabriel now changed his mind. A lie of location might suffice.

The sergeant repeated his name as he wrote it. "Gabriel Scriven. Also of the Indian Territories."

In the back room, men took off their clothes and put their valuables into cloth bags they were instructed to hang around their necks. They covered their crotches with their hands. Some had hairy bodies, some not. Most had buttocks white as biscuits. But Gabriel's skin was darker than any of them.

A doctor cupped Cloud's testicles in his palm then told him to turn his head and cough. After Gabriel had also done this, the two of them were directed to the next line. Behind them, a bow-legged cowboy protested. "Doc," he complained loudly, "how you expect me to cough when you got ahold of my privates? I just cain't." This broke the tension and many of the nervous recruits laughed.

"You cough, or you're out," the doctor snapped. "Now take a deep breath and try one more time."

Suddenly Gabriel felt the floor shaking. At the head of this line, a naked recruit was jumping up and down. The examiner made him jump two hundred times, then jammed his cold stethoscope against the man's heaving chest.

At each juncture, men were eliminated and told to dress. Some swore, and a few cried. But none were permitted to argue. The scrappy recruit who had trouble coughing passed the jumping test and now stood behind Gabriel. In such close quarters, the men tried not to touch. "Scuse me," "beg your pardon" and "sorry, pardner," filled the air along with the sharp odor of trail-worn bodies.

Ahead of T. T. Cloud, in the last line, another cowboy complained to the doctor—"I can SEE that bottom line just fine- but I never seen them exact letters before."

Then it was Cloud's turn to cover one eye and read. Before he did, a trooper changed the chart and Gabriel heard a groan from a cowboy behind him who had better memory than eyesight.

By the end of the examinations there were only a dozen men left. But Cloud and Gabriel were among them.

They were sent to a tent out in back. There, a sweating lieutenant with a neatly trimmed mustache recorded each man's name, age, and place of birth. The officer asked Cloud if he had brought a letter of recommendation. Gabriel saw Cloud's jaw tighten and he knew he must speak up. "T. T. Cloud, sir, has been my bunk mate for a long time. I'd trust him with my life." The lieutenant regarded Gabriel coolly. "If he's not qualified," Gabriel snapped, "then I'm not either."

"You come as a matched set then," the lieutenant said.

They answered as one. "Yes sir."

"Well then," the lieutenant smiled, "When you get to San Antonio, maybe they'll put you in the same troop."

Excited, but not knowing what to expect, Gabriel stood with the others, raised his hand and swore a solemn oath to God and country. He hoped Cloud would not try it in Lakota.

Afterwards, the lieutenant gave them train tickets.

The tickets were one way and written across them, in a sure, firm hand, "U.S.V. 1."

CHAPTER 7

May, 5, 1898

Neither President McKinley nor the members of his cabinet had gotten much sleep. They had been informed that the Spanish fleet under Admiral Cervera had left the Cape Verde Islands on April twenty-ninth. But there had been no word of it since. Had Cervera headed for Cuba? For Puerto Rico? To bombard New York? Where?

But Theodore Roosevelt knew much of the Spanish fleet had been sent to the Philippines. Cervera's smaller Atlantic squadron consisted of four out-dated armored cruisers and three torpedo boats. Roosevelt was keeping it to himself that there was not much to worry about. This furor could be used to his advantage. Congressmen who had recently opposed funds to build an adequate Navy were now insisting that they get a personal warship to protect their own district! Mayors were losing their heads too and prevailed on the President and Secretary Alger to do the most foolhardy thing in a time of war—to distribute the American fleet thinly along the coast. Furthermore, Roosevelt had just had some unwelcome news about the trial voyage of the battleship *Indiana*. She had developed leaky boilers and required a costly refitting. That would cost money. So he hoped this panic might bring emergency appropriations.

In the past days, as Roosevelt haggled with manufacturers and railroad men to get supplies to San Antonio, he kept himself amused by reading of how the entire eastern seaboard was thought to be defenseless against the Spanish "Armada." One wealthy matron, a Republican contributor, threatened to withdraw her support unless the President sent a warship at to protect the large beach hotel that bordered her summer mansion. And the Navy Department was almost hourly besieged by reports from Maine to the Carolinas of sinister vessels, "probably torpedo boats." He laughed when he read that even Bostonians, normally not given to panic, had transferred their assets inland to the city of Worcester, completely overflowing that smaller city's bank vaults. On the beaches of Long Island any man of swarthy complexion was likely to be arrested for being a Spanish spy.

Roosevelt could see that the President was tired. The already prominent rings under his eyes had grown darker. Roosevelt left the circle of fretting men, stripped off his jacket and jogged to the Navy Department. It was time to clean out his office.

Once within its dark and secure confines, Roosevelt stared at the photograph of his father he kept on his desk. At the time it had been taken, Theodore Roosevelt Senior was the healthy age of forty-five. He seemed to be giving a look that Theodore had always read as a command—"Remember the Roosevelt family name." His father's stern yet pleading expression summed up a year when his job had been killing him. Now, Theodore would right the Roosevelt name in history.

After a few moments, Theodore strode to the closet where that morning his tailor had placed the results of several fittings and a week's furious work. There hung his freshly pressed khaki tunic, complete with the yellow shoulder epaulets of a Lieutenant Colonel. The Assistant Secretary of the Navy, with the thrill of a boy peeling for a plunge into his favorite swimming hole, began to hurriedly undress.

Some moments later, Roosevelt studied the uncertain soldier in the mirror, searching for that resolve he worried was sometimes lacking. He had worked at a resolute look since college, growing side-whiskers and affecting a scowl. Now, Roosevelt placed his fists against his hips and gave the look decidedly his own—that toothy grimace. Yes, perhaps he could do it! Spinning on the balls of his feet, he affected a somewhat clumsy "right face." Now he faced his desk, bare except for the photograph. Lieutenant Colonel Theodore Roosevelt gave his first salute—to his father.

*

Even on the two-day train ride to San Antonio, Gabriel and his fellow recruits got constant news of the war. At every train station, excited operators leaned out the windows of their telegraph offices like newsboys to broadcast the latest Spanish outrage.

Gabriel loved the speeding cars as they rushed on polished rails, moving them toward a destination and a great, national cause. As he watched the landscape slide by, the wheels clicked against the track joints and created a tempo that inspired music in his head, tunes of action and purpose.

But there were challenges ahead. There would surely be difficult tests for them both in San Antonio. And with recruits coming from all directions, might he or Cloud yet be eliminated?

Soon, Gabriel and Cloud were collaborating on a scheme. They began to forge letters of recommendation on Union Pacific Railroad stationery. Posing as headmaster of the non-existent Pine Ridge Indian Academy, Gabriel attested to T. T. Cloud's exemplary character. Knowing the Cowboy Regiment stressed physical skills; he praised his friend's ability to play baseball. He cited Cloud's fast ball as the deciding factor in winning the Christian Baseball League Championship. Proud of this wonderful lie, Gabriel shoved the stationery to Cloud, and he began to dictate a letter. Cloud wrote in a slanted hand.

To Whom It May Concern:

As Registrar at Oberlin College, I must first apologize for not using the school letterhead. I was on my way to accompany Gabriel Scriven to the College when I learned that he has enlisted in the Army. It seems that the President's Call to Arms has been heeded. For Gabriel Scriven, a very promising young musician, is also a young man of character. Not surprisingly, he has decided to postpone his education until this

Cuban affair is settled. So please accept my admittedly hasty but truly heartfelt letter to affirm that for almost a year Mister Scriven has eschewed the gentle life to harden his body as a common cowhand. In the precious few hours between a hard day and well-deserved sleep, he has strengthened his mind. His excellence in Latin has enabled him to become quite proficient in the Spanish tongue.

Gabriel Scriven has prepared himself for the rigors of the campaign in Cuba. The First Volunteer Cavalry will certainly reap the benefit of his dedication and character.

Your Obedient Servant,

But here, Gabriel's inspiration vanished. Cloud dipped his pen and waited. Then a name came to him. He said it aloud as Cloud rolled his eyes.

Washington Lincoln Jones, Registrar.

Cloud practiced the name on a separate piece of paper until he could pen the registrar's impressive but slightly illegible signature.

Who would doubt a letter from a man who had been named after two presidents, Gabriel explained. Besides, a common name like Jones would difficult to doubt or to trace.

This was but a half lie, since Gabriel had been offered a scholarship. But he knew a letter lauding musical skills alone would not impress the men training a cowboy regiment. He doubted he would ever see action if he were relegated to a regimental band.

*

Snake, the cowboy who had trouble coughing, sucked on his cheroot as he told the recruits how he earned his nickname. He had once stepped upon a pair of diamond-backs "while they were a-makin' babies." Bitten by both, he nearly died. But after two days, he had recovered and his amazed trail mates had given him the handle of Snakebite. In time, that had been shortened to Snake, a name he still went by. Snake drew them all close and as he watched the recruits with his beady eyes, and hinted that he had a price on his head back in Kansas. Then he took out a pack of cards.

The men bet tobacco until it ran out, then pennies and finally, when he had won those, matches. Then he let the men bet the scalps of some of the "Spanions" they intended to kill.

*

It was a blistering hot afternoon when the train pulled into San Antonio. There, on the platform, Gabriel could see a squad of bluecoats standing at attention.

An officer wearing a dusty Stetson and riding boots with blunt, iron spurs rested his hand on his saber as the recruits filed off the train.

A sergeant lined up the recruits, then did a crisp about-face and saluted. The tanned officer addressed his new charges. "Gentlemen," he said, "welcome to the training camp of The First Volunteer Cavalry. I am Captain Maximillian Luna. Colonel Wood sends his regards. Soon, Lieutenant Colonel Roosevelt will come from Washington."

He appraised the half dozen men before him, from the tall Indian to the short, bow-legged cowboy with the constantly moving jaw. "You have to work hard. We have just weeks to make you into soldiers who can take orders and act as a unit."

Captain Luna seemed to be looking directly at Gabriel when he said, "Fifteen thousand men have applied for a regiment of one thousand. So one of the first things we will do here is to thin our ranks to leave the very best men. Some of you will not make it."

Then Captain Luna smiled. "But *caballeros*, your horses will be even more ignorant of military life than you. And they have yet to come, so you'll get a head start." He waited until the nervous laughter had subsided then said, "Pay attention and obey every single order without question. Then, and only then, do you have a chance to make our final roster." Captain Luna paused. "Sergeant, march these recruits to camp."

"Camp Wood," was a city of five hundred white tents pitched in neat rows in the sandy plain of the fair grounds. In the center, a large wooden building served as mess hall. Surrounding it stood several sheds and a grove of trees, offering some relief from the sun.

Seven hundred men had already arrived; most of them already organized into troops. But some, like Gabriel, Cloud and Snake, had yet to be assigned to a troop.

The new recruits were marched to the Quartermaster's tent where they were passed between two lines of sergeants and corporals. Each man called out his size for a hat, britches, shirt, and finally, shoes. Then each stepped aside to see if they fit. Snake laughed when he was given a yellow rubber raincoat.

The Quartermaster, a lieutenant with a walrus mustache, watched as each item was handed out. It was clear that some of the men did not know their sizes. Wives or mothers must have seen to such things. And others had worn the same trail outfit so long they had forgotten.

Gabriel saw that his shirt was too small. Somehow, he had grown at least an inch in the neck and the shoulders were too tight. The baffled orderlies handed Cloud the biggest size they had. Meanwhile, the fastidious Quartermaster checked off each item.

Snake made a fuss about his hat being too big. A corporal pulled him aside. Gabriel heard the warning. "Don't get Lieutenant Hall mad at you," he said just loud enough for every one to hear. "He issues the camp passes," the corporal warned. "And you boys are assigned to L Troop, I believe. That's Hall's troop besides. He's a spit and polish West Pointer. So you boys better look sharp."

Snake flapped his arms in frustration. His shirtsleeves hung over his hands. He shot Lieutenant Hall a poisonous look, then clamped his mouth shut.

After his bath in a watering trough, Gabriel pulled on his new cotton underwear, then the stiff, khaki pants. His wool shirt was heavy and hot. Its Navy blue color soaked up the Texas sun. The wide, gray suspenders barely held his pants up, for they were at least a size too big. Gabriel screwed his feet into his hobnailed brogans. Finally, he laced the canvas leggings.

Cloud's trousers barely met the tops of his leggings. The Indian undressed and folded his clothes neatly. He then made a breechcloth with a towel and set his hat squarely on his head.

Despite the Corporal's warning, Cloud decided to go see Lieutenant Hall. Gabriel and Snake followed. Lieutenant Hall seemed not to see the men approach, for he did not look up. When he did, and saw Cloud, he barely suppressed a smile. Then he cleared his throat.

"What is your name, trooper?" he asked the Indian.

When Cloud told him, Hall stood. In a somewhat easier tone, he said "I don't want to hurt your feelings, Mister Cloud, but it is simply not proper for you to come into an officer's tent like you did."

"But, my uniform does not fit."

His mustache almost hid the smile, but Gabriel caught it. "I was not referring to your attire, Cloud. But the way in which you men approached."

Lieutenant Hall regarded the tall recruit for a moment. "From now on, when any of you men approach an officer's tent, halt at the entrance, salute, and wait until you are spoken to. If the officer has not heard you or seen you come; rap lightly on the tent pole. He will then ask what you want. Now go back out and try that."

T. T. Cloud did as he was instructed and Lieutenant Hall, who had sat down again, looked up as though it was the first time he had seen him.

"Yes, Private?"

Cloud held out his folded pants. "Sir, my uniform does not fit."

"But we have none larger at present. You will have to make do until Lieutenant Colonel Roosevelt arrives with additional supplies. And you may not wear that towel."

Cloud stepped back, and drew himself to attention. "Yes, sir."

Hall got up, led the Indian out of his tent and stopped before Gabriel and Snake. He unbuttoned two of the brass buttons of his tunic and wiped the sweat from his neck with his yellow kerchief. "Look, men. I don't mind telling you I was not planning to be a Quartermaster. Not when I have already served as an officer with the Tenth Cavalry. But this is a 'hurry up' regiment, and it is my job to help recruits make the distinction between officers and enlisted men. For instance, an officer eats with officers. The enlisted men always eat at a different time and place. An officer will rarely take cover during a battle, although he may very well command his men to do so. Officers give orders which must not be questioned."

Lieutenant Hall sighed and shook his head. "Just imagine. In every troop, we've got men who in civilian life were more used to giving orders than taking them. Scions of rich families who've never heard the word no. Men who ran banks and mines. Champion athletes. More than one mayor and a few characters who have probably killed someone. Yet, each once stomps into my tent the way Cloud just did, like he is the exception to the rule." Hall took off his hat. His black hair was plastered flat with sweat. "In addition to everything else I have to do, Colonel Wood wants me to teach every man, as I encounter him, military protocol. So, Cloud, when I snap at you, like I just did, it is to make you as good a soldier as any regular." Lieutenant Hall spoke this last word with emphasis.

"So, in that regard," he continued, "Atten SHUN!"

Gabriel and T. T. snapped to, as they had seen some of the sergeants do. Jumping to his place beside them, Snake was almost bent backward in an exaggerated pose.

"Right FACE!"

Snake turned left and since Cloud and Gabriel were now behind him, did not realize that he was wrong.

"About FACE!"

As Snake spun, tripping over his own feet, his eyes were level with the leather pouch on Cloud's bare chest. Lieutenant Hall grabbed Snake by the shoulders and spun him into position. Then he barked, "Forward—MARCH!"

Many a trooper hooted as these three recruits, skipping to stay in step, were marched by Lieutenant Hall down the street of the tent city, past a row of red and white company pennants. Finally they came to a pennant with an L upon it—their troop.

There were twelve of them, Hall explained, Troops A through M, omitting Troop J. He did not explain why. He then said to Cloud, "Now get into uniform."

Later that afternoon, L Troop's forty men filed into the mess hall. Troop K had just eaten, and it was their turn to serve the men of L.

The men were all trying to look like soldiers but rivers of sweat ran down their bodies. K Troop joked in their quick, New York accents as they ladled beans into tin bowls for L Troop, plopped cornbread on top, then sloshed their tin mugs full of coffee.

When every man in the troop had found a seat at one of the long tables, Hall gave an order he seemed to enjoy. "*Bon appetit*, gentlemen." Hungry men began to slurp their beans, to dip cornbread, and eat. Gabriel noticed that several of the troopers ate politely, spearing upside down forks with modest bites, the way he had seen his mother eat.

After L Troop had finished, it was their turn to serve M Troop and to wash dishes.

Gabriel found himself beside a tall trooper who looked down at the tub of soapy water with disbelief. "Here," Gabriel said, realizing that this astonished young man had never washed a dish in his life, "you dry." The trooper introduced himself as "Bill" Tiffany, from New York. But Gabriel could see by his clumsiness with the dishes that he was no "Bill." He was definitely a "William."

Later, when they were resting in a slab of shade beside the mess hall, T. T. cut a plug of tobacco and offered it to a recruit who announced he was half Crow. Other men rolled cigarettes, wasting not a shred of tobacco. Most of L Troop, the men learned as they got acquainted, were from Oklahoma—known as the Indian Territories. Snake was teasing a whiskered trooper he'd given the nickname of Prayerful Jones. It seemed that Jones had been a Hell-raiser in his youth, but the Lord had finally got his attention. He had been struck by lightning while plowing. "It was God's call to preach," he said, casting his eyes on the sunburned faces of his comrades. "And I'll be holding Bible study every Sunday. You boys are all invited."

"Well I 'kin hardly wait," Snake chided. "Always heard of that book. But," he spit a brown glob into a can for effect, "never seen it yet."

Too concerned with his potential convert to get the joke, Prayerful murmured, "Praise the Lord."

That evening, many of the men were given nicknames because it was too hard to remember so many new bunkmates in so short a time. But the Indian boys resisted the nicknames the cowboys gave them. Tom Isbell was a Pawnee, known for his keen eyesight and fine marksmanship. Gabriel noticed that he and Cloud seemed to give each other a wide berth. A few others were part Cherokee.

Outside the mess hall, Gabriel found a crate and sat on it. He blew softly into his mouthpiece. Then, squelching burps from his undigested meal, he began to struggle with a tortured version of "Battle Hymn of the Republic." It was nearly impossible to play without the valves of a coronet.

A tall ruddy-faced officer in his late twenties had come over with Captain Luna. One of the sergeants stepped forward and saluted him. "Capt'n Capron, sir," he said, "will you be our company commander? We do not want

Lieutenant Hall."

Capron looked uneasy. "I am honored, sergeant. But Colonel Wood decides such things."

The sergeant grinned. "He will accept our vote, sir. He said so."

Allyn Capron thought for a moment. "Then vote in private, so as not to embarrass Lieutenant Hall." Captain Allyn Capron Jr. came from a fifth generation military family. Allyn Senior commanded an artillery unit and father and son hoped to meet in Cuba. Capron was one of only three West Point men in camp, the others being Colonel Wood and Lieutenant Hall. He had commanded the Pawnee scouts of the Seventh Cavalry, and had practically memorized the Cavalry manual on Indian sign language.

The two captains watched the dark trooper coaxing notes from his mouthpiece. Captain Capron thought he might be Creole. The trooper poured passion into the tiny bit of brass while the tall Indian beside him tapped his foot. The Indian, Capron thought to himself, looked like a Cheyenne or Sioux—one of the northern plains Indians. Capron made a mental note. If he indeed were given command of L Troop, he would need a guide-on, the front corner of the column to carry the troop pennant. He realized the Pawnee Isbell might resent it. The Sioux and Pawnee had been enemies for a hundred years. Pawnees lived in huts, farmed corn and squash. The Sioux lived in teepees and roamed with the buffalo. During hunting season, Pawnee and Sioux competed for the same meat. The Pawnees had long ago deeded what they felt was their land to the government. The trouble was that the nomadic Sioux never considered it their land. To make matters worse, the Sioux hated "the Wolves," the derogatory name they had given the Pawnee regiment, for they often tracked breakaway Sioux bands. It was no wonder that the bow-legged Isbell and the tall Sioux never spoke.

Capron approached Gabriel just as he stopped blowing and began to curse the mouthpiece. "Tell me, trooper," he asked, "did you lose your horn?"

"I left it at home, sir."

"Well that's a shame. For a minute there, I was beginning to believe I was back in New Orleans."

So complimented by an officer, Gabriel tried again. His mouthpiece made hollow music, but Capron and Luna listened with great interest and began to hum along to the tune.

Gabriel squeezed his eyes in concentration. He seemed to be speaking the words through his mouthpiece.

Too bad, Capron mused that Hall had already given a Muscogee man the job of troop trumpeter.

*

That night, Gabriel and Cloud lay on new blankets in their new tent. As taps played, Gabriel winced. Whoever was playing had not even warmed his bugle.

Soon, Cloud's even snoring began. In the distance, a mule brayed a question and a pony seemed to whinny an answer.

Gabriel lay there under the canvas. The smell of waterproofing and the sense of being with hundreds of men made him feel safe. Then, Gabriel imagined Aura's hand on his as he stared into her eyes.

If he slept soon, he might draw her into his dreams. Burrowed into his new blanket, Gabriel closed his eyes.

*

Every night after the officer's mess, Captain Capron held classes for the other officers. He used his dog-eared copy of the United States Cavalry Drill Regulations. He explained that Colonel Wood had decided that officers would have sabers, but that such an unfamiliar weapon in the hands of a cowboy was a menace. Capron told of how one trooper had sharpened his saber and while testing it, had accidentally cut the ear off his horse. But each man would have a Colt revolver and, once they arrived, one of the Norwegian carbines designed especially for the U.S. Cavalry.

During those scorching days in San Antonio, each squad carried their log-like Springfields, learned to stand at attention, at parade rest, and to present arms. Cloud insisted on using his Winchester, preferring it to the Civil War blunderbuss.

And they marched. "Column left," "column right," "to the rear," and "to-the-winds." The men learned to peek from the corners of their eyes without turning their heads as they spaced themselves at arm's length in straight lines.

For Cloud and Gabriel this was not difficult. But for many of the others, including Snake and Isbell, their awkward attempts were pitiful.

Unregimented lives—the very experience that qualified them in the first place, made these individuals question every order.

Soon, L Troop excelled at skirmishing. This amounted to running in a crouch, some men falling prone to fire, while their companions ran ahead. Then as the first line fell and fired, the second ran past them and did the same. A mixture of tribal yelps always accompanied the running charge.

Capron had told the men that the Spanish like to fire in volleys. So the skirmish would be an effective counter to this tactic.

Soon, Cloud was wearing a broad corporal's stripe. When L Troop marched, T. T. Cloud was the anchor of the four-man column.

Their black powder Springfields made an awful racket, and the men choked in the thick, white smoke. They joked that each shot from the Springfield was guaranteed to kill two men: the one aimed at and the one firing. But Captain Capron promised his cursing, coughing troopers that new smokeless carbines would be arriving with Lieutenant Colonel Roosevelt any day now. The rumor quickly spread that whatever a trooper lacked, from bullets to beer, from saddles to soap, from marmalade to a decent mount, from toilet paper to medals—this ROO-za-velt fella would bring it soon. And by the trainload, to boot.

The men were drilled in squads of ten, then by troops of fifty officers and men, and finally, the full regiment of fourteen troops, including the general staff. The regiment created a cloud of dust a mile high.

*

On May tenth, the First Volunteer Cavalry marched for their first review. And still, only the officers had mounts.

The men marched to sharp commands, troop pennants fluttering. Colonel Leonard Wood, riding his spirited chestnut, looked over his command. He sat ramrod straight as Lieutenant Hall, now Regimental Adjutant, walked his mare a few paces behind.

To Colonel Wood's consternation, the journalists had already renamed this array of men before him- this Volunteer Cavalry. It was the first special forces unit ever commissioned by Congress, so some western newspaperman, unable to resist alliteration, had dubbed it "Roosevelt's Rough Riders." It was as though Colonel Wood never existed, and he was furious that Theodore had done nothing to refute it. The Hearst papers were already predicting

"Roosevelt's Rough Riders" would beat the Spaniards single-handedly.

But Leonard Wood remained outwardly calm, a skill that every doctor learned early. And when his blustery friend did arrive, finally bringing the Norwegian carbines and other items Wood had painstakingly requisitioned before he left Washington, Wood would remind Theodore that he was only a "light" Colonel. If Roosevelt hoped to succeed in the military, he would have to learn that insubordination, or any appearance of it, is strictly forbidden.

As the First Volunteer Cavalry waited, each troop drawn up smartly, lieutenants in front of the men, half a horse behind their captains—the mounted captains saluting him with drawn sabers, Colonel Leonard Wood was filled with pride.

But he worried that the Cuban rainy season would begin all too soon. Although the theory that mosquitoes caused malaria had not been fully accepted, Wood suspected it must be true. In every Cuban puddle, Anopheles larvae would hatch. Once the mosquitoes swarmed, the men, no matter how rigorous the training, would sicken and some would die. Over a hundred years ago, a British invasion of Cuba had been defeated more by malaria than by the Spaniards.

Theodore had cabled he would be arriving tomorrow. Once Roosevelt got to camp, Wood knew he would be upstaged. That was precisely why he had held this drill today—to demonstrate to his men who was in command. Theodore did not know, would never know, that he, Leonard Wood, would have refused a subordinate rank in the First Volunteer Cavalry. That would be no way to reach his goal.

The Colonel swept his gaze down the ranks of troopers. Then he presented them with the only reward they sought for their weeks of drill—he brought his glove to the brim of his Stetson and saluted.

*

May 16

Snake had just reached the trench of the latrine when the assembly bugle sounded. He let go a long, amber arc and sighed, "Hear that boys? Colonel's even got a bugle call for takin' a piss." He shook off and glared at Prayerful. "Next one'll be for takin' a shit. Listen up, boys, 'cause we all gotta let go on command."

Again, the bugle called and Snake began to unbuckle his belt. Cloud grabbed his arm. "Get moving. Roosevelt's here."

And it was so.

The troopers watched a dozen men gallop into the camp. Gabriel had never seen anyone like the leader. His hat brim was pinned up on one side. The man's too many teeth were framed by a sandy mustache. His spectacles caught the sun. Unlike the blue-clad officers in camp, this ROO-za-velt wore a tan military blouse. A blue and white polka dot kerchief hung at his neck. Beside Roosevelt's pinto ran a barking wire-haired terrier.

The usually stern Colonel Wood shook his head in amazement. Roosevelt reined his pony to a halt and leapt down as his panting dog sat in the dust. "Here now, Little Cuba," Roosevelt commanded loudly, and slapped his thigh with his gloves. "Salute the Colonel, boy." To the men's amazement, as Roosevelt beamed, the dog sat up.

Wood saluted back, laughing in spite of himself.

The two men shook hands. Then Roosevelt addressed him, but loud enough for the throng of troopers to hear. "Sir, I have come with saddles." There was a cheer as he beckoned to one of the mounted civilians behind him, who handed Roosevelt a short rifle. "And the Krag-Jorgensons!" Roosevelt declared, holding the carbine high. "And gentlemen, what your tired feet have been waiting for—the best ponies money can buy!" At this, the men roared and his hat flew into the air. Snake and Prayerful danced a jig.

Wood raised his hand to quiet the troopers. He stared at the strangers who had come with Roosevelt, neatly dressed young men in city clothes and straw boaters.

Roosevelt looked over his shoulder, then coughed into his fist. "Oh yes," he said, "and I've brought volunteers from New York. For each man I will personally vouch. Furthermore, not one of them requests anything more than to serve as a common private."

The Colonel watched the New Yorkers dismount, greeting each man with a handshake. Gabriel was turning away when he heard a familiar voice.

"Marcus B. Hammer, Colonel Wood. I have come with the Columbia contingent."

*

Gabriel got little sleep that night. He lay his lips against the cool mouthpiece. Although Marcus had not seen him, they would eventually meet, at the mess or the latrine. And then Marcus would tell Colonel Wood that Gabriel was from Fort Chambers and God knows what else. Whether the Colonel believed Marcus or not, his falsified letters of recommendation would be discovered and Gabriel knew he would be cut from the regiment. So would Cloud.

Just when they were becoming soldiers, Gabriel realized, Marcus Hammer could take it all away. He closed his eyes and saw Aura's face. Then Gabriel breathed a promise. He would not let Marcus B. Hammer ruin this chance to make a name for himself. Even if he had to kill him.

CHAPTER 8

This morning, Corporal Cloud's squad lay in a line on the firing range. Gabriel closed his right hand around the pistol grip stock of the new Krag-Jorgenson. He rested his left arm against a sandbag and gripped the routed groove of the walnut hand guard. They waited for Lieutenant Day to give the order to load. When it came, each man rolled onto his side, picked a brass cartridge from his bandoleer, then fed it into the loading gate.

Gabriel flipped the gate up, then the bolt down. As the Lieutenant counted in his Oklahoma drawl, each man fed in four more rounds, working the bolt each time. Know your load, the Lieutenant shouted. In battle, a trooper who fired on an empty chamber might not live to tell the tale. Gabriel aligned the notches of his rear sight with the vertical pin at the end of the barrel. He aimed at the heart of a pasteboard torso a hundred yards distant and tried to imagine a Spaniard there.

"Fire!"

Gabriel squeezed the trigger and his Krag-Jorgenson barked. He flipped the bolt up, ejected the spent cartridge, then flipped it down.

Again the order came. "Fire!"

After five volleys, Cloud led his squad out to inspect their targets. Prayerful's target had been penetrated with five separate holes near the heart. Gabriel had missed the center with three shots, but hit with two. Cloud had scattered his shots, but all were within the tight circumference of the center ring.

Gabriel's heart sank. T. T. Cloud deserved his corporals' stripes—the men willingly carried out his orders. But so far, Gabriel was known only for a tooting mouthpiece. What he really wanted, was to become one of the sharp shooters of L Troop.

By the time the squad had emptied their bandoleers—a hundred rounds for each man—Gabriel's shots were nearly as good as Cloud's. The corporal grunted encouragement and then, in a totally uncharacteristic manner, praised Gabriel's improvement to the other men. Prayerful Jones, a man who had weeks earlier said Christians ought not to kill, had the tightest pattern of hits.

Captain Capron told them there would be no saber training. Snake remarked about what a man might cut off in such perilous drill and Prayerful moved his lips in a silent supplication.

As the men took a rest, Roosevelt marched back and forth, giving commands to an imaginary troop. The men did not laugh, for they could see their peppery Lieutenant Colonel was practicing, totally unaware that his men overheard him. They seemed to appreciate that he was learning with them.

*

Despite Colonel Wood's advice, Roosevelt did not always eat with the officers. Instead, he liked to pop in and dine with an astonished table of enlisted men.

Tonight, he slid his plate next to Hamilton Fish. Roosevelt joked with Fish, who had been blessed with his mother's square, handsome face, but had his father's athletic frame and protruding ears. Fish had been the first New Yorker to volunteer. He had called on Roosevelt and explained that he wanted to serve without any privilege—and to be treated like any one else. He had already been offered a place with Captain Woodbury Kane's Knickerbockers, K Troop. But Fish declined. Roosevelt admired the lad for that. Here Hamilton Fish was, just having served kitchen duty, stirring pots of beans and cutting cornbread for gamblers and cowboys. That very afternoon, Roosevelt had ordered Lieutenant Hall to assign Fish and Hammer to I Troop, Captain Schuyler McGinnis's New Mexico recruits.

As he chewed a mouthful of beans, Roosevelt noticed that Hammer was not eating. How could the lad be so sour-faced among such splendid comrades? And in such a remarkable place! Although sweat rolled down his face, and his beans were watery and undercooked, Roosevelt had never in his life been happier.

The Lieutenant Colonel wiped his mustache and, as he always did when broaching a delicate subject, began to polish his spectacles. "Methinks young Marcus looks unwell, Mister Fish."

Marcus's face flushed, and he took a tentative spoon of beans.

Now Roosevelt's eyes bored on Marcus through clean glasses.

Something is not right, Roosevelt mused. Why, the whole table seemed ill at ease. Usually, the men would ply him with questions. "Colonel, what do you think of this? When do we get to Cuba, Colonel?" But tonight he heard only slurps, the occasional burp, and the discreet passing of wind. Roosevelt grunted, then intentionally farted. "The expulsion of one's methane," he explained to the embarrassed men, "is nothing to be ashamed of. Indeed, it breeds health, although," he laughed, "it does present a shock to the olfactory gland." This had broken the silence, and some of the men began to talk.

Trying to swallow the very beans he had been forced to stir hours before, Marcus Hammer was sullen. Why had Fish turned down a place for them both in Kane's Knickerbockers to join this band of misfits? He wondered if Roosevelt would grant him a transfer. .

As he had been taught to do, Hamilton Fish chewed politely. He realized this adjustment must be hard for Marcus. At Columbia, the bull-necked lad had been the frontiersman—a character out of dime novels. But now he must feel cowed, eating with real westerners.

He realized already that bringing Marcus had been a mistake. Why had he weakened the night Roosevelt promised him a place? Between sobs Marcus begged Fish to take him too, showing a scathing letter from Judge Hammer. If Marcus did not apply himself more to his studies, the Judge threatened to cut off his funds. Marcus told Fish that before he went back to Fort Chambers, he would jump into the East River. So Hamilton Fish pleaded his case to Roosevelt.

Marcus was immature and willful, but Fish had been touched when Marcus showed such vulnerability. Judge Hammer's tyranny had not given Marcus a chance to develop anything but muscles. Under that swaggering exterior Fish could see that Marcus was just a boy trying to live up to his father's expectations.

But for Fish, there had never been any question. His family had always answered the nation's call. The challenge was as natural as breathing. His father was openly proud that Fish had been the first to be accepted by Roosevelt, ahead of a Roosevelt's own police sergeant! But Hamilton Fish realized that his father might have had a strong influence on the decision, and the family name was to be honored at any cost. In a way, he had as much to prove as Marcus Hammer.

None of these New Mexico boys, he knew, would be fooled by "Wildcat" Hammer. Troop I had brought a mountain lion cub as their mascot. They did not need another. Besides, he had always suspected Marcus' story was sheer braggadocio. But now he was annoyed that Marcus Hammer seemed to be sulking.

*

Lieutenant Hall awoke in the moonlight. It was unbelievable that a thousand men and as many horses could be so quiet. Then he heard the stamp of a sentry as he reversed his direction. A moment later there came a sharp crack and a heavy grunt and Hall knew a mare had chastened a stallion's attentions by kicking his ribs.

Hall could not get back to sleep without a drink. He reached under his pillow, found the bottle, and studied its contents in the moonlight. He had rationed himself, and tried only to drink before going to bed. But that noon, Colonel Wood had smelled whiskey on his breath, and had cautioned Hall that the men should have no alcohol and that the officers were to set an example.

There was one swallow left, but perhaps it would be enough.

It was amazing how these men, hand-picked for their resourcefulness, were like children. Men who had been used to disciplining others were so eager to succeed as soldiers that they wore him out. Day and night, he had a line of supplicants following him. Men he was embarrassed, yet obliged, to deny. As Adjutant to Wood and Roosevelt, as well as Quartermaster, Hall's job was nearly impossible. He was personally responsible for every detail of this regiment—from saddles to toothpicks.

And Colonel Wood and Roosevelt were difficult masters, for they were opposites. Wood spoke quietly when things were going well, but if things went wrong, or a man did not do his duty, Wood's temper could flare. On those occasions, everyone including Roosevelt jumped to do his bidding. For Wood there were two ways to do things, the Army way, and the wrong way.

Roosevelt, neither hampered nor informed by a military education, was unpredictable. His enthusiasm was infectious. Everyone, including Hall, found himself carrying out the most outlandish commands. But because Roosevelt led by example, Hall and the men were all mesmerized—were swept along by his enthusiasm.

It was the very absence of duty that summoned Hall from sleep. Night was the only solitude he could expect and solitude had always been the source of his poetic thoughts. As a shave-tail Second Lieutenant in Arizona, he had savored nights like this.

The sleeping troop beneath a starry canopy conjured metaphors. His poems, written at first in courtship, had finally been sent to a publisher. Now they were in their third printing. With the Indian Wars won, the army trimmed its bulk and Hall resigned his commission to write full time. His verses never strayed far from the plight of a young officer on a lonely mission, or the innkeeper's daughter at an isolated watering post and her sudden love for a soldier passing through.

Tom Hall's books had just begun to make money when the *Maine* blew up. The call of drums had been irresistible. Already established as a best selling author, he would now have the chance to distinguish himself in war. He could feel the ground swell. He would write the definitive novel about the war and the best part was that his publishers had already vowed to publish it.

This sleeping regiment. Yes. Hall pulled a worn journal from his bag and angled it to catch the moonlight. He remembered a popular children's rhyme and began to alter it.

> *Rich man, poor man, Indian chief,*
> *Doctor, lawyer, not one thief...*

All right, there were signs of thievery in camp. But, when the thief was caught, Roosevelt dismissed him as quickly as he had a morphine addict. Yet, "thief" rhymed prettily with "chief" and warmed by the whisky, Hall relented. He continued writing.

> *Merchant, sheriff, artist, clerk,*
> *Clubman, quite unused to work,*
> *Miner, ocean gondolier,*
> *Broker, banker, engineer,*
> *Cowboy, copper, actor, mayor,*
> *College athletes, men of prayer,*
> *Champion amateur sports, to boot—*
> *And all of them can ride and shoot!*

Satisfied, Lieutenant Hall closed his journal. He was lucky to be here, even in the thankless role of Adjutant. He had tried every avenue for a commission without success until someone had passed one of his letters to Colonel Wood. Thankfully, both Wood and Capron remembered him from Arizona. And Roosevelt had read him! And now he was more than Tom Hall, solitary author. He was glad to be part of a regiment again. And especially, the colorful First Volunteer Cavalry.

Tomorrow promised to be a long and exhausting day. He was surprised by the resentment of men toward him. Colonel Wood did not draw their venom, but his Adjutant did. And Theodore Roosevelt was everywhere at once, barking orders, cajoling, making men laugh, forever the populist. But even Roosevelt made a few cry when they were dismissed for a forbidden deed. Then came his shout—"Hall- take down this order. And see to it that it is carried out—at once!"

Lieutenant Hall dreaded the dawn. He was not sleepy, and worse, out of whiskey. As he lifted the bottle and sucked the last drop, the silhouette of a stocky trooper parted his mosquito netting.

Marcus Hammer stared at the bottle and then allowed a conspiratorial smile. "I got caught in town, Lieutenant. Lost my pass. The sentry sent me to you."

This trooper knew it was forbidden to drink in camp and now the very officer that was responsible for reprimands and kitchen duty had been caught taking a nip. Hall also knew that Hammer had never been issued a pass, and as he slipped the bottle under his bunk, he said so.

"I went with two boys from New Mexico," Hammer explained. "They wanted to desert, and I thought I could talk them out of it."

Hall wondered what to do. Hammer had a mean streak and if he gave the boy too strong a punishment now, he might tell Roosevelt that he had caught his Adjutant finishing a bottle of spirits.

"How about the other two men?"

Marcus Hammer stared at the bottle. "They deserted sir. But I just needed a little female company. Once I got that, my first thought was of the regiment." Marcus Hammer's voice was firm. "When a man needs something," he said, spinning the bottle out from under the bunk with his boot, "he just has to get it, doesn't he?"

"All right, Hammer. Let's just keep this between us, shall we? As long as a man puts the regiment first, minor transgressions must be overlooked."

Marcus Hammer's leer was not pretty. Hall knew this one act had made them equal. He no longer had any power over Hammer, and the boy knew it.

"You sleep well, sir," Hammer said, backing out of Hall's tent.

*

The new mounts were Western horses that would eat anything and endure hostile environments. Even so, a few officers had purchased thoroughbreds. To save confusion, Colonel Wood instructed Hall to distribute the horses by color. Each Captain was given a vote and Capron quickly chose roans for L Troop. A Troop, F Troop and K Troop chose bays; B, E, and M sorrels; C, G, and I browns; and the remainder, D, and H got grays.

Although Cloud and Gabriel had broken a few ponies, they were no match for forty neighing young mounts. So Roosevelt held "auditions" with a dozen of the meanest, wildest ponies. When the test was completed, he had identified a few wranglers. They got the bone-crushing job of breaking horses for the entire regiment.

Bill McGinty was barely five feet tall, and could not keep up in marches anyway. But the man rode like he had been born on a horse. Three of the full-time broncobusters were Indian, and they quickly worked their way through the unbroken horses.

Colonel Wood took particular interest in watching how the men handled their unfamiliar mounts. It seemed to be the only recreation he allowed himself. As the regiment assembled for the first mounted drill, Snake tried to mount his willful roan. Each time he put a foot into the stirrup, the filly would lie down. Time after time, cursing under his breath, Snake tried again. But each time, with a great sigh, the mare lay down and, as Snake leaped away, she rolled over. Officers were biting their lips, trying not to laugh, but the troopers were less thoughtful. Snake looked appealingly to Captain Capron for help, but got no response. He threw his hat into the dust. At that instant, the mare got up. Snake gingerly put his foot into the stirrup and swung into the saddle. Then the roan trotted into the line.

Capron took the men through the same drills they had learned on foot. The drills were not easy considering the skittish mounts. Despite the horsemanship of nearly every Rough Rider, it took days of hard work under the relentless sun before they could begin to perform anything resembling a mounted drill.

Gabriel's colt obeyed until another horse bumped him, then he would buck. Still, L Troop mastered their mounts so quickly that Roosevelt had them lead the regimental mounted drill. On this day, Captain Capron wore regulation blue. His two lieutenants, Day and Thomas followed him. Behind them, L Troop rode two abreast in a long line. Cloud carried the troop pennant. Behind them, the other troops followed.

Today, each trooper had outfitted as though for battle. Behind Gabriel's saddle a rolled tent half contained his blanket. His carbine was sheathed near his right knee and a bandoleer of ammunition weighed his shoulder. At his waist, he wore his Colt 45.

The regiment rode in a cloud of dust, creaking leather and clanking canteens. With Cloud and Snake flanking him, Gabriel Scriven felt invincible.

Because of their sloppy drill, Troop I brought up the rear. In end of the line, far away from Sergeant Hamilton Fish, Marcus Hammer jerked the reins. His chestnut, flanks bleeding from frantic spurring, bucked out of line.

Colonel Wood watched his men ride past. Nobody dared call them Roosevelt's Rough Riders to his face. Beside him, half a length back,

Roosevelt grinned and nodded to the Captains. Wood realized there would be no First Volunteer Cavalry without Roosevelt, but he was learning slowly. A few days ago, Wood had admonished him for providing a keg of beer at the enlisted men's mess. Even though Roosevelt paid for it out of his own pocket, such unadvised behavior by an officer resulted in a reprimand. Then there was the concert. The regiment had been invited to the San Antonio fairgrounds for an evening of band music. Wood had been unable to attend, but Theodore took the regiment. As part of one composition, band members fired their revolvers, loaded with blanks. The men of the town, all of them wearing side arms, took this as an invitation and followed suit.

The next day the newspaper printed a tale of how the Rough Riders had shot up the concert, how they had jumped their horses over streetcars and caused general mayhem. Lieutenant Hall came to the regiment's defense, swearing that all weapons had been locked away, as was common practice unless the men were drilling. Roosevelt had said nothing, and Wood had apologized. It turned out that the editor of the newspaper had been denied access to the Rough Rider camp, and was trying to get even with his story of cowboy mayhem.

Wood realized Roosevelt would never look like a soldier. He sat his horse like a mounted fire plug. He resembled an unkempt boy. His Stetson looked like Little Cuba had been chewing it but Wood realized this might be Roosevelt's attempt to look experienced.

*

That night, the officers had a congratulatory mess. Across the table from Roosevelt, Captain Bucky O'Neill held forth in his Irish brogue. Regimental Surgeon James Church congratulated Lieutenant Hall on his appointment as Adjutant, since the Quartermaster's duties had now been assigned to Jacob Schwaizer. Hall, enjoying his third glass of port, was having an enjoyable discussion of the novels of Andre Balzac with Church.

Roosevelt listened with interest, then interrupted. "As you all know," he said, "for a time I dedicated my life to the solitary pursuits of ranching and literature. Actually made a decent living with the books. Not so, the ranching. Both volumes of *The Winning of the West* sell vigorously, I am told. But gentlemen—my tomes on Thomas Hart Benton and novelist Gouveneur Morris are another story. They have," he moaned, "underwhelmed readers by the score."

Roosevelt looked thoughtful. "I even considered," he nudged Hall with his elbow, "taking up the novel. But my thoughts," his hands flew up in mock confusion, "were far too abundant to get onto paper."

He raised his glass. "So I defer to Crane and Hall here." Roosevelt emitted a theatrical sigh. "I shall just have to live life rather than invent it. Lacking, as it were, the ability to do otherwise."

At that moment Colonel Leonard Wood strode in and Hall called the officers to attention. Wood wore a tight-lipped smile. He clutched a yellow telegram in his fist.

Roosevelt knew what it must contain. At Wood's command, he had cabled President McKinley that afternoon, declaring that the Rough Riders were ready.

"Gentlemen," Wood announced, "Secretary Alger has ordered us the to the disembarkation port. The First Volunteer Cavalry leaves in twenty-four hours for Tampa, Florida."

After the cheers and applause had eased, Roosevelt bellowed, "And then gentlemen, to CUBA!"

CHAPTER 9

At midnight, the two trains of Rough Riders stopped in a sleepy delta town. Both Wood and Roosevelt, each in charge of a train, warned their men to catch up on their sleep, but their spirits had been too high. Now, a thousand complaining ponies and a hundred and fifty protesting mules had to be unloaded and manure shoveled from their cars. Then the animals had to be fed, watered, and reloaded. The fire hydrant was opened but the horses could not drink the gushing water. One resourceful woman ran to her house and brought back her copper bath tub. Soon, other people came with buckets and hastily rinsed chamber pots. But the watering, feeding, and reloading of animals who wanted no part of the cramped box cars was a Herculean task. Afterwards, the exhausted troopers were lucky to catch an hour of sleep in their cramped, hard seats.

The next day, as the bunting-draped trains chugged along the Gulf of Mexico, throngs of well-wishers crowded every station. Girls handed tired but happy troopers ladles of milk and slices of pie. Snake was nearly dragged out of the window when a buxom lass threw her arms around his neck. Gabriel grabbed his suspenders and pulled him back in, but Snake's polka dot kerchief was taken. As the train pulled away, the girl clutched the kerchief to her breast and Snake observed that he'd rather be that bandanna than some "shit shovellin' soljer."

In the next car, the troopers were practicing a new cheer.

TOUGH!
We're the STUFF!
We're goin' to fight
And we won't get
ENOUGH!

The cheer was followed each time by cowboy yips and blood curdling Indian whoops.

As the trains crossed the Florida panhandle, the troopers sang, one car louder than the other, "Oh Susanna, The Girl I Left Behind Me," and their favorite, "There'll Be a Hot Time in the Old Town Tonight." The singing was a harmless battle that everybody won, and occasionally, in a briefly pious mood, they would lapse into hymns like "Onward Christian Soldiers."

Roosevelt visited each car, boisterously singing off-tune. His fist pumped the air as he led their songs.

Jammed in the seat between Snake and Cloud, Gabriel yawned. Lieutenant Hall had told them that two things a soldier rarely got were sleep and food. They might as well get used to scarcities of both, and consequently, when there was the opportunity for either, a man had to take it.

The rumor had spread that Colonel Wood had drawn his revolver on an engineer who refused to leave early. And with his own eyes, Gabriel had seen Roosevelt threaten prison for a switchman who wanted to divert his train onto a siding for a freight to pass.

This was a train to glory. No matter that the aisles were slick with tobacco spit and the toilets were overflowing. The train made its motion, cut the thick air and hurtled them along with power and purpose. Under such circumstances, it was impossible to look back.

As Gabriel experienced his first gulf dawn, the coral light and the damp sea air, he tooted reveille on his mouthpiece. But harmonicas and a loose-stringed banjo soon drowned him out.

Their train arrived in Tampa and discharged steam in a swirl of confused soldiers, spooked horses, and clattering wagons. Unable to get clear orders, Colonel Wood led most of his men into a field, while the others stabled the animals. The nervous Rough Riders, conspicuous in their tan britches and polka dot kerchiefs, struggled to join their shelter halves into tents and then to pitch them in the sandy soil. They heard the regulars taunting, "Well ain't they PRETTY! In them summer camp uny-forms and all! How come you boys ain't wearin' specs like ROO-za-velt? Hell, we might as well go home. Old Four Eyes' boys is here!"

Across a stream that separated them from their white comrades, the Tenth Cavalry had already pitched a tidy tent city. The dusky veterans watched, at least trying to hide their smiles and laughter as these cowboys, who must have been better at riding and shooting than setting up camp, struggled. Lieutenant Hall galloped here and there, trying to keep lanes open for horses and men. More than once, to the laughter and jibes of the regulars, Hall made men rip out their stakes and start over.

Gabriel and Cloud had joined the halves of their tent and were driving the last stakes when Roosevelt trotted up on his pinto. He stopped at the stream, dismounted, and placed his fists against his belt. He beamed across at a gray haired Negro in civilian clothes who was wading toward him.

Roosevelt pumped the old man's hand. After they had conversed a few minutes, Roosevelt brought him over. "Julius," Roosevelt said, "I want you to meet Corporal T. T. Cloud. His father helped defeat Custer at the Little Big Horn."

Julius shook hands with Cloud.

"He is both friend and soldier," Roosevelt said.

Julius's yellowed eyes danced as he gestured toward the Tenth. "Served fourteen years with that outfit." After a little good natured banter, Julius turned serious. "Sir, Mizz Edith sent me to fetch you for dinner. She has reserved a suite at the hotel. I'll go ahead and draw your bath."

Roosevelt seemed embarrassed. He looked off toward the hotel's silver domes that rose from the dust like a mirage. "Well, Julius, I am not free to honor her invitation. Colonel Wood and I have been trying to find General Wheeler. Do you know if he has arrived?"

The servant shook his head.

Roosevelt stroked his mustache. As he did, his eyes fell on Gabriel.

"Aha!" he blurted. "I have it! I'll send Scriven with you, Julius. Don't worry, Scriven, the more disheveled you are the better. When you get to the hotel, inform my good wife of how very busy I am." His face broke into that many-toothed grin. "Lay it on a bit—you know, orders from Washington—all that. She'll believe a trooper from my command before she will me. Or even Julius." He winked. "You see, over the years, Julius and I have, how shall I put it—tested our credulity with Edith. Ha, ha, ha.

"Then, when you have finished that, find General Wheeler. And inform the General where we have bivouacked."

Gabriel saluted and followed the old servant. They threaded their way through regiments of bored regulars, squatting beside teepees of stacked carbines; state militia, dressed like the regulars, but with some incongruous detail such as bright blue pants. The militia carried on the self-conscious banter of men who were nervous in the presence of real soldiers. Officers and orderlies trotted their mounts back and forth, trying to undo the chaos of a disembarkation point with a single rail line, and the subsequent bottle neck that it had caused. With no orders, regiments claimed space wherever they could. This caused heated arguments between officers who had once been friends and who knew better.

"You will move your regiment at once, sir," a red faced Lieutenant shouted from his horse.

A stocky Colonel stood in the dirt with his arms crossed. "I shall not, John," replied the Colonel. "without orders from General Miles."

The Lieutenant retorted, "General Shafter is in command, not Miles. And the Ohio Militia has claim here."

"This, Johnny, is not Ohio. You weekend warriors had better learn to deploy first. Ask questions later. I assure you, I shall not move."

The Lieutenant galloped toward the silver domes of the Plant Hotel.

When they left the dusty camp and entered the gate of the hotel grounds, Gabriel thought he had died and gone to heaven. The hotel, a red brick, five story palace, was ringed by a wide verandah that followed the contour of the building. There were acres of gardens. Beyond a curved bridge, two officers in shirtsleeves swung clubs at a tiny white ball. Sparrows and seagulls called above the tall pines and the palm trees shot up like green rockets. A profusion of flowers and shrubs grew everywhere. Officers and their ladies strolled along the gravel paths as though the chaos outside the gate did not exist. The verandah was overflowing with officers who sat in wicker rockers and sipped iced lemonade against the heat.

It seemed to Gabriel that this reunion of officers, consoling each other on the dearth of promotions over the past twenty years, were completely unconcerned with the regiments outside the gates who struggled to find the order they had been trained to expect.

The Plant Hotel, with its minaret towers, gothic windows and keyhole arches reminded him of the stereoscope he had seen of the Alhambra Palace. The hotel seemed big enough to house the entire Rough Rider regiment. As his dusty hobnailed boots clomped on the polished porch, Gabriel straightened his tunic and removed his sweat-stained hat. As he raked his mustache, he realized his fingers smelled of manure. This was no way to meet a lady, much less Mrs. Roosevelt.

Gabriel had just paused on the verandah behind Julius when he heard glass break.

"Sorry, General Shafter," a waiter said to an extremely fat officer sitting in a wicker rocker. "My fault. I'll fetch another." Near General Shafter, several officers huddled in animated conversation. They seemed to be arguing amongst themselves. Then Gabriel saw a sparrow-like man in a tropical suit step from behind Shafter's chair. The white haired man leaned over the sweating general and engaged him in conversation. The little man saw Gabriel, jumped up and announced in a southern accent, "Well, I declare, Leonard's outfit has arrived! Where's your regiment, son?"

As Gabriel told him, his eyes danced with merriment. "Innybody teach you to salute an officer?" Gabriel raised his hand tentatively.

"At ease, son," Wheeler chuckled, "you were not to know. My uniform arrived this morning, but in the wrong coluh. I shall wait for the version you wear as it suits me better than blue." He laughed as though at some joke. "I am the General of the cavalry, Joe Wheeler."

Gabriel jerked a salute. Then he told General Wheeler that Roosevelt was trying to find him. During his explanation that the Rough Riders were setting up camp as best they could, General Wheeler shot a glance at Shafter, who was now surrounded by protesting officers. "Thank you, son. I shall go to him at once."

Following Julius, Gabriel stepped into the cool lobby and stood near a giant palm frond. Officers who must have overheard were staring. Gabriel drew himself up and tried to walk purposefully among the ornate furniture, tall Chinese vases, and marble statues. Brass stands held placards that touted the hotel's conveniences. Completely Fireproof. Five Hundred Luxurious Rooms. Modern, Steam Heated. Fully Electrified. First Electric Elevator in the South.

Foreign officers argued excitedly. One with a plumed cap appeared to be Japanese. Another, in a band-box cap spoke French. Then there was a German with a huge mustache and a spiked helmet.

As the electric elevator climbed, Gabriel's nervous stomach churned. He looked at the filthy, unshaven soldier in the mirror, spit on his fingers and tried to subdue his cowlick. When the elevator jerked to a halt, the operator opened the scissored gate.

And there stood Marcus B. Hammer.

Beside him was Lieutenant Tom Hall, the Adjutant. "Scriven," Hall blurted, "what are you doing here?"

"Colonel Roosevelt sent me with a message for his wife," Gabriel said, watching Marcus Hammer's shocked face, and his hand that raised to the stub of his ear.

Hall cocked his head. "But I do not understand. We've just come from her suite. She expects the Colonel at any moment." Then, Hall turned to the Negro servant. "Are you Julius?"

"Yessir."

"Mrs. Roosevelt requests medical attention. Have you come with news from Doctor Church?"

This time Julius spoke up. "No doctor is required, Lieutenant."

"But—"

As Julius stepped past Hall, Gabriel followed. His eyes met Hammer's for an instant, and what he saw was gratifying. The bully looked confused and even a little fearful.

Lieutenant Hall had caught the uneasiness between them, but as the elevator door closed, Hammer remained uncharacteristically silent. Hall concluded that these two troopers were intimidated by both the posh hotel and meeting their commander's wife.

At the end of the carpeted hallway, Julius paused at a mahogany door and knocked. As they waited, Gabriel first rubbed one boot on his leggings, then the other. His heart was still beating hard from the encounter with Marcus. So, he thought, Marcus had just realized what he had himself known since that Marcus rode into San Antonio with Fish. Two arch enemies were in the same regiment!

The door swung open and amid the sudden smell of perfume, the expectant smile of the handsome woman in the doorway turned into a disappointed grimace. She was a woman of thirty-five, with a simple face—straight eyebrows and honest, dark eyes. Her auburn hair had come undone a little and she pushed it back with an impatient hand. Her long neck, framed in a square bodice, glowed with light perspiration. She fanned herself vigorously.

"So," Edith Roosevelt said, her quick eyes flashing, "my husband has sent one of his boys to bring the news." Then she forced a smile. "Don't be offended, young man," she said, "do come in."

Behind Edith Roosevelt, was the largest four poster bed Gabriel had ever seen. Except for his mother's, he had never before been in a lady's bedroom. Despite the soothing chop of the electric ceiling fan and the presence of Julius, he felt uncomfortable—a dirty trooper in a lady's boudoir. "I am Private Scriven, Ma'am." Then, with sudden inspiration, he added, "the Colonel's bugler."

Edith Roosevelt's look of annoyance faded as she tilted her head back and gave a laugh that ran the full length of her long neck. Dabbing the tears from her eyes, she finally said, "Well, Private Scriven, I am not surprised. Do you know," she shot Julius a hard look, "I have been here for nearly a day and my husband has yet to walk a hundred yards to welcome me? Three trying days and nights by train from Sagamore, leaving our protesting children in pandemonium, worried sick that their father is going off to battle. You would think Colonel Roosevelt would have the decency to come himself to tell me what I suspect is true. That he is too busy playing soldier to bother with his wife." Her good humor was gone now and the color had risen in her face. She had taken on a strong, no-nonsense countenance that reminded Gabriel of Thelma. "Well, you can tell my busy husband that even if he sends his regimental band, It would not assuage my very deep displeasure."

When she realized how uncomfortable her words had made Gabriel,

Edith Roosevelt sighed and offered him ice tea. "You can go, Julius," she snapped. "I shall send a note with this young man."

Edith pulled a chair close, patted it for him to sit, then poured Gabriel's tea. The first swallow tasted like nectar to his parched throat and before he realized his bad manners, he had drained the tumbler and was gasping for breath.

Edith Roosevelt laughed, but this time with open pleasure. "Isn't this Florida heat absolutely disgusting," she declared, pouring Gabriel another portion. "It is just like a man to leave the comfort of home to don a uniform and to camp in a swamp." Then, her face sobered, as though she had just remembered something. "But Theodore..." She gave Gabriel an encouraging smile. "I must admit," she said, "the cause is just."

As he drank, this time more slowly, Gabriel was composing a few words to convince her that his Colonel was indeed too busy for such niceties. But before he could speak, shesuddenly asked, "Tell me, young man, what caused you to volunteer?"

Gabriel considered her question. He had never been asked it and he had thought little about an answer. "Well, ma'am, the Spanish started it."

Edith looked doubtful but she did not follow this line of discussion. She fixed her clear, somewhat heavy lidded eyes on him. "You must have left a family, perhaps a sweetheart behind. You have been taught by someone to use a napkin. And you must be a musician, are you not?"

Gabriel allowed himself to smile. "Why, yes ma'am. I was headed for music college."

Mrs. Roosevelt pursed her lips. "But you chose to shoot other young men instead."

Gabriel liked Edith Roosevelt. He could see that she was a match for his feisty commander. He would not be able to deceive her. "Mrs. Roosevelt, the truth is that things down here are a real mess. And only a man like the Colonel can straighten it out. Plenty of officers are taking it easy in this hotel while their men shift for themselves. But not Colonel Roosevelt. The orders are not clear and he is having to improvise. It is a twenty-four hour job, ma'am. He will not have his own dinner until his own men are billeted and fed. That's just the way he is."

As he spoke, his words rushing, Edith Roosevelt nodded. Then she rose, went to her wardrobe and withdrew a letter. As she handed it to Gabriel, he noticed a child's scrawl on the front. "Give Theodore this," she said. "And tell him I have others from the children." Then she gave a knowing smile. "He'll come when he can, I am sure. And thank you, Private Scriven. Will you please be careful when you get to Cuba? Theodore can be quite brash, you know. And even foolhardy. We want him back with as few holes as possible. And your own mother will want you back just as you are."

As he tucked her letter into his tunic, Gabriel wondered that this woman had so easily sensed how much his mother meant to him. He realized how long it had been since he had written her.

Downstairs, Gabriel lingered in the lobby. He did not want to encounter Hammer again, and the guise of official business gave him protection. The sound of tinkling of glasses spilled out of a smoky parlor. Drawn by the sound, Gabriel edged into a bar packed with men, their voices amplified by alcohol. Near the bar, a broad shouldered gentleman who looked like he had stepped from the haberdashery pages, raised his shot glass. "A toast, gentlemen of the fourth estate, and to the worst newspaper in New York, *the World!*"

Amid jeers and laughter he drained his glass. A thin, unshaven man with a narrow nose climbed slowly up onto the bar. "Sir Richard The Lion Harding Davis," he boomed, "has fired his usual shot heard around the bar." The drinkers all groaned at his pun. "But he writes for *the Journal,* William Randolph Hearst's rag of a paper. And for that, I award him the Yellow Badge of Courage!" Even Davis laughed at this and edged in closer.

"Have one on me, soldier," the unshaven man coughed. "You'll be doing the dirty work. Scribes like me just write about it. What'll it be?"

"Why, a whiskey."

"Name's Stephen Crane. You're with Roosevelt, aren't you?"

When he nodded, Crane leaned closer. "The Dandy boys. But you don't look like you were born with a silver spoon in your mouth."

As they sipped their whiskey, Gabriel explained that most of the Rough Riders were cowboys.   He enjoyed Crane's sudden interest when he described T. T. Cloud. The reporter opened a pad and began to take notes, licking his pencil during pauses. "I've been accused of making things up," Crane explained. He swallowed some whiskey and coughed again. "Have you read *The Red Badge of Courage?*"

Of course, Gabriel realized. The Stephen Crane. Every school boy had read the popular novel of a young Civil War soldier who had first run from battle, then returned to fight bravely.

"Why yes. And I loved it. I'm honored to meet the author."

Crane gave a sardonic smile, revealing yellowed teeth. "Well, soldiers think it authentic. Others, jealous writers, mostly, claim foul—that I have never seen battle and so could not possibly write about one. True, I was too young to witness the Civil War. But I did cover the Crimean affair. And a war is a war. Boys becoming men, way too fast." He caught the barman's eyes and ordered another round, but Gabriel deferred. He didn't want to return to Roosevelt drunk.

"Take *Moby Dick*," Crane continued, "Ol' Melville knew little of whaling. Direct experience might have produced a more authentic fishing book, but hardly a tale of obsession. Details can be made up by a good writer, but not the challenges a man must overcome."

A glass of whiskey slid down the bar and stopped in front of Gabriel. He looked in the direction from which it had come. The dapper Hearst correspondent who had made the first toast eased onto the next stool and extended his hand. "Richard Harding Davis," he said, "and the whiskey is a bribe. Drink it and take me to Roosevelt."

Crane gave a low laugh. "*The Journal* seeks its own kind. You can have the Rough Riders, Dick. I'll cover the regulars."

Davis seemed not the least bit offended. "Yes, Stephen, let's stick with what we know best. While you cover the poor, unwashed ranks," he said, lifting his cleft chin, "I shall cover the brash and daring. Besides, we know what Theodore thinks of you. You caused him enough embarrassment with that case you reported when he was Police Commissioner."

"Roosevelt is an amateur and a *poseur*. He deserved it."

Gabriel did not touch the whiskey. As though Davis was reading his thoughts, he slid the glass to Crane. "Take me to Theodore, son. He has promised me an interview."

"I don't think he'll see you. The Colonel has a lot on his mind."

Richard Harding Davis' smile telegraphed confidence. "But of course ill, my boy."

ago Rag

They left the bar, crossed the vestibule and went out the back of the hotel into the garden. There, four first class railroad cars sat on a track. Richard Harding Davis said, "Mister Plant's railroad runs from New York to this, his most lucrative last stop. A case of predestination." Davis spoke as though he could imagine each word appearing in print.

*

Later that day, Roosevelt took a few men to inspect the transports that would take them to Cuba. A dozen black steamers were tied up along a pier south of the hotel. The single rail line, jammed with box cars, ran to the end of the pier. The empty transports rode high in the water, and marines guarded their gangplanks.

Box cars of unidentified goods simmered in the heat. Bacon grease dripped from one car. Lard melted through the seams of another. As they worked their way down the pier, an explosion sent animals and men flying. In the aftermath, splinters fell, then, oddly, pop corn. They ran toward the noise and among the dazed and bleeding men, saw that a boxcar of corn had blown up. The wreckage and kernels covered the tracks. Roosevelt stooped and examined a handful but it burned him and he flung it away. "Spontaneous combustion! This is sabotage of the worst sort," he fumed. "Sheer neglect and worse, rampant inefficiency! I shall cable Alger about this!"

*

Marcus had been too astonished to say anything. Gabriel Scriven, a Rough Rider? It seemed like years ago that they had fought. But on closer inspection, he saw that behind the mustache, beard, and long hair was the school marm's mulatto boy. His anger had been dampened by a question. Why was Scriven in the hotel? And why would Roosevelt sent him to his wife's hotel suite?

Marcus thought he saw something new in the eyes that had once showed fear. Now they held something else. Marcus still hated him—perhaps even more now that Gabriel no longer seemed to be afraid. Scriven was the only man in camp who could refute the wildcat story Marcus had now told a dozen times. Fish had chastised him for it. For once, Marcus had kept his mouth shut. And Marcus would make his silence pay off.

Judge Hammer sent messages, both silent and verbal, that Marcus took after his mother's side. Her French Canadian family of furriers had

A Gathering Storm / 87

descended from trappers—French Canadians that had long mingled too closely, the Judge inferred, with Indians.

Back in San Antonio, Marcus had visited a photographer who offered bogus uniforms and swords as props for the ordinary soldiers to impress their families. Against a backdrop of palmetto, Marcus struck a proud pose, resting his hand on an officer's sword. He had sent the photograph to his father.

When the Judge got the picture, he immediately wired,

Perhaps the war will make a man of you. Do not shame me. —*Father*

CHAPTER 10

Sensing that it might very well be the last great cavalry maneuver, General Wheeler had planned an elaborate drill for the five cavalry regiments in his command. Two thousand men would participate. The flat Florida landscape and its widely spaced young palm trees made maneuvers possible that Wheeler had only studied. Now, he had the chance to execute them all.

Days before, he notified his old Confederate comrades and today they were here, shoulder to shoulder with Yankee officers, openly gleeful to see what they had only seen in their dreams of retribution—a Rebel general once again in command of a mounted brigade. As the troopers worked through their drills, the old soldiers bragged it was better than anything they saw during what they still preferred to call "The Great Rebellion."

A somewhat annoyed Edith Roosevelt sat under a wide parasol held by Richard Harding Davis. As far as she was concerned, Theodore had asked her to come out into the hot Florida sun to watch a lot of nonsense. But the foreign dignitaries around her were anticipating this much touted event.

Soon, Davis pointed his walking stick at a long line of troopers in tan tunics, trotting their mounts through the young palm trees. They were led by a phalanx of officers. Davis handed her his binoculars and saw among them a proud figure on the dark war horse Texas.

The sun reflected from his spectacles. Edith was overcome—as her breast filled with pride. The crowd broke into applause. Then the Rough Rider bugler stood in his stirrups and sounded a musical call. With a resounding hiss of steel, the Rough Riders drew bladed machetes that Theodore must have commandeered for the occasion. When the bugler sounded the charge, the officers and men emitted the most uncouth cowboy yips, rebel yells, and war whoops, and with their machetes drawn, galloped toward their imaginary enemy.

To the crowd's applause, the regiment reigned to an abrupt halt in a cloud of sand and dust. When it had cleared, she saw that the Rough Riders had squared off into twos and to growing applause, they began a sham machete fight, steel clanging against steel.

Beside Edith, a French officer guffawed his disapproval. "Ridiculous," he roared, "whom do these amateurs think they are fooling?"

"Oh do be quiet!" Edith snapped, "that is my husband's regiment."

*

That evening, Captain Maximillian Luna was beside himself. Tomorrow the Rough Riders were to load onto their transports but Hall had told him that due to a shortage of vessels, their horses must be left behind. The First Volunteer Cavalry was being turned into an ill-prepared infantry! Luna's men, chosen for their horsemanship, would become little more than pack animals, heaving heavy equipment and ammunition.

Trudging through the grass toward Colonel Wood's tent, Luna surprised a group of armadillos. Grunting like armored pigs, they bumped into each other and scattered into the brush. The pathetically stupid animals reminded Luna of bungling bureaucrats. And amateurs like Roosevelt, who had no business in uniform.

Roosevelt and Wood were waiting. As the captains assembled, Wood set his jaw. Roosevelt looked in a foul mood. As usual, Colonel Wood did not mince words. The officers would take their mounts. A dozen mules would be shipped, split between the hospital corps and the kitchen staff. Teamsters from other units would haul the Rough Riders' heavy supplies and provisions.

Colonel Leonard Wood was not finished. The worst news, Roosevelt had decided to let Wood deliver. Theodore was, for the first time since Wood had known him, too furious to speak.

The shortage of transports, Wood explained, was worse than anyone anticipated. General Shafter had just handed down the order. The First Volunteer Cavalry could board only half of their force. Five troops must remain in Tampa until further notice.

Luna and the other Captains were stunned. Such, the Colonel reminded them, was war. Those who waited also served. Then Colonel Wood, reading from a prepared list, named those who would be left behind—Joe Alexander's C Troop, George Curry's H Troop, Schuyler McGinnis's I Troop, Robert Bruce's M Troop, and finally, Luna's F Troop.

Captain Luna started to protest, but Wood's hand silenced him. No argument would be tolerated.

Those captains chosen to go were elated, but out of sympathy for their comrades, they tried not to show it. It was obvious to Luna that Roosevelt's favorites were going and the rest were not.

They filed out. Although Wood gave him a sharp look, Luna stayed behind.

When the others were safely out of earshot, Captain Luna, his face anguished, finally spoke. "Colonel Wood," he said, "I have a right to go to Cuba. You are going to fight Spaniards. I have Spanish blood. I am the only officer in camp who understands our enemy. Furthermore I am completely fluent in their language—good, upper-class *Castilliano*." He took a deep breath and exhaled to calm himself. "The Spanish hold honor above everything. Even though they are my enemy now, I do as well. This is my fight, Colonel, more than any man in camp. In the name of God, sir, you cannot leave me behind."

During the silence that followed, Roosevelt scuffed his feet. But Wood held the line. "Surely, Captain, you don't expect me to give you another man's troop. I would have to attach you to the general staff."

Luna raised his chin. "Forgive me, sir. In my disappointment, I have not been clear." He took a deep breath. "I speak for my men. If I am to go, they must as well. It would be unthinkable otherwise."

"Then it follows," Wood said, his face beginning to color, "F Troop stays in reserve, Captain. And consequently, so will you."

Luna had no chance to reply, for at this point Roosevelt stepped between them. "Leonard, Luna has a point. If I can find us a bigger vessel, will you take him? "

Wood was clearly annoyed. "Theodore, that's most irregular! We can't change orders for personal reasons. It is unfair to the others."

"But the others," Roosevelt said, "did not stay and fight."

Wood felt like strangling Roosevelt, the very person who had suggested eliminating Luna in the first place. Now, Theodore had suddenly made himself the man's champion, and Wood had been cast as the villain. Going back on an order would be unthinkable. If word got out, he would spend the night arguing with bitterly disappointed men. And Leonard Wood was tired, dead tired "Leave us, Captain," Wood commanded. "Colonel Roosevelt and I will discuss your request. Mind you, nothing is promised."

After Luna left, Wood slammed his fist on the table. "Damn, Theodore! Don't ever do that again! Five minutes at West Point would have taught you that the very worst thing an officer can do is to rescind a combat order. Men must be led, not pampered."

Roosevelt said nothing. He took Wood's anger with a bowed head.

Finally, Colonel Wood broke the awful silence. "Can you really deliver better transport?"

Theodore Roosevelt's contrite expression quickly changed to a grin. "Leonard, I was not Assistant Secretary of the Navy for nothing. Don't worry. Leave it to me and do not ask too many questions. If my plan goes awry, I shall accept the full responsibility."

Wood shook his head in disbelief. "Theodore, Theodore. You are quite impossible. Well, go ahead. But you must make me a promise, right here and now. My command must never again be questioned, especially in front of the men."

Roosevelt bit his lip and nodded curtly. "You have my word, sir."

The Colonel passed his hand across his face, as though to erase an unpleasant thought. "Send Luna to me. I want to tell him myself. You are to say nothing, is that clear?"

"Yes, my Colonel. And thank you, sir."

After Roosevelt had found Luna, he returned to his tent and lit the lantern on his folding desk. As bugs bounced off the glass chimney, he read a handful of hurriedly scribbled notes Hall had placed there, along with pitiful entreaties from men whose handwriting was so shaky he could barely read it. Several reminded Roosevelt of their prominent relatives. Although Roosevelt could imagine a mother's relief at her son being left behind, he was not willing to face the wrath of some of the fathers. After raising the expectations of the best families in New York, indeed after garnering their first born sons, he would have to make a few changes.

Roosevelt penned a transfer order to Adjutant Hall. Lieutenant John Greenway of Hot Springs, Arkansas was to join Bucky O'Neill's A Troop. To Allyn Capron's L Troop, he assigned the sons of his strongest political allies— William Tiffany and Hamilton Fish. Tiffany had personally crafted Roosevelt's spurs and belt buckle, and through his son, had donated the regiment's Colt machine guns. Hamilton Fish, Senior would be a force in politics he could not ignore. A request by Marcus Hammer to be appointed sergeant to Woodbury Kane's Knickerbockers Roosevelt crumpled and tossed into the waste basket.

When Julius had finally taken his orders off into the night, Roosevelt lifted Little Cuba onto his lap. As he often did before sleeping, he began writing a letter to his oldest child, Alice. He told her to read it aloud to Theodore, Jr., Kermit, Little Ethyl, Archie, and even to baby Quentin.

As the crickets rasped, Roosevelt drew in the margins. He described the camp and the thirty thousand troops, and the gray warships in the bay. Roosevelt explained how his commander, General Wheeler, had fought against the Union in the Civil War. As a Confederate officer, Wheeler had been wounded many times; had a dozen horses shot out from under him. So wasn't it splendid, Roosevelt wrote, that former enemies were going to Cuba as comrades?

The children had a house full of animals, so he told them how Little Cuba had tried to pick a fight with the I Troop's lion cub. And mother Edith was quite comfortable in a big hotel nearby that looked like a sultan's palace. And Julius was taking good care of his two horses, Texas and the pinto, Rain-in-Face.

When Roosevelt finally extinguished his lantern, parted the netting and lay back on his cot, his mind swam with thoughts as thick as the mosquitoes. Both he and Leonard were disgusted with Shafter. Their Falstaffian General swore in all directions, but that was hardly leadership. Tomorrow,

Roosevelt vowed to cable his dear friend Henry Cabot Lodge. But first he would secure a bigger vessel and he had a plan to do it. Convinced he would but rest his eyes, Roosevelt let them close.

*

On the dock, Marcus smoked impatiently as he waited for Lieutenant Hall. Then he heard a dog barking and the cadence of marching feet. Down the pier, led by Roosevelt on his favorite pinto, the tan clad Rough Riders marched four abreast. Little Cuba barked, and the commotion parted the New York Seventy-First blue-shirts, who were lined up to board. Roosevelt stopped in front of a formation of the Seventy-First, who recognized him and cheered. He turned in his saddle and held up his hand. His order, "column right," echoed down the ranks as the Rough Riders, heavy blanket rolls over one shoulder and their Krags over the other, turned, apparently to march off the dock into the harbor. But a tall trooper held the Regimental flag at the gangplank of the *Yucatan* and Bucky O'Neill led A Troop up it before the astonished marines could stop them.

As his men filed onto the *Yucatan*, Roosevelt lifted his hands. From the rear, the Rough Rider band struck up "Hot Time in the Old Town Tonight."

A Captain of the New York Seventy-First galloped up to Roosevelt. Between the cadence of marching feet and the beat of the drums it was impossible for Marcus to hear anything, but he saw the Captain lean out of his saddle and push his face toward Roosevelt's, who cupped his hand to his ear and motioned that he could not hear. The Captain galloped away, nearly trampling some of his own troopers. Minutes later, as Captain Luna's Troop, the last of the Rough Riders, headed up the gangplank, three officers rode up.

Roosevelt dismounted, handed the reins of his pinto to Julius, and stepped onto the gangplank. He jammed his fists against his belt and gave his defiant, toothy grimace.

"Sir," an angry Colonel shouted, "this vessel is reserved for the Seventy-First! Have your men disembark at once."

Roosevelt's posture and expression was that of a small boy who had just won at King of the Hill.

Marcus Hammer, certain that Roosevelt would let him board,

rushed through the New Yorkers. He reached Roosevelt just as he had turned up the gangway, and grabbed his sleeve. "Colonel, Colonel!"

Theodore's smile vanished.

"The transfer," Marcus blurted.

Roosevelt pried Marcus' hand from his sleeve, and the boy took a step backward. On deck, the Rough Riders seemed to be mocking him.

We're Rough!
And Tough!
We came to fight
And we cain't git enough!

The band played as Marcus B. Hammer and the cheated men of the New York Seventy-First wondered what to do.

Lieutenant Hall trotted his bay up the dock, his roster under his arm. Hammer saw him and spread his palms in helplessness.

Hall quickly sized up the situation. To the men he had to leave behind, he was a fiend. To those transferred, he was a hero. Although he merely bore the news—the tendency was to shoot the messenger. That's why he had let Hammer tag along, and had had him to wait at the pier. This will-ful boy could hurt him, yet if he took him under his wing now; Hall had a body guard and a grateful sycophant as well. He could use both.

Lately, Hall had witnessed the tension between Roosevelt and Wood. Now, staring at Hammer's pathetic face, he had an idea. And he was sure Colonel Wood would approve, even if Roosevelt objected. "Marcus," Hall said, "if I give you one condition to board that ship, will you take it?"

Hammer seemed ready to do anything.

"We've had an ambulance man fall sick," Hall told him. "Surgeon Church needs a replacement. Will you volunteer?"

At first Marcus hesitated. The hospital unit seemed women's work. But then, Marcus remembered that Church had once rowed for Princeton. The Ivy-Leaguer would no doubt see Marcus as an equal. Why, Church might even single him out for promotion!

Lieutenant Hall watched Marcus' scowl turn into a confident, lop-sided grin.

As they climbed the gangplank, Lieutenant Hall congratulated himself. Marcus Hammer's broad back would make the Rough Riders an excellent stretcher-bearer.

PART II *To Cuba*

CHAPTER 11

Gulf of Mexico
Sunday, June 19, 1898

It was before dawn on the stern of the *Yucatan*, and Gabriel was seasick. He leaned over the rail and let go. Above him a flag with forty-five stars luffed her stripes in the breeze. Suddenly, the flag's wire halyard twanged against the steel mast. The *Yucatan* was turning into the wind.

Cloud bumped Gabriel's arm and whispered, "We're going west." He pointed in the darkness and had it not been for his wide corporal's chevron, Gabriel would not have seen the arm, then the hand. The transport took the swells at an angle as her stern rose. A new spasm gripped Gabriel's belly as he spread his legs to counter the ship's sickening roll.

Cloud burped and pressed his mouth to the sleeve of his tunic.

The two troopers clung to the mahogany rail as the freighter fought to hold her place in a triple column of ships twenty miles long. There were thirty-seven fat transports, a dozen sleek war ships, and the wallowing coal tenders that made the going so slow. Despite orders from Admiral Schley, the transports ran with full lights. Evidently, their civilian captains considered collision more likely than an attack from Spanish torpedo boats.

But at least the convoy was underway. The invasion fleet had sailed a week ago, but a few miles outside of Tampa Bay, had turned back. The Spanish feet had been found, then lost again. The order came from Washington to wait. And so, while the rainy season began in Cuba, thousands of men and hundreds of mules and horses were imprisoned for a week aboard steel ships in the heat of a Florida summer, riding at anchor in a harbor choked with flotsam and sewage.

The heavy engines of a warship approached and Gabriel's stomach seemed to burst into his throat. Her searchlight washed the *Yucatan* for a blinding instant and her rakish hull sped past, making the transport shudder in her wake. The *Segurança*, General Shafter's flagship, was keeping the convoy in formation.

Below, five hundred seventy-one Rough Riders were jammed into the *Yucatan's* former coal deck. Men tossed in tightly packed bunks three high, choking in the suffocating stench that a seasick regiment makes.

On deck, Gabriel hooked his elbow through the railing. His trousers were loose, very loose now.

"Look," Cloud said. "The Maysi light."

The *Yucatan's* yaw made it hard to track the lighthouse, yet Gabriel remembered that Captain Capron said the light marked the eastern tip of Cuba. Maybe they would get off this prison hulk today. The ten days aboard had been hell. And since he had never before sailed anything rougher than the chocolate eddies of the Missouri, *terra firma*, even teeming with enemy, would be like balm. His stomach was like an animal trapped within him. Maybe he'd get wounded in the first wave so that he'd have it over with. He was sure glad Aura couldn't see him now—vomiting over himself until his suspenders stuck to his chest.

Gabriel wiped his face with his kerchief and groaned, "I didn't sign up for this." He had learned to interpret Cloud's silence as agreement, what was said was both heard and understood. Then what was meant by it and what consequences the words might have. To Cloud, words alone meant little, and after the past year with him, Gabriel could imagine a group of Sioux sitting for hours, listening to the night, without any talk at all.

Since it was against orders for them to be on deck, silence was a good idea anyway. The breeze was cool, and anything beat going back to the stifling heat below decks.

Cloud touched his arm and as two men approached, they crouched between the smokestack and a lifeboat. Gabriel recognized Roosevelt's peppery voice and Colonel Wood's Boston accent. The two officers leaned on the rail and looked out at the lights of the ships and the white wakes they made.

Wood was the first to speak. "The delay in Tampa cost us. Mosquitoes are hatching in the puddles of Cuba. But we mustn't blame Shafter, for he's inherited a difficult situation. One day, Alger says go, the next, he commands him to stop."

Roosevelt grunted. "Shafter is too skilled at stopping. He was once a railroad brakeman."

"But," Wood countered, "a man who came up through the ranks. A Medal of Honor winner in the Civil War."

"The man's a buffoon," Roosevelt said, "a cartoonist's dream."

"The heat will be hard on him," Wood acknowledged. "General Miles would have been a better choice to command. But Shafter has a few months' seniority. Shafter has enough on his plate without those correspondents. Richard Harding Davis galls the General even more than Harvard men like ourselves. To gain Shafter's favor, we'll have to keep Davis out of his way."

Theodore disagreed. "Why, Hearst pays Davis hundreds just to cover the Yale game because the man is *read!* He will make our boys famous! Davis's dispatches have already helped us catch the imagination of the American people!"

"Yes," Wood grumbled, "and helped dub us as Roosevelt's Rough Riders."

"Well I want you to know that I am no more comfortable with that appellation than you are."

Wood managed a dry laugh. "Come to think of it, I suppose it may be better that way. If the Rough Riders fail, history will blame you, not me."

"We will not fail," Roosevelt blurted. "To be fair, we'll invite other reporters to accompany us as well. Harry Scovel and Ed Marshall. A cable from any of them means that within hours, the presses are running and, and by morning, the nation is reading the exploits of our boys."

"Now, Theodore," Colonel Wood cautioned, "we're about to attack an island the Spaniards have successfully defended since Columbus. A week after our arrival our men will be coming down with fever. Even if the Negro regiments are immune, and I doubt they really are, we are still outgunned. And don't think the Spanish are not counting on fever beating us They'll most likely fight a long, defensive campaign if we let them. And we'll have Davis and your magic lantern fellows recording our demise."

Roosevelt laughed. "Kinetoscope men, Leonard. Not magic lantern. The Kinetoscope shows us in action! This will be the first war where the press takes a part. Why, Hearst himself has joined the convoy."

"Disgusting," Wood said. "We've got more correspondents than cannon. What if we are driven back? That will be in Mr. Hearst's paper too. Imagine, a retreat recorded in motion!"

Roosevelt seemed deep in thought. Then he reminded Wood of Admiral Dewey's victory at Manila.

Wood chuckled softly. "It was your victory at Manila, Theodore."

A coral wedge glowed against the horizon. Gabriel could see the whites of Cloud's eyes under his hat brim, and the forms of the two officers alarmingly close. Roosevelt's pinched, oval glasses caught the color. "I don't think our boys can even imagine defeat."

Colonel Wood squinted into the dawn. "Ultimately, men are drawn to a chance for glory. For others, the security of pay and regular meals is the goal. If a man feels two of the three is unlikely, he sometimes gives up. And this will be America's first amphibious invasion since Washington crossed the Delaware."

"Good," Roosevelt huffed. "We'll whip Spaniards the way Washington walloped those Hessians."

"Ah, but General Washington," Wood cautioned, "had one advantage we will not. Surprise."

Around the *Yucatan,* the convoy was becoming visible; bulky black transports, and the shark-gray warships. Gabriel watched his commanding officers walk away, Wood erect, his tunic pressed. Roosevelt's looked rumpled and he waddled against the *Yucatan's* slow roll.

Cloud crept down the aft ladder and Gabriel followed.

*

Below decks, William Tiffany lay reading in his bunk. Although he had been transferred to L Troop at the last minute, the troopers knew him because he had the finest horse in the regiment, a thoroughbred. But his horse had been left behind. Now, he passed the time reading from a thick edition of *Don Quixote*.

"HEY trooper!" Snake kidded, "Don't you know this here's a war? Put your darned Bible down!"

Tiffany, who wore riding boots over his longjohns, calmly lowered the book to his chest. "I wouldn't blaspheme the Word, until we're through with the *Peninsulares*," he said.

"The who?"

"That's what the Cubans call the Spanish. Because they come from the peninsula of Spain."

Snake snorted. "Well, if you ain't a walkin' encyclopedia."

Tiffany returned to his book.

"Well, all I know," Snake sang out, "is I'm about to mess my pants and there's no place to go but on Prayerful's bunk."

"Prayerful'd forgive you," another trooper jeered.

L Troop was still laughing when Adjutant Hall backed down the ladder. His pockets bulged with lists. "Religious services will be held on the foredeck in half an hour. Sergeant Fish?"

Fish sat up in his bunk, bending his muscular neck and close-cropped head to one side to avoid the steel deck struts. "Sir?"

"See to it that your men are properly uniformed before they come up. General Wheeler is expected and we want to look sharp."

"Yes sir," Fish said.

Hall turned and started back up the ladder. Complaints cut the heat for an instant, and then the heavy air fell back on the men. The canvas vents that had been attached to some portholes so that air could flow into the deck lay flaccid and empty. The heat was made worse by the prospect of donning stiff britches, wool shirts, and canvas tunics in such close quarters.

"You heard the Lieutenant," Fish snapped, "but skip the tunics."

The whole troop cheered.

Snake took this instant for a complaint. "Sarge, how come L Troop always has to eat last? Why cain't they put us first in line once in awhile?"

"We're right lucky, Snake," someone called. "That way there won't be any grub left to poison us."

"Heck, Snake's poison proof anyway," another man laughed.

Snake spat a stream of brown tobacco juice through the porthole. "Not to that canned Japan beef. I ain't never et anything worse, 'cept maybe rotten Gila monster. At least that stuck to my ribs."

*

Chaplain Brown gave a long but moving sermon, urging the men to don the armor of righteousness. Even Snake gulped a few times and joined in the hymn singing.

After the church service, Gabriel and Cloud sat on their haunches in a strip of shade made by the smokestack. The men ate their rations, canned beef, canned tomatoes, and a piece of hardtack biscuit. But today, Roosevelt had promised each trooper would get a heaping spoonful of sugar in his coffee and as much salt as he wanted over his rations. The salt helped, for the beef was sometimes fatty and rancid and the tomatoes had an acrid, tinny taste.

Roosevelt brought his plate over and sat down next to T. T. Cloud. His shirt was open and he had pinned his hat brim up on one side with his cavalry pin. Roosevelt slapped his hands on his knees. "Well, then. How's the chow, Cloud?"

"Not too bad, sir." Cloud's muscular jaw worked on a lump of resistant beef.

Roosevelt's eyes danced light blue and penetrating behind the spectacles that doubled their size. "And how are you this morning, *Trumpeter* Scriven?"

Gabriel stopped chewing.

Roosevelt chomped happily and then took a swig of coffee, making a face because the rim of the tin cup burned his lips. When he had recovered he said, "Captain Capron suggested that I make you regimental bugler, son. In the cavalry, buglers are called trumpeters."

"But sir," Gabriel said, "I want to stay with L Troop."

Roosevelt was not taking no for an answer. "Tell me, is not your name Gabriel?"

"Yes, sir, but a bugle is much different than a trumpet."

Roosevelt nodded. "Well, if I let you stay with L Troop will you agree? Wait, before you answer. I intend to stick close to Capron myself. We will never be far apart and I'll need a trumpeter who can sound the calls immediately and unambiguously. I trust you have them memorized."

Gabriel knew a dozen, since the men had to respond to them or face punishment. But he did not want this job. "Mostly reveille and taps, " he said.

"You'll need more, of course. I'll send Platt to teach you. We shall not need 'boots and saddles.' Nor will we, I think, need 'retreat.' 'Charge' is one command you should learn to blow in your sleep." Roosevelt signaled up to the bridge and Lieutenant Hall brought down a wooden case. He handed it to Roosevelt, who passed the case to Gabriel, who freed the clasp. Inside, in the crushed velour hollow lay a C Crook trumpet, with the second, detachable crook of brass tubing to help with the difficulty of blowing from the saddle. As Gabriel lifted the trumpet from the case, two cloth patches fell out. Roosevelt quickly stooped to the deck and picked them up. He held the patches up for the men to see. Against a blue background was a triple v of gold stripes. Above the v, and just under the rainbow- shaped top stripe was nestled a stylized, rounded horn.

"A Chief Trumpeter's chevrons, Scriven. You can blame Cloud for this," Roosevelt said. "One brave to another, he convinced me you ought to have some responsibility."

Roosevelt glanced around to make sure he had an audience. "Do you know the Sioux once made me a blood brother? Gave me a tribal name. Tell them, Cloud."

Cloud looked uncomfortable.

"How do you say it in Lakota" Roosevelt prodded.

Cloud said something they did not catch. "Laughing Horse," Roosevelt translated. Theodore slapped his thigh and laughed "Yaah-nah-nah-hah-hah! Isn't that splendid? Laughing Horse! And some believe the red man to be without humor. Quite untrue, I'll tell you. Well, a horse has large, strong teeth, doesn't he? And so, gentlemen do I. Hah! All the better to masticate Army rations in their most obdurate state, don't you think?" He bit off a knot of beef, and chewed vigorously, his jaw working under his mustache.

Gabriel warmed the mouthpiece of the trumpet. He had to confess he was pleased that Capron, a man they all respected, had recommended him, although he was a little annoyed that Cloud had not warned him first. But he would be near Colonel Roosevelt when they met the Spaniards. He wondered how he'd sound the commands and still fight, managing Krag and bugle both.

Captain Capron squatted beside Cloud, and the two began to make exchange silent gestures.

Cloud pointed to his own palm, then closed his hand over his finger, moving both slightly side to side. Then Cloud pretended to drink from his open palm.

Allyn Capron laughed.

Roosevelt stopped chewing. "Allyn, what are you saying?"

"Just practicing, sir," Capron said. "Cloud will be my point. We'll have to communicate this way."

"But," Roosevelt asked, "what is so funny?"

Capron coughed. "I don't think that it is very translatable sir. You might say it is a kind of joke."

"Good God, man, I can take any joke."

Capron took off his hat and parted his damp, blonde hair with his fingers. "Corporal Cloud wishes we had some cold beer, that's all. Like the beer you brought us in San Antonio."

"Ahah," he grinned, "Yes. Well, I'm afraid that was the last beer any of you will imbibe for the duration."

"It was good, sir," Cloud said. "We still think of it."

"Yes," Roosevelt agreed, "worth every inch of epidermis Colonel Wood chewed off my *gluteus maximus*, eh boys?"

*

Stripped to the waist, L Troop trotted around the deck in close order, each man with his hands on the shoulders of the trooper ahead. Colonel Wood and Captain Capron watched from the shade of the bridge where the Kinetoscope men worked with their camera, cranking, panning, and following the snaking line of men. Roosevelt ran at the head, sweating and counting cadence, as their hobnailed brogans hit the deck.

K Troop was cooling after their run. To the New Yorkers, L Troop must have looked like a controlled war dance. Someone would let out a whoop, and then a ripple of cowboy yips would go down the line.

After the exercise was over, a trombone sounded the Rough Rider band into life and soon the ships were competing, snatches of music bouncing, making a collage of sound. Gabriel warmed the mouthpiece of the bugle and joined in, but without the valves, he had to strain to make clear notes. But echoes distorted the songs. The westerners sang "Clementine", which was answered by easterners singing "East Side, West Side." Then, they were brought back together by a series of rounds, ending with one they had sung with certain knowledge since the swamps of Tampa. The tune was "Row, Row, Row Your Boat," and the men called it "The Skeeter Song."

> *Chew, chew, chew your food,*
> *Gaily through the meal;*
> *The more you laugh,*
> *The less you eat,*
> *The better you will feel.*

It was during this concert that a powered longboat chugged alongside the *Yucatan*. The boatswain piped a party aboard. As Gabriel watched a diminutive officer climb the ladder and salute, he recognized General Joe Wheeler, this time looking very much the soldier in his tan tunic. The little General's saber nearly touched the deck. Wheeler greeted Wood, then Roosevelt, and the three officers strolled the deck, talking with the men. As they passed, Gabriel heard Wheeler quip, "I'm right indebted to you, Theodore, for pickin' these summer uniforms, " he laughed and pointed to his collar. "These yella epaulets are just like what we Rebs wore."

CHAPTER 12

Monday, June 20

Through the porthole, Gabriel saw a cloudless, azure sky. Yet thunderous booms came in cadence, followed by sharp reports that ran along the surface of the calm sea, finally slamming against the hull of the *Yucatan*. Was this a thunderstorm? His view, but a foot in diameter, yielded only cobalt waves and clear sky. Then came the thunder again and troopers below decks of the *Yucatan* braced themselves for the shock wave.

Lieutenant Colonel Roosevelt scrambled down the ladder, stopping on the last rung, hanging monkey-like. He held his hand to his ear and rolled his eyes. "Hear that, boys? The battleships *New York* and the *Oregon* have begun shelling the Cuban coast. Our first shots against the despots of Spain. Shots now heard around the world!"

"What we shooting at, Colonel?" a trooper asked.

"The Morro Castle, boys, the gateway to Santiago Harbor."

"Tell them Navy Jacks to leave us a few Spanions to hunt."

Roosevelt beamed. "Don't worry, trooper, there will be Spaniards aplenty once we get ashore. But alas, it will not be today. Uncle Sam's Navy wants to give the Spaniards religion first." He screwed on his battered campaign hat. "Meanwhile, gentlemen, I trust you'll forgive the racket and the inconvenience." Roosevelt disappeared up the ladder, his thick calves working the rungs.

At noon it was too hot. Below decks, L Troop lay in their bunks, stripped to their underwear. Either the shelling had ceased or at least they were too far away to hear it. There was no room to stand. All a trooper could do was lay on his bunk, sweat, and pray for the order to go up onto the deck.

From his porthole, Gabriel scanned the shoreline with Fish's field glasses. Beside him, Sergeant Fish traced his finger along a hand-drawn map of Cuba. On Fish's instructions, Gabriel swung the glasses, following a curved white strip of beach, separating aquamarine shallows from the emerald jungle and a wall of feathery, lime-green palms set against blue mountains. The Cuban shoreline seemed to glide by, as the *Yucatan* seemed to sit still. Then a conical mountain slipped by to reveal a high iron pier. On it, a rusty ore car stood, high over the aquamarine tide. Below that, a narrow wooden dock jutted out from the beach. Then the mountain gave way to a large shed, surrounded by a dozen huts with shiny tin roofs. Above the beach, the mountain rose from the sea and flying from a blockhouse on its peak Gabriel spotted a yellow flag with two horizontal, red stripes in the center. He dialed the magnification, bringing it closer. "I see a Spanish flag!"

Cheers followed Gabriel's announcement.

"You see any garlics, Gabe?"

"Naw, they sleep off the heat of the day," a trooper called.

"Not a bad idea, if you ask me," someone quipped.

Snake rolled his chew to the other cheek. "Gimme a peek, Gabe." Gabriel passed the field glasses, and Snake pressed them against one eye and squinted. His jaw froze. He was quiet for long time. "Lordy, I don't know how anybody could ever die in such a purty place," he whispered. He handed the glasses back to Gabriel and lay back on his bunk, gophering his cud under his whiskers.

Cloud lay on one side, wiping his Krag with an oily cloth.

Scanning the village before them, Gabriel wished they had a better map. He could probably find where they were: the conical mountain and the way the beach curved and the land rose steeply to the higher inland mountains would be a dead give-away. "Hey Tiffany, do you have those charts?"

Tiffany had brought nautical charts of the waters around Cuba, but when they were handed over, the rolled charts were too large and cumbersome to read in the confines of a bunk. And with only one man able to look out the porthole at a time, each gave a completely different version of what they saw.

But no matter. They were off Cuba. And to Gabriel the island looked beautiful. He imagined springs of cold water and shady groves.

*

From the bridge of the *Seguranca,* General Wheeler scanned the shoreline with the captain's mounted telescope. Daiquiri seemed deserted. Here and there a fire burned—a small steam engine, a low shed, and several huts. He knew the signs—the Spanish had pulled back, destroying any means of pursuit. He raised the telescope and scanned the hills above the crescent beach. The navy gunners had thrice hit the blockhouse on the mountain and the hills behind were still being shelled. But navy guns would not be as effective as they looked. Explosions on the ridges gave the troopers who watched courage. But Wheeler had seen many bombardments during the Civil War. And no matter how many barrages were fired, after the smoke cleared, the Yankees were still there, firing over the breastworks. In fact, the shell craters afforded an enemy shelters and rifle pits better than they could themselves dig. No matter how much bombardment, the battle would have to be won hand to hand. He saw no breastworks on the ridges—no fresh earth indicating rifle pits.

Wheeler knew the Spanish artillery would be further back, where the Navy could not see them. They had been a defensive army for hundreds of years and they would be so now.

They were waiting for the Fifth Corps in the jungle. Wheeler knew that in their position, he would follow the same strategy. Let the enemy land, and get a false sense of victory. And when they advanced along narrow trails, cut them down. Once defeated in that manner, especially if they suffered heavy losses, the American people would lose interest and Congress would never fund a second amphibious invasion.

General Shafter had yet to decide where the troops would land. This decision would depend on a meeting onshore with the legendary Cuban rebel

General Calixto Garcia.

Later that day, accompanied by a contingent of marines, Generals Shafter, Wheeler, and Lawton were taken ashore thirty miles west of Santiago harbor. Admiral Sampson came in another boat. As their longboats steered into the shallows, Wheeler was amazed by the transparency of the tide. Every sea creature was visible against the white sand, and the depth was deceiving, as he discovered when he stepped over the gunwale. The warm surf came to his waist rather than his boots, as he had expected. This depth would certainly fool his cavalrymen too.

Unloading the bulky General Shafter took some doing, but four swarthy marines that made a seat of their arms and politely averted their eyes as they hoisted the portly general ashore managed it. There, a hundred well-armed Cubans greeted them. The Cubans wore white cotton uniforms and straw sombreros with their brims pinned by cloth badges of the red, white, and blue Cuban flag. General Wheeler noted each man had a machete at his side as well as a mixed array of carbines— mostly single shot Remingtons, old Winchesters, some Navy Lee rifles, and a few captured Spanish Mausers. American gunrunners had likely supplied the Remingtons and Winchesters.

Through an interpreter, the dark skinned Cubans explained that they were General Calixto García's *escolta*, or personal bodyguard. Wheeler worried that Spanish snipers might be near, mercenaries who tied themselves high in royal palms and shot men in the back with brass-tipped bullets intended to make horrible wounds calculated to cause gangrene.

The Cubans put General Shafter onto a small mule they swore had a stout heart, and they began their climb up the heights.

An hour later the exhausted little mule deposited his burden in a palm grove, and General Calixto García Iníguez greeted Shafter in almost perfect English. Across his chest, General García wore a sash with three gold stars. The mustachioed Cuban General removed his Panama and bowed deeply to the American officers. As he straightened, Wheeler saw a very deep declivity in his forehead—a bullet wound if he ever saw one. Wheeler had heard stories about how García, facing capture during the Ten Years War had put his pistol under his chin and fired. The bullet went up through his tongue, then behind the nose, exiting the skull. Unbelievably, the officer who found him wounded saw the wounded Calixto raise his arms across his face and recognized that this Cuban general was a fellow Mason. Rather than execute García on the spot, the officer insisted that a Spanish surgeon save him. After his recovery and a few years of house arrest in Madrid, Calixto García escaped and returned to Cuba.

Now the Cuban general introduced his dark skinned host, General Jésus Rabí, whose headquarters they were using. Next, García introduced his son, Colonel Raúl García. With obvious pride, he explained that Raúl, a lean man with a pencil-thin mustache, had been educated at Oxford.

Here in this cool glade, one would never know there was a war on. General Calixto García seemed perfectly at ease, although the Spanish must certainly be near. Soon the delegation was drinking coffee and eating white Camagüey cheese, which they dipped in guava jam. As they dined, General García and Raúl, taking turns, brought them up to date on what Lieutenant Rowan had brought some months before- in his famous "Message to García."

The Spanish troops were well armed but nervous. The Cubans had harassed them with raids and the Spanish dared not make a fight on the beaches. They feared the Cubans would attack them from the rear, or cut off their retreat to Santiago.

Both the Spanish and Cubans had followed a scorched earth policy— burning everything as they retreated. Pointing to maps, General García explained that the Americans would not find much shelter. There was but one rail line along the coast, from the Carnegie Iron Works at Daiquiri that had been wrecked by his own troops to stop armored Spanish trains.

Colonel Raúl García, sounding very much like a Sandhurst officer, traced his finger along the coastal plain running east to west toward Santiago. The few roads, he told them, were narrow and rough, except for the main road that passed through El Caney. There, the Spanish had established a strong defense and some artillery. Despite his attempts and the loss of many of his men, Colonel García had not yet been able to cut the road between El Caney and Santiago. He suggested that American ships could transport the Cubans to where the Spanish least expected them. If General Rabí's troops, guarding the west, could be landed in the east, the combined Cubans could easily take and hold the road between El Caney and Santiago.

General Shafter nodded his assent to this plan.

The next task, Colonel Raúl García explained, would be to stop

Spanish reinforcement columns that the Spanish were sure to send from Manzanillo in the west and Holguín in the north.

General Joe Wheeler, who had tried to stop Sherman's columns as they swept through Georgia, appreciated García's hit and run plan. But General Shafter was scowling as he dipped another piece of cheese into the guava jam.

Wheeler realized that the American officers were patronizing this Cuban general with a hole in his head that had stalemated the Spanish army in Oriente Province.

With an ornate letter opener, General García indicated where the Spanish had entrenched on a crescent height overlooking the southeastern outskirts of Santiago. And the Spanish had deployed units in the jungle, at a ruined sugar plantation named for a cluster of large Guásimas trees.

Lately, Colonel Raúl García admitted, the Spanish were moving so many troops that Cuban scouts were not able to keep up. But he could assign Cuban scouts to each American column. In that way, he suggested, the absence of American mounted cavalry reconnaissance might be overcome.

Obviously, Admiral Samson had been sent with orders from Commodore Schley, for he reminded them all that since the Spanish fleet was bottled up in Santiago Harbor, the Navy believed General Shafter should attack the Morro Castle at the entrance. Perhaps, Samson suggested, as Shafter reddened, the army could form a pincer movement from both west and east. That, the Admiral allowed, would bring about an immediate surrender of both naval and ground forces. And without losing a single American vessel. Ships, he explained coolly, were more difficult to replace than men.

In a fury, General Shafter put down his half-eaten cheese. In front of his Cuban hosts, he reminded Admiral Sampson that Secretary of War Alger and President McKinley had not appointed an admiral to lead this invasion. He had appointed a General of the Army. Samson bit his lip. Although he clearly did not like it, he deferred to Shafter for the rest of the conference.

Colonel García warned that a direct attack on Santiago would be foolish. The Spanish had already taken heavy guns and sailors from their ships and mounted them at the mouth of the harbor and in the heights around the city. A direct attack would have to pass through crossfire of artillery. "No," he demanded, moving his finger along the coast. "You must land here, further east."

Shafter was not sure of the terrain, for the Americans had been able to get nothing but sketchy maps.

"It is time to put a face on your invasion," Colonel Raúl García said. He hovered over the map and pointed to a curved beach near a conical mountain. "You should land here."

Joe Wheeler could not suppress a smile. He liked this young Cuban's decisive manner.

General Shafter squinted at the map, then glanced at his second in command. "What do you think, Joe?"

"I would have chosen exactly that place, suh! A two day march from Santiago."

With great effort, General William Shafter lifted himself from his chair. He clasped his hands behind his thick back and took a step or two, staring out toward the aquamarine sea. Then, surprisingly quick for such a big man, Shafter spun and snapped, "then so be it."

And so, the American invasion would land in the village of Daiquiri, after which, the Bacardi family would eventually name a popular rum julep. .

But the battle plan could not be complete without the Navy. Admiral Sampson told Shafter that warships would steam up and down the coast, bombarding fifty miles of Cuban coastline. That way, the Spanish could not know where the Americans would land.

Tonight, he explained with recovered dignity, the Navy would pull out to sea. Then before dawn tomorrow, the fleet would come back and the warships again would bombard the coast while the transports put the men into longboats, which would then be pulled to shore by steam lighters.

It seemed a good plan, and they all shook on it. As General Wheeler congratulated the Cubans for their excellent advice, he noticed that General Shafter looked worried.

That night, aboard *Seguranca,* Shafter announced that General Lawton's infantry division would land and deploy to the right. Then General Bate's brigade would hit the beach behind him. With his thick finger, Shafter pointed again. Wheeler's cavalry division would then occupy the center. "Joe, I have no worry about the Ninth and Tenth. But your Rough Riders better hold their fire until ordered."

Wheeler nodded. "Do not worry, *suh.* They will have regular officers with them at all times."

Shafter grunted and returned to his map. "General Kent's division will land further west." He dabbed his brow with a kerchief and then straightened. "It is settled then, gentlemen. We land at dawn."

*

From the sick bay of the *Yucatan*, Marcus Hammer cheered as each shell exploded on the shore. He could not contain his enthusiasm. Even though Fish had abandoned him, Marcus likened his chances for glory to that of a substitute, sitting on the bench during a most important football game. At least he was in uniform. And when the coach called on him, Marcus Hammer intended to play hard.

Lieutenant James Church seemed less enthusiastic. There was something about Hammer, something Fish had barely hinted at. But, he reminded himself, this was no time for reverie. Today there would surely be dead and wounded to attend to.

*

Gabriel set the bell of the bugle on his knee. At first the sky above the darkening mountains remained blue, then a sinking, orange sun tinged it almost green.

Colonel Wood let the men stay on deck until taps, and they were making the most of the breeze and the first Cuban sunset any of them had ever seen. Sergeant Fish stretched out on the deck, his hat brim tilted down on his nose, shielding the sun's slanting rays. "You know, Gabriel," Fish murmured, "This could be a man's last sunset."

Gabriel did not answer, but he had realized with each bursting shell that men would die. And that he could be one of them. But he tried to put it out of his mind.

Fish rolled on his side. "Is there someone special? I mean, for me to contact, just in case?"

Gabriel saw her, then. Fish had brought Aura back, that oval face crowned by dark hair. Right there, where the sun was setting. But he didn't want to talk about her. "T. T. Cloud knows how to reach my folks."

But Fish was in a pensive mood. His normally open face seemed to be pinched with worry. "Captain Capron says a sergeant ought to have the names of next of kin. That's definitely my duty."

"Lieutenant Hall has the list."

Fish lifted his Stetson and stared at Gabriel. "Would you want Hall in your parent's sitting room, informing them of your death?"

Gabriel hadn't thought of that, but he pictured it now. The thought left him uneasy. He did not know Hall, really. But he seemed more like a clerk than an officer. "Maybe not. It would be better to have a friend who saw you go down."

Snake had been listening to them and cut in. "You'd do it right, Sarge, telling how a man went clean, with no hollering. Even if a man did holler a little."

Fish nodded. "Yes, but I may go down."

Snake made an impatient grunt. "Naw. You won't. None of us will. We're just talkin' fillysophical, is all. A bullet's either got your name on it, or it don't."

Fish hugged his knees. "Umm. The belief of a fatalist. Well, I've had a premonition. It's been nagging me since Tampa. " He and looked Gabriel oddly. "Somehow, I can't imagine going home again."

Gabriel felt his insides churn. He didn't like the sound of Fish's talk. "The scripture says nobody knows when or where."

Sergeant Fish smiled. "Yes. Anyway, I want you to know I am not afraid." He lay back on the deck. The sky above them had now deepened to purple, the riot of color of a rapid, tropical sunset. And the emerging stars seemed to pulse with the throb of the *Yucatan's* engines.

Gabriel regretted now that he had not memorized some of the constellations. He wondered only at this sea of stars, likening their number to cottonwood in the summer air, floating by the billions, one bright and shimmering; others, pale and weak. Some of us will no doubt die. But, he thought, there are thousands of us. Probably not me.

As though reading his thoughts, Cloud broke the silence. "This kind of talk is bad medicine."

"So how would a Sioux warrior prepare for something like this?"

"With days of fasting and dancing," Cloud said. "Then medicine marks painted on you and your horse too, to protect you from bullets."

"With all due respect," Fish said, "I can't see how that would help."

"It only works if your medicine is very strong."

"Like Crazy Horse," Gabriel added.

"And others," Cloud added. Then he grew silent.

Gabriel welcomed the silence. If he listened to any more of this talk, he'd be able to hear the clods of dirt hitting his coffin.

Just then, Colonel Wood, Roosevelt, then Captain Capron stepped down from the bridge. "Gabriel," Roosevelt said, "better sound 'Assembly'." Gabriel put the bugle to his lips and blew the peppy cadence, once in each direction as he had been told to do. Within minutes the regiment had formed by troops, all five hundred and seventy-one of them, standing tightly packed on the deck of the *Yucatan*. Lieutenant Hall put down a box and Colonel Wood stepped up on it. He told the men that tomorrow morning at reveille they were to assemble on deck, in full battle gear. He hesitated, but seemed unable to think of more to say. Then he yielded the box to Lieutenant Colonel Roosevelt.

"Stand at ease, men," Roosevelt barked, then waited for the mumbling men to quiet themselves. "Well," he clapped his hands together and wrung them, rocking back and forth on the narrow box, "if we can believe the veracity of the communications from the *Seguranca,* tomorrow morning we land with General Wheeler."

A great cheer arose and Roosevelt, raising his hat, slapped it against his thigh. Then, his smile gone, he spread his arms, asking for silence, and got it. There was no sound but the throbbing of the steam engines as the *Yucatan* crept along, parallel to the dark shore, under a canopy of stars.

"A man only earns his freedom, his freedom of existence, who daily earns it anew." Roosevelt let that soak in. "A great German philosopher gave us those words, boys. And we, tomorrow, are going to prove his words true!"

Again, the rousing cheer of nearly six hundred men who had waited for this moment. Roosevelt, visible in light from the bridge, took his Colt revolver from its holster and held it high. For a moment, Gabriel expected him to fire, but he did not.

"This, gentlemen, is not regular issue. It is a Navy Colt. Yes, that's right. Why?" He waited, master of timing, working the men, spellbinding as a revival preacher. "Because this forty-four caliber pistol, with its rude wooden handle, is the very symbol of why we have trained so hard in the heat of a Texas prairie. Why Colonel Wood and I have gathered you from the towns and cities, the farms and the reservations of the nation. But, why, you ask, does Colonel Roosevelt carry a Navy revolver? A very good question." He drew himself up. "This revolver, gentlemen, was recovered from the oily filth of Havana Harbor. This very six-shooter was taken from the blackened, twisted hulk of our proudest fighting ship, the USS *Maine*!" Again the roar, the cheering men calling out in cadence, "Remember the *Maine*, to hell with Spain!"

Roosevelt let them shout and stared at the pistol, as though it alone had caused their reaction. Finally, he slipped the Colt into his holster, closed the flap and slapped it.

The men wanted more and Roosevelt braced his shoulders to give it. "Will that infamous Spanish act of dirty treachery, gentlemen, go unpunished?" Roosevelt held his hands high.

"HELL NO!" The Rough Riders shouted.

"Indeed not, gentlemen! Not when the First Volunteer Cavalry lands tomorrow!" Again they yelled and whooped. When the troopers had finished one salvo of "ROUGH, TOUGH, WE'RE THE STUFF," Roosevelt put a finger to his cheek and shifted thoughtfully. When he spoke again, his voice was soft.

"Not a decade ago, boys, our Census Bureau, in its *infinite* wisdom, declared the great American frontier officially closed!"

The troopers laughed.

"Yes, you heard me, they said the West had been completely won, thank you. Wrapped up and tidy." He cocked his head and grinned, "Although there is nothing tidy about the Dakotas, *is* there boys?"

More raucous yips and yells under the stars.

"What then, do we do? Raise sheep? *Become* sheep?"

"BOOOOOOOOOOOOOOOOO! FIGHT! FIGHT! FIGHT!"

Gabriel could see the flash of Roosevelt's grin.

"Fight, you say? Well, boys, that means nothing unless a man has a just cause. Now I am generally opposed to war, as such. Those of you who know me, can see that I am a peaceful man." Sniggers of laughter. "That is, when not thrown into the company of bullies, thugs, and tyrants! No, generally, I go about doing quietly what I think is right. But certain principles guide my life, gentlemen. These principles are not unlike those of our founding fathers, and, of course, those held by Colonel Wood and President McKinley.

Let's review them. I think you'll agree." He brought a fist down hard and smacked his palm. "First, don't flinch, don't foul, but hit the line hard! Then, build a vigorous body, mind, and character. But I forget gentlemen, to whom I speak," he chuckled, "I hardly need tell any Rough Rider that!"

The men cheered and laughed. Some of them sat on the deck. Others lit cob pipes or started fresh chews, enjoying Teddy's show.

"The fate of a new century looms before us, boys. And not just for the Cubans, but for many nations. This calls not for a life of ignoble ease, but a life of strenuous endeavor! If we, as a nation, sit idly by and seek only swollen, slothful ease, why then we shrink from the contest that men and women must win at the very hazard of their lives! Hah! Why then, stronger peoples will pass us by and win for themselves domination of the world! Far better it is to risk mighty things, to win glorious victories, though checkered with defeat, than to take rank with those poor spirits who neither enjoy much or suffer much. Why? Because they, gentlemen, are quite content to live in that gray twilight that knows neither victory or defeat. No! I preach not the doctrine of ignoble ease. Let the somnolent Dons of Spain do that, as they violate Cuba, the Queen of the Antilles, as they outrage her innocent women, as they herd Cuban farmers into concentration camps to starve while the Dons dine on the very beef and drink the very rum these heroic people have produced. Ah! But their heinous acts are well known to you gentlemen, for you have read the papers and seen the illustrations of Freddie Remington, showing, indeed *proving* through his personal ocular testimony the horrible evil that has been visited on our tiny neighbor, Cuba."

"But lest you think I am alone in these views, let me just close, boys, with a few words from one of our Senators, days after he had buried his beloved wife."

He paused, now and rubbed his eye with a knuckle. Lieutenant Hall had already told the troopers how Roosevelt's wife had perished in childbirth just hours after his mother died, and how, to "heal up" Teddy had gone west and founded Elkhorn Ranch near the fork of the Little Missouri and Beaver Creek in North Dakota. "The senator's good wife had visited the camps in Cuba," Roosevelt said, "and the shock of what she saw literally ended her life. The Senator addressed the congressmen and, with tears of grief streaming down his cheeks, reminded them that in the nineteen hundred years since

Christ died, Spain, a *Christian* nation, had set up more crosses in more lands, beneath more skies and yet had *butchered* more people than all the other nations of the earth combined! He begged the assembled representatives of the people, implored them, that before another Christmas morning, the last vestige of Spanish tyranny and oppression would vanish from the Western Hemisphere!" Roosevelt pulled on his cavalry gloves and cupped his palms to his mouth.

"That, boys," he shouted, "is exactly what we came to bring about!" Then he quickly softened his voice and said, "I thank you and wish you Godspeed tomorrow."

Then Roosevelt had the band play and he led the worried troopers in the song they had already sung a hundred times.

> *When you hear, them-a bells go ding, a-ling,*
> *All join 'round, and sweet-ly you must sing,*
> *And when the verse is through,*
> *In the cho-rus all join in,*
> *They'll be a hot time, in old Cuba, tonight!*

Then the trombones razzed them all into another chorus while the band music from other ships scattered across the luminous sea. After a medley of popular songs, "Hello Ma Baby, The Man On the Flying Trapeze" and cavalry standard, "The Girl I Left Behind Me."

The opening bars of "Hail Columbia" signaled the end of the fun.

> *Oh Columbia, the gem of the ocean,*
> *The home of the brave and the free...,*

As they sang it, Gabriel blew silently into the mouth piece of his bugle, warming it so that that when the last cymbal crashed and the final note had been played, he could begin playing taps seamlessly in the same key.

> *Thy ramparts make tyranny tremble,*
> *When borne by the red white and blue!*

Then, Gabriel began, blowing sweet and clear.
Ta ta TAAAA,
Taa ta taaaaa...

With each note he was imagining himself anointing the regiment. They were committed now and Gabriel blew no turning back. His bugle carried across the calm water, eventually silencing every ship, hushing an entire flotilla. Tonight the sixteen thousand men of The Fifth Army Corps would rest more easily under the Southern Cross. Perhaps, Gabriel hoped, they would even sleep.

CHAPTER 13

Tuesday, June 21

Captain Bucky O'Neill swore, coloring the air with good Irish oaths. "By the Holy Mother of God," he wailed, "if this were Golgotha, our Savior would still be waiting for the nails to pin His blessed extremities to the cross!" O'Neill had just heard the news. No troops were to be put ashore today.

The *Yucatan* was out of sight of land. The troopers heard the salvos of the heavy guns in the distance.

"Gol'danged war's a-passin' us by," Snake whined.

Colonel Wood addressed the men crowding the rail, officers and troopers alike. "We'll know General Shafter has decided to land us when the *New Orleans* hoists her signal flag. They call it the Blue Peter. Then, we'll lower our boats and go right in." Wood made the landing sound like a drill.

Gabriel looked off the port rail, then to starboard. So long aboard the *Yucatan*, the men had learned the navy terms for left and right, front and rear. Most troopers used nautical terms constantly, although Snake usually got them wrong.

Roosevelt lowered his field glasses and bellowed, "The *New Orleans* is with the destroyers, farther in. They're shelling the coastline. That way, the Spanish won't know where we'll hit the beach. Anything can happen now. So when our men-o-war come back out, putting us between them and the shore, we'll see the signal. You boys be ready, " he said, "every man jack of you. Blanket rolls, haversacks, and lard in your barrels. You don't want the brine to clog your carbines."

Theodore made this sound like a war.

"Hell, we're ready now, Sir."

"I'll be dead, dried, and cured by then," Snake said. "Lordy, what I wouldn't give for a shot of whiskey."

"You'll get lead poisonin' if you don't quit bellyachin'," Prayerful taunted, patting the stock of his carbine. It seemed to Gabriel that the preacher had lately shed some of his religion.

"Bust him Snake," a trooper chided, "bust him you-know-where!"

But Fish grabbed Snake and Prayerful by the hair and with a resounding crack brought their heads together.

Snake rubbed his head. "Hell, Sarge, says in the Holy Scripture that fightin's good."

Prayerful reached for his breast-pocket Bible. "Is that so! Well you point me out chapter and verse."

Snake frowned. "Sez somewhere, I forget where, to turn the other cheek, don't it?" He looked at Prayerful. "Well," he continued, "if a man insults me and is dumb enough to turn his face my way, I just can't resist doin' the Lord's will, can I? Lord, forgive him, fer he knows not what he says... Eh? What's that, Lord?" Snake cupped his hand to his ear, as though listening to heavenly advice. "Sure thing, Thy will be done." Then, Snake punched Prayerful in the nose.

As Prayerful looked at the blood in his hand, Snake quoted scripture. "Vengeance is mine, sez the Lord."

*

Clouds blew in from the southwest, bringing a hard brief rain. Troopers stripped off their shirts and boots. Gabriel had learned to carry a slice of soap in his pocket, for the almost predictable evening rain was his only chance to bathe. Cloud stood in the rain, letting his uniform get drenched. Then, as suddenly as the rain had come, it stopped, leaving the deck a rainbow of steam. .

In five minutes the deck was dry. Most of the troopers draped their soggy shirts over the whale-boats or tied sleeves to the ship's railing.

Near the funnel, Tiffany read aloud from an old newspaper. "Since April twenty- third, when President McKinley called for 125,000 volunteers, a million men have responded. Of men requesting officer's commissions, nine of ten were refused."

"Officers cain't cough, I reckon," Snake quipped. He was in the midst of a poker game, and was counting his take. "Seventeen dollars." He rolled the treasury bills tight and tucked them under a stained suspender, next to his chest. "Guess I'm out."

At his point a well dressed stranger in a white suit leaned over them, putting his weight on his silver handled walking stick. Tipping his crisp Panama, he said, "Mind if I sit in, boys?"

Gabriel had seen Richard Harding Davis come aboard that morning from a steam lighter. He had gone straight up to the bridge, where he laughed and joked with Roosevelt and Wood.

Sitting in the newcomer's shadow, Snake squinted up. "I don't believe I know you, mister."

Davis took a Rough Rider polka-dot kerchief from his breast pocket, leaned on his stick and dusted a spot the deck. With some effort, he sat down and rubbed his thigh. "Dick's my name, boys. And my sciatica is flaring up. I need a spirited game of chance to get my mind off it."

Davis shook hands with each player. "We might as well get acquainted. I'll be in the first boat when you disembark, just as I was when the marines took Guantánamo a fortnight ago."

"Where?"

"Guantánamo. A harbor superior to Santiago. And our marines safely secured it, with few wounded and fewer killed. So it looks like you boys will have to out-do the marines." Davis had won them over already.

"So you been ashore," Snake asked in a skeptical voice.

"Why certainly. I've visited all sections of Cuba a good many times. Of course, now that we've declared war, I'm no more welcome behind the

Spanish lines than you are. We are all in the same boat, as the phrase goes."
Davis took a twenty dollar gold piece from his vest and placed it on the deck.
"Whose deal, gentlemen?"

CHAPTER 14

Dawn
Wednesday, June 22

The men were ready, fully equipped, and sick of waiting. There was not a trooper or officer onboard the *Yucatan* who was not ready to try to walk the gray chop of ocean all the way to the Cuban shore.

Lieutenant Colonel Roosevelt was ebullient. He gripped the rail, lifted his heels and chuckled as a turreted warship cut across the *Yucatan's* stern, hundreds of sailors lining her decks, all waving and cheering the Rough Riders. Heartened by the greeting, the troopers cheered back.

"The heavy cruiser *New York*," Roosevelt bellowed. "You see, boys, three stacks, two masts. Admiral Sampson's flagship. Now, the rest of the squadron will follow her out to sea. Yes! See out there?" He shouted as the *New York's* wake lifted the *Yucatan*. "There, further east. Two high stacks, one mast. Modern gun turrets. Now that's our battleship *Iowa*." He made wings with his arms, setting his fists on his hips. "I helped get her built. Why,

I know every vessel and their skippers. Look, there, coming up to port, that saucy yacht with her slanted stacks." He put his hands to his walrus mouth and shouted as the speedy vessel drew close. "Ahoy, *Vixen*."

"Ahoy, Colonel Roosevelt," the cry came back from her wheel house, "you'll give them hell, won't you sir?"

"We certainly shall, Lieutenant Sharp!" Then as the *Vixen* came about and headed back toward shore, Roosevelt explained, "The owner of that brave little yacht was my aide in Washington, gentlemen. At his own expense, he fitted his ship with guns and we got her commissioned. Captain Sharp will fight. By God, he'll be in the thick of it."

The gray warships continued to steam past them, knifing the swells, heading out to sea. Roosevelt named each one. Next came the *Oregon*, a monster like the *Iowa*, but with one less gun turret, her smoke stacks shorter. Gabriel's heart leaped when Roosevelt identified the *New Orleans*, the merchant cruiser that would give their invasion signal. The mighty *Indiana* steamed past, belching heavy smoke from her stacks, then the cruisers *Detroit* and *Castine*. The last vessel to pass them, the sleek *Wasp*, hardly left a wake.

*

Silent white smoke puffed from the sides of the war ships. They were stretched out behind the transports in a line. The delayed roar of shells screamed overhead, hurtling for the beach. Each time a shell exploded the men cheered. Palm trees were thrown into the air along with spurts of red earth. The bombardment seemed to release something in the men. They screamed until they were hoarse.

Snake took bets on which shell would hit the block house on top of the mountain.

Woooooooooo sssssshhhhhhh. Silence, then *KA-BLAM!* Rock splinters and dust made a crimson cloud a dozen yards below the summit.

Snake jumped. "Higher, you goldarned jacks! Aim higher. That's it. Hell NO, the other way!"

Gabriel had never felt so alive. It was wonderful, after so much waiting, to be close to the beach.

High above the water, an ore car burned on the iron pier. Below it, the wooden dock jutted out, black and crested by waves.

Ka-bloom! A shell hit the gray cliff overlooking the town. A cascade of rock dust slid down, rocks rattling on the tin roofs. One shed was burning. To the right of the mountain, away from the village, two dark caves overlooked the sea.

Blammmm!

Delayed reports from the salvos shot along the water and slammed into the men. Then the overhead whooshing, silence for a second, and the shells exploded magnificently on the beach. Every Rough Rider, a few hours ago dog-tired from lack of sleep, was alive and filled with anticipation.

A lone rider galloped down the beach on his mount, dodging shells, carrying a flag with a large white star set in a red triangle that led a half dozen blue stripes.

"A rebel, sir," Gabriel reported.

Roosevelt grabbed Gabriel's binoculars. "Look, boys, he's waving a white flag. There, on the end of the dock. The Spanish have withdrawn! We're going in! We're going in. OH Bully!" He danced up and down. "But..." Roosevelt suddenly froze, "where are our boats?"

The *Yucatan* was turning, not toward the beach, but out to sea.

Roosevelt was stunned. He screamed up to the bridge, "No, Captain Jenkins, damn it, NO!" he bellowed, dashing for the ladder, "You will *not* ruin my war!"

*

The *Vixen* drew alongside. Lieutenant Sharp saluted smartly up to Roosevelt, who stood on the bridge with a sullen Captain Jenkins.

A large Negro, naked except for his dirty trousers, waited beside Sharp. He stared up at Roosevelt.

"Sharp, isn't your pilot a Cuban?" Roosevelt called down.

"Yes sir!"

"Then he knows these waters, does he not?"

Lieutenant Sharp nodded. "Why, of course, sir."

Roosevelt glared at Jenkins. "Then, Lieutenant Sharp, send him aboard! Our good Captain has developed a sudden aversion to Spanish lead. You're a witness to this, Sharp. He refuses to bring us in to our rendezvous with the steam lighters! Can you believe it? While America holds her breath, Captain Jenkins *vacillates!*"

"Then go, Manólo," Sharp commanded.

The Cuban took the line and, cupping his bare feet around it, pulled himself up to the gunwale. Gabriel took one of his hands and Cloud the other, as they pulled him aboard. Manólo, mistaking Cloud for a Cuban, grinned. "*Buenvenídos, amigo,*" he said.

*

The shelling stopped. Smoke hung on the water, thick and acrid. Gabriel adjusted the heavy bulk of his blanket roll and cinched the strap of his Krag tight. He would need both hands to scramble down the rope ladder into the bobbing whale boats. From below, the brawny tars laughed as the Rough Riders gaped at their tiny moving targets.

Tiffany swung down the ladder, ducking his head in time with the wave motion. He hugged his carbine and counted. The whaler was thrown up, shivered on the crest of a wave, then ground with a sickening rasp down the barnacled hull of the *Yucatan* into a trough between waves.

Calmly counting, Tiffany watched the boat rise, then he jumped, landing in a crouch, his hands clutching the heaving gunwales.

"Hell, it's like mountin' a bronco," Snake yelled. Then he jumped too, catching the bobbing, shooting boat, and falling in a heap into the bottom. Roosevelt leaped next, his saber clattering noisily. He stood and yelled up. "Now jump! There's nothing to it. Colonel Wood will not disembark until the last Rough Rider has been loaded."

Cloud and Fish scrambled down, then Gabriel and Snake.

Finally, the Rough Riders were loaded nine troopers to a boat, each boat secured by a rope hawser. The steam lighter blew her high-pitched whistle, pulled the lines taut, and Gabriel's boat was towed with the others through the waves.

But halfway to shore, the speedy *Seguranca* cut them off. On her bridge, General Shafter scowled from under a white pith helmet. "*Mister Davis, sir!*" he bellowed into a megaphone, "you will not land with those troops!"

In the bow of the boat, Richard Harding Davis lowered the notebook in which he had been scribbling. He wore a yellow pugaree on the back of his pith helmet to shield his neck from the sun. "General Shafter," he replied, "I am under orders to report the first landing of troops."

"Not from me, you are not, sir."

"But Mr. Hearst...."

General Shafter's face twisted. "I have had quite enough of Mister Hearst! He is a civilian, *Mister* Harding, and so are you. My skiff will bring you aboard, sir, where you will remain, with the rest of the reporters, until we have occupied Siboney."

Davis set his boot casually against the gunwale and smiled. "Ah, but I am not a reporter, General. I am a descriptive writer."

The General slammed his megaphone against the rail and barked to a subaltern. Immediately, a skiff loaded with four marines swung out from the *Seguranca's* davits.

Davis turned to Roosevelt, who had been uncharacteristically silent. "General Shafter has made his first tactical error, Theodore. I want you to know that."

Roosevelt did not speak, but he stared hard at the portly General.

As the marines rowed toward him, Harding stood up in the boat. "Well, then," he intoned loudly, "so be it. But I shall annihilate that fat pig in print."

Richard Harding Davis handed his cane to a marine, and with exaggerated lameness, he lifted himself over the gunwale.

From the *Seguranca*, Shafter watched, making no sign to the men he commanded. Only when the skiff pulled away did the General lumber toward his cabin.

"Amazing," Roosevelt remarked, "the man has no joy for war."

*

Ten steam tugs pulled eight hundred screaming men through the heavy swells through patches of smoke, troopers bailing and cheering. Gabriel saw their lighter pull away from the others and veer right, heading for the wooden pier. A red flare arched high into the blue sky, the helmsmen cast off hawsers in each of the whale boats and troopers began to row.

"Keep bailing, or we'll sink," the cockswain guiding Gabriel's boat yelled. "Pull together, you danged landlubbers. Ain't you never rowed a boat before? Look, we're zig-zaggin'!"

As Cloud, Tiffany and Snake pulled against the creaking oar locks, Gabriel's oar shot its lock and he swept air just as the whaler crested a wave. "PULL. Two, three, PULL!"

As spray dashed over him, Gabriel tasted the warm brine. Then they shot off a crest and, with a loud crack, hit the dock. "Now hold fast. No! Not like that," the cockswain cursed. Other boats were banging into them and the dock seemed a rearing monster, lurching crazily sideways, forcing the whale boats with board-splintering cracks against mossy timbers. The whaler bolted up. Gabriel looked down on the pier, with half its cross-boards missing. Without thinking, he leaped, groped air, and his water-logged brogans stuck wood. He clawed for a handhold as a wall of water knocked him flat. But he had landed. Yet the pier seemed to heave with a life of its own. Around him, boats and men and waves collided.

"*Yaaaaaa heeee!*" he bellowed in delight. The boat hurtled past and he saw Snake's astonished face disappear, then up the bow shot again, depositing Cloud beside him, drenched and coughing brine on the splintery dock. Each rising wave brought another knot of scrambling men, grabbing anything, cracking each other in the face with elbows and carbines.

"God damn, son of a bitch," Snake wailed, "I dropped my gun. In the God damned ocean." He pointed, disbelieving, between the planks. "Hey, I see it." he pointed, "there, on the bottom. I'm goin' in."

But Fish had grabbed Snake's suspenders. "No you don't. That water's deep and with your load, you'll sink like a rock. Let's get off of this dock. Out here, we're sitting ducks. Watch out for loose boards, boys!" Fish led as they ran in a crouch.

When they had reached the sand and fallen flat, they clutched the beach, for the land seemed to be bucking under them, a result of having been at sea for so long. When they got up, it was hard for Gabriel to walk a straight line. He suddenly understood the peculiar gait he had observed in sailors.

Fish called, "Listen. I don't hear any fire."

Cloud squinted up the beach into the line of leather-leafed trees.

Roosevelt huffed down onto the sand. "Isn't this wonderful!" he said. "It's just..." Then he whirled and looked out toward the transports. "Sergeant Fish!"

"Sir."

"Your binoculars please."

Teddy dialed the range, then exploded. "Damn! Three, four, five... Oh no! I see a horse swimming OUT, there's another. Oh my God. This is a disaster!"

Snake threw down his campaign hat. "Steamin' buffalo shit!"

Roosevelt handed the glasses to Gabriel, then ran down the beach, yelling at surprised men, gesturing wildly out to the *Yucatan.* "The horses, the horses! Get me out there. Get a boat! Do you hear?" But the regulars were not obliged to obey this frantic officer with the polka dot kerchief.

"Damn Jenkins," Roosevelt screamed. "Will you look at that, men! He's opened the high cargo doors. I told him to use those near the water line. Those horses are weak and scared already. They'll drown if they jump that far."

Cloud took the glasses. "Here they come. Texas first. He's shaking his head. He's got water in his ears! Where is Rain-in-Face?"

Tiffany cried, "The swells are confusing them. They can't see the beach. Lord, what if they swim in the wrong direction!"

Gabriel swung the glasses, counted a dozen horses, nostrils flared, eyes white in terror. They swam in a pack, first one way and then the other. On the *Yucatan,* he could see the teamsters screaming at the mounts, confusing them even more.

Tiffany yanked off his boots. He slipped out of his blanket roll, gave his haversack to Snake, peeled off his longjohns and sprinted into the surf.

Gabriel, watching the horses round the stern of the *Yucatan* and swim out to sea, knew Tiffany would not reach them in time. In one instant he knew what to do. He hoped the wind was right. He unwrapped his bugle. Cloud stared at Gabriel like he'd gone loco.

"Keep your eyes glued on the horses, Snake. You tell me every move they make." Gabriel blew right wheel, the first command an army pony learns, hoping instinct would prevail. He blew it again; praying the wind would carry his bugle over the din of steam boat whistles and cheering men.

Snake banged on Gabriel's back. "Them cayooses is turnin' Gabe! *Yaaa hee!*" Then, "No. Wait; don't blow right wheel no more. They turn each time you do. Hell's fire, Gabe, there they go again!"

Gabriel lowered his bugle. "Do you see Tiffany?"

"No."

Gabriel said, "Listen Snake, I'll blow 'right wheel' one time. That should turn 'em parallel with the beach. You tell me if it does."

"Okay, Gabe. But hurry! Them ponies is crazy spooked. We're

gonna lose 'em all!"

Gabriel blew. "Did they turn?"

"Yaaahooooo!"

Gabriel blew 'right wheel' again, keeping the notes crisp.

Snake whooped. "They're swimmin' in, Gabe! But some of 'em is goin' under."

Gabriel filled his cheeks, hardened his stomach, and blew, sounding "charge."

"Yaaaa heeeee! That did it Gabe! Man, look at 'em come!"

"Bully, Gabriel," yelled Roosevelt. "Absolutely bully! Look, here comes Texas! Now, the others will certainly follow!"

Gabriel's bugle crushed his lip as the sour-smelling Colonel squeezed him in a bear hug. "Brilliant, Scriven. Absolutely brilliant. You've saved both my horses!"

*

Two naked troopers staggered from the breakwater toward the tall grass. Gabriel hesitated, then saluted, recognizing Captain Bucky O'Neill. Tiffany squatted beside him, gasping for breath.

Roosevelt's face was grave. "Did you find them, Bucky?"

Bucky knelt on the sand and shook his head.

Tiffany, his sunburned face pained over a marble white torso, gestured back toward the crowded dock. "Captain O'Neill dove down so many times we had to make him quit," he gasped. "But they must have been crushed between the boat and the dock. Sank fast with no struggle. Knoblauch was there. He's is a champion swimmer and even he couldn't find them. Water's too stirred up."

Roosevelt chewed his lip. "Did you know either man?"

Bucky shook his head. "Tenth Cavalry," he gasped.

"Well," Roosevelt said, "how about the horses?"

"We roped most of ours and towed them in," Tiffany said, "they're feeding in the grass below camp. But other regiments did not fare so well. The water is full of dead ponies."

Bucky O'Neill slapped his neck and stared at the bloody mosquito. "My boys made it fine. But one of the Tenth's boats capsized," he gasped, "not many swimmers. Didn't know how to hold their breaths and slip their gear."

Roosevelt shouted, "Lieutenant Hall! Bring Captain O'Neill's clothes." Then he said, more softly, "Overall we've done well. Just lost two Negroes and a few horses. One of them, I fear, was Rain-in Face."

Gabriel felt sick and Roosevelt must have noticed his reaction. "Eh, by that I mean- if the Spaniards had actually fired on us, we'd have many times the losses. Hah! Why we might be dead too!"

Bucky O'Neill took his folded clothes from Lieutenant Hall. "We brought up a Krag and a few canteens."

Snake grinned. "My gun!"

Hall squinted down the beach. "Here comes General Wheeler!"

Fighting Joe Wheeler, flanked by two tall regular officers, labored through the sand. As he approached, the General was staring, somewhat bemused, at the two naked men, both of whom had leaped to attention. "At ease, gentlemen. Adorned as Adam, I see," Wheeler said.

Roosevelt blurted, "My compliments, General. An excellent operation, so far."

Wheeler made a face. "More like vaudeville, than a war," he observed. "We have nothing to ride and, look, " he pointed his saber up the mountain, "is not that an enemy *bannuh* up there?"

Roosevelt hurriedly cleaned his spectacles, and put them on. "Why, I believe you are right, sir."

The General spun, fixing his eyes on Roosevelt. "Then why do you have your troopers makin' bivouac?"

"Colonel Wood's orders, sir."

"And where, may I inquire, is the *Cunnel?*"

"Conferring with General Lawton," Roosevelt answered. "Sir."

Wheeler's saber flashed in the sun, pointed accusingly at the blockhouse on the summit. "Well, *Cunnel*, we've got to get that down, and raise our own colors. It is imperative that we insult our enemy. At once."

Roosevelt saluted. "Immediately, General Wheeler."

Fish stepped forward. "I'll take Cloud and Scriven, sir."

Snake kicked the trampled grass.

After General Wheeler had left, Roosevelt sent Hall for a large, triangular bundle. When Hall returned, Roosevelt unwrapped the bundle and gave it to Fish. "From the ladies of New York," he said, "the biggest in Fifth

Corps. Now get up there, boys. Stay on this side so we can see if you get into trouble. Signal by heliograph if you need help."

*

Cloud led, picking his way up the steep, rocky trail, cratered by shells and sharp with the smell of cordite. Gabriel's Krag weighed heavily and the strap rubbed his wool shirt against his neck. The men had to crawl, using both hands to grasp at the scrub brush. Often, the loose rock gave way, and even the sure-footed Cloud slipped. The sun hammered down on them like a fist. The only sound was the sliding shale and their labored gasps. Then, the wind shifted and from below, they heard steam whistles cut the air.

"Keep your eyes ahead, Gabriel," Fish snapped. The trail, barely wide enough for a goat, twisted and turned back on itself. Cloud stopped, wiped his face with his kerchief. "We can't stay on this side, Sarge," he panted. "Trail winds around."

Fish squinted up the slope, then nodded. "Take a breather." He took a mirror out of his breast pocket, glanced up at the sun and began to flash a heliograph message in Morse code.

Below them, boats worked the sapphire bay, running white wakes from the anchored transports. Farther out, the cruisers steamed in dark water, their gun turrets screwing toward the hills behind the troops. On the yellow beach and in the umber grass and dotting the green jungle, rows of white tents were springing up, identified by regimental banners, with soldiers working like ants among them.

Fish had been reading the return flash from the Rough Rider's camp. "Colonel says the blockhouse looks abandoned. Let's go."

They worked up, then down, then up, scrambling, trying to keep the summit in view. On the shaded side of the mountain, the sea breeze chilled them. Cloud held up his hand and they stopped. He put his finger to his lips. Fish nodded, then leaned close to Gabriel. Gabriel slipped the Krag from his shoulder and eased the bolt back. Fish did the same.

Then Cloud signaled them forward.

The trail widened, then flattened and they crouched, making better time. Then Cloud stood, and Fish did too. There it was, the wooden blockhouse, with its pyramidal tin roof blazing in the sun, surrounded by three barbed wire fences. From the crest of the roof rose an empty flag pole.

Something moved in the doorway and Gabriel instinctively brought his Krag up and sighted down the barrel at a handsome young man in a white cotton uniform, with a straw sombrero with the Cuban cockade on the front. A machete hung at his belt and against his chest he held a bundle of red and yellow shreds—the remains of the Spanish flag.

"Welcome to Mount Losiltares," he said, stepping out into the sun. "I am Colonel Raúl García of the army of *Cuba Libre*. My father, Mayor General Calixto García Iníguez, commander east of the *Moron trocha*, sends his very highest regards."

Fish stepped forward and was stopped by the barbed wire that was wound like a silver nest around the blockhouse.

Colonel García tossed the shredded flag to the ground. "So much for the *Peninsulares,*" he said. Then he gave an ironic smile. "What do you want?"

Gabriel and Cloud exchanged glances. Fish set his jaw, and reached inside his haversack for the flag.

When he saw it, Colonel García stiffened. "How very *Yanqui*, no? You want to raise your flag over our island, and yet you have not killed one man, except two of my *mambises* who died from the barrage of your naval guns. Also a few innocent cows. Yet, you want to play the conqueror, no?"

Fish was losing patience. "Listen, mister, it is not our fault the Spaniards ran. We've had nothing at which to shoot."

García smiled. "Of course not. Because our men have driven the *Peninsulares* back. We have attacked them repeatedly, losing thirty of our own a day. So you see no Spaniards, *Yanqui*, because while you were sailing back and forth in your ships, singing your songs," he withdrew his machete and chopped the air with it, "my *mambises* were spilling blood."

Then Colonel García's shoulders relaxed. "I hate to see the first American flag raised on Cuban soil because I know it may never come down. If I had a Cuban flag at this moment, I would raise it. But I was too intent to get up here before you did."

Fish adjusted his hat, tilting it forward until the brim as low over his eyes. In a steady voice he said, "I have orders to raise our flag. It is not for me to interpret the politics, despite the fact that your flag of Free Cuba was designed in New York by my father and Jose Marti."

García sheathed his machete and stepped to the fence. F

To

Fish through the barbed wire as he continued.

"And furthermore, Colonel García, we *Yanquis* have been supplying you with rifles and ammunition at great peril to ourselves. " Fish withdrew his pliers and snipped a strand of barbed wire. The wire snapped and whipped against his cheek. He raised his hand, rubbed the cut and stared at the blood on his glove.

Colonel García grunted. "So. You have finally shed blood on Cuban soil. Now we have something in common. All right, Sergeant Fish. You may raise your *Yanqui* flag, but consider it temporary. When we have together beaten the *Peninsulares* and the flag of *España* comes down for good, the flag of *Cuba Libre* will take its place. Not yours."

Fish nodded. "That is my government's every intention, Colonel."

It took some time to cut through the wire. Then Gabriel and Cloud scrambled up onto the hot tin of the blockhouse roof. The lanyard on the flag pole had been slashed, so Cloud threaded the ends through the brass eyelets off the flag and tied it off with two half hitches. Then, Gabriel hauled the lanyard hand over hand and the heavy flag caught the breeze. Gabriel's throat thickened.

They slid down and slumped in the shade of the blockhouse, passing Fish's canteen.

"You'd think somebody would notice," Fish said.

Below, a swarm of boats cut the bay as naked, pink men dragged mules through the surf and hauled wagons out of soft sand.

Cloud went into the block house, then stepped out with a long necked green bottle. He sat down beside them and bit the cork out.

"Wait," Fish said.

Cloud sniffed the open bottle. "It's rum, Sarge."

Fish grabbed the bottle, then took a very small sip. He made a face and spit it out. "No good," he said. "Poisoned, more than likely." Then Fish side-armed the bottle down the mountain. As it shattered on the rocks, Cloud muttered in Lakota.

Below, a ship's gun fired and the shell whined high over their heads. "Down!" Fish yelled, and the three of them hit the ground. His face in the dirt, Gabriel waited. But there was no second shot.

Then it came, slowly, a familiar tune broken now and again by the fitful wind that carried it up the mountain. "Listen," Gabriel said, raising his head. "Stand up, boys, they've seen the flag. That's the National Anthem."

The three of them stood up, brushing dirt from their uniforms.

From below, the regimental bands aboard the transports played, but Gabriel realized there was no reverence in it. Steam whistles laced the air. The troopers on the beach leaped about, throwing their hats into the air. All the launches had stopped. Gabriel knew every eye was fixed on the flag atop the blockhouse.

Then amid the swell of noise and music below, came the popcorn sound of rifle fire. Below, the Cubans rode their ponies down the beach, carrying a faded Cuban flag. They spurred their horses hard as they fired their carbines into the air.

*

"Why they're nothin' but bums," Snake snorted, watching the Cubans leap their ponies over tents, kicking sand everywhere. "Too ragged to fight." He drew a bead on one of them and pulled the trigger of his Krag, but the pin clicked on an empty chamber.

"Hey!" Fish snapped.

"Jest practicin', Sarge."

As the Cubans rode by on lathered ponies, they yelled "*Vivan Los Americanos!*" The troopers had learned to yell back, "Beeba Cuba Librey," a corruption of "*Viva Cuba Libre.*"

A Cuban reined his lathered pony to an abrupt halt before them. The pony's mouth foamed and his ribs bled where a single spur, tied to the Cuban's bare foot, had dug. The Cuban threw back his unraveling straw sombrero and gave them an almost toothless smile. Then he raised his carbine to show it off. "*Americano legítimo!*" he said.

"Yeah," Snake snarled. "Stole, I bet."

"No," Fish corrected. "that is one of the Lee rifles we shipped down to them."

"They ain't fighters," Snake spat. "You can tell."

"*Legítimo,*" the Cuban insisted, shaking the riffle over his head. His smile dissolved as he looked from one man to the next. Clearly offended, he dug the spur, forcing his pony to leap a pup tent and gallop off down the beach.

Snake spat a stream of tobacco juice. "Son-of-a-bitch should be shot, mistreatin' a horse like that. Even if his horse looks like a big rat."

*

Colonel Raúl García posted in his stirrups, trotting his stallion among his men as they hacked palm branches with their machetes.

The Rough Riders watched the Cubans from a hillock. "Hell's fire, Sarge," Snake snarled, as he lay in the long grass, "they're making camp upwind of us!"

Fish squinted into the sun. "Then Wheeler ordered it."

"But they're Nigras!"

Gabriel pinched Snake's arm and Fish caught the reaction.

"Yes," Fish said, "not pure like you. Now shut your mouth and watch. You might learn something."

The Cubans, some barefoot, others wearing straw sandals, were dressed in rags. Yet they wielded their machetes expertly, slashing thick branches with a single cut, then shaving bark with the next, talking excitedly all the while.

Tiffany crawled up, for the tall grass offered shelter from the sun.

"Ain't they got no tents?" Snake asked.

One of the Cubans spotted the Americans and called up to them, "*Vivan Los Americanos!*"

"*Viva Cuba Libre,*" Gabriel called. The Cuban grinned and dropped his machete.

Tiffany laughed. "Well, you got his attention. Here he comes."

The Cuban's arms and legs were covered with scabs. Ribs showed through what had once been a strong torso. Gabriel could see the Cuban was young, yet he looked twice his age. He crouched beside them in the grass and offered a modern carbine to Gabriel.

Gabriel drew the bolt and removed a clip of five cartridges.

Fish took the clip and examined it under the Cuban's proud smile. "Ask him where he got this, Gabe."

"*De dónde enquentralo?*"

"*Los Peninsulares,*" the Cuban said.

A shadow fell across the troopers and Gabriel looked up to see Colonel Wood, who reached down and took the carbine. After working the bolt, which kicked out a cartridge, he spoke. "A German Mauser, boys.

Smokeless powder, a clip of five steel-jacketed cartridges. Range two miles. And every Spaniard has one."

Wood tossed the carbine back to the Cuban. "Scriven, ask how much ammunition the Spanish have."

When Gabriel asked, the Cuban drew his hand from his shoulder to his opposite thigh, indicating a bandoleer. *"Ellos tienen mucho parque."*

Wood scratched his sandy mustache.

"Scriven, show this man your carbine." Gabriel reluctantly handed over his Krag. The Cuban accepted it, whispering to himself. He opened the chamber and his cracked lips moved as he counted the shells. *"Ay, carajo,"* he exclaimed with wonder.

Wood nodded with satisfaction. "Now he'll tell his *compañeros*. Soon as a Cuban gets captured, the Spaniards will know they are up against a carbine as good as theirs." Wood put on his hat and tilted it smartly. "Watch your gear, men. Now that they know what we've got, these rebels might make a few trades. And probably when you're not looking."

*

At twilight the Cubans began to string hammocks between the trunks of the palms as fireflies floated lazily. Then they wove grills of green twigs, built fires under them and laid strips of meat on to roast. Soon, staccato voices and laughter surrounded each fire.

Meanwhile, the Cuban officers lay smoking under palm-thatch roofs. It was hard to distinguish the ends of their cheroots from the fireflies.

The smell of grilled meat drifted up to the Rough Riders. None of the men had eaten since they left the *Yucatan*.

Gabriel's stomach growled. "Wonder if they'd trade for some?"

Snake looked interested. "What'd we trade? Ain't no tobacco left. Did you see the way that feller eyed our 'quipment? He didn't have but a flour bag for his gear. And jest a coconut shell fer a cup. An 'ol bottle fer a canteen. I'll bet we could git a belly full of beef fer, say, fer Prayerful's mess kit."

"Not on your life," Prayerful said. "You can go to—you know where."

"Too late," Snake laughed, "I'm on my way already."

"It is probably iguanas they are cooking," Cloud said. "They get big down here."

Snake got up. "I don't care if'n it's armadillo. C'mon, Gabe. You do the talkin' and I'll do the dealin'."

Leaving their carbines behind, Snake and Gabriel hauled four haversacks of camp junk down the hill. They were soon greeted by the click of a bolt, then a voice shouted, *"Alto!" Quien va?"*

"Americanos," Gabriel answered. *"Tranquillo!"*

"Americanos! Bien! Passe, y bienvenídos!" A sentry stepped out of the high grass, and in the dim light from a fire Gabriel saw a sawed-off shotgun slung across his arm. He wore no trace of welcome on his Oriental face. Another sentry, so dark they could only see his teeth, sheathed his machete.

Gabriel explained that they came to trade. Within minutes, the negotiations attracted a crowd of eager Cubans, who began to finger the troopers' shirts, suspenders, and cartridge belts. The Chinese stared at Gabriel's boots. Soon, Gabriel and Snake had traded for a big wad of cooked meat wrapped in banana leaves. They put it into one of the haversacks and traded the other three sacks which were full of tin plates, bandages, a canteen and a few oil cloth ponchos.

Gabriel saw several of the Cubans smoking cheroots. *"Amigos, damos tobacco?"*

He made the motion of packing and lighting a pipe. Although several of the rebels were smoking, this request went ignored.

"My men have orders," a familiar voice said from the darkness. "not to do certain things." Colonel García stepped into the fire light. "They do not have much tobacco, and they have orders not to trade it. It helps them to fight hunger. Rarely do we have the meat such as we eat tonight. And the tobacco ash is often our only medicine. You may laugh, but we have found it is very effective against infections."

García said something in Spanish and the three haversacks were returned. "The meat is yours, because in a way, you gave it to us. Besides, you look hungry. We know the feeling very well."

Colonel García was not finished. "Another thing. Tell your officers that my men have orders not to dig your latrines, carry your loads, or in any way, be your servants. We have done away with that in *Cuba Libre*. It is written in our new *Constitución* that no man will be a servant to another. Please, do not think these things as unfriendly. You must remember, that despite our lack of supplies and what must seem our pitiful condition, some of us left a privileged life to fight the *Peninsulares*. There are men here who would trade you their dignity for a carbine. There are others, quite frankly, who would cut your throat for one *Yanqui* souvenir. But we shoot our men for such things. For we are soldiers first. If ever you are in doubt, simply ask a man for his *cedula*, his pass. If he does not have one, he is surely a Spanish guerrilla, the very lowest form of human life. The *Peninsulares* hire them to do what they themselves do not have the stomach to do. Such animals do not deserve the price of a bullet." García spoke in rapid Spanish and a man stepped forward with two coconuts. He dropped one on the ground, took the other in his palm and brought his machete down hard. Then he chopped again and Gabriel saw that a wedge had been cut. The man handed the coconut to Gabriel. "We find them, sweet and cool, growing near water."

Gabriel took a deep drink of coconut milk, strange but gratifying to his thirst. He wiped his stubby beard and handed the coconut to Snake. There was pride in the Cuban' eyes as they watched the thirsty *Yanquis* drink.

When their haversacks were full of coconuts, white strips of cane, and the bundle of meat, Gabriel thanked the Colonel. "Tell your men they are very kind," he said.

"They understand your feelings without any words. It is an instinct illiterate men have," Colonel García explained. "They miss nothing and can even recognize my signature." Again, he translated and his men laughed.

"You are not curious about the meat?" García asked with an amused smile and raised eyebrows.

"Don't tell us," Snake drawled.

García laughed. "It is one of your *Yanqui* horses that drowned today. Thank you very much, *amigos*. The spotted one that belonged to your Colonel Roosevelt."

*

Prayerful squinted in the fire light, aiming the unfamiliar machete at a green coconut on the ground. He brought his blade down hard but the glancing blow did not affect the coconut one bit.

" 'Sposed to hold it in between yer legs, stupid," Snake said, grease running down his chin.

Fish chewed appreciatively on a piece of sugar cane.

Whaack! Prayerful's machete chopped off a slice of the green husk, but the hard, inner shell of the coconut remained unscathed. The grizzled trooper ran his thumb along the machete. "It's like cuttin' a boulder. How they do it?"

The meat was soon consumed. He had never eaten horse before, and Gabriel did not reveal its source, except to say that their own officers had made the tender, thick meat possible.

*

Due to the hilly ground, the Rough Rider's camp was established in uneven rows. There still was no source of fresh water.

Near midnight, Roosevelt came up from the beach with a mule loaded with canned goods. The regiment built fires from small branches and twigs, and set their cans over the heat.

"Despite the horrendous logistics," Roosevelt vowed, "my men will not spend their first night on Cuban soil hungry." Then he swatted at the mosquitoes that arrived in swarms.

During the night, beads of moisture collected on the underside of the tent. The drops gathered weight and one dropped in Gabriel's face "Snake?"

"Huh?"

"I can't sleep. Let's volunteer for picket."

Snake groaned. "We'll get our turn soon enough."

Gabriel crawled out of the tent. The moon was high in an indigo sky. A meteor shot from behind the mountain, then disappeared again. The Cubans could still be heard talking below, but their camp was dark now.

Suddenly Gabriel heard a rustling sound. His first instinct was to challenge it. "Halt! Who goes there?"

"Listen," Tiffany whispered. "Do you hear something?"

Gabriel listened, and then he heard a clicking, grunting, and a heavy rustle just below the knoll. He fixed his eyes on the spot, and saw two eyes reflecting the moonlight back.

The breach of Tiffany's carbine clicked.

Blam!

"I think I got him!"

"There are more out there, listen!" The rustling filled the grass and

Gabriel heard another trooper challenge. "Halt! Who goes there?" Then another sharp rifle report. In the silence that followed, Gabriel heard the Cubans laughing.

"They're playing some trick on us, Bill."

"If they do, they will take the consequences."

"Who fired that shot?" It was Captain Capron's voice.

"Sir, we're surrounded!"

"Hold your fire, damn it!" Capron commanded.

But other men were already firing and Gabriel scrambled back to his tent for his carbine. Snake was wide awake now. "Sneaky garlics!" he swore.

The two of them crawled back up the hill. Captain Capron had deployed a few men, so that they could fire from an angle. Each time a shot rang out, the rustling stopped. Then, from every side, the noise began again.

"Why ain't they shootin' back?" someone whispered.

"Cain't see us, prob'ly!"

Fish crawled up. "Just wait. They eventually got to move."

Gabriel cocked his Krag. From behind, someone lifted a lantern. "Here," Theodore Roosevelt whispered hoarsely, "put this on the ridge. See if it draws fire."

Fish bellied forward with the lantern. Then, setting it on the knoll, he scrambled back. The men waited, but there were only bursts of giggles from the Cuban camp.

"Apparently, our enemy has no guns," Roosevelt speculated.

"Tiffany killed one, sir. I saw it!"

After some moments of tense waiting, Capron had Fish and Tiffany creep down the hill, just beyond the lantern's light.

Fish straightened up. "We found our victim, sir," he called. Then the two men came back, Fish holding an enormous crab. The men gathered around the lantern. The thing measured two feet across, with eyes like black berries on the ends of red stalks. Its color was black and yellow and orange. Two claws, one bigger than the other, clicked open and shut. The thing had a mouth that stopped Gabriel's heart.

"Our enemy," Roosevelt declared. "Of the family *Gecarcinidae*, gentlemen. Not Spanish at all."

"Lordy," Snake exclaimed. "What do they eat?"

Roosevelt winked. "You, if you let them," he laughed.

It was impossible to sleep after that. Gabriel knew how green and ridiculous the Rough Riders must have seemed to the Cubans. And this was not a story he would ever tell Aura.

CHAPTER 15

Thursday, June 23

The thunderheads piled up over the flat turquoise sea. At the tops they were fleecy, but underneath they were dark as rotten wood. A yellow horizon between the great clouds and the sea was being squeezed to a narrow strip.

Gabriel enjoyed his first bath in weeks, lathering himself in the lapping, warm salt water. But he noticed buzzards fighting up the beach. At first, he could not see against the glare of the sun and he turned away.

When he had rinsed off and wrung his shirt, he roped his wet clothes around his neck and waded toward the commotion. The black, red-necked birds scattered noisily.

It was then that he saw what they had been fighting over. One trooper floated, face down, nudging the sand, over and over, as though trying to grasp the beach with his lifeless hands. A few feet away, belly up, the other lay half out of the water. The buzzards had taken his eyes. He wore corporal's stripes and had woolly gray hair.

Gabriel had seen drowned bodies before, bloated, floating high in a stiff embrace with the river, bursting their clothes, rotted green and yellow. But these had their mouths open as though in sleep. And they were almost touching. The sockets where the eyes had been sickened Gabriel. *Mine eyes have seen the glory,* he thought, then his torso heaved. His vomit, the horse meat of the night before, sunk in a brown scum. Instantly, tiny, iridescent fish darted to feed on it. *They'll eat you, if you let them.*

He grabbed a shell, hurled it at the circling buzzards. They parted easily, moving just a few feathers like fingers, then resumed their watchful spiral.

Lieutenant Pershing panted up the beach. He knelt and recognized both of his men. He called them by name—Corporal Cobb and Private English, the two troopers that had perished in the water near the pier.

Pershing pulled the trooper in the water onto the beach and lay him beside his comrade. He covered their faces with his blue tunic.

"I'll help bury them, Lieutenant," Gabriel said.

Pershing's Missouri twang betrayed his anger. "No thank you, trooper. The Tenth Cav buries its own." Then he seemed to realize the harshness of his tone. "But will you keep the buzzards away until I get back with a detail of men?"

"Yes sir." And Gabriel swung his shirt at the vultures and the flies.

Soon, a dozen Rough Riders were gawking down at the two dead men. Most of them were respectful, but a few, Gabriel noticed with rising anger, laughed behind their hands.

*

As a detachment of Negro troopers carried the dead away, the Rough Riders cleared the grass so that they could cook their rations. The wooden crates of hardtack had been soaked with sea water and the outer part had turned to a briny paste. Gabriel had noticed that green mold had grown in his boots during a single night.

The Rough Riders watched a tall, bearded General Lawton lead two regiments of regulars off toward Siboney. "We'll be marching, sooner or later," Cloud said.

Snake sucked noisily at a cup of beans.

Cloud poked the fire, chewing a blade of grass. "Lieutenant Hall came looking for you, Gabe."

"What for?"

"He didn't say. But he wants to see you."

Gabriel buttoned his damp shirt, then knotted his kerchief loosely. The wool, where the salt water had begun to dry, scratched his skin. He draped his long johns over the tent. Gabriel saw a new pair of brogans on his blanket. In one of them he found a note.

We are both size eleven—- Fish

*

Even in the high humidity of the morning, Hall wore his tunic buttoned. He looked up from his folding table as Gabriel knocked on his tent pole. "Where have you been, Scriven?" he asked.

"I sounded reveille, then went down to bathe."

"Without permission, it seems."

"Sergeant Fish gave me permission, sir."

Hall's eyes were bloodshot. "All right. It's just that Colonel Wood needs you. You speak Spanish, don't you?"

"A little."

Hall rose wearily and took his Stetson from a peg. "All right. Then follow me."

General Wheeler and Colonel Wood were seated at a field table in the shade of a large, open tent. Roosevelt stood behind them.

Gabriel stopped in front of the table and saluted. "Private Gabriel Scriven, Chief Trumpeter, First Volunteer Cavalry, reporting, sir."

Wheeler returned his salute. "Good mornin' Private. We need you to interpret. The Cubans have some advice for us. Sit down, son. It's hot."

But Gabriel could not sit in the presence of Wheeler. "General, their commanding officer speaks better English than I do. My Spanish is very limited, sir."

"Just the same, you've met the Cuban already and he asked for you. We've got to get to the truth right quick."

Roosevelt nodded encouragement to Gabriel.

Colonel Raúl García rode up, followed by two aides on foot. Gabriel watched General Wheeler assess García's stallion as though to judge the rider.

García dismounted as General Wheeler rose.

Colonel García did not look at him, and Gabriel realized this was officer's business.

General Wheeler unrolled a map, flattened it on the table, and weighted the corners with his field glasses and an inkstand. He poked his pale finger. "Colonel García, I believe I know where the enemy is not. But I must know where he is. Now normally, we'd reconnoiter the enemy ourselves. But", he gave an exasperated sigh, "my cavalry's horses are still in Tampa. We've got to attack soon. I've just sent General Lawton off to take Siboney. We will follow shortly, but may have to turn off to the north."

Roosevelt could contain himself no longer. "The Rough Riders have come to fight. We didn't pick the toughest men and the best shots just to sit around and wait."

García ignored Roosevelt. "General Lawton is wasting his time. Our General Castillo occupied Siboney last night."

Wheeler smiled. "Then I'll be expecting Lawton's report sooner rather than later."

Colonel García stepped around the table. "General, there are three ways to Santiago." He pointed with his riding crop. "The first, the railroad, is not possible. The *Peninsulares* have burned the locomotive and have torn up the tracks. Even before that, we destroyed the bridges. So, look." He touched the map where two thin lines converged. "This road, *El Camino Reál*, winds away from the beach, up through the hills to Santiago de Cuba—here. But," he smiled and his aides did too, "despite the impressive name, this is no royal highway, I can assure you." He moved his crop an inch lower and began to trace another line, so faint it could hardly be seen in the bright sunlight. "The only other road is more like a path, barely wide enough for a *burro*, but it goes straight, almost as the crow flies, I believe you say. All the way to Santiago." Again he tapped the map. "Here, four miles past Siboney, the two roads come out of the *Guásimas* forest and they converge." He looked at Wheeler, then at Wood. "Here is where the *Peninsulares* wait for you."

Wheeler nodded gravely. "We'll send scouts to verify."

Colonel García stiffened. "General, during the Ten Years War, our General Máximo Gómez fought at Las Guásimas for seven days. There he killed over three hundred *Peninsulares*. In that case, we were the defenders. If I tell you it is a bad place to place to attack an enemy, you can believe me. My own scouts have seen the *gringos* digging in there."

Roosevelt grunted. "I thought we were the *gringos*."

Colonel García smiled. "You must forgive me. It is a habit. You see, we call any foreigner *gringo;* even the *Peninsulares*. In a war, there must be formal and informal names for things, no? Do you know what the *Peninsulares* call us, the army of *Cuba Libre? Mambises.* A *mambi* is an uncouth person, a savage, someone of low birth, of doubtful breeding, so to speak. Well, somehow, this name struck our Cuban funny bone, as you would say. So we proudly adopted the name. For when we fight, we can be very savage and very uncouth. In this case, the *Peninsulares* are quite correct."

As Wheeler motioned García aside, Wood and Roosevelt took the hint and walked up the beach. Gabriel followed a few steps behind them. "Well, Theodore, what do you think of our little Confederate fighting cock ?"

"He's a man of action."

Wood nodded. "A different cut than Shafter. He's a lot like you, Theodore. You both have the gift of impatience. He too, would build Rome in a day."

Roosevelt stopped and scowled back to where General Wheeler and Colonel García were conferring. "But, I do not trust either of the Garcías."

Wood was at first silent. "I'll admit, it is poor strategy to entrust the lives of our men to Cuban reconnaissance. We will verify everything, of course."

Roosevelt ground his teeth. "If the Cubans were so smart, they would have beaten the Spanish. And the simple fact is—they have not. Ten Years War, my backside! We'll lick the Spanish in ten days!"

Gabriel noticed that Colonel Wood did not seem to share Roosevelt's optimism.

*

Stephen Crane and Sylvester Scovel waded in the surf as their gear was unloaded from whale boats. Richard Harding Davis directed from a dinghy. "Easy boys," he said, as two troopers hoisted a heavy trunk. "You're carrying destiny on your back." One of the Kinetoscope men laughed. Davis lifted his white pith helmet and fanned his face. "That's the way, lads, but do be careful. That trunk was made for me in New York and it has, up to now, withstood the rigors of travel on four continents. I should not like to lose it to the Caribbean."

Scovel hoisted his own battered haversack. He had an easy way with the troopers, and, as they worked, he touted the passion of Cuban women. Gabriel listened as he lifted yet another of Davis' chests. Scovel, he knew had, months ago, interviewed the Cuban leader General Gomez. It was clear that Scovel was a man of action, and that Davis liked to pontificate.

Another correspondent, dressed to fight, stuck out his sweaty hand. "I'm Ed Marshall of the *New York World*," he said.

"Gabriel Scriven. Put 'er there."

Marshall watched as the troopers completed the unloading of saddles and bags of gear. Then he invited the troopers onto the porch of the small house to which the correspondents had been assigned. Marshall reached into one of his many pockets and produced a pint of whisky. He pulled the cork out and lifted it. "We owe ya, boys. Have a snort."

Snake took the bottle, downed a gulp, then handed it to Cloud. Then Cloud passed the bottle to Gabriel. He put the bottle to his lips, tilted it back and drank deeply. He handed the bottle to Fish but the teetotaler gave it back to Marshall.

It was still hot, even though they sat in the shade. Marshall tossed the empty bottle into the brush, causing a land crab to scuttle for it. "Lesson one. Destroy all evidence."

"Let's destroy some more," Snake encouraged, licking his lips.

Marshall's field jacket had plenty of pockets and several contained bottles. He opened another and spit the cork over the rail. "Sorry there's no ice, gentlemen."

"I take two pieces, usually," Snake said, raising his pinkie. He had just reared his head back to drink, when his eyes popped open and he let out a blood-curdling scream. Snake was staring up into the cane roof of the porch. There, watching the men, crouched a hairy spider, larger than a man's hand.

Marshall grabbed his hat and scooped the spider up.

The troopers stared at the horrible thing, its legs drawn up tightly in the well of the hat.

"Jésus B. Christ!" Snake whistled. "I knowed they was big. But that thing's a giant!"

Marshall grinned, reached in and to the horror of the men, picked the spider up by its thick torso. Its legs moved frantically as Marshall turned it, examining closely. "Yep. Just as I thought. *Tarantulus Runnicus.*"

"Huh?"

He held the spider out and Snake fell off the porch, much to the general hilarity of the troopers. They were giddy from whiskey, the heat, and lack of sleep. "What's the matter, Snake. Thought you wuz immune to poison?"

Snake got up, dusting himself off. "Not to no spiders, I ain't."

"Boys, this is a particular kind of arachnid, " Marshall said. "The racing variety of tarantula."

Snake's little eyes showed interest.

"Now," Ed Marshall continued, "if we can find another one—they got to have this yellow marking on the legs—then we could have us a real serious race."

Snake chewed his jaw and looked around. "Ain't no such thing as a racin' spider."

But Marshall would not be denied. "They travel in pairs, I'm told. To practice, no doubt. Now, shall we find this *Tarantulus Runnicus* a suitable contender?"

By the time the third bottle had made its rounds, the idea seemed feasible. Even Snake was crawling in the bush, knocking land crabs away. "Here boy," he called out, "I got you a nice juicy bug to eat."

"They don't eat bugs."

"What then?" Snake said, peering up from all fours.

"Balls," Marshall said.

The troopers cackled. Then Gabriel put his hand on something furry and felt a sharp sting. "Hey, it bit me!" Marshall and Fish ran over to him. "They ain't very poison," Marshall said. "Don't worry. Hey! Don't let him get away." Marshall rubbed whiskey into the reddened place on Gabriel's thumb. "Antidote," the grinning correspondent said. "Here, take some internally as well."

Soon the tipsy troopers made a crude race course of two planks. The first spider Marshall named Lightning. The other, bigger than the first, and deemed a fighter since he had bitten Gabriel, they dubbed Tecumseh, the middle name of the same General Sherman who had ravaged Georgia.

Marshall collected bets, allowing anything from a penny to a slice of tobacco. Marshall wouldn't take sides, but put up his last pint of whiskey for the winner. This skewed the betting heavily toward the frantic Tecumseh, who scrambled about in his board pen. Lightning, hardly living up to his name, cowered against the boards.

"Don't fret," Snake called, "he's just savin' his wind."

Marshall looked at his pocket watch. "All bets in? Good. Now boys, the first spider to reach the end is the winner. But if one won't run or gets away, he's disqualified. The other wins by default, just like a horse race. We're gonna hit the plank with a board, to get 'em started. That's just like firing a gun to a racing tarantula—really gets their blood up."

A crowd of troopers from all units had gathered for the race. The hairy racers were much discussed and hotly debated. The men crowded in on either side of the planks.

"Get up to the startin' line, Lightning! Come on, boy!"

"Settle down, Tecumseh! Easy boy. Easy. Whoa!"

Marshall slapped the plank and both spiders leaped straight up. Lightning landed on Snake who screamed, but managed to knock him back into the race way. Tecumseh headed for parts unknown.

"It's Lightning, by default," Marshall declared to general jeers of the men who had bet otherwise.

"He didn't win. Snake throwed him back in!"

But Marshall would have none of it. "Boys, a bet's a bet. Now pay up." Cloud doled out the winnings, and the prize whiskey was opened, passed, and gone in a minute.

Marshall was about to organize a land crab derby when Lieutenant Hall came running up, holding his saber to his side.

"Scriven," Hall panted, "sound 'boots and saddles.' Wheeler has ordered the Rough Riders to Siboney."

"Yaaaaa hooooo," the troopers shouted.

Gabriel tried to make his lips move. His hand no longer hurt and he never felt better in his life. He took a deep breath and staggered up the hill, where he fumbled with his bugle, then put it to his lips.

A few moments later, Roosevelt came charging up the knoll. "And what," he demanded, "was *that?*"

" 'Aura Lee', sir."

The peppery Colonel was beside himself. "I can't believe this! My drunken bugler plays Stephen Foster instead of the command to march."

"Trumpeter, sir," Gabriel hiccuped.

"And another thing," Roosevelt fumed, "I don't even *have* a saddle. "

"Marshall has plenty of saddles," Gabriel said.

"Then sound BOOTS AND SADDLES," Roosevelt commanded. "NOW!"

Roosevelt's fury helped Gabriel remember, and of course, he blew. But this was, he realized, a very ludicrous command. Their boots were on. And except for the officers, there were no mounts to saddle.

An hour later, Roosevelt stared at his unsaddled Texas and swore. "Captain Jenkins," he vowed, "will be tried for treason! He has sent us nothing."

Ed Marshall had a solution. "Well, like your bugler says, the press has a porch full of saddles, but not a single nag. Seems like we could do a swap."

Roosevelt put his fists against his hips, and sucked the sweat from his mustache. "With what? We have damned few horses. Colonel Wood has already forfeited his Kentucky thoroughbred to carry regimental cooking gear! I loaned our last horse to our color bearer. And you need a mount!" Roosevelt thought for a moment. "How about a mule?"

Marshall grinned. "Guess that'd be about right."

*

To Gabriel's call, the Rough Riders formed up in a column of twos. A Cuban boy, mounted on a small pony, headed their column. Then rode Colonel Wood and Ed Marshall. Next, in regulation blue, rode Captain Rivers and Captain McCormick, the two regulars General Wheeler had added as observers in deference to General Shafter's worry about Rough Rider discipline.

Tiffany rode a mare and carried the flag they had planted on Mount Losiltares.

"Hey Killer," Snake jeered. "You cut a notch on your stock fer each o'them Spanion crabs you kilt last night?"

Behind Tiffany, Colonel Roosevelt led Texas. Captain Allyn Capron marched in front of his sorrel mare. Behind him, Cloud carried the L Troop pennant.

But the rest of the Rough Riders walked, laboring under the weight of carbine, full cartridge belt, blanket roll with both poncho and shelter-half rolled inside, a haversack containing five days rations, mess kit, personal belongings, and a half-full canteen, tin cup dangling next to it. Their marching produced grunts, and a rhythmic tinkling. It was a curious sound, Gabriel thought. But the men were quiet, putting all their energy into the hot march. They had a goal, for the Tenth Cavalry had marched out an hour before them.

Gabriel was soon drenched with sweat. San Antonio had been hot but dry. Tampa had been hot and humid. Cuba was a steaming hell where cicadas screamed with the heat. The troops labored through the jungle along an almost impossible foot path. Parrots squawked in the heavy air. The troopers' unwieldy loads slipped around, breaking blisters on their tortured shoulders.

Snake trudged next to Gabriel. "I got more than a hunnert pounds."

"We all have the same," Gabriel reminded him.

"Well, I drew double weight, if you ask me." Snake retorted. "And no chew. Ain't a plug left anywheres."

"Don't talk so loud, Snake My head feels like a bucket."

Prayerful shifted his blanket roll. "You'll have to just walk your sin off, trooper."

"Maybe bein' spider-bit gives a man extry muscle, " Snake said.

It was then, struggling in the awful heat, throats swollen with thirst, that the Rough Riders overtook the first of Lawton's stragglers. A few men sat beside the trail, dazed from heat exhaustion. Beside them, cast-off blanket rolls, haversacks, and tunics lay in a heap.

There were no wise cracks from the Rough Riders. These loads were designed for the backs of horses, not men. But the abandoned equipment gave Snake an idea. Without missing a step, he slipped his blanket roll off and dropped it. Soon, several other troopers did the same. Roosevelt glared, but said nothing. It was commonly known that a man who left his gear would not be permitted to borrow.

The trail dipped and wound through the trees. The men slopped through mud, then struggled through vine-tangled ruts. The dense foliage was alive with buzzing insects; swarms of gnats that hovered in the men's faces, bright moths, beetles big as eggs scurrying across the path. The hot air was heavy with the rot of the jungle.

"Smells like a funeral parlor," Prayerful said.

Snake and Gabriel stepped into a muddy hole worked smooth as batter by the boots and hooves of two regiments before them. "Now this is plain unhealthy," Snake whined, wading in the sucking mud. "I remember Doc Church lecturin' us on keepin' our feet dry. At all times, he said. use foot powder. A good soljer's a healthy soljer. Hah! Well my tootsies ain't been dry since we left the *Yucatan.*"

The intervals between the men grew greater. Now and then a trooper collapsed with a heavy sigh and the rattle of gear as he fell. These men were examined quickly by Surgeon Church, who followed with his hospital corps. The fallen men were given precious water and a little salt and left behind, with instructions to catch up with the unit as soon as they could.

Marcus Hammer helped drag the fallen troopers into the shade. He was hot, but his footballer's body and the Princeton rowing team had built his stamina. Besides, he was so eager to please Surgeon Church that he leaped to the aid of any dazed trooper.

Eventually Colonel Wood rested his men near a small stream. The troopers began to discard their canned goods and anything else they thought they would not need.

Wood dipped a cup into the creek and studied its contents. The men waited, licking their parched lips while Wood's horse sucked water downstream. Wood had warned his men against fever from contaminated water. He let them drink nothing until he had tasted it himself. He looked up from his cup, addressing Roosevelt. "I do not think it has been fouled. Have the men pass canteens forward. The first troopers will fill them."

A weak cheer rose from the exhausted men, who fell where they stood, half in and half out of the jungle.

Gabriel held his canteen below the stream's surface and watched the bubbles rise. Then, from up stream, they heard splashes. Colonel Wood snatched the canteen and motioned for Cloud and Gabriel to go look.

They kept to the bank, trying not to muddy the water. Gabriel parted a curtain of vines and there in a widened stretch of creek, several half naked troopers of the Tenth frolicked in the water. On news of this, Wood ordered the canteens emptied. The Rough Riders resumed their march, hot, dehydrated, and with little love for the regiment they followed.

"Don't want no Nigger juice anyways," Snake said.

Before he knew what he was doing, Gabriel had taken Snake by the throat and was squeezing off his wind. The surprised trooper's eyes bugged out and his cracked lips tried to form a plea for air. It was T.T. Cloud who finally pried Gabriel's hands away. Snake sunk to his knees..

"Don't you ever, *ever* use that word again," Gabriel shouted.

The troopers were surprised, for they had all used the word at one time or another. Gabriel Scriven, usually an easy-going fellow, had suddenly gone berserk.

By the time Captain Capron had come to see what the ruckus was about, Gabriel had helped the baffled Snake to his feet.

Snake massaged his neck as he stared at Gabriel.

But Gabriel realized it was natural for troopers to resent the few troopers of the Tenth and their lack of consideration for the regiments behind.

Soon the men were marching again, Snake shooting glances at Gabriel as though he expected another outburst.

Then the Cuban guide held up his hand and word was whispered back to halt.

A hot wind blew in from the sea, moving the leaves so that their bluish-white undersides showed the same color, the men knew, of Spanish uniforms.

Carbine breeches clicked until Wood ordered the men to cease. The guide whispered something to Wood, then trotted on ahead. After some moments, he cantered his pony back.

By now, Gabriel's mouth tasted like rotten corn.

Finally, after a half-hour's march, the trail widened into a grove of palms, which opened onto the sea. The Cuban slid off his horse and began to hack at coconuts. During his short rest every man in the regiment got a drink of cool coconut milk.

After their rest, the Rough Riders caught up with the main body of the Tenth. On seeing the Rough Rider column, one of the dusky troopers threw down his carbine. "Five o'clock, boys. I'm out." He held a paper up. "Official. July twenty-third, eighteen and ninety-eight. And it's five pee emm. Hallelujah! Ain't marchin' no more." A few of his comrades looked like they wanted to kill him. Gabriel did too.

Colonel Wood grabbed the man. "You speak desertion, soldier!"

"No, I ain't. Here, read my papers!"

"I will not."

The rest of the Tenth had written him off. They turned and resumed their march.

But Roosevelt was seething. "Do you know that under fire I could shoot you, trooper?"

The trooper smiled. "But we're not fightin' yet." He angled past Roosevelt and pried his way back along the trail. .

Roosevelt wiped his hands as though contaminated, then called back, "All right boys. Let's give this coward a hand. He has decided he wants to go home!"

Gabriel could hear the trooper protesting as he was buffeted and shoved to the rear.

Marcus Hammer had just given water to a prostrated man, when the deserter from the Tenth was thrown at him. The man's arms were covered with scratches and one eye had begun to close from a blow. Surgeon Church, normally courteous to everyone, snapped, "If you're quitting, then go. But don't expect any help from us. We're here to help soldiers. And you are a soldier no longer."

Marcus Hammer stepped forward. "Beg your pardon, Doctor. The man is hurt. Let me give him some bandages and help him to the rear."

Church looked suspicious. There were many other stragglers to help at the moment. "All right. But quickly. Get him out of here."

Marcus helped the grateful trooper, one arm over his shoulder, and staggered down the empty path. "Thanks, I'm plumb bushed," he whispered into Hammer's damaged ear. Suddenly, Marcus threw the man down, and he kicked him, again and again, feeling his boot go deep.

Moments later, when Hammer caught up with the column, he fell in beside Church.

"You needn't have helped that man," Church said.

Marcus Hammer summoned a look of dismay. "But sir, didn't you tell me some time ago that it is our duty to relieve a man's suffering? Why I would have done the same thing, even for a Spaniard."

Church gave his young stretcher bearer a sidelong look. Maybe he had been wrong about Hammer. The boy seemed to have a heart after all.

*

It was dark when the Rough Riders stumbled out of the jungle onto the long beach at Siboney, and into the powerful search lights of the fleet. The beach was crowded with men and wagons and further out, the bright transports waited their turn to be unloaded. Aboard them, regimental bands played, and snatches of song carried across the dark water.

Blinded by the light, Gabriel wanted only water and a piece of ground to collapse.

Fish scratched his head. "Is this a war or a dress ball?"

"I reckon it's a party and we're late," Snake said.

*

Gabriel was dreaming under his half-shelter when he was jarred awake by a sharp pain. Someone had stepped on his leg.

"Sorry, trooper," the intruder grunted. Gabriel could only make out his silhouette against the searchlights sweeping the sea. Then the light flashed off a gold tooth.

"I'm lookin' for Trooper Scriven," the shadow said.

Gabriel sat up. "That's me."

"My name's Biddle. Eli G. Biddle, Jr. Tenth Cav." Biddle sat down on the shelter half and sighed. "What's your daddy's name, son?"

Gabriel was surprised at this question. "I don't rightly know," he finally said. "My father died a long time ago."

"It's just that I used to know a trooper with your name." Biddle spoke in a raspy voice. "Claimed he had a boy somewheres near Fort Chambers. I plumb forgot about it, bein' a good many years ago, but when Lieutenant Pershing told me Roosevelt's trumpeter found Cobb and English in the surf this mornin'. I wanted to come and thank you. Cobb was my friend and I even liked English a little. Your Adjutant told me your name. Lordy, I thought to myself. This boy's done passed for white. Colonel Roosevelt would have a real conniption."

"I never knew my daddy," Biddle continued. "Died with the Fifty-Fourth Massachusetts at Fort Wagner. You know, the big war." The trooper spit into the night. "So I know how wonderin' can chew you up from the inside."

It was as though Biddle knew what he was thinking. There many things Gabriel wanted to ask Biddle, and he hardly knew where to begin.

"Bleak country, the Dakotas. I know. The Tenth worked the North Platte."

But now Gabriel had a question. "Did you tell Lieutenant Hall my father was ..."

Biddle's head shook. "No, I didn't. Besides, I wasn't sure. If you was really his boy." Biddle struck a match and the two men stared at each other across the flame. Biddle's round face, fringed in gray, was encouraging. "Yeah," he said, "you have his eyes. But them freckles must be your momma's."

The match burned Biddle's fingers and he threw it down. "I got to get back."

Gabriel grabbed his arm. "No you don't! I've got to know some things."

The dusky trooper sighed. "Yeah. I reckon you do."

"Tell me," Gabriel asked, "did he ever mention his wife?"

Biddle thought a moment, then nodded.

Gabriel's heart was beating hard. "What was her name?"

"I don't recall he ever said."

Now Gabriel felt sick. His father had not given the girl he had made pregnant a face.

Biddle continued, "Your momma was our Lieutenant's sister."

And there is was. "Biddle," Gabriel pleaded, "what was my father like? Tell me everything."

And as the searchlights played across the beach, illuminating the men who struggled with gear and munitions in the surf, light was thrown by Eli Biddle on the secret of a young volunteer from Baltimore who carried a fiddle and liked to recite Shakespeare. A good soldier, the troopers of the Tenth knew, would have been an officer but for the color of his skin. And a man who suffered because he had left a girl rather than disgrace her—a tortured man who wrote letters he would never mail.

When Biddle had run out of words, Gabriel took a deep, long breath. The searchlights could no longer block the canopy of stars over them. It seemed to Gabriel Scriven that the whole firmament had brightened.

PART III *Las Guásimas*

CHAPTER 16

Friday, June 24

General Wheeler's riding crop shook as he traced a line on the field map. In the ring of lantern light on the porch of his Siboney headquarters, General Young, Colonel Wood, and Theodore Roosevelt bent forward, listening hard against the driving rain for General Wheeler's soft voice.

Gabriel had slept little, for in his dreams he been following his father in a thick, dark forest. Once, the trooper he had followed turned, and had sung out his name. Then Gabriel awoke to the noisy gathering of officers and the urgencies of the day.

Now he was waiting to blow reveille. He could not hear what the officers were saying, but the consultation had to mean one thing— the Rough Riders were moving out.

When the officers had finished, Lieutenant Hall brought Wheeler's horse, made a stirrup of his hands and helped the little General up into the saddle. Once mounted, Fightin' Joe's eyes flashed in the lantern light. He set his Stetson, motioned to his aide, and together they galloped off to reconnoiter.

Colonel Wood motioned to Gabriel. "Summon Captain Capron."

The dawn had pushed the rain out to sea and Siboney revealed a dozen shacks, a sawmill, and an empty storage barn. Behind the beach, swarms of mosquitoes rose from a brackish pond. Out in the shallow surf, engineers and artificers struggled to bolt together a makeshift wharf. Higher up the beach, regiments began to crawl out of their wet tents.

Colonel Wood chewed his bacon slowly. Roosevelt slopped back and forth in the mud. Finally Wood wiped his lips. "Young is taking the First Infantry and the Tenth Cavalry," he said. "We'll march with him until the roads separate. Then Young's two regiments will take the high road. We take the trail to the left." Colonel Wood put his hand on Capron's shoulder. "Allyn, I understand today is your birthday."

Capron shifted his weight. "I'm, twenty-seven, sir."

"That's young for a Captain these days. Well, I have a present for you. I want L Troop to take the point."

Capron smiled. "I am honored, sir."

Wood took a sip of coffee. "Now, Allyn, our trail may look too narrow to send out flankers. But we must remember to do so. General Wheeler reconnoitered this morning. If we can make it through the jungle and take the high ground, there is a meadow with good forage and drainage where we can accommodate the entire invasion force. Our objective is to establish a base camp there for the final assault on Santiago."

"Yes sir."

"One more thing. General Wheeler intends for the cavalry to get there before the infantry."

Roosevelt bared his teeth. "But Young's infantry gets the highway and we get the cow path."

Wood looked up. "I imagine we must have impressed Fightin' Joe yesterday. We lost fewer men to the heat than Lawton's regulars. So we've drawn a tough mission," Wood said with gravity. "A real compliment from Fightin' Joe."

Captain Capron nodded gravely. "I'm surprised General Shafter is permitting an engagement before we have artillery. I understand the batteries are still at sea."

"Wheeler got a dispatch late last night from the *Seguranca*. Shafter ordered the cavalry to stay put, and to back up the infantry." Wood looked around. "But," he chuckled, "by some act of Providence, General Shafter's dispatch was sent to Daiquiri by mistake!"

As they were laughing at their luck, the sun broke through a cloud. Roosevelt squinted up at a Cuban rainbow.

Now the officers and men could see earthen slashes dug into the green hills above Siboney. But the fresh Spanish trenches seemed empty. A sharp white light like the sun itself flashed from one of the hilltops. The Spanish were using heliographic mirrors to send signals.

"They know our position," Wood said, emptying his coffee into the fire. He stood and nodded to Gabriel, and the trumpeter blew assembly.

*

Except for Colonel García, who rode his stallion before them, the Cubans were on foot. Their ragged column loped past, taking a path up into the hills. Two ponies passed loaded with the carcass of a cow the Rough Riders had watched the Cubans kill with machetes. Colonel Wood warned his men against accepting any of it, explaining that in this climate, fresh meat had no chance to cool. He knew the meat might be loaded with debilitating parasites.

Despite his robust frame, Richard Harding Davis had trouble mounting his mule. He could not manage to throw his leg over the saddle, yet angrily waved off the help Lieutenant Hall offered him.

Hall could not suppress a smile at Davis's efforts, while the whole regiment waited.

Davis twisted around and sneered, "It's my sciatica, Hall. One leg is practically numb. Meanwhile, I do not appreciate your smirks." This retort, and the side-stepping of Davis' stubborn mule made the incident downright funny, and this time Lieutenant Hall could not suppress a laugh.

Wood snapped his watch shut and turned in his saddle. "Any man not ready in five minutes will be left behind."

At last, with a mighty heave, Davis mounted. But as he glared at Lieutenant Hall, he seemed to be making an entry in his mental notebook.

Colonel Wood's hand dropped, Gabriel's bugle sounded, and the column moved out.

Ed Marshall, riding his mule next to Davis, leaned in his saddle.

"Where's Crane? I'll bet he's covering General Young, hoping that they'll draw first fire."

Davis jerked his head angrily. "If you're worried, go with Young."

Marshall spurred his mule. "And let you beat me to this story? Not on your life!"

Davis lifted his cleft chin. "Just because my paper has doubled circulation while yours lost proportionately, you needn't be petty. You'll no doubt have a few readers left."

"Your Hearst is an arrogant ass," Marshall said. "I'll work for Pulitzer any time. Freddie Remington cabled from Havana in February that nothing was happening—didn't look there was going to be a war. Told Hearst he was returning to new York. Do you know what Hearst replied?"

Davis smiled. "Yes. Mr. Hearst told Remington to stay put and to supply the illustrations, and he, Mr. Hearst, would supply the war. And so he has."

To Gabriel, marching behind the two reporters, this did not seem like a war at all. It was almost as though they were all going on a muddy picnic. Where were the colorful battle lines he had imagined as a boy? He had seen Matthew Brady's photographs of cannon drawn up in a menacing line. The Rough Riders had been two days ashore and had fought nothing but heat, rain, land crabs, and mosquitoes.

The unmounted cavalry panted and slogged along the path, past ruined plantations overgrown with creepers and over the bones of cattle.

The column halted at a burned-out hacienda where a palm tree grew through its broken roof. Roosevelt rode through the gate, and when he returned, he had two rusty shovels tied across the pommel of his saddle. Roosevelt leaned down from his saddle. "There is a dead Spaniard in the path ahead," he whispered. Then he barked, "Fall out, boys! Ten minute's rest."

*

Before Gabriel saw the body, he heard the buzzing flies. The dead man wore a light blue, seersucker uniform. On closer inspection, Gabriel saw that on his collar a red cloth badge spelled out his regiment—*2 Peninsular.* His rope-soled shoes were made of canvas. Someone had already taken the Spaniard's carbine.

Fish rolled him over. He was clean shaven, just a boy. Ants covered his open mouth. A machete blow had severed his jugular vein and he had bled to death on the spot.

Roosevelt handed shovels to Prayerful and Snake.

While the troopers dug, Roosevelt summoned Colonel Wood to the barbed wire fence.

"Look," Gabriel heard Roosevelt say, holding two broken strands, "freshly cut. The enemy is nearby."

A few feet away, standing over the body of the Spaniard, Richard Harding Davis clicked the shutter of his box camera.

Further down the line of men, a trooper tightened the ropes holding one of the Colt machine guns to a pack mule. The mule protested and Roosevelt tramped over and vehemently whispered, "Quiet that animal!"

"Silence in the ranks," Colonel Wood ordered.

*

Off to the right, Gabriel could see Young's column, the Tenth Cavalry leading the First Ohio Infantry. Some of them already lay in a skirmish line in the pale grass and they seemed to be making progress toward the stone breastworks.

Wood directed the Rough Riders to the left, toward a path that tunneled through a thicket of trees between two high hedges. The Cuban guides crept cautiously into the tunnel, their rifles at the ready.

Wood looked at his watch and counted. Then he signaled Capron to take the point.

With five men, Capron started forward. In the lead, Fish and Cloud moved slowly, a few yards apart. Gabriel and Tiffany followed close behind. Crimson and yellow blossoms glowed like lights in the dense green foliage and Gabriel could not help but muse that they were the colors of the Spanish flag. Occasionally the sun penetrated the thicket and when it did, the light caught droplets of moisture and turned them to jewel-like points of light. But is was deathly quiet in the green tunnel.

Tom Isbell followed Captain Capron, who wanted to stay in view of his point men as well as the main body of troops that followed.

Cloud and Fish set their boots down like cats. Gabriel heard the buzzing of a mosquito, then sudden silence and a sharp sting as it bit his neck.

A cicada rasped sharply in the green tunnel and Gabriel froze, mouth like cotton, his stomach like an iron spring.

Moving again, he parted dense undergrowth that closed again behind him. Sticky, sharp-edged leaves scratched his face and he considered that it might be poison sumac. Then, someone touched his back.

Tiffany's face was tense. Somewhere ahead, a branch broke.

Gabriel walked faster, hoping to catch view of Cloud's Stetson, easy to recognize because of the way had begun to turn it up in the back. For moments now, there had been silence in the tunnel. Just behind him, Isbell cocked his head and listened. Then it came, the clear, soft, almost sleepy call of a wood dove. *Cuu coo coooo!* Capron and Isbell exchanged a quick series of hand signals.

Cuuuuu coo cooooo!

Capron leaned close to Gabriel. "Wait here," he whispered. "I'll take Isbell and catch up to Fish and Cloud." The Captain and the Pawnee stepped into the jungle.

Suddenly, the silence was split by the unmistakable bark of a Krag, quickly followed by a far-off, popping sound. Immediately, a wind of steel seemed to pass through the foliage.

Whit. Whit. Z-z-z-zeuuu.

A twig snapped next to Gabriel. All around him, leaves floated down, as if cut by insects.

He and Tiffany dove through the underbrush, running toward the gun fire.

Isbell lay curled in the path, his teeth clenched in pain. Gabriel knelt beside him. He had been grazed along the face and shot in the buttock. One of his thumbs lay dangling by a strip of skin. Then another whistling zip, the sound of a fist against a sack of flour, and blood spurted from Isbell's neck in a pencil-sized stream. Gabriel tore off his kerchief and tried to plug the hole.

Ahead the gunfire was heavy now. Branches fell, cut by a swarm of whizzing Mauser bullets.

From the jungle ahead, an anguished voice cried, "The Captain's shot!"

Fish stumbled onto the trail. He took a quick look at Isbell then dragged him behind a rock. Isbell groaned, opened his eyes. "This is good cover, pardner," he said.

Then, something knocked Fish onto his back. Gabriel saw a clean hole over his heart. Fish opened his astonished eyes, stared at his bleeding chest then fell back.

Ahead, the gunfire stopped.

Cloud beat the brush back with his carbine. His right thigh glistened with blood. He stared at Fish and Gabriel. "Capron's hit in the lungs," he said.

Colonel Wood came jogging up the trail, followed by a dozen anxious Rough Riders. "Load your chambers and magazines," Wood ordered. "Pass it along. And get those Colt machine guns up here, on the double."

Roosevelt came crashing through the brush, jumping one way, then the other. "Why don't they show themselves," he cried, "and fight like men!"

Colonel Leonard Wood gave his second in command a silencing stare.

"*Hey! Yip, yip, yip!*" A teamster rode fast up the trail, pulling a mule laden with the machine gun behind him. Wood stood in the path, arms crossed. "Set your pieces over there, in that clearing. " he said. "Begin firing dead ahead, across the gully, toward the hill."

"*CHUGA-CHUG-A-CHUG!*" The hand cranked Colts spat lead into the jungle. In the intervals between bursts, there was smoky silence. No birds called out, and there was no return volley of enemy fire. Just the flutter of falling leaves the Colts had cut. They floated lazy and dreamlike to ground.

Ahead, Captain Capron knew he was dying. The sucking sound came from his own chest, and it was getting harder to breathe as he searched the familiar faces surrounding him. There was Isbell, his face twisted in torment. And Scriven and Cloud. Roosevelt and Wood, all bending over him.

Church tried to plug the holes, but the bullets had penetrated both lungs and Allyn Capron was drowning in his own blood. Finally, Church lifted his head from Capron's chest and said, "He's gone."

Tom Isbell swore softly.

As the sound of heavier machine guns began on their right, Roosevelt jumped up.

"Calm yourself, Theodore," Colonel Wood snapped. "That's Young's Gatlings engaging the enemy." After a pause he said, "Take three troops into the bushes on our right flank. Try to close with Young if you can. "

Roosevelt stepped calmly over the barbed wire fence. Captain Llewellyn heard Wood give the order and led his company close behind Roosevelt. The determined troopers from New Mexico swept Gabriel along with them.

As Roosevelt's men broke through the trees to an open field, they began to draw fire. Next to Gabriel, a trooper fell like a clod of dirt.

"Hold your fire," Roosevelt yelled. "That's L Troop, thinking we are the enemy."

But before the volley, Gabriel had heard a shout, *"Fuego!"* Gabriel grabbed Roosevelt's sleeve. "No sir! They're Spaniards."

Roosevelt motioned his men to crawl forward on their bellies, yet he paced back and forth, watching them. "Get down, sir," Gabriel yelled.

Roosevelt's teeth flashed in the sun. As Gabriel watched in horror, he strolled to higher ground and presented an easy target. Bullets cut the grass around him, and not two feet away a trooper fell with a rattle of gear. Roosevelt shielded his eyes and pointed up into the tree line. "I see them, men! Fire and advance. Fire and advance!"

But there was too much noise for the men to hear, and to his horror, Gabriel saw Roosevelt, thinking the men were following, walk forward alone. Gabriel reached into his haversack and grabbed his bugle, then blew charge.

Hearing the bugle, the Rough Riders opened up, firing from a prone position, then running ahead a few yards, flopping, firing again. Meanwhile, Roosevelt walked back and forth on the hillock, spinning his saber in the sun, urging his men toward the tree line.

The guidon of Company K ran to high ground and planted his red and white pennant. On Roosevelt's right, the Tenth's Hotchkiss gun began its chatter and then came the Comanche cry the Negro troopers screamed when they charged.

The Rough Riders were advancing steadily now, yard by yard, firing, running, falling prone to fire again. But some did not rise again from the tall grass that waved from a breeze of another Spanish volley.

Colonel Wood rode out from his two columns of reserves, calmly dismounted, and leaned against his horse. He studied his men under fire as though this were a training drill. Seduced by Wood's manner, correspondent

Ed Marshall, also wearing a Rough Rider tunic, joined him. Roosevelt, seeing that his men were pinned down, ran over to consult with Wood. A sweaty aide jogged to Wood and panted that yet another officer, Major Brodie, had been badly wounded and needed attention.

At this point, Lieutenant Hall ran through the tall grass in a crouch. "Colonel Wood," he gasped, "we have three officers wounded or killed— for God's sake, sir, take cover!"

Colonel Leonard Wood appeared to not hear Hall, who had not been able to get rid of the image of his colonel lying dead since the Spanish ambush began. "Please, sir," he pleaded, "take cover."

"Tom," Wood said, "Major Brodie needs a first aid package. Go back to the field hospital and get one."

Just as Lieutenant Hall had run halfway to the thicket where he had tied his mule, he heard another Spanish volley and turned to see his tan-clad commander stiffen, then fall. "My God," he cried. "They've killed Colonel Wood!" Hall fumbled to untie the frightened animal's reins, then threw himself into the saddle and galloped back along the trail. Hall knew that General Wheeler had more than likely taken to his bed, and Young's headquarters were but a few miles away. Only a general could order reinforcements, and Hall had to get word that the Rough Riders were caught in a cross fire and Wood had been killed.

Lieutenant Hall rode hard, bent low in the saddle, whipping his mule. He knew he could not allow a Spanish sniper to stop him. He galloped by the field hospital near the giant mango tree and there saw Surgeon Church working on a wounded trooper. "Church," he shouted, "Colonel Wood has been killed! I'm riding to get reinforcements."

Gabriel Scriven had heard Hall's alarm. Ducking the hail of bullets, he crawled to where Wood's horse stood chewing grass. There, kneeling over the fallen man, was Colonel Wood himself! He looked up at Gabriel. "Ed Marshall has been hit in the spine," Wood said.

Marshall lay in the trampled grass. "Colonel," he groaned, "I can't feel my legs."

Richard Harding Davis had by now joined the group trying to help Marshall. "Did you see Hall run," Davis snapped. "The man is a coward."

Roosevelt shook his head then rushed out into the field. He drew his saber and waved it. "Come on boys," he shouted to his men who lay in the grass, "let's get them." Gabriel blew the charge, then through tears of anger that blurred his vision, he emptied his Krag into the Spanish lines. He had just stood up to feed a new clip into the breech when a plank hit his belly.

*

Fever shook his thin frame. Despite the heat, General Wheeler buttoned his tunic and shielded his eyes. He scanned the road for the three troops of Ninth Cavalry he had just ordered up to reinforce the Rough Riders. He saw Lieutenant Hall ride by, yelling, hell bent for leather, Wheeler supposed, to hurry the Ninth along. The Rough Riders appeared to be caught in the jaws of a v-shaped enemy ambuscade. It was his own fault, Wheeler realized. He should not have sent untried volunteers into the breech. It would have been better to send them to the right, close to General Young. As Wheeler second-guessed himself, the report of a bugle charge made him turn with renewed hope. He lifted his binoculars and saw the Rough Riders rise from the high grass, and along with the Tenth, they began to advance on the stone breastworks they could not see.

Wheeler spurred his horse and closed the distance. He pulled up beside Roosevelt and Wood as they watched the advance. The three officers trotted out so that they had a better view and just then, the Spanish volley ceased. General Wheeler raised his binoculars and saw, on the summit, the enemy had leaped up, and begun to run in total disorder. He stood in his stirrups and beat his hat against his thigh. "YEEEEE-HAH!" he screamed, "now we've got those Yankees on the run!"

*

Marcus Hammer combed the tall grass on the hillside for wounded. Then he came upon a trooper who had fallen on his knees. Marcus Hammer rolled the wounded man over and cut away his shirt. It was Scriven, shot in the side. He quickly inspected the wound, half hoping it was fatal. The Mauser bullet had penetrated Scriven's side and had come out his back. He had to smile because Marcus was not going to risk his life saving the bastard who had disfigured him. Scriven could just bleed to death where he lay. The fighting had moved up the hill and nobody would know. Marcus was rising to go when he saw Lieutenant Church looking at him from where he had just lifted a wounded man onto his back. Church's gaze seemed to say, "what are you waiting for?" And so Marcus Hammer picked up the man he wanted to die and followed Church to the field hospital. But he angrily grabbed Scriven's carbine. Marcus Hammer intended to be a non-combatant no longer.

*

Gabriel opened his eyes in the shade of a mango tree. Lieutenant Church bent over him. As his vision cleared, he saw Marcus Hammer smoking nearby. Church pressed a cotton swab to the opening of a bottle of carbolic acid, and went to work. Gabriel felt no pain, just a curious numbness.

I'm going to die, he thought lazily, and Marcus will bury me. The thought brought him back, and now he felt pain as Church probed his wound. To keep from passing out, Gabriel turned away from the sun. He saw wounded men laying dazed in the grass. Not far away, a gray tarpaulin lay on the ground. Sticking out from under, he counted six pairs of brogans.

Gabriel closed his eyes and saw Thelma's face.

"You're one lucky trooper," Church sighed. "It's a clean wound. You're going to live."

Marcus Hammer ground his cigarette out in his own palm.

*

Lieutenant Hall cantered his mule along the trail, shouting to anyone he passed to spread the word. He knew he should have reported this only to a ranking officer, but if Young were not in his headquarters, word might get to another General officer in time.

But Hall was relieved to find General Young was in his tent, reading a dispatch he had just received. Hall quickly related the news, and pleaded for reinforcements.

General Young frowned. "Tom, are you sure about Colonel Wood?"

Hall knew he had to convince the General. "Yes," he found himself saying, "I took Colonel Wood's dying statement to his wife."

Young's eyes widened in realization. "My God. That leaves Roosevelt in command!"

Assured that reinforcements were on the way, Hall galloped back toward his regiment. He was beginning to shake and he didn't know why.

But Hall's alarm had spread along the road to Siboney as fast as aides could ride. Soon the rumor had reached General Wheeler's empty headquarters, where a band of reporters, angry they had not been allowed to accompany the battle column, pounced on the news.

The newsmen bolted for the telegraph shack, intent on filing the first scoop of the war.

*

A sharp whiff of ammonia brought Gabriel back. Snake knelt beside him. "Yer plumb lucky. If that had been a lead slug, it'd taken your belly out, bunkie." Gabriel looked down. A cotton worm protruded from a hole in his side, and another from his back. There was very little blood but it hurt when he breathed.

Church staggered in, a limp trooper across his shoulders. He lay the man down gently and lifted his eye lid with a finger. "Gone," he said softly. Then he jumped up. "Come on, Marcus! There's plenty more." They ran back into the jungle.

The staccato of the Colt machine guns filled the air. Then, over their racket, came a bugle call

Snake yelled, " I got to git back, we're beatin' them."

Gabriel grabbed Snake's arm and the movement nearly made him faint. " Snake, don't you know 'cease firing' when you hear it?"

A dazed trooper led a mule out of the jungle. His arm was bound in a bloody bandage. Another trooper sat on the mule, holding a broken pipe in his teeth. He had been shot in the thigh.

One of the wounded in the grass called out weakly to them. "Killed 'em all, did ye?"

The rider removed his broken pipe with his good hand. "They shot this out of my mouth. Got so mad I brought down four or five."

"Then I hope you got the one that shot my backside."

The trooper put his pipe back between his teeth and said, "Truth was, you can't see 'em," he mused, "I never did see 'em."

On the other side of the tree a delirious trooper began to sing.
My Country 'tis of thee...

He groaned, then skipped a few lines as though to finish before his breath ran out.

Land of the pilgrim's pride,
From every— moun-tain...side...

But the last line never came.

Gabriel watched the dressing station fill with wounded men, many expecting amputation, a few praying. Then he felt a new pain and saw that a land crab, its antenna waving, was trying to make a meal of him. He beat at the thing and it scuttled sideways into the brush.

Damned if he was going to lie here. Off to the right, the bugles and gunfire resumed. He rolled onto his side, and sat up. He was dizzy, but he got to one knee and fought the nausea. Finally, he stood amidst wounded and dying men who lay scattered in the grass. The shelter-half covering the dead moved and a crab scuttled out, an indistinguishable prize in its claws. .

Gabriel took a Krag from a dead trooper. Then he unbuckled the man's cartridge belt and looped it around his neck. Maybe he would live and maybe he wouldn't. But he intended to die with the regiment, not here.

*

The Rough Riders inched forward in the tall grass. They could see nothing but the tree line where the Spaniards had retreated. Roosevelt and Wood had dismounted and walked, leading their horses. The grass still moved to the whipping of Mauser bullets.

Behind the troopers, Richard Harding Davis aimed a carbine into the tree line and fired.

Gabriel got to the skirmish line just as the troopers came in view of the stone breastworks, and their Gatlings and Colts opened up. The Spanish sombreros could be seen bobbing as they withdrew. With a roar, the troopers stood and began to fire after them.

*

Two exhausted troops of the Ninth Cavalry arrived on the run, but Las Guásimas had been won. They were frustrated that they

Las (

help in the fighting. Colonel Wood thanked them, and deployed them along the top of the hill. Then he ordered the Rough Riders to make camp, but they had all thrown off their gear at the outbreak of the fighting, and the Cubans had taken it.

Gabriel wore a dead man's shirt, carried a dead man's carbine.

Roosevelt, his eyebrow bleeding slightly, knelt beside Gabriel, and lifted his shirt to examine his wound. "Get back to the hospital, Scriven. You'll get gangrene."

"Sir, I'm all right. But Church has his hands full with the badly wounded."

Roosevelt seemed dazed. He took off his hat and ran his fingers through his hair. "You know," he said, shaking his head, "they got Hamilton Fish. And Allyn Capron."

Gabriel still could not imagine Fish dead. "Has anybody seen T. T. Cloud?"

"I saw an Injun go down," Snake said. "Shot bad."

Just then, Cloud stepped through the grass. He and sat down cross-legged, as though he had been gone but a few minutes. He told them that Isbell might make it and that Lieutenant Day had already replaced Capron.

Roosevelt looked at his Indian Corporal, then said "I'm promoting you to Sergeant, Cloud."

Cloud's expression did not change. "Nobody can take Fish's place."

The Colonel nodded. "But you must. L Troop took the brunt of this fight. I know Hamilton Fish's parents and will eventually have to comfort them." Then he lifted his chin. "But Hamilton Fish would want the next man to step right up, fill his place. In a war, this is what they call a battlefield promotion." Roosevelt grinned. "There are likely to be a good many before we are finished with the Spaniards."

*

Snake and Cloud took their turn hauling Marshall's stretcher toward Siboney, trying to hold him steady and level over the root-tangled trail. Gabriel followed. Tiffany and Prayerful carried the extra carbines, ready to spell Snake and Cloud on the three mile ordeal. Marshall sang weakly, halting only when one of the bearers stumbled. As his hand reached over his head,

Tiffany took it and held tightly.

When the moon...comes out...tonight...
upon the Wabash—
In the heart of my Indy-ana home.

Gabriel could feel a sticky ooze where his wound had started to bled again. But if he walked a bit bent over, the pain wasn't bad.

"I'm glad we ain't haulin' that lard ass Shafter," Snake said.

A trooper of the Tenth caught up with them, sticking his bandaged hand up proudly. "I got mine," he grinned. "No need to take a trooper off the line to carry me neither. I'll git to the hospital on my own."

"What's your hurry," Snake drawled. "They just gonna saw yer arm off when you get there."

Considering this possibility, the trooper slowed down.

Gabriel kept talking to Ed Marshall. "You'll make it, Ed. I'd bet a month's wages on it."

Marshall's pained eyes rolled toward Gabriel. "How much is that?"

"Fifteen dollars and fifty cents."

"Oh great!" Ed Marshall groaned.

*

They deposited Marshall in the care of Chief Surgeon LaMotte at the makeshift hospital in Siboney and were assured he would soon be transferred to a hospital ship. "Now clear out of here", LaMotte warned them. "We're starting to get boys with malaria. Yellow fever will be next."

On their return trip, they rested at the dressing station. under the mango tree. Late that afternoon. Captain McClintock of B Troop had come in. He lay against the trunk, his face expressionless. His left ankle was a pulp of blood and bone. Further away, wounded men watched the buzzards that circled ever lower.

Nearby, Gabriel heard Roosevelt laugh. He was standing with Richard Harding Davis near the tarpaulin covering Fish and the others. A reporter he didn't know aimed his camera at Roosevelt. Davis heard the shutter and he snarled, "Burr! Surely, you won't use that."

"The Hell I won't."

Roosevelt walked to the photographer. "What is your name, sir?"

"Burr McIntosh."

"Mister McIntosh," Roosevelt explained, "I fear you misunderstand. These fallen men are our comrades. We do not joke about their deaths, but were just congratulating ourselves that we are still alive. If you would be good enough to bring your camera back tomorrow, you may very well take a picture of my boots sticking from this very canvas."

McIntosh was having none of it. "In this camera," he said, tapping it, "is the last photograph of Hamilton Fish alive. He was at the rail of the *Yucatan*, and I liked him. You are callous beyond belief to laugh so close to his body."

Just then, Colonel Wood trotted his horse into the shade of the tree. "I understand," he said to Roosevelt, "your bugler has been shot. Is he bad?"

Roosevelt chuckled. "Apparently not bad enough," he said, nodding toward Gabriel. "He discharged himself from the hospital to return to the line."

A shot rang out and Wood's mare flinched.

"Snipers!" Captain McClintock yelled, grasping his leg. "They've been shooting at the wounded all afternoon."

Gabriel cocked his Krag. Cloud and Tiffany were already fanning out, staring up into the royal palms. .

A shot rang out and Tiffany fell.

Gabriel and Cloud both shot at the source of the report, the thick fronds of high above them. They emptied their chambers into it, then quickly reloaded.

Gabriel aimed his Krag while Cloud walked over to Tiffany. Cloud bent over him, then got up slowly, staring up into the tree. He walked straight to the trunk, put his hands on it and stared up, as though contemplating a climb. Then he drew his hand away, pointing to where blood was dripping down the tree trunk. They backed away and Snake joined them as they again emptied their Krags into the tree top. In the silence afterwards, a canteen clanged to the ground. Then a Mauser fell, sticking barrel-first into the soft earth. Gabriel went over to where Tiffany lay. He had been lucky, the bullet just grazed his forehead.

Back at the mango tree, Marcus Hammer knelt beside the tarpaulin, keeping the crabs away and waving his carbine at the vultures. He stared at the boots of Hamilton Fish. Marcus had carried him to the tree himself, refusing any help. Now, fighting back tears, he vowed to make some Spaniard pay. Marcus tucked the tarp around his friend's cold feet.

CHAPTER 17

Saturday, June 25

A thick fog blanketed the encampment. During the night, volunteers from every troop had dug in shifts, but the long, mass grave they had hacked from the rocky ground was only two feet deep.

The sun burned through the mist like the end of a smoldering cigar, and then the fog began to evaporate. Soon the diggers could see each writhing beetle, every centipede scuttling from their picks and shovels.

Gabriel unwrapped his bugle and tensing his gut against the pain, blew reveille.

At first, there was no response in the tents. The troopers lay as though dead.

Gabriel put down his horn and stared at the tarpaulin. As his bugle call echoed off the hills, he half expected Fish to rise, stretch, then arouse his men.

Gabriel bent stiffly and tied the brogans Fish had given him. He knew there were other size elevens in the troop, but Fish had singled him out to get these. They could talk—almost guessed each other's thoughts. Cloud's friendship was as solid as oak, but the Indian's long silences sometimes seemed cool. And Fish was a talker. They had what the Mexican ranch hands called *simpatico,* a natural ease between men.

General Wheeler rode slowly over the hillock, followed by Colonel Wood and Roosevelt. The General reined his sorrel and took off his hat. He sat silently while the horse snorted and stamped the ground. Wood dismounted and stared at the shallow grave.

Cloud saluted. "Colonel, we need more time."

Wood nodded. "Yes, we've got to go deeper." He stepped to the long tarpaulin, cleared his throat and spoke in a strange, faraway voice. "Remove their boots, will you Cloud? I don't want any Cuban scavengers."

Other officers soon joined them. Wheeler saluted first. "Good mornin', General Lawton."

Lawton summarily returned the salute. "I'm glad to see the losses Lieutenant Hall reported were greatly exaggerated. Until this moment, Colonel Wood, I had reason to believe you were dead. Hall swore he took your dying statement, and he had Lieutenant Colonel Roosevelt here shot through the brain."

Roosevelt glowered and muttered to himself.

Lawton stiffened in his saddle. "But no matter. I have a bigger fish to fry." He turned to General Wheeler, then took a dispatch from his saddle bags. "Apparently, General, you ignored a direct order."

Wheeler glanced at the dispatch, set his jaw, and quickly handed it back. "I did nothing of the kind, *suh.*"

"You deliberately sent your troops into an ambush, General. A skirmish at most. General Shafter..."

Wheeler interrupted. "May I remind you, General, that I am the rankin' field officer on shore, not you." The little general paused. "You may report whatever you see fit to General Shafter. But you should know, *suh,* that we had a battle, not a skirmish!" His eyes flashed. "It is no skirmish when three troops rout a superior force of entrenched enemy and establish a base camp within strikin' distance of his capital! I wouldn't insult the forty Rough Riders killed and wounded by calling this any ambush! Colonel Wood was beaten by most odds, yet he triumphed. You cannot deny that." Wheeler's eyes narrowed in accusation. "I think your usual good judgment has been affected *suh*, by one somewhat panicky report."

General Lawton was unmoved. "I shall record the truth as I see it, General!" He saluted curtly and rode away.

General Wheeler eased down into his saddle, then wheeled his horse sharply the other way.

Roosevelt watched the two generals ride in different directions. "Where *is* Hall! Look at all the trouble his panic has caused."

Wood rubbed the back of his neck. "Easy, Theodore. Frederick the Great ran from his first battle."

"But Hall has disgraced brave men. I intend..."

"Theodore," Wood said evenly, "think. We will not sully the reputation of The First Volunteer Cavalry by an official reprimand. Besides, Hall is responsible for most of the reports we must sign. Lists of killed and wounded, posting sentries, the business of running the camp for which you have neither time nor inclination. In short, Theodore, we need him."

"But," Roosevelt protested, "he sets a poor example for the men. I understand now why they have never much liked him."

Wood stroked his sandy mustache. It seemed to Gabriel that he seemed to enjoy Roosevelt's discomfort. "Tell me, Theodore, are not you curious to know exactly where that Spanish bullet entered your skull? I can tell you," he smiled " that I'd be most interested in what message Hall took down for my wife from my dying lips."

*

In the first light of dawn, Lieutenant Hall crossed and recrossed the battle site. He could feel fever gripping him but he fought the shivers. He could not face Colonel Wood until he understood what had really happened. The confusion could happen to any man amid flying bullets and shouted orders.

This morning, Hall's eyes, although aching from lack of sleep, were especially sharp. His commanders would want nothing but empirical truth. He was still convinced the Rough Riders had entered an enemy trap, the very kind of ambuscade he had been warned about at West Point. And with no flankers, they had fallen for it. Surely there had been Spaniards flanking both sides, and if he could find evidence, he might vindicate his actions. He caught the glint of brass and stooped to examine it. Then, near the empty shell casing he found a rifle ammunition box printed in German. And further on, another box containing German machine gun bullets. Hall gathered up the boxes and began to make his way through the wet grass. Surely Wood would believe him now. Only a miracle had saved Wood. And no man in Cuba was more glad than he himself! The Rough Riders had stood in the jaws of death and had escaped. And now, Lieutenant Hall had the evidence.

*

At noon Gabriel sounded assembly. He stood at one end of the long trench, now lined with fresh ferns. Beside it lay seven dead troopers, each rolled in a clean gray blanket. Their carbines had been fixed in a row, bayonets stuck into the diggings. Each man's hat, shaped by his own hand, had been set at the angle he had worn it on the stock of his Krag. In front, six pairs of empty brogans stood at attention.

At the other end of the trench, the flag they had raised over Mt. Losiltares draped the only officer to die, Captain Allyn Capron.

Chaplain Brown's pink head glistened with sweat as turned the pages of his bible. Officers and men waited, bareheaded in the blazing sun, holding their hats. The cicadas shrieked the scorching heat while ever-present vultures, like angels of death, floated above them.

No more than half the troopers had answered Gabriel's call. Many of the men had a strange chill. Still, there were enough to crowd the grave site.

The Chaplain stepped in front of the first Stetson; the brim set at a sharp angle on the carbine. "Hamilton Fish," he announced, as though addressing the dead sergeant. Brown stepped to the next carbine. "Tilden W. Dawson."

A macaw squawked obscenely from the thicket. "Edward Liggett."

"William T. Irwin." Brown paused, then stepped again. "Henry J. Haefner." The full names sounded strange. Gabriel knew the dead by the nicknames they had earned in San Antonio.

"Marcus D. Russell."

The Chaplain turned and marched stiffly to the bright folds of the silk flag. "Captain Allyn K. Capron, Junior." Brown paused, gathering his voice. "He was twenty-seven on the day he gave his life. His father has not yet landed. But we will consult him as soon as possible as to where to bury his son. All officers as well as the men of L Company are invited to attend that service, once it is announced."

Gabriel shifted in Fish's boots.

At Wood's nod, Gabriel, Cloud, Snake, and Prayerful lifted Fish's body. Trying not to grunt, they slid the body onto ropes, then lowered it gently down into the ferns. Gabriel and Cloud eased the ropes, but when they came away, Fish's body slid. A bare foot showed beneath the gray blanket. Gabriel tried to drop a palm branch over it. Prayerful, conjuring a silent prayer, completed the job. He handed the ropes to the Chaplain.

When the dead had been laid end to end in the narrow trench, rolled in their blankets, they reminded Gabriel of spent cartridges in a chamber of of soft green.

Chaplain Brown read a passage from his Bible, "I am the Resurrection and the Life, saith the Lord."

When he had finished the reading, he knelt and prayed silently. The men bent with him. Afterward, still kneeling, a cowboy quartet sang "Rock of Ages." The men joined in, singing low and hesitantly in the sun, with the vultures flickering over their heads.

Next, Colonel Wood dropped a clod of dirt into the trench. Roosevelt, his face fiercely reverent, bit his lip and did the same.

The clods stirred flies, already working under the palm branches.

As the spades of earth were thrown into the trench, Gabriel readied his bugle and blew taps.

Ta ta TAAAAA.
Ta ta TAAAAAAAAA.
Ta ta TAA, ta ta TAA, ta ta TAAA...

A breeze moved in the mango tree and whipped Capron's flag.

As the men filed away from the grave, a white-clad figure remained, sombrero under his arm. Colonel García stood over Fish and crossed himself. He bent over the dead Sergeant's carbine. When he stood, Gabriel saw a white camellia in the trigger guard.

Cloud nudged Gabriel's arm. "I'll go to Capron's service. You look none too good." When Gabriel opened his mouth to protest, Cloud said, "That's an order."

"Who will bugle for the regiment?"

"The Colonel can find someone else. Kelly, maybe."

"Then take my bugle. Tell Kelly..."

"You have been shot. Stop acting like you're not. Get some sleep. Captain Capron was my friend, more than yours."

As Gabriel watched his new sergeant step out into the sun, he propped his back against the bullet-scarred tree and slid slowly down. In the grass lay pieces of make-shift stretchers. Bloody bandages buzzed with flies.

Colonel García walked over to him. "I am sorry to see that you have been wounded. It very bad?"

"No, I was lucky."

"Nevertheless, you will be sent back on the next ship. Tell me, will you do the honor of taking a letter for Sergeant Fish's family?"

"I am staying, Colonel."

Colonel García shrugged. "I would do the same. But of course, you are like Sergeant Fish. But take this anyway." He handed Gabriel an envelope. It was addressed in ornate script "To the family of Hamilton Fish."

"I'll pass it to Colonel Wood."

"No," García protested. "He is sure to get a bullet sooner or later and I do not want my message detained."

"Then Roosevelt. He knows everybody in New York."

"I do not like the man," he spat. "Take it yourself. That way, you can tell the father how it was his son died. That he was a leader despite his rank. You will give Señor Fish my very deepest gratitude for his sacrifice toward a free Cuba."

"All right, Colonel, I'll do my best."

García nodded. "I go now to Sevilla. We have dead to bury too."

"How many?"

"Two. But one was my best man—but you *Yanquis* would not appreciate him."

"I do, whatever his name," Gabriel said.

García's lip curled. "Yes, *amigo*. I wish there were more men like you, on all sides. *Adios,* Private Gabriel."

When the Colonel had gone, Gabriel lay back, panting. The trench had been filled in and the earth mounded up. Buzzards clawed the dirt, scattering the small stones troopers had gathered and placed in the shape of a thin cross.

*

At twilight, Gabriel awoke with a start. Snake crouched near him, chewing a cud of tobacco.

Snake snarled. "I been beatin' the crabs away. They're plenty hungry and I kind of know how they feel. We got nothin' to eat again. This afternoon, a trooper auctioned off two ounces of tobacco. Got near fifty dollars. I bought five dollars worth. Figure it costs me a penny a bite. So I chew slow."

Gabriel was stiff but he felt better. Snake gave him a drink from his canteen, then led him to the Rough Rider encampment. The command tent glowed like a lantern. Gabriel ducked painfully under the flap. Colonel Wood and Captain Llewellyn sat behind a camp table. Roosevelt paced behind them. Lieutenant Hall waited at attention.

Wood returned Gabriel's salute. "Son, this is an informal hearing pursuant to Lieutenant Hall's leaving the scene of battle yesterday. Captain Llewellyn contends that Lieutenant Hall ran from the field. The Lieutenant denies this. So, we'd like to clear things up. Did you see Lieutenant Hall leave the field?"

Gabriel glanced at Hall, who looked hopeful.

"Yes sir. The Lieutenant saw a man fall. I did too. Then the Lieutenant rode to the rear to report it."

"You are sure of this?"

Gabriel shifted in Fish's boots. "Yes sir."

Wood put his palms on the table. "Did Lieutenant Hall say anything as he passed?"

Gabriel thought for a moment. Roosevelt leaned forward, his knuckles on the table.

"Yes sir. I thought I heard him say you had been shot."

It was silent in the tent, except for a huge moth that repeatedly butted the lantern chimney.

Roosevelt's spectacles reflected the light.

"Thank you, Scriven," Colonel Wood said, "that will do for now." Then he addressed Lieutenant Hall. "Tom, you've lost credibility with the men. They expect their officers to be steady. What you thought you saw got the better of you, I suppose."

Tom Hall's voice broke as he said, "Colonel Wood, I will not deny that I knew fear at that moment. But more than for my own life, I feared for the regiment. I was convinced we were being slaughtered in a cross fire. When I thought I saw you go down, I had to..."

Roosevelt cut him off. "But you told a lie, Tom. Why?"

"That's enough, Theodore," Wood snapped. "It is water under the bridge now. A man does strange things under fire. Sometimes, he has to convince himself that he did the noble thing. The realization of a mistake made can be too painful to admit. As I see it, Lieutenant Hall's unruly imagination is the culprit here."

Lieutenant Hall saluted. "Thank you, Colonel Wood."

Roosevelt stormed out of the tent, and Captain Llewellyn followed.

Colonel Wood's voice was soft but firm. "That will be all, Tom. I want you to go to Siboney tonight. You are responsible for getting our supplies up here by morning. One-third rations is no way for our men to fight a war."

Hall saluted and rushed out of the tent.

Then Colonel Wood stepped around the table and unbuttoned Gabriel's shirt. He brought the lantern closer and poked the swollen welt with his finger. Gabriel winced.

Wood took his finger away and sniffed it. "Tomorrow morning, get yourself to the hospital. Have LaMotte purge this with carbolic acid; give you a fresh dressing."

"But sir, there's fever down there."

Wood sighed sat down in his chair. He rubbed his eyes with the hand that had not touched the wound. As Gabriel left, Colonel Wood was watching a flurry of moths fighting for the lantern's killing flame.

*

The First Volunteer Cavalry had camped in plain view of a ridge with three Spanish blockhouses. Although out of carbine range, the enemy could see them. And tempers were hot. The second brigade of cavalry, mounted regulars, passed the Rough Riders that afternoon and camped nearer to the front. Wood could see that the regulars were insulted that they had been denied the first battle, and doubly so because some of them had been called up to rescue the "upstart" Rough Riders.

Now, each regiment posted pickets and refused to let anyone pass through their territory. The Rough Riders were envious that the second brigade had mounts. As a consequence, they refused to let the regulars water their horses in the stream that ran through the Rough Rider encampment.

During the afternoon rain, the second brigade watched while the Rough Riders dug drains with shovels and picks they had hustled from headquarters. The regulars had no digging equipment. As a result, their tents filled with water.

As if things were not bad enough, that afternoon Hall brought news of the first Rough Rider death from fever. The man had been safely isolated and died aboard a ship in the harbor at Siboney. Yet, the fever had begun.

Wood had given strict orders that there would be no drinking or washing utensils in the stream, and under the watchful eye of Surgeon Church made sure it they were obeyed. The immunes, the Ninth and Tenth cavalry, were under no such orders. Now, Wood realized, the specious immune theory would be tested with men's lives.

Tomorrow he would send a detail into the forest to hunt for mangos, bananas, and limes. Perhaps the men could make a drink with the small supply of fresh water they had. That would give them something to do besides defend their perimeter.

CHAPTER 18

The *State of Texas* dropped anchor, a slab of white in a harbor filled with sooty transports and gray war ships. Gabriel watched from the window of the ramshackle house commandeered for the American hospital. Tom Isbell, like the other badly wounded, lay naked on the board floor. His bandages were brown and caked. He closed his eyes from time to time and bit hard on his knuckle to fight the pain. He had been shot through the neck and through the hip. Another Spanish bullet had nearly cut off his thumb. With so many wounds, there was no position that provided any comfort.

Chief Surgeon Winter stepped to the window beside Gabriel. His apron was smeared with blood. "As if things are not bad enough," he growled, "we must now contend with that Barton woman and her confounded bevy of nurses!"

Clara Barton? A murmur passed among the waiting wounded, for they had heard of her in Tampa and knew of her concern for real hospital beds and good food. Even Tom Isbell perked up at the name. It was better to think of the American Red Cross's intrepid founder than surgeon Winter's scalpel and possible amputation.

Gabriel bent over Isbell. "Now maybe we'll get something to eat!"

Surgeon Winter wiped his sleeve across his brow. "I'm sending your friend Marshall out on the next ship. His spinal cord is severed. Even if he survives, he'll certainly never walk again."

Gabriel saw Isbell wince in a spasm of pain. He ignored the surgeon, who turned away from the window and went back to his grisly work. "Miss Barton's got a boat down, Tom. I can see them loading! Biscuits and gravy. Eggs. Hot Coffee. Look at that, will you? A whole boat load of..."

Isbell's mouth was a black hole, but his dark eyes were bright. "Peaches?," he asked hopefully. "I want me a peach."

"Sure, peaches," Gabriel told him. "A whole skiff full."

Just then, a wounded trooper Gabriel did not know limped to the window. "They ain't even finished the dock," he said. How's Miss Barton goin' to unload?"

"I'm going to help her," Gabriel said. "Tom, don't you worry, You are going to get your peach."

*

She was a little lady of seventy. Above a lace collar, her thin lips made a straight line. Miss Barton's quick eyes missed nothing—even the naked men who were embarrassed they could not cover up. She had brought several Red Cross officers and five sturdy looking nurses, who did not avert their eyes. Clara Barton stopped beside a patient and wrinkled her nose. "Dysentery, Doctor Hubbel, make a note." Her Red Cross doctor nodded and made a notation on his pad.

Now, Clara Barton paused over the thrice-wounded Isbell.

As Hubbel bent over the now unconscious Pawnee, Chief Surgeon Winter came back into the room. "Ah, Miss Barton," he said with no particular feeling.

She turned to face him. "We came as soon as we got word, Doctor Winter. The Navy refused our help at Guantánamo. Perhaps the Army will be more receptive."

Surgeon Winter took a deep breath and his words came out in a hard stream, giving Miss Barton no chance to question or interrupt. "You know that we forbid women in any Army hospital. It is an embarrassment to the men. The seriously wounded have already been treated and I am attending to the lesser cases now. Our beds and other supplies are at the dockside. We have a hospital ship on the way. The Army has things under control."

Clara Barton knew there was no dockside. "But Doctor Winter," she replied, "these men are practically naked. Let us set to work. We'll clean them up and bring blankets. Obviously, you are needed in the surgery. You can't be expected to worry about amenities for these boys."

Winter stiffened and said, "Soldiers, madam. Not boys."

But Clara Barton was already rolling up her sleeves. "Nevertheless, their spirits will be improved with a clean ward and proper linen."

Surgeon Winter crossed his arms. "Miss Barton. The Fifth Army does not recognize your organization. I command you to leave. Perhaps," he forced a smile, "you'd be more useful elsewhere."

Clara Barton did not move. She looked at him squarely as she said, "Doctor Winter, when we received the telegraph that the Rough Riders had been hard dealt by at Las Guásimas, I came. I knew that our help would be somewhat rough, but I vowed, by the grace of God, sir, to come."

"Noble sentiments, Madam. As you can see, your help is not needed."

Clara Barton turned and looked out the window. "That house next door. Is that your facility?"

"No, Madam. I believe it is for the Cubans."

She turned abruptly. "Well then, we shall go help them. Come, Doctor Hubbel. Begin unloading with the flat-bottomed scows. We shall not wait for the Army to complete the dock."

Later that day, Gabriel entered the Cuban hospital. The plank floors were still wet from scrubbing. Miss Barton's nurses scurried about, setting folding cots into rows. A mountain of blankets lay stacked on a table and Clara Barton, her skirts tied up above bare feet, stepped from behind it. Under her direction, the abandoned house had been transformed into a thirty-bed ward with white sheets and gray blankets on each cot.

When she had inspected the ward, she nodded. "All right. Bring them in."

Her orderlies carried in a Cuban with a bandaged stump where his right arm should have been. The man was nonchalantly smoking a cigar. Miss Barton snatched the cigar from his mouth and threw it out the window as the Cuban protested.

Gabriel knew it was time to execute his plan for Isbell. He went next door and bent over he delirious Pawnee. "Come on, Tom." he whispered. "We're going back to the regiment." Isbell's eyes fluttered open and he tried to rise, but he had lost too much blood. Gabriel's belly seemed to be on fire, but he knew Isbell might die if he stayed here much longer. "Come on, Tom," he urged. Isbell grunted with pain, but sat up. Soon, with Gabriel's help, he was standing on his one good leg. Gabriel put his arm around Isbell's waist and they hobbled out into the sun.

In the Cuban hospital, Gabriel eased Isbell onto a cot. Clara Barton hurried over. She eyed the naked Indian and Gabriel's dirty Rough Rider uniform. "So," she pronounced loudly enough for everyone to hear, "you've brought me another Cuban."

Gabriel was relieved. "Yes ma'am," he smiled, "Full-blooded."

Miss Barton's steamer trunk was a wonderment to Gabriel. He watched her unbuckle the straps, then, with the help of Dr. Hubbel, unfolded the contraption. The top was hinged so that it swung back and doubled the length of the trunk, providing her bed. Along its sides, drawers stored clothing, personal items, and books. Doctor Hubbel strung a sheet across a corner of the ward and Gabriel was amazed to see that Clara Barton intended to sleep but a few feet from her grizzled charges—and with only a flimsy sheet for privacy.

Satisfied with her abode, she commanded Gabriel to build her a fire for cooking.

When the fire crackled, Clara Barton unpacked her iron kettles. Meanwhile, her orderlies had managed to unload a scow of foodstuffs— meal, flour, rice, condensed milk, tea, coffee, and canned goods. These Clara Barton arranged neatly on a plank. "I don't know much about what a Cuban prefers," she winked at Gabriel, "but I am quite certain what he should eat. I'll make plenty. Do you think you could convince Doctor Winter that a cup of Red Cross coffee would not poison him?"

Gabriel brought her buckets of water, which she set over the embers to boil. Then Clara Barton began to open cans and to measure meal.

The smell of the bubbling food brought tears to Gabriel's eyes.

When the hot gruel was ready, Gabriel took a bowl for himself and a cup for Isbell. When they had eagerly devoured every drop, he went back for seconds. Then he took a bowl of gruel and a pot of coffee to Doctor Hubbell. He found Hubbel dispensing medicine to the wounded Cubans. Hubbel replaced the cap carefully. "Our best Shaker opium," Hubbel said. "from Massachusetts. Now that your Cuban friend," his eyebrow raised in amusement, "has eaten, I'll give him some as well. He'll sleep peacefully tonight. Then I want to have a look at your wound."

*

Gabriel wrote by the light of a candle Miss Barton had given him.

A *Sunday night in Cuba*

Dear Aura,
Did you get the letter I wrote in Tampa? We got here a nearly a week ago, but it seems much longer. If it were not for the war, Cuba would be a beautiful place to visit. But we are here as soldiers. I've been shot but it is just a small wound and it doesn't keep me from fighting.

In that battle my captain and sergeant were both killed. We had a service for them, and I played taps.

Some others died too, enlisted men I didn't know. But most of us just got shot up a little.

It is hot and rainy here. Not like home. We have land crabs big enough to drag off a sleeping man so we don't doze much. Then there're the ants. They'll fell a tree and carry it off. They'll eat people too.

Gabriel realized he was boasting. Marcus must have written Aura already, and he might need to counter whatever lies Marcus had told her.

I am now Colonel Theodore Roosevelt's bugler.
He's quite an interesting man.

But Gabriel couldn't write what he felt, that he had dreamed of her, had held her in his arms and kissed her and had entered that mysterious portal of her womanhood.

I never saw so many stars in my life.Stars we do not have at home.

Colonel Wood thinks we will beat the Spanish in another week. Tonight I met famous Clara Barton. She actually gave me this paper and told me to write my girl before I go to sleep. Perhaps I presume too much. You may not consider yourself my girl at all.

But Miss Barton is a very convincing lady, and it would have been impolite to go against her.

War is nothing like I thought it would be. You never know what will happen next or if you will get anything to eat. Nothing is regular. You can't even see the enemy. You shoot at trees and bushes.

I wish I had some of your cherry cobbler.
What do you sing at church now?

I bugle at least ten times a day. The Army seems to have a bugle call for everything, but not for missing someone.

If they did, I would blow it right now.

God Bless,
Private Gabriel Scriven,
Trumpeter, First Volunteer Cavalry

CHAPTER 19

Monday, June 27

"Rough Riders? Why, they broke camp two hours ago. Moved north." The trooper was working on a sketch pad laid across his lap. He, like the rest of the New York Seventy- First, wore sky blue britches.

"Say," Gabriel asked, "Are you some kind of artist?"

The trooper looked up and a smile split his beard. "Sure am. I'm Charles Johnson Post."

Gabriel shook his hand. "Sorry we beat you boys out of the *Yucatan*."

Post shook his head. "Never mind, we got a better boat out of the deal. Say, why don't you let me draw your picture?"

"Not like this. I look awful. I've got to catch up with my outfit."

"Let me make a sketch first. Just take a jiffy. You're the first Rough Rider I've seen standing still." The artist took a cigar, slipped it between his lips and flicked his cotton-flint lighter until it smoldered. He blew the spark to light the cigar, then regarded Gabriel. "Now just stand natural. Talk all you want."

Gabriel watched Post's eyes dart between him and the pad, as his hand and the pencil in it moved rapidly.

"You boys ate some lead at Las Guásimas, didn't you?"

"A little," Gabriel answered.

Post's cheroot glowed, then he exhaled. "We saw the Rough Riders turn into the jungle." He turned his pad as he sketched, squinting critically. Then he went back to work.

"How about you?" Gabriel asked out of the side of his mouth, "been shot at yet?"

"No, but we're itchin'."

"I wouldn't be in any hurry, If I were you."

In what seemed to Gabriel like minutes, Post cocked his head at the sketch. "Guess I'm done. Here, have a look."

The trooper Post had sketched pad looked like an old forty-niner, not a boy of eighteen. "But this doesn't look like me," Gabriel protested.

Post grinned. "Yes it does. That's a portrayal of a trooper who has faced the grim reaper."

Gabriel looked again, this time, more carefully.

"There," Post said, pointing with the pencil, "you can see it in his eyes."

*

Storm clouds gathered as Gabriel walked into the Rough Rider camp. In their tent, Snake lay shivering. Gabriel slumped beside him as the sky opened. It rained buckets, then barrels, like the ocean itself had fallen on them. The rain beating on the canvas deafened the two troopers. They watched tents collapse with men still in them, then begin to slide down the hill. Luckily, Snake had lashed theirs to a palm tree. A trooper tobogganed past them on his mattress, his eyes wide with disbelief.

It kept raining. Finally, Gabriel dug through his wet blouse and handed Snake the cheroot the artist had given him. Snake took one surprised look and bit off a chunk, he gave the rest back to Gabriel. The rain made too much noise to say anything. Snake put his arm around Gabriel's shoulder. Then the two men rolled onto their sides, doubling their legs and laying back to back for warmth, waiting for the rain to stop.

*

Gabriel awoke stiff and soggy. In the steamy aftermath of the storm he could see that they were once again camped beside the thatch shelters of the Cubans, whose hobbled ponies, still saddled, limped toward their forage—a bundle of young cane leaves.

In the Rough Rider's camp, troopers struggled to erect fallen tents, which were sopped with mud. But the ground was too spongy to hold stakes. The men were sick of being wet and hungry.

"We come to fight spanions, not suck mud and swat skeeters," Snake complained. He slapped his neck. "We ain't nothin' but a bunch of latrine maggots," he snarled.

Then two Cubans came into camp. Gabriel had noticed that the quickly erected palm thatch of the Cuban camp provided better shelter than the tents. Besides, a man could stand up inside. He asked them in Spanish if they would build one for him and Snake. He offered to trade their tent for the work. The Cubans argued first between themselves, but finally agreed.

Gabriel watched them work, first scuttling up a palm tree to choose particular branches, then hacking notches into the woody stems. The branches were tied to a horizontal ridge pole and hung downward. More palm branches were added so that they overlapped. Finally, the ridge pole was raised and secured with long stakes. Then the sides were raised, propped to a wide angle, and tied. The whole process took less than half an hour. One of the Cubans brought a piece of sticky hide and tied it under the ridge pole. Within minutes, it was covered with flies. Gabriel pointed and asked, "*Por qué?*" The Cuban explained that the flies would be attracted to the hide, and be stuck in the pine tar—a kind of fly paper.

Gabriel inquired about Colonel García and the Cuban said he had not seen him. Major Miguelín commanded this *fuerza*, or brigade. The man, thinking Gabriel had asked to have the Major brought, trotted back to his camp.

Major Miguelín wore officer's whites, but his straight black hair was as long as a woman's. He was flanked by two of the biggest Negroes Gabriel had ever seen. The way the two guards stared at the Rough Riders, it was clear they did not trust them. But Miguelín seemed friendly enough. He nodded at Cloud and asked, "*El alto es Indio, no?*".

"*Sí,*" Gabriel answered, "*de los campos del norte.*"

Miguelín pointed to his chest. "*Yo soy Taíno. General Rabí también.*"

Cloud looked at Gabriel for an explanation.

"He sees you're Indian," Gabriel translated. "Says he is too—a Taíno. And so is his General Rabí."

Miguelín spoke to Gabriel in rapid Spanish, making gestures toward his long hair. Gabriel had to ask him to speak *con despacio*, more slowly. Then he understood, as Major Miguelín made scissors of his fingers.

"The Major swears," Gabriel explained "that he refuses to cut his hair until the *mambisses* march into Havana."

Cloud grinned. "Then tell him, me too."

Just then, the clatter of a mess triangle penetrated the air. It was the first call to chow the men had heard in three days, and they left the Cubans standing in their tracks.

Their cook, a little New Yorker they had not seen since the *Yucatan*, had prepared an enormous pot of beans, seasoned with bacon and onion. As he ladled out the meal into proffered mess tins, the men thanked him.

"Don't thank me," he jabbered happily. "From Siboney Colonel Roosevelt brought two sacks. Porkchop, he tells me—you cook 'em up quick. His own money, he paid. That's right! So eat, boys, eat! No, no coffee. No biscuits. Just beans. And listen, be thankful you got even the beans!"

Gabriel held the hot tin plate. The aroma rose and mingled with smell of unwashed men in dirty woolens. The men crouched in groups, sipping, happily cursing the hot bean broth, for they were like dogs burning their mouths on hot bones—too hungry to wait for their meal to cool.

Gabriel went back and Porkchop scooped the scorched paste from the bottom of the pot. But this was a feast.

As Colonel Roosevelt passed among the troopers, he paused beside Gabriel. Roosevelt removed his saber and lay it in the grass. His hat looked chewed off—was missing part of the brim and his glasses were steamed. "We must set up our artillery before we attack Santiago. Why, just today twelve hundred Michigan Volunteers arrived. If the sea is calm tomorrow, we should get another three thousand. Shafter wants to finish the cable connections with Washington before we attack."

"Smoke, Sir?" A trooper offered Roosevelt one of the twisted, Cuban cigars.

"No thanks, son. Incidentally, I checked on Isbell today," Roosevelt said. "He seems to be holding his own. Doctor Hubbel saved his thumb. Do you know the Cubans mistook him for one of their own? But Winter's hospital is better organized now. His tents have finally arrived."

"Many with fever, sir?"

Roosevelt pretended to ignore the question. "Miss Barton. God bless her! She wouldn't take money for these provisions. I wish she were commanding Fifth Corps."

Snake belched. "Don't worry about us, Colonel. We can take it."

Roosevelt leaned closer and whispered, "Boys, I want no talk of fever, do you hear? There may be a case or two, but that's all. Any of you feeling ill?"

They answered in unison, as much to convince themselves as anything. "No Sir!"

"Then bully!"

When Roosevelt retrieved his saber, a land-crab was clinging to the tassel, tangled in

the silver threads. Roosevelt was as excited as a small boy who had found his first bug. He removed it gingerly and placed it, almost lovingly in the grass. "Remember, boys—the first order of nature is to eat. This crab has a right to do it to. "

"And what's the second, sir?" a trooper called.

Roosevelt's eyebrows shot up. "Reproduction, gentlemen. And may we soon be home to fulfill it."

Then he looked down the road. "Good! Here comes Captain Capron." Then realizing the troopers were confused, quickly added, "Senior. Allyn Capron's father. I shall go fetch his son's belongings."

But later, when Roosevelt offered the trunk of belongings, the gray-haired Captain brusquely refused. "No sir," he vowed. "Not until the Spanish have paid," he said. Then, he turned and busied himself with his guns.

Nearby, Richard Harding Davis set a telescope on a tripod and was describing the Spanish lines to a group of troopers. He leaned over, one hand behind his back, swinging the telescope to the left. "Their white sombreros bob against the yellow dirt," he intoned. "Yes, they are digging furiously, boys, digging for their lives. They've already cut a long trench along the heights, the last hill that overlooks their capital, Santiago." He adjusted his telescope as the troopers waited, hanging on every word. Gabriel had to admit that Davis's description was like looking through the glass himself. Snake stopped chewing and squinted his eyes.

"There is a blue bungalow on the hill to the right. Then in the center of the last hill, a blockhouse, much like a Chinese pagoda."

Snake grunted, trying hard to imagine such a thing.

"And behind the pagoda, not more than three-quarters of a mile, boys, I see the long white walls of the Reina Mercedes Military Hospital. The outskirts of our goal—Santiago de Cuba!"

"Yeeeeeeeee hah!" yelled Snake.

"Theodore," Davis demanded, "come look at this!" Roosevelt shoved his spectacles up and bent to the level of the telescope. "Jove!" he uttered. "We could blast them right now. Gabriel! Get Colonel Wood!"

*

Gabriel blew taps. The encampment had been restored from the storm. Tents lay muddy white against the dark earth. As yet, there had been no cannon fire on either side. Mist hung on the stagnant pools, and from them rose clouds of hungry mosquitoes. Deep into a hard shiver, Gabriel endured their bites.

As if in answer to his bugle call, the hills beyond echoed with trilling Spanish trumpets. The musical answer seemed beautiful and sad. These were difficult notes Gabriel could not play. They overlapped each other like the strings of a guitar and sounded like they came from the past. Gabriel tried to imagine his counterpart, dressed in the light blue cotton uniform of the dead Spaniard they had seen at Las Guásimas, taking off his rope-soled shoes, cleaning his Mauser. Gabriel found himself wondering what the Spanish bugler had eaten and whether he had a girl waiting for him across the ocean.

In that instant, he was angry that thousands of boys were shivering in the mud just for the chance to shoot each other at first light. War was beginning to seem pointless. He would give anything for a cup of hot cocoa and a dry blanket. But in the same instant, Gabriel was ashamed of such unsoldierly thoughts. He wrapped his bugle and crawled under their thatch *rancho*. As if in answer to the Spanish bugles, the sleeping Snake farted a long, tuba-like b flat.

*

During the night, Gabriel was awakened by a noise. In one movement he had cocked and aimed his Krag at the source, somewhere above them. "Snake?"

When the trooper did not respond, Gabriel jabbed him with the butt of his carbine.

"Huuuuh?"

"I hear something."

In an instant, Snake sat up, his carbine at the ready. They both listened to the rustling sound above them.

"Sounds like some critter," Snake breathed, laying his Krag aside. Gabriel heard him pull the cork on his bottle of matches. When the match flared they saw three tarantulas, hanging upside down, eating the flies on the sticky cowhide. Snake cursed as the match burned his fingers.

Gabriel covered his head with the blanket. A shiver began at his toes and worked up his body and heard his own teeth chattering like bones.

*

Well beyond the Rough Rider camp, near the Camino Reál, Colonel Raúl García wrote a dispatch to General Wheeler. The American Cavalry commander seemed to understand García's impatience to get his men into the fight. García was fed up with the secondary role he had been forced to play and now was the time to act. General Rabí had told him that the *Peninsulares* were sending a large reinforcement column from the west toward Santiago. That column must be cut to pieces. It must never reach the already demoralized Spanish garrison.

García had seen the signs of Spanish panic. Several of his men had gone into Santiago and come back with reports, most of which he had not shared with General Shafter. His men had witnessed Spanish sailors marching from the ships, bringing more deck guns from their fleet to mount in the squares of Santiago for a final defense. And Colonel García had heard of the first cases of fever at Siboney. Besides, it would be hurricane season soon. The *Yanquis* would be falling in droves to fever and they would all, including his own men, run out of ammunition before the Spanish would release their hold on Santiago.

He finished the dispatch and handed it to his aide, a quick-witted young Lieutenant with the *cajones* to deliver it through the snipers. It was no use, García had already decided, to try to meet General Wheeler face to face. Such a meeting would be noticed, resented and the General would be compromised. No, García reasoned, this request would surely win a favorable response. He was merely asking permission to join up with Rabí in the west to help destroy the relief column. He would need a brigade of Americans to hold the road in the meantime. He had asked for the Tenth Cavalry. García had watched them fight at El Caney. The *"Smoked Yanquis"* had the discipline to hold the road and not rush in pell-mell like the impetuous Rough Riders.

Raúl García knew that General Toral meant to obey the mandate of Queen Cristina—to hold Cuba against the *Yanqui* army. To the last *peseta*, to the last man! But there was another reason the *Peninsulares* would fight feverishly. If they surrendered, they believed the *mambises* would show them no mercy. Well, let them believe it. Perhaps it would be true.

CHAPTER 20

Tuesday, June 28

As the prisoner ran from the Cubans, Prayerful twirled a coil of rope above his head and tossed it. The rope fell over the prisoner's shoulders, then tightened at his knees as he fell.

Captain Luna rose up just as one of the Cubans raised his machete. "No!" Luna commanded. *"Tranquilo!"* And the *mambi* reluctantly lowered the blade.

Then Luna began to question the prisoner, who was so afraid he began to mess his pants.

The Cubans who had brought him reacted by again drawing their machetes. Luna's revolver stopped them. "This is a Cuban, not Spanish. Says he just borrowed a Spanish soldier's clothes."

But the *mambises* were not convinced. They told Captain Luna that they found him climbing out of a tree. So he must be a *mercenario.*

Now Luna looked at the prisoner with new interest. Snipers were held in low regard in every camp. They shot the doctors as they tried to operate and picked off the wounded as they stumbled toward aid stations.

The commotion had drawn a ring of angry men by now, some of

them Rough Riders. Luna was somewhat relieved to see Colonel Wood approaching.

"Says he's Cuban, sir. But I am not sure."

But Wood was watching the *mambises*. "What do they think?"

"They think he's a guerrilla. He has no papers on him."

Wood shifted his hat. "We have no provisions for prisoners. Better give him back."

Luna hesitated, then spoke to the prisoner who immediately fell to his knees. "*No, hermanos. Por favor. Yo soy Cubano como tuyos!*"

Luna appealed to Wood. "They will hack him to pieces, sir."

Wood stared down at last night's mud, which was already baking to clay. "I can't guarantee our own men might not shoot him. Then I'd have to discipline a good soldier. We need every man."

"But this man is a human being," Captain Luna protested.

Gabriel watched Wood's jaw set. "So was Allyn Capron."

But it was Luna, speaking to the Cubans, who saved the man's life. He did it with a neat trick. Luna began to ask him about his family and it turned out that he was indeed married to a distant cousin of one of the *mambises*. A few weeks back, he had made the mistake to go to Santiago to get some rice and beans and the Spanish, he admitted, had conscripted him to be a guard at the prison.

As the Cuban went off with his captors, they plied him with questions. In a friendly way, they were seeking news of family members who were still prisoners of the Spanish.

*

Clara Barton hiked her skirts against the mud. She was followed by her phalanx of nurses. Lieutenant Church, wearing his peeling yellow poncho, brought up the rear.

The cadre of medics was caught in a tangle of braying mules and drivers. Officers berated their half-starved men. Rivers of mud slid down the hillsides. The sun cooked the men in their steaming clothes. But Miss Barton was determined, and the men stepped aside for her as she strode, her elbows flying.

Church explained to the troopers that Miss Barton had come to assess the conditions at the front.

"That's easy." Prayerful sucked on an empty cob pipe. "Tell her it's nothin' but starvation, shakes, and shit."

In his command tent, Colonel Wood could see that Hall was not well. The man was sweating and shivering as he tried to deliver his report. "Tom, go to your tent. I'll have Lieutenant Schwaizer assume the Adjutant's duties. Stay out of the sun. I need you to assemble the lists of killed and wounded. Verify every name, because I've got to dispatch them to General Shafter. And our boys dropped most of their equipment along the way. I'll need to see what has been recovered before they will resupply us from Siboney."

Hall felt relieved as he left Wood's tent. It was true, he felt like hell. And Jacob Schwaizer had been quartermaster for some weeks, so he would do a good job. The events of yesterday had become cloudy in Hall's mind and the sun made him sick, like an accusing eye. Making lists is something he knew he could still do. He had always believed that if a thing were written down, you could determine whether it was true or false.

*

Gabriel recognized the gaunt figure of Stephen Crane. The reporter stood in the shade of a palm tree and coughed into his handkerchief. Next to Crane a pink-faced officer in a British uniform fanned himself with his pith helmet. Despite the heat, a huge cigar protruded from his mouth. "Theodore," Crane said, "I'd like to introduce Leftenant Winston Churchill of Her Majesty's Fourth Hussars."

Roosevelt extended his hand. "Aha! Delighted, sir! So the English have come to see our fight!"

Churchill removed the cigar and regarded the dirty officer with the torn hat. "I am honored to meet you sir. I have read your books. And but for an accident of birth, I would be fighting with you. For my mother was born in Brooklyn."

Roosevelt laughed. "Then you are American enough."

The young officer fingered a medal on his chest. "The Spanish General Valdez would not decorate an American," Churchill bragged. "I was with him at the battle at Iguara."

Roosevelt blinked. "Never heard of that engagement. Who won?"

Churchill raised his chin. "Valdez, of course. And against a greater number of savage Cuban Colonials."

Roosevelt cocked his head.

"You must understand," Churchill sniffed, "Cristina of Spain is our beloved queen's niece. Spain and Britain are friendly, with a good deal in common."

Roosevelt's fixed smile began to dissolve. "You mean that blood is thicker than water."

The young subaltern colored, but held his aplomb. "I was sent to investigate the Cuban insurrection. I've seen the Spanish version. Now, as a journalist, I would like yours, sir."

But Roosevelt deferred. "No, you should talk General Wheeler."

The English lieutenant sucked on his cigar, but the fire had gone out. "I'm afraid, *shir*," he slurred, "I have not the time. Mister Crane and I have plans to move on."

From where he leaned against the trunk of the palm, Stephen Crane grinned. He had the look of a man who had set two fighting cocks against each other.

Churchill dropped his dead cigar to the ground. "Colonel Roosevelt, I hope your life is spared and that your losses are not great. But I must tell you that British sympathies lie with the Spanish. Between England and Spain, we have brought civilization to most of the uncivilized world. It is most unfortunate that American arms have escalated this rebellion into full scale war. Otherwise, the Spanish would have placated or subdued the Cubans by now. General del Rey assured me of that only last week."

Roosevelt had begun to scowl. And it seemed to Gabriel that in the grimace, his colonel's teeth multiplied. Gabriel felt suddenly sorry for him, with his polka dot kerchief pinned to the back of his battered hat, a sweaty field officer, addressing a tailored aristocrat.

Roosevelt raised his heels. "My young lieutenant, it seems that all you have acquired on your sojourn so far is a taste for Cuban panatelas."

As Churchill's face turned red, Stephen Crane laughed outright.

"You should know, sir," Roosevelt said, "that I am a Harvard man. And may I remind you that a few hundred feet from where I got my education, Colonel Washington took command of the Continental Army. That was well before he cooked your British goose at Yorktown. Some years later, after your continued bullying, John Paul Jones did it again! In the past, Britannia has dominated the world. But this island, my young subaltern, is ours! This will be our century. The tired potentates of Europe have had their day."

Churchill was at first speechless. "Colonel Roosevelt," he said, his voice faltering, "I shall report your words to the Queen, although they sound more like a President's, sir, than the second in command of a citizen regiment. By the time I see her, I shall likely be compelled to report your defeat. Nevertheless, my mother would wish for your personal safety. And, so sir, the best of luck." He turned to go, then said, "I've seen the fortifications in Santiago. You shall dearly need it."

"Get him out of here, Crane," Roosevelt said, "before I thrash him," his arm swept his circle of grizzled troopers, "and they will if I don't."

As they mounted to go, Stephen Crane wore a satisfied, yellow-toothed smile.

*

Snake and Gabriel were sharing some cold beans when the Generals rode up the hill. In the lead, general Shafter dwarfed his bay. Beside him, General Wheeler looked dried out. With Wood and Roosevelt, they rode out to a high point of ground and surveyed the enemy positions.

Shafter took his telescope, peered through it for some minutes, then handed it to Wheeler. Wheeler, after steadying his prancing mare, swept the terrain. Wood took it next, peering at the distant ridge. Then he passed it to Roosevelt who dismounted, dropped to one knee and pushed up his spectacles to take a look. Roosevelt looked ridiculous, crouched in the mud, his dirty blouse open at the neck. Were it not for the yellow stripe on his britches, Gabriel would have taken him for a teamster rather than an officer. Yet, it was this gritty quality that the men loved. While they respected Colonel Wood, they did not love him. .

On the hill, Shafter nodded.

Next to Gabriel, Cloud grunted. "Looks like we attack."

CHAPTER 21

Wednesday, June 29

The Cubans trotted by, but it was clear that Roosevelt did not expect much of them. At Las Guásimas, he remembered that the Cuban scouts disappeared as soon as the first shots were fired.

But to Colonel Raúl García, who led the Cuban column, the fight at Las Guásimas had been a case of *machismo*. Although the Americans had somehow won the day. But his *mambises* had been trained to hit and run when the *Peninsulares* least expected, not to hurl themselves at an entrenched enemy with repeating rifles. Such a charge was an act of selfishness and stupidity. A Cuban would think—who will take care of my widow and your children? And how will we recover our dead and wounded, something the Cubans did immediately. At Las Guásimas, García watched in disbelief as the *Yanquis* stepped over dying comrades to take a few yards of earth. Only later did medics hunt for the wounded. But by then many had bled to death, never knowing whether their sacrifice had meant anything.

His father, General Calixto García, had been too trusting. He had quickly placed five thousand Cubans under General Shafter's command, then had withdrawn to his headquarters to await the results. The old man's head had begun to ache again and he had taken to chewing coca leaves to ease the pain. As a result, Colonel Raúl García was supposed to obey any *Yanqui* officer who gave an order.

General Shafter decided that García should take some of his men and harass the Spanish as they withdrew. The rest were to cut Spanish supply lines. It was not a brilliant idea. His *mambises* had already done this many times, had been doing it for years. As a result they knew every foot of jungle trail and each ravine in the crease of the mountains.

García urged his horse ahead of the column of men who had so often fooled the Spanish with their rapid mobility. They could trot for five miles before they rested. They could do this because they carried very little with them and because they were peasants and farmers. Not one of them was slow and heavy like some of the *Yanquis*.

But today Colonel García was enraged. He had been sent far too late to cut off a force of eight thousand *Peninsulares*. According to General Rabí, the *Peninsulares* were marching from the Manzanillo in the west toward Santiago. Along the way, his largely barefoot *mambises* were to demoralize a well-heeled army. They would kill and wound many Spaniards. But General Shafter had refused García the repeating rifles or a troop of cavalry he needed to guarantee success.

The General did not understand that were too many Spaniard in Oriente to defeat by direct attack. Besides their superior numbers at Santiago and the column now advancing from the west, the Colonel knew there were ten thousand *Peninsulares* in nearby Holguín.

*

Gabriel bathed his wound. The redness had gone and it no longer hurt when he breathed. Now, his joints ached and his bowels were grumbling. He had begun to pass what looked like coffee grounds. Chills and headaches came when he least expected them. He began to feel bites all over his body.

Snake swore at the thermometer. "A hunnert and ten. And you shiverin'." Snake laughed, then began to shake too. "Y'know, a feller gits chilled goin' from a hunnert and twenny into the shade, ten degrees cooler."

They saw T. T. Cloud carry a protesting hen up the hill.

"Lordy, we'll have some meat," Snake cried.

"Not yet," Cloud said, stroking the chicken, "take off your clothes."

"But Sarge, we're both a'freezin'."

"You heard me," Cloud commanded. "Everything. Long johns too." Cloud stooped and picked up their filthy blanket.

When Gabriel and Snake had peeled everything off, Cloud wadded their clothes into the blanket and walked away. Snake's jaw dropped. "What the hell....?"

Gabriel stumbled out of rancho.

"Where you going, Snake?"

"With Cloud. I don't aim to fight the rest of this war nekkid!"

At the top of the hill, Cloud dropped the bundle onto the clay chimneys of an ant hill. He seemed to be talking to the chicken as he stroked it.

"I didn't know you wuz a medicine man," Snake said.

Cloud watched intently as the black ants swarmed over the trooper's filthy clothes.

Gabriel squatted on his heels. Suddenly, he felt a stinging pain in his penis. He leaped up, clawing at his groin. "They're biting!"

Snake laughed. "No, you burned your pecker on the ground. I tolt ya to tuck it under yer arm."

The two troopers shivered in the sun, wearing nothing but their brogans and sweat-stained hats, watching ants crawl over their duds. To make matters worse, Cloud wouldn't talk. He lifted the clothes with his bayonet and flipped them back onto the ant heap. The hen clucked, struggled. A few feathers floated lazily to the ant-covered earth. Now, Cloud seemed to be talking directly to the hen, holding her over Gabriel's yellowed long-johns. Then the Indian set her down and she began to peck.

Cloud stepped back. "Now you have seen a Lakota delousing station," he explained. "First, the ants eat the lice. Then the hen eats the ants." He grinned, looking more like the old Cloud, before he had become their sergeant. "Once you boys have had a bath and scrubbed your heads good, maybe we'll eat the chicken."

*

Richard Harding Davis read his account of Hall's ride aloud.

At Las Guásimas, while brave men lay dying, men like Captain
Capron and Sergeant Hamilton Fish, our Adjutant fled.

Although he claimed his intent was to save the regiment, his flight was
no way to do so. In fact, his action might well have panicked men who
saw their comrades fall in a hail of Spanish bullets. And this battle,
which was brilliantly won, might have been lost. The Adjutant has more
than the yellow stripe an officer wears on his trousers. His is very wide
indeed and every Rough Riders knows it runs right down his back.

Of over five hundred men fighting at Las Guásimas, only one ran.

Colonel Roosevelt looked doubtful. "I don't think you should print
that, Dick. We know that Hall broke and ran. But the fact remains that he is
an officer of our regiment. And such a dispatch will hardly help anyone's
cause. I have suffered more than most from Hall's mistake." He grimaced.
"Can you imagine how Edith must have felt when she read of our annihilation? Well, I blame Hall for that, along with the sour-grapes reporters in
Siboney who filed such hasty cables."

Richard Harding Davis thought for a moment, then he tucked his
dispatch away. "As you wish, Theodore. But I'd watch the man."

*

Back in New York, Julius thought it best to hide the morning newspaper. He was doing so when Edith Roosevelt caught him and snatched it
away. There, on the first page, she saw a small box with just a few lines, but
as she read, Edith felt faint.

Initial reports from Cuba indicate rash action by Roosevelt's Rough
Riders, which may have cost their commander's life. Colonel Leonard
Wood was fatally wounded during an ambuscade in the Cuban jungle,
according to a cable received yesterday. Some of Roosevelt's many critics
are calling for either his resignation or a court martial.

Edith read it again, then lifted the heavy telephone. "Operator," she
said breathlessly, I must speak to the War Department in Washington.

Secretary Alger's office. Yes, at once. I shall be waiting."

As she replaced the phone, her knees felt weak. Then she grew angry. But for a correspondent's tag given months ago, this story could just as well be about "Wood's Wranglers," or "McKinley's Mauraders." But no. "Roosevelt's Rough Riders" had stuck. She hated the name, and Theodore had made a grave mistake by not refuting it. Now Theodore was being blamed for an ambush and he did not even command the regiment! How could they court martial a man who was second in command?

Slowly, Edith's anger turned again to fear. It could just have easily been Theodore who had fallen. She heard the laughter of the children from the next room, and Edith Roosevelt had to fight back her tears.

*

Gabriel was hunting for Surgeon Church, hoping to get some quinine, when he heard Lieutenant Hall call.

"Scriven," Hall whispered from his tent, "do you have a minute?"

Gabriel hesitated. But he realized it was too late to pretend he had not heard. Besides, he could hardly ignore the command of an officer, even a chastened one.

Hall's normally fastidious cot was a mass of papers. As Gabriel stepped in, Hall ran his fingers through his hair.

"How can it be," Hall wondered aloud. "Men I turned into soldiers now shun me." He looked up with bleary eyes. "It simply is not fair. They have written me off. Have you, Scriven?"

But Gabriel was hardly listening. He had been transported back to that night when he too, had run. In that instant, his life had been changed. He had faced Spanish fire. He could die any day now, from fever or from a sniper's bullet. But he felt his death would mean something. He was part of something bigger. But, he realized, Hall had been cut out of it.

Without thinking, Gabriel lay his hand on Hall's shoulder, and he felt it shake as the Lieutenant began to sob.

PART IV *San Juan Hill*

CHAPTER 22

Thursday, June 30

Yellow fog hid the meadow where the regiment slept. But the hills were islands of green above the blanket of mist. The sky was pure and clean.

Gabriel pressed the bugle to his lips and puffed his cheeks. The notes tumbled into the fog. Soon, he began to hear coughs, curses, the rattling of gear—sounds of a rousing regiment.

On the next hill, the officers were already conferring. The figure of General Shafter dominated them all. Gabriel didn't see General Wheeler among them.

"What's old fatso lookin' at now?" Snake sneered over his cold bacon. "We know right where them garlics is at! Hell, with yer nekkid eye you can see their hats bobbin'."

T. T. Cloud chewed a blade of grass. "Yesterday, I counted twenty-five blockhouses. Every one inside a nest of barbed wire."

Off to the east, above the tops of the palm trees, against the blue-green slopes of the Sierra Maestra, a huge lopsided ball rose into the air. They watched in amazement as the thing struggled higher, quivering like an upside-down, floating pear.

The generals had turned and were watching their observation balloon's ascent. From his perch in the gondola, an officer shouted through a cone. "More line. That's right, pay it out!" As the huge orb lifted higher, Gabriel saw troopers paying out lines from the wagon to which it was tethered.

At the sound of Spanish rifle fire, all the troopers hit the dirt.

"Pull back! Shorten tether!" The balloon dipped, then descended and the gondola skidded through the brush, finally coming to rest. With his aides sitting on the sides of the gondola to hold it down, the officer ran around the still-inflated balloon. "They missed us! Well, we'll keep behind the rise." He threw a leg over the wicker gondola and riding it like a pony, clung to the shrouds. As the balloon lifted, two officers called out excitedly, one in Spanish and one in English.

"Looks like more fun than a barrel o' monkeys," Snake said.

Another trooper retorted, "You couldn't git me up in that thing in a million years."

"I'd love to ride in it," Gabriel admitted.

"Yeah, and git yer ass shot off by the garlics," Snake laughed.

When the balloon landed again, Gabriel ran over to help with the lines. "I'm Colonel Roosevelt's bugler and I'd sure like a ride."

Colonel Derby, chief engineer and map maker for the Fifth Corps, laughed. "This is not Coney Island, son. But tell you what. If you will help us deflate and roll the balloon, I'll take you up first."

Gabriel tossed his hat to Snake and climbed into the gondola. Derby nodded and as the men paid out the line. He felt himself jerked up and then the gondola swung over a circle of squinting Rough Riders.

The men grew smaller, and Gabriel could see the panorama of green hills was cut by yellow dirt paths and the white tents of the camp below him. The wind caught the balloon and Gabriel's stomach tightened. They moved silently, high along the tree tops. Gabriel heard the whinny of a horse, the sneeze of a trooper, the clank of tin cups. He and the Colonel were free of mud, bugs, and heat. A breeze pressed his cheek, and the gondola spun. Beyond Derby's shoulder, the mountains looked like giant green fingers plunging into the turquoise sea.

The horizon seemed to spin and Gabriel saw yellow gashes in the hillsides filled with white maggots. But he was seeing thousands of them and they were Spaniards. Their trenches were at angles to the road and punctuated by blockhouses surrounded by barbed wire that caught the sun. Below them, further down the shadowed slope of the hills, lay the terra-cotta roofs of Santiago. Beyond, the narrow harbor was sheltered from the sea by more mountains and Gabriel saw half-a-dozen warships anchored in the harbor.

Then something hit the balloon with a pop and it began to descend. Gabriel Scriven's world was again shrinking.

*

As soon as the brief downpour stopped, General Lawton's column moved out. Teamsters snapped whips and urged their mules through the mud. When the artillery had passed, churning the mud into soup, the infantry and dismounted cavalry came in columns of two, with the *squish, suck, squish* of boots in muck, clinking dangle of tin cups, the clack of bayonet scabbards. The troopers were silent as they struggled under soggy blanket rolls and bulky haversacks.

Men were so tightly packed that the press of those behind forced them onto the heels of those in front. As the Rough Riders fed into the column, Gabriel's eyes, like those of his comrades, were on the balloon at the head of their great blue and tan mass, a clanking serpent coiling up into the hills, its sinew mauling the earth, tearing bushes, and always the teamsters' whips, cracking like fireworks.

Aides rode back and forth along the narrow trail, splashing the men. "Will you bring your regiment up at once, sir!"

"General Wheeler's compliments, sir, but you are not to enter the trail yet."

Now they were at the grim business of war.

From the lip of the hill, Gabriel looked back. The column snaked back as far as he could see, a belt of bobbing Stetsons, gun barrels catching the sun, horses neighing. In that moment, sandwiched among thousands of marching troopers, he felt almost invincible. It was easy to believe that this army would march right over the Spaniards. They a huge, unstoppable machine, as irreversible as a steam engine. Gabriel's heart had sunk, when, from the balloon, he had seen the thousands of Spanish in their trenches. But now, from his perspective on the hill, with the Fifth Army stretching out so far ahead and so far behind, this mass of men, animals, and cannon, the enemy seemed puny.

As the balloon raced its shadow over them, he saw Colonel Derby unfurl Old Glory from the shroud lines, and the deep roar of a happy legion filled the air.

In the rear of the Rough Rider column, Marcus Hammer trudged through the mud with the hospital unit, shouldering Gabriel's carbine. He knew Lieutenant Church had noticed his rifle, but with so many enemy snipers about, he convinced Church to let him keep it. If the snipers were not observing the rules of war, Hammer had argued, why should the hospital corps? Why should he?

When the column passed the cooking fires of a Cuban camp, the aroma of roasting meat drifted toward the hungry troopers, and they began to jeer. The Cubans sat in small groups, intent on their eating. One man rose from his fire, pointed toward Santiago, then, smiling broadly, drew a finger across his throat.

Roosevelt rode back and forth, encouraging his men. He glanced over at the Cuban camp. "When we have won, we'll have to bar them from the city," Roosevelt said. "Left to their own devices, they will perpetrate a blood bath."

"What'd he say," Prayerful whined, hiking his blanket roll to a new spot against his neck.

Snake turned, "Colonel says get ready for perdition."

Prayerful quoted the Bible. "Narrow is the path of righteousness and broad is the road to destruction."

That evening the exhausted Rough Riders camped near an abandoned sugar factory on a hill the Cubans called El Pozo. Above, the sky held blue-white stars. But three miles away, across the misty basin where the Fifth Corps camped, the men could see the sulfurous lights of Santiago flickering.

As soon as Wood had set up headquarters in the factory building, he sent Gabriel to blow taps, then to fetch Roosevelt. When they returned, Wood was sitting behind his folding desk. "Well, Theodore," he smiled, "we have gotten our wish!"

Roosevelt looked puzzled.

Wood stood up. "Promotion! I've just come from General Young's headquarters." Wood looked pleased. "He has been brought down by fever. General Shafter has promoted me to Brigadier. As of tonight, I command the Second Brigade."

"Bully! Brigadier General Wood," Roosevelt grinned. "Has a nice ring, doesn't it?"

Wood accepted Roosevelt's pumping handshake. "And so, Theodore, you are now a full Colonel, in command of the Rough Riders."

Roosevelt shook his head, and grinned. It was the first time Gabriel had seen him speechless.

Wood turned serious. "There is more. How do you feel?"

"Splendid, sir!"

"Good. The fever is beginning to take its toll. Wheeler is down. General Sumner has been put in charge of all combined cavalry. He'll be your new commanding officer."

Roosevelt cleaned his glasses longer than usual. Finally, he set them over his nose. "The men will miss you, sir. And so shall I."

Brigadier General Leonard Wood smiled. "I don't believe you'll have time for such sentiments. Shafter has finally released his brake."

Roosevelt stiffened. "We'll be ready. I shall inform the men at once."

Wood waved his hand. "Let them sleep. They'll need it. Tomorrow will be the day of reckoning and we must win."

Then Wood's face took on a hopeful look. "The Cubans say Santiago is in a state of starvation. The Spanish are running out of food. The victors in this war will be famine and fever. Let's get all the quinine we can. Hall is too sick and dispirited to help much."

"I can get it from Miss Barton," Roosevelt said.

Wood nodded, "As you wish, Colonel."

It was the first time Wood had called him that and Roosevelt's chest swelled with pride. He quickly clasped Wood's forearm, then, uncomfortably moved, he dashed out of the tent.

CHAPTER 23

Friday, July 1

Crouched under the flap of Roosevelt's tent, Gabriel readied himself to blow reveille. Then the Colonel lay his hand on Gabriel's arm. "No, Gabriel. The enemy is too close." He grinned. "We mustn't spoil our game plan."

In the lantern light Roosevelt removed his Navy Colt from its oil-soaked rag and wiped it clean. Laying the revolver on his campaign table, he fed six forty-four caliber bullets into the cylinder and snapped it shut. His spectacles kept fogging in the humid air. Squinting, Roosevelt aimed the Colt at the San Juan Heights and puffing his cheeks, made a shooting noise. Then he sheathed the Colt and buckled the flap.

He opened his foot locker and removed extra spectacles. One pair, Roosevelt buttoned into his tunic. The other, he wedged inside the brim of his battered hat.

Acknowledging that Gabriel watched, the Colonel winked. "Just in case. The Rough Riders can little afford a myopic Colonel, can they, Scriven?"

*

They looked grimly eager, hovering over the lantern, almost like footballers forming an intricate play. Rain dripped from their hatbrims onto the map as the captains huddled close, watching their new Colonel put his finger on closely parallel lines like fingerprints that indicated the San Juan elevations. "General Sumner has relegated us to a secondary role," Roosevelt told then. "We are to support the Ninth Cavalry, here."

But he cut short his captains' protest. "We're soldiers, are we not? And we'll do as we're told." Then he raised his eyes and they saw the set of his jaw. "But I assure you, gentlemen, if the slightest opportunity presents itself, we'll pass the Ninth or any other outfit that gets in our way!"

Roosevelt straightened. "General Lawton will take two battalions of infantry and a battalion of Cubans." He waited for their reaction but there was none. "He'll attack El Caney, up here, along this road. That should take two hours. As soon as Sumner gets word of Lawton's victory, he'll send us across the forks of the San Juan river." His stubby finger poked the hills, whose elevation lines made them look like so many centipedes on the map, "We are to take these heights, above Santiago. At the same time, Lawton will swing southwest to close the line, along this road." He leaned back, his fists against his belt. "And we will have a strangle-hold on Santiago."

Captain Luna stared at the map. "And the enemy's strength, sir?"

"According to the Cubans, ten thousand," Roosevelt said. "But you know how they exaggerate. I doubt if the Spaniards have half that many."

Hoof beats and the rattle of heavy caissons ended their conference.

Roosevelt lifted the tent flap. Against the brightening sky, Captain Grimes's battery, three teams of six horses each, distinctive because of their crimson saddle blankets, hauled cannon up the hill.

It took the Rough Riders a while to form up. The cowboys had learned something from Las Guásimas, that bulk—the new shelter halves and blankets, were unnecessary. They went into a pile and the troopers concentrated on bare necessities—full bandoleers of cartridges, canteen and, carbine.

Finally the column began to move—slowly at first, gradually picking up speed, men stepping with purpose.

After an hour's march, the Rough Riders paused on a low ridge. Ahead of them the heights of San Juan rose from the mist, fortified with three blockhouses, rows of glinting barbed wire and behind breastworks, and a double row of the conical white sombreros.

A score of reporters and foreign military attaches watched Captain

Grimes position his cannon. Crimson saddle blankets seemed to glow in the mist as Grimes's lieutenants aligned the three guns, pointed them west, and began to calculate the range. When they had finished, Grimes opened his watch and spoke quietly to his cannoneers.

Gabriel and Roosevelt were watching this when distant thunder broke their concentration.

Roosevelt's head snapped up and his greasy glasses caught the sunrise. He lifted his telescope and pointed it north, gnashing his teeth as he focused in the dim light. "Lawton has begun." And indeed, the attack on El Caney sounded like the crackle of brush fire. Thick, white smoke, made pink by the rising sun, rose over the hills to the northeast.

An officer Gabriel at first did not recognize trotted his mare up the slope. "Lieutenant John J. Pershing, Tenth Cavalry, Colonel. Sir- I hate to intrude, but I do not advise setting up artillery in our ranks. The resulting smoke will make us a target for the enemy."

Roosevelt stared at this trim officer he knew commanded a company of buffalo soldiers. His big eyes narrowed behind his oval glasses.

Pershing pointed to Lawton's distant smoke. "That's what our position will look like after Grimes begins firing. The enemy artillery will train on our smoke and we will pay for it dearly."

Roosevelt saw that the Tenth was deployed to the right of the hillock, a contingent of Cubans in front, while the Rough Riders occupied the left slope. He paused, and his voice took on an uncertain, high pitched tone. "But Grimes requires this high ground, does he not?"

"Some other hill," Pershing urged, "not this one."

The voice of Grimes ended their debate. "Range two thousand five hundred yards!" The breech on the first cannon closed with a clang and the gun was swung into position. A trooper squinted over the sights. Cranking, he lowered the barrel an inch. Number two gun was adjusted in the same manner.

Captain Grimes raised his chin. The cannoneers stood ready. "Number one FIRE!"

A mighty report shook their muddy hillock as a shell went soaring over the valley, beyond the first ridge, then burst, sending a fountain of yellow dirt into the air. Coughing in a cloud of smoke, Gabriel heard Grimes bark, "Too much elevation! Number TWO. Two-four-five-c' ' ¯

San Ju

Again the blast, and the screaming shell whistled ever lower, then exploded, this time on the ridge. A roar arose from the men.

"Same range. Fire three!"

The third shell screamed high into the sky. The men's eyes burned in the smoke, but they followed its dying whistle. It hit a Spanish blockhouse, sending roof tiles high into the air. A cheer, greater than the first, tore from the throats of the troopers.

Roosevelt surveyed the damage as each shell exploded. Between shots the men heard what at first sounded like the echoes of their cannon.

Grimes had ceased shelling long enough for the smoke to clear. "Lawton is still heavily engaged," Roosevelt yelled. "And we've already sent the enemy nineteen projectiles!"

Captain Grimes stormed out of the smoke, his saber raised as though to strike. He bellowed at the reporters and foreign observers who had been distracting his gunners, pointing out likely targets. "Get off my hill! Go file your blasted reports!"

Conditioned to obey, the foreign officers withdrew a respectful distance. But the reporters were another matter. An exasperated Grimes finally enlisted Roosevelt's help in persuading Davis, whom the other reporters would follow, to leave as well.

"You can come back when Captain Grimes has finished," Roosevelt promised. "You shall certainly be advised before when we attack."

The hill had no sooner been cleared of civilians when the report of the Spanish Mausers began. Now familiar with the sound, Gabriel hit the dirt. Roosevelt did not order return fire.

Snake lay on the ground swearing at the zinging bullets as they hit the ground around him. Grimes was about to resume firing, the smoke having cleared somewhat, when a loud pop from the Spanish lines, defined by a tiny bluish ring of smoke, grew into a screaming projectile, ever louder until it was directly over their heads. Following the deafening blast, there was silence, then screams of agony. Shrapnel had wounded a dozen men. Another enemy shell screeched in on them as Grimes brought his saber down.

Lightning had twice struck in their midst. Roosevelt, seeing the men confused and horrified at the effects of aerial bombardment, sprang into the saddle of the frantic Texas. The Rough Riders had already begun running in all directions. "Scriven! Blow!"

Roosevelt galloped among the men, yelling for them to get behind the hill, for in their haste some had run into the open.

Below the hillock, a Spanish shell burst directly on a farmhouse where Cubans had taken shelter, blowing men out through the windows like limp sacks. In the scorching smoke, dead and wounded Cubans lay everywhere.

Roosevelt reared his horse. "No, no! BEHIND the hill! Scriven, for God's sake. Blow retreat."

But Gabriel's horn had been punctured and would make little more than a bleating sound. He closed his finger over the hole and this time the bugle responded.

Roosevelt took a glove in his teeth and jerked it off. He stared at his hand and saw blood. He seemed awed and proud of his slight wound. The Colonel's teeth flashed until he heard the approaching screech of another Spanish shell.

In the piercing silence that followed the blast, a trooper stared at the stump where his knee had been. The hideous shrapnel wound spurted blood. The trooper opened his mouth to say something, then fainted.

With a grunt another trooper fell. Gabriel thought the man had been hit, but when the man turned, he saw Eli Biddle's face. "Now don't you run too," Biddle growled. "Whatever you do, don't, or my boys might shoot you." Biddle drew the bolt on his carbine and slammed it shut. Then he aimed at the distant ridge as though his shot would protect them from the fiery bursts over head.

Gabriel started to get up, but Biddle shoved him flat.

"I've got to get back to Roosevelt!" Gabriel protested.

"Forget that glass-eyed dude," Biddle spat. "Unless you want to be minced meat, stay put! The Tenth Cav is gonna hold this hill."

Gabriel lay his head against the dirt, waiting for the next shell. But instead, he heard the earth reverberate with pounding hoof beats. He looked up to see Colonel Wood jerk his horse to a halt near the cannon. Wood gestured to Captain Grimes, then pointed east.

A shot rang out, and Wood's horse staggered and fell. Without thinking, Gabriel jumped up and, despite Biddle's protest, ran toward the fallen Wood. His leg had been pinned under the fallen animal. Gabriel got the terrified horse to roll enough to extricate Wood's boot from where it had been tangled in the stirrup. Wood struggled to his feet, avoiding the mare's flailing hooves. Her eyes were white with terror and a bloody froth issued from her mouth. Wood borrowed Gabriel's bayonet, cut the bridle and slipped the bit out of her mouth, all the while stroking her head and speaking softly.

Then he drew his Colt, cocked, aimed at her forehead and fired. One reflexive jerk and the mare was dead. Leonard Wood turned on Grimes, his face furious. "I said, Captain Grimes, withdraw your pieces! At once!"

*

In the shelter of the hill, Roosevelt rode about, rallying his men. He soon formed the Rough Riders in a column of twos. Just ahead, the Ninth were loading their carbines. The column of blue shirts and dark faces stretched down the road and into the tree line.

The troopers made way for the wounded, stepping back as they hobbled toward the rear on crooked sticks, some helped by comrades. There was no bantering. The impersonal slaughter of artillery had shocked everyone and many troopers could not hear because of the concussion of the shells.

Three Cubans carried a wounded officer in a hammock slung on a pole. His white uniform was splattered with blood. A barefoot rebel trotted alongside, trying to hold his commander's tunic closed over a loop of intestine. The wounded man cried, *"Madre de Dios!"* as the straining men who carried him fiercely repeated the rosary.

*

The men were waiting in the double column that could not move. Above the trees, against the steep mountain, they saw the observation balloon shiver, then rise. Colonel Derby shouted to his ground crew as they worked the lines, tugging him toward the head of the column, stumbling past impatient, wise-cracking troopers.

"Well, I declare, if it ain't Derby's circus a-comin' to town."

"Where's the peanuts?"

"Be ridin' elephants next!"

Lieutenant Hall rode up the hill. His horse had finally recovered from sea sickness and he had given his mule to Stephen Crane. Hall wore a clean uniform, for he had an important dispatch from General Sumner.

Roosevelt discarded his tunic and hastily pinned his Colonel's epaulets onto the shoulder of his blue shirt. He looked more like a scavenger than an officer. Roosevelt studied the dispatch for a moment, then turned to Captain O'Neill. "It seems they doggedly resist at El Caney. Shafter is sending them reinforcements. We're to cross the Aguadores River, wherever that is, and from there, on Sumner's signal, support the attack on the San Juan heights." He removed his battle map from a saddle bag and flattened it against the flank of Texas. "But gentlemen, I see no such stream."

"It's dead ahead, sir," Captain Luna said. "Aguadores is the Cuban name. Your map has it as a continuation of the San Juan."

His task done, Lieutenant Hall tried to swing himself up into the saddle, but something had gone out of him. Again, white faced, he tried to mount. No one stepped forward to help him but Gabriel. The troopers muttered dark curses as they watched him spur his horse to the rear.

*

Colonel Derby's balloon, flanked by a squadron of vultures, led the long column. As the Rough Riders waded across the shallow Aguadores river, they dragged their canteens in the muddy water to fill them. General Sumner called to Hall. "Make those men stop, Lieutenant. They are holding up the advance." So as each man hesitated, trying to fill his empty canteen from the stream, Hall commanded him to stop. Under General Sumner's eye, the thirsty troopers cursed with frustration.

The road widened and followed the creek through a valley of scorched guinea grass.

Ahead, Gabriel could hear Derby's shouts, but with the aftermath of the bombardment still ringing his ears, he could not distinguish the words. Balloon tenders pulled Derby back along the line. From his gondola, a hundred feet up, Derby shouted, "Is there a General Officer down there?"

Roosevelt bellowed, "I am the ranking officer, sir!"

"I am to report but to General Sumner or General Hawkins."

Roosevelt cupping his gloves next to his mouth. "You'll find Generals further to the rear. Perhaps you can tell me what you see?"

The balloon was over Roosevelt now, and he stood in its shadow. Colonel Derby pointed west. "Nearly a mile up, just before the river forks, a trail splits off to the left. Heads southwest of the heights. Get word to General Kent."

"I shall certainly do so, Colonel."

Derby signaled his men to tow him back to the head of the column.

The Rough Riders were moving again when the Spanish artillery again opened up. Officers shouted encouragement. "Steady, men. Do not break rank."

They came to a turn in the trail and waded into the shallow creek. To the left, the New York Seventy-First had been hit with a shell burst, and the men had taken cover in the brush. When they saw Roosevelt on Texas they recognized him and began to cheer. "Hip, hip, hooray. Its Roosevelt!"

But Theodore was not pleased. "Why are you not advancing? Are you New Yorkers or not?"

The cheering died and the Seventy-First, all spit and polish back in Tampa, sat on their sky-blue britches and let the Rough Riders pass.

Roosevelt turned in his saddle, as if to apologize to Bucky O'Neill. "It's not their fault. They are good men, but poorly led."

From the tree line ahead, the Spanish were firing at the balloon. Troopers had learned from the screech of the shells whether they were coming close and when a burst exploded in the air, near Colonel Derby's balloon, Snake yelled out. "They got the goldanged circus! Sure enough, Gabe! Hell, that's what they're shootin' at. Look, she's hit and she's a-comin' down!"

Derby's gondola sank a little, then, like a kite that had caught a breeze, rose again. The men at first cheered, then, as they realized the balloon was drawing Spanish fire down on them, they began to shake their fists at it.

The enemy rifle fire was like sleet as L Troop reached the fork of the river. Wounded men floated in the water, which was turning purple with blood. The column was jammed up and could not move. There was nowhere for the men to take cover. The sun glared off the water and it was hotter than a prairie fire.

Gabriel stood waist deep in the stream and let his bladder empty. The blank expression on Snake's dirty face indicated that he was doing the same, then Snake pitched forward and his hat floated away.

"He's been hit," Prayerful yelled, diving into the shallow water. He soon hauled Snake up by his suspenders. He had been hit in the right shoulder.

"I'm punctured," Snake coughed, as Gabriel and Prayerful held him above the surface so he could breathe.

Roosevelt waded Texas into the stream. The horse held steady as Roosevelt, his teeth set, unsheathed his navy Colt, laid the long barrel across his fore-arm, and to the men's delight, fired at Colonel Derby's balloon. But his gesture was one of frustration rather than effect. The balloon was well out of pistol range. The Spanish had done better. Now the balloon was full of holes and it sagged and began to sink.

Roosevelt had seen enough, and he led the Rough Riders out of line. "Follow me, men!"

Gabriel and Prayerful tried to walk with Snake, but he cursed and fought them. Finally Prayerful stooped, and taking Snake's good arm lifted him across his back.

Roosevelt took his column to the right of the position he had been ordered to hold. There the Rough Riders would receive less of the arching fire. The Colonel, ignoring the whizzing bullets, rode among his men, shouting encouragement even as some were hit and slumped to the ground.

"Steady, boys. When we see them, by God we'll make them pay!"

"Then let us shoot, sir!"

But there was nothing to shoot at. The Mauser fire came from over the trees.

Prayerful eased Snake to the ground. Unsheathing his bayonet, he cut snake's shirt away from his shoulder. The bullet had caught him below the socket, and had missed the bone. Snake kept up a steady threat. "Show me those God damned garlics!"

Spanish bullets rained on the Rough Riders. At the ford, the Ninth had moved to get out of the withering fire. But now, with the Seventy-First still cowering beside the trail, there was no attacking column at the center.

*

The wounded continued to pass, stumbling, some groping like blind men. An ambulance wagon rattled by, loaded with bleeding men. One trooper rolled off and the teamster of the following wagon did not see him in time. After the wagons had passed, the dead trooper's back remained dented where iron-clad wheels had crushed it.

Another unconscious trooper was carried by on a stretcher. His white belly was exposed, and on it Gabriel saw that someone had laid a severed finger. Then, Gabriel realized that the brown, truncated thing was not a finger after all.

At the ford, Surgeon Church and his men were overwhelmed with wounded. Some floated, face down in the river. On the bank, Church saw one of the dead move. But the corpse had merely been struck again by a sniper.

Marcus Hammer hauled one trooper after another from the water. He laid each down in the grass and headed back for the next, as Church bent over each victim.

As the Mauser fire poured in over the trees, Prayerful bandaged Snake's shoulder, using a first aid kit from Church's haversack. Printed diagrams on each bandage showed how to tie a tourniquet, splint a compound fracture, and sling a broken arm. Gabriel read while Prayerful worked. The wound was ugly, black, and swollen and had not bled enough to purge itself.

"Not so danged tight," Snake complained.

Gabriel helped Snake to his feet. Somehow, through the wounding, Snake had kept a grip on his carbine.

"Better git," Prayerful said, nodding toward the rear.

Cradling the carbine with his good arm, Snake grinned. "Here's jest fine."

Gabriel could see that Church's men, wearing white arm bands, were getting hit. Two of them lay wounded and Snake saw it too.

Snake shook his head. "I ain't a-goin' from the frying pan to the fire. I'll take my chances here."

Lieutenant Hall waded his horse across the ford and dismounted where Church bent over one of the wounded medics. They lifted him and lay him across Hall's saddle. Then Church helped Hall up behind the saddle and slapped the horse's flank.

Snake's angry eyes watched him go. "That's the last we'll see of Hollerin' Hall."

*

All the bandages were used up and the Rough Riders had not yet fired a shot. Roosevelt moved them a few hundred yards, below the first hill, the summit marked by a giant, overturned kettle. "Two hours as sitting ducks!" Roosevelt fumed.

Bucky O'Neill removed his Stetson, wiped his brow with a sleeve, then carefully set it back to the same angle. "Colonel Hamilton of the Ninth is waiting for Sumner's order."

"Damn those West Pointers," Roosevelt swore. "And where is General Sumner? CONFERRING, no doubt. And well in the rear. We know we are supposed to advance. But our boys are dying needlessly."

A squadron of Cubans loped by, surprisingly graceful for such ragged men. Gabriel recognized the Chinese-Cuban and shouted, *"Amigo, qué va?"* The Cuban pointed up toward the kettle, and the long trench with fire coming from it. *"Mariánje,"* he said, and Gabriel knew the name of the hill they were going to try to take.

The *mambises* seemed to sense victory. And why not, Gabriel thought—so close to Santiago, with thousands of *Yanquis* at their backs. Gabriel watched them splash across the stream, each man scooping a palm of water for a quick drink, losing not a breath of time.

But Roosevelt could hardly contain himself as he watched the Cubans trot past the Ninth, veer left, then round the base of a hill he already considered his private objective. "Scriven. Sound the advance."

As Cloud and his squad crawled through the guinea grass, Spanish bullets sang over Gabriel's head. Above them, the Spanish fired in volleys then fell back into their trenches while their second line stood and waited for their officer's saber to drop. They fired and more troopers fell.

Ignoring the Spanish volleys, Roosevelt rode back and forth. "Stay low, boys. But advance steadily. " Gabriel wanted to pull him down, thinking that he would be hit.

But now that they were somewhat protected from the angle of fire, Roosevelt rode to each captain, making sure they edged their men into a massed position at the foot of the hill.

Gabriel leaned up on an elbow and found a Spaniard in his sights. He squeezed the trigger, the man pitched backward and Gabriel felt a rush of blood, exactly like the first time he'd shot a rabbit. That's it, he reasoned. These are just rabbits, deadly rabbits in white hats.

The Rough Riders' brown britches blended with the grass; their Stetsons, too. But their navy blue shirts looked almost black. Their side gray suspenders, bracketing vital organs—almost begged for bullets by Spanish marksmen. The trick was to hug the grass, and to crawl in a jerky pattern.

Gabriel, cradling a borrowed bugle, tried to stay close to Roosevelt, but the Colonel kept riding off, shouting orders. "When, in God's name, will Sumner give his signal?"

"I'm ready to blow the charge, Sir."

Roosevelt watched as his troopers crawled like turtles in the grass. Halfway up the kettled hill, he could see many strands of barbed wire glistening in the sun.

"We've got to move," Roosevelt said. "To hell with Sumner. Cloud! Pass the word!"

Trotting Texas back and forth, standing in his stirrups to see his men,

Roosevelt called, "Gabriel! You may blow the CHARGE!"

Roosevelt could barely hold the horse, trained to bolt at the thrilling call to close with the enemy.

Four hundred blue-shirts rose as one and began to wade forward in the knee-high grass, Krags across their chests. They walked first in single file, troop by troop, then fanned out, as the Spanish stood and fired their Mausers down into them. The footing was slippery and the Rough Riders crept up the slope like men on ice.

Roosevelt rode through the men, while his officers waved their sabers ever forward. Mauser bullets singed the tops of the grass. Men fell, but the slow, deliberate stroll toward the crest continued.

Finally Texas scraped the first barbed wire barrier and Roosevelt jumped down, slapped his gloves against his horse's flanks, and sent him off. Then he tied his kerchief to the point of his saber and circled it over his head.

At the barbed wire fence Prayerful stabbed L Troop's pennant into the ground and worked his wire cutters. One strand snapped into a coil as the bullets kicked up dirt around him. The second strand gave, then the third, and Roosevelt stepped calmly through. Gabriel and the blue-shirts stumbled forward, faster now, falling to shoot, then running again. Roosevelt's powerful legs worked like pistons as he puffed ahead of Gabriel.

Most of the men were caught at the wire. They began to beat the wire down with their rifle butts. Just above them, the top of the hill roared and flashed with flame. The Rough Riders seemed to waver and Roosevelt screamed, "I'll shoot any man who retreats."

Ahead of him, Gabriel saw a trooper fall. As he stepped over him, he was sprayed with the man's blood.

Just ahead, Roosevelt's glasses had been knocked off. Blindly guiding his saber with his fingers, he sheathed it, opened his breast pocket, and blew the dust from his reserve spectacles. Under deadly fire, calm as a banker, he fitted them over his nose and squinted up the hill. Then he drew his Navy Colt and Gabriel heard him yell, "To the summit, boys!"

Then, the Rough Riders were over the crest, screaming and jumping over Spaniards laying dead and wounded in their trenches. Bucky O'Neill's pistol barked and a Spaniard dropped. Cloud knocked one of the enemy down with his rifle butt, then shot him in the chest.

But above them, on the San Juan heights, the Spanish directed a withering cross fire down on the Rough Riders. Yet, as bullets pinged off the iron kettle, Roosevelt walked back and forth like a rooster. Now, troopers from the Ninth ran up and planted their standard. One elated, blue-pants sergeant tore up the hill with a squad of Seventy-First New Yorkers.

But the Spanish continued to make the men who had taken the kettled hill pay. Roosevelt rallied his officers near the iron pot. Bucky O'Neill conferred with the Colonel briefly, then stood up, pacing back and forth.

Mauser rounds pinged off the kettle and Captain Luna yelled, "O'Neill, take cover, or Prescott will have a new mayor."

"Max," Bucky scoffed, "the Spanish bullet has not been made that can put me out of office!"

No sooner had he spoken these words than his head burst open.

Roosevelt ran to him, bent down, then rising, rubbed his bloody hands on his shirt.

Now, crouching in the shelter of the kettle, Roosevelt had his first good view of the main Spanish fortifications on the long, s- shaped heights of San Juan. There were three blockhouses, the biggest commanding the southern end. He was heartened to hear the heavy drumming of American Gatling guns as they kicked up dust near the blockhouse. Spanish sombreros ducked.

A bugle sounded from the left and as the staccato cadence of the Hotchkiss guns joined in to make the Spanish duck, the Rough Riders watched Hawkin's Eighth and Ninth Infantry march out into the open ground between the hills and begin to advance. In the center, the Negro Twenty-Fourth Infantry filled the gap and began a slow advance.

Roosevelt jumped up. "Egad! The INFANTRY is moving."

Just then, a Negro trooper of the Tenth Cavalry ran up to Roosevelt. "Our colonel has been killed, sir."

"Then have your men follow me. We'll take the right flank! Come on boys," he said in his high-pitched voice.

As Roosevelt started forward, followed only by himself and a few troopers, Gabriel realized that neither the Rough Riders nor their captains had understood their colonel's intention. Roosevelt had gone a hundred yards before he turned, and seeing that his men had not followed, began to admonish them.

"You gave no command sir," Gabriel shouted. The Colonel made an exasperated gesture and screamed, pointing toward the San Juan Heights,

"Then forward, MARCH!" To make sure they heard over the crackle of gunfire and the drumming of the Gatings, Gabriel blew the advance. And the Rough Riders arose and followed Roosevelt.

Gabriel dropped to one knee and squeezed off two rounds. The Gatlings were raking the hill in front of them, in effect cutting off their advance. Roosevelt, furious that his men were not following fast enough, waved his Colt and pointed it toward the block- house, where the infantry had already covered the southern end of the s-shaped hill.

The Spanish returned fire, but were falling back as they saw two regiments of Negro troopers, bayonets fixed, charging the center. With the Rough Riders closing on one side and the Ninth Cavalry on the other, the hilltop seemed to burst with flame as the Spanish fired one last volley. Many troopers fell, but the eyes of the rest were on their goal and they doggedly waded through the high grass as though it were water, hacking at the barbed wire with bayonets and rifle butts, ripping the posts on which it was strung from the ground, and when all that failed, falling across it as men stepped over them. Whether following officers or not, whether in columns or alone, the troopers continued to come, although they seemed not enough to take the hill in the face of such deadly fire.

The Spanish line broke first where the Ninth Cavalry led the advance, and as they turned and ran, Yankee troopers—men of all colors and units—swarmed up the slope and onto the sweeping double curve of San Juan Hill.

As the Ninth concentrated on clearing the blockhouses, Sergeant Eli Biddle planted the Tenth Cavalry standard. Next to him, the Rough Rider First Volunteer Cavalry pennant went up and further down, some troopers of the First Cavalry speared the bloody soil with their own.

The exhausted troopers began to cheer and congratulate each other.

But Roosevelt, still not content, watched the Spanish run down the back of the hill into a palm grove. "After them, boys!" Roosevelt screamed to his exhausted men.

Gabriel followed the indefatigable Colonel as well as he could. Running under constant fire had turned his legs to rubber. But he soon reached the shade of the grove.

There, Roosevelt put his finger to his lips and motioned for the handful of men who had followed to fan out.

Ahead, through the maze of gray trunks, Gabriel saw a slight movement. A horse whinnied, then came a shout, "*Carga!*"

Their sabers drawn, the Spanish cavalry galloped out of the grove toward the troopers. Gabriel fired but his second shot was a click as the hammer fell on an empty chamber. Roosevelt's Colt was empty too.

A Spanish officer galloped toward Roosevelt with his saber pointed for the kill. On instinct, Gabriel stepped in front of Roosevelt and raised his trumpet, catching the point of the saber. The Spaniard's arm cracked as the saber pierced the horn, knocking both Gabriel and Roosevelt to the ground. As Gabriel shook off the blow he saw the Spaniard wheel his horse and stare at his useless arm. Then someone shot him out of his saddle. Gabriel swung up onto the officer's horse. The Spaniards scattered and rode pell-mell into the grove. Gabriel followed but quickly encountered a troop of Spanish infantry who immediately threw up their hands in surrender.

Roosevelt was examining the saber-imbedded bugle when the Spanish prisoners walked out of the trees, their hands on their heads. Behind them rode his trumpeter.

He could barely speak. "Scriven, I believe I owe you my life."

Gabriel dismounted near the wounded Spanish officer, who had been shot in the other arm. Amazingly, he had red hair and blue eyes. Gabriel offered him a drink from his canteen. His face was a mask of disbelief. "*Gracias, caballero,*" he gasped, after he had drunk, then he said, "It must be the will of God, for you have beaten me with *musica.*"

Roosevelt made an unusual decision. "Let the prisoners take him to their hospital. We cannot care for him properly here."

When Gabriel had translated this, the Spaniards made a seat with their hands and took their red-haired Colonel into the trees.

*

The cross-fire was heavy. At the south end of San Juan Hill, below the captured blockhouse, the New York Seventy-First marched out into the open and massed against the barbed wire. Under heavy Spanish fire, the first rank knelt, shouldered their ancient Springfields and fired a black powder volley at the Spaniards. As they bent to reload, engulfed in white smoke, the Spanish returned a volley and a dozen of them fell.

Watching from the San Juan heights, Roosevelt sputtered, "do they think this is Gettysburg?" But the New Yorkers did not break rank. Tightening their archaic formation, they held the position long enough for the Gatlings to move to a safer position.

*

Gabriel gulped a mouthful of water. Roosevelt had given him the saber-impaled bugle and now he stared at it, hardly believing what had happened. It was as though the movement had been a musical score and he had raised the bugle to blow at exactly the right interval. It was like a dream now and he was a player in it, certain that he had saved a life, but certainly no hero.

Along the three hundred yards of San Juan Hill, troopers lay completely spent. Few had eaten or drunk anything all day, and the rush of battle over for the moment, they could only fall and pant. The wounded and dead men and horses lay around them. A thousand yards before them, across the valley of palm trees, the red tiled roofs of Santiago shimmered in the heat.

*

The usual afternoon downpour did not come. Time refused to pass. The men squatted in the trenches listening to Spanish snipers shoot at corpsmen as they tried to get the wounded to the dressing station behind the hill.

Roosevelt, with Captains Luna and Llewellyn, patrolled the crest, soberly tallying their losses. They stopped at Gabriel's trench and crouched in the dirt. Luna told of how a wounded Spanish officer explained that the Gatlings were very bad. If a man put up a finger, the officer had told him, it would be taken by sheets of bullets. Until then, the Spanish were sure that they had the *Americanos* beaten.

Roosevelt's glasses were opaque with dust except where a rivulet of sweat had cut a path. There was a large welt on the back of his hand. "We started this morning with five hundred men and twenty-six officers," he said. "Now O'Neill is dead and five more officers have been wounded. I can only count about four hundred men." He put his glasses on and cocked his head up, calculating the angle of the sun. "Five more hours of daylight. We could lose even more."

Snake had stuffed his kerchief into his wound. "Colonel, some of our boys got mixed up with the colored boys. I saw Cloud leadin' a bunch of 'em when we took the hill."

Roosevelt nodded vigorously. "Yes, men of every persuasion. This has been magnificent. When Davis gets here, I shall make sure that every one gets the credit he deserves." He turned to Gabriel. "A Chief Trumpeter who foils death with his bugle. First he saves my horses with it, then my very life!"

Roosevelt clasped his arm around Gabriel's shoulders. "This was my hour, my wonderfully crowded hour, and it shall never be forgotten."

All over the hill, men, lying in the trenches, troopers called out. "Hey Jim, you make it, Jim?"

"Who's that? Yancee?"

"Why no. Its Silas."

After a pause came the reply. "What outfit?"

"Why A Troop, what else?"

"I'm in L. Anybody seen Jim?"

Soon, Eli Biddle put his shining face down next to Gabriel's.

"We've come up to relieve you boys. Go git yourselves some grub."

Gabriel was glad to see him. "I saw the Tenth on our left. You boys scared the pants off the Spanish. One of the captured said they thought you were Haitians."

Biddle chuckled. "Yeah, they get spooked by darkies."

Slowly, the Rough Riders dragged themselves up, encouraged by the prospect of their first food in over nine hours. After a handful of soggy hardtack and a cup of warm water, Gabriel tried to sleep.

*

Behind Kettle Hill, three large tents and half a dozen smaller ones marked the field hospital. There were many wounded and dying. Unlike the troopers at Las Guásimas, shot clean with Mausers, many of these men groaned, clutching blasted limbs.

In the large tents, surgeons worked on the worst cases. The smaller tents held men they thought could wait. Then there were some who had walked in who were sitting in the grass, waiting to be classified.

When a sniper's rifle shot rang out, the wounded jerked as though they had been hit again.

Gabriel recognized Snake's voice. "You're a goddamned liar! You ain't puttin' that on me!" A young orderly struggled to pin a red, white, and blue ribbon to his suspenders.

"Gabe," Snake begged, "No! That's how they tag the dyin'!"

The orderly lifted his knee from Snake's chest and handed the ribbon with a twist of copper wire to Gabriel. "Then you do it. Get it on his right suspender quick. Left side means he's a goner."

In one row of half-naked men, most had ribbons pinned on the left.

Snake closed his eyes. "Each time I conk out they drag me closer to the deads." Then opened them and gazed at Gabriel. "Gabe, you look none too good, pardner. Like death warmed over."

*

This time, she had commandeered a wagon. Clara Barton and Doctor Hubbell sat on boxes of supplies, and Gabriel heard her remark, "If there was anything more terrible than this in the War between the States, I did not see it. Why, we must have a thousand wounded."

"I think more," Doctor Hubbell said, as they watched men still staggering into the hospital.

If she heard, Miss Barton made no sign. She seemed to be praying.

*

In the purple twilight, Gabriel fed Snake a gulp of Red Cross cider. Then he took one himself and savored the stewed apples and prunes, mixed with lime juice.

Miss Barton brought a coconut cup full of gruel and Gabriel and Snake shared it. Ignoring groans and occasional screams from the surgery tents, Gabriel sipped the hot liquid.

In the darkening tents, surgeons turned on their lanterns. Then, a shot rang out and the order was passed to extinguish all lights. Grim-faced, Clara Barton palmed dirt onto her cooking fire.

As soon as the moon was full, surgeons took their tables out of the tents and they probed, operated, and amputated as best they could. Now and again, despite the sniper fire it was bound to draw, a candle flickered as orderlies shielded the light so that they could work.

By then, Gabriel had moved Snake to a tent farthest from the dead.

With Snake taken care of, Gabriel returned to his trench and lay back between the piles of dirt. He was staring up at the full moon when the silhouette of a head with a tall feather appeared against the disk of white. Cloud was back! "Where have you been," Gabriel asked. "I thought you'd been hit."

Cloud squatted in the trench. "With the Tenth. They lost half of their officers, thought I was one of them. Shoved me some dead Lieutenants bars and told me to lead the charge."

After a very long silence, Cloud said, "I'm going away for a few days. And I don't want anybody to know but you." He fingered the pouch that hung from his neck.

Gabriel started to speak, but Cloud held up his hand. "When I came of age," he said, "I intended to go on my vision quest. And come back marked with the signs of it." T.T. Cloud let out a long, sad sigh. Then he muttered something in Lakota that trailed off into the night like vapor. Finally he spoke again, in a flat lifeless way. "The government agent put me into the Indian school. There they tried to purge the tribal ways from every Lakota boy. I did not realize we could never get them back." Cloud shook his head. "They promised the old ones blankets and cornmeal through the hard winters. And the price was for their sons to wear stiff collars and new shoes the agent provided.

"Still, I vowed I would go on my quest as soon as I had the chance. Then I got lost in the way the Indian School worked. They said I was a good student, gave me awards. This clouded my mind. And soon, I had forgotten my promise." After a long pause, Cloud stood up. The moonlight fell on the planes of his face. "Now I must do it. I can feel a vision, but it cannot reach me among so many men."

A heavy, dark smell hung in the night air. Gabriel realized they were in a place of ripening fruit and ripening bodies.

"Not every Oglala seeks a vision," Cloud said, "But I knew I must. And now I will." He lay his cool, hard hand on Gabriel's arm. "I'll need a horse," he said, "Roosevelt's horse."

"Have you gone loco?"

As Cloud's smiled, his teeth caught the moonlight. "Maybe," he said. "But we have taken the last hill before Santiago. Now, as the braves used to say after a battle, is the big bellies' time."

"Huh?" Now Gabriel was thoroughly confused

"Chiefs," Cloud explained, "generals. Now there will be plenty of talk and not much fighting. That's when you go—not when your tribe needs you. And I need a strong mount that will not be missed."

"But Roosevelt's horse!" Gabriel gestured toward the sky. "You might as well ask for the moon. You'll just have to steal a pony. Or walk."

Touch-the-Cloud shook his head. "No, it is too far. And Texas has the lungs for it.

Wait until after I'm gone, then tell Roosevelt I have gone to speak to the fathers. And that I needed a horse with good medicine. He'll know what I mean."

Despite his surprise, Gabriel was intrigued with Cloud's idea. He began to realize that each of them had a quest and that his own was to pump Biddle for everything he could learn about his father.

Gabriel asked, "Where are you going?"

Cloud did not reply, but he was looking east toward the hump of mountain that blocked the stars.

At least, Gabriel thought, Cloud won't be going toward the enemy. He allowed his friend some silence, wondering how he could ever get Roosevelt's horse.

Finally Cloud spoke. "I would ask Roosevelt myself, but that would put him in a bad position."

"Oh, but it's okay for me to risk court martial by stealing his horse."

The Indian smiled. "They think you're white, remember? You know what they do to Indians who steal horses. Anyway, you saved his life. and he owes you. Tell him I was pressed into service by the Tenth, and that got me thinking. " He grunted as though satisfied. "Both things are true. You will not have a lie on your conscience."

But Gabriel was not convinced Roosevelt would take Cloud's departure lightly. He might even want to pursue him. Yet, Gabriel decided to help. To refuse would be unthinkable. Gabriel's mind was already working fast. "All right. When?"

"Long before dawn," Cloud said. "I need the darkness."

"But you'll need a saddle, water and food," Gabriel protested.

"No," Cloud said. "I've already begun my fast. And no saddle."

And Gabriel could see that in his mind, Cloud was already on the trail. He was already staring toward the mountain.

*

It was almost easy. Gabriel told the sleepy picket the Colonel wanted his mount, slipped the bit into his mouth, and led Texas away. The mustang followed until Gabriel turned off the path to Roosevelt's tent. Then he stopped and snorted. "It's okay, boy," Gabriel whispered, stroking his nose. Then he shook the reins and led the mustang into the palm grove where Touch-the-Cloud waited.

CHAPTER 24

Saturday, July 2
Daybreak

In his dream it was snowing. Gabriel rode behind the dusky trooper, but he was far ahead and at each turn in the trail, Gabriel lost him. Compelled to ride on, to follow but somehow unable to call out, Gabriel spurred his horse, but the pony was slow and dreamlike. When he had given up hope and was ready to turn back, there would come from somewhere ahead, the thump of a hoof in the snow or a glimpse of a dark form—just enough to keep Gabriel going. He would see smoke rising straight and white through the dark pine forest and that would mean the rider ahead had made camp. Then Gabriel knew he would at last sit across the crackling fire from his father and meet those eyes that were like his own. And he would hear every word the trooper spoke and they would talk of his mother.

Then Marcus leaped into his path, his machete raised, and Gabriel felt the cut against his neck and downward, splitting him like a log.

Gabriel awoke, a half-buried man; his limbs numb and lifeless. Beside him, Prayerful and Tiffany snored.

The troopers had dug all night, using the only implements they had, bayonets and canteen cups. And now, nestled in a few new feet of trench where a sniper's bullet might not find them, they slept.

The hill was shrouded in mist. To the south, the captured block-house rose through it like the bridge of a ship. A sentry moved in the horizontal gun slit.

To the north, on the lip of the hill, the Ninth still slept in the mist. Beside Gabriel, L Troop's pennant hung limp.

A rooster crowed. To the east where Cloud had gone, the sun warmed the mist and on Kettle Hill, the overturned pot protruded like the snout of a whale.

*

The correspondents were just waking on El Pozo, where General Shafter made them wait. Stephen Crane had just ridden from El Caney, and was reading his dispatch aloud as he hastily penciled edits.

> *Pushing through the throng in the plaza, we came in sight of the door of the church, and there was a strange scene. It had been turned into a hospital for the Spanish wounded who had fallen into American hands. The interior of the church was too cave-like in its gloom for the eyes of the operating surgeons, so they had the altar table carried to the doorway, where there was a bright light. Framed then in the black archway was the alter-table with the figure of a man upon it. He was naked except for a breech-clout, and so close, so clear was the ecclesiastic suggestion that one's mind leaped to fantasy that this thin, pale figure had just been torn down from the cross.*

Crane paused, penciled an edit, and gathered breath.

> *The flash of the impression was like light, and for this instant it illuminated all the dark recesses of one's remotest idea of sacrilege, ghastly and wanton.*

Not far away, Richard Harding Davis shaved his chin and wiped it with a towel. "Not bad, Stephen. But a bit heavy handed, don't you think?

Just then, great iron bells began to ring-- an almost funereal sound. And below them, through the mist, the correspondents could make out the

ago Rag

ornate white and yellow towers of Santiago's cathedral.

"The death knell of Spain," Davis intoned.

Crane looked up from his notebook. "Now look who's being melo-dramatic. More likely, it is a last mass before General Toral counter-attacks."

"Captain Best's battery has moved up," Sylvester Scovel snapped. "So the Spanish must be up to something."

"You are right," Davis said. "Shafter will have to hurry to put the fear of God into our enemy, whom we have by no means beaten."

The correspondents watched the teamsters drag the cannon, backing each piece into place. Burr McIntosh set his camera on a tripod and clicked the shutter.

*

Gabriel sank down in his trench, dreading another artillery duel. If Cloud had made it through the lines, he would be up the mountain by now, away from all this. Gabriel was both cold and hungry. He made himself think of pancakes. Stacks and stacks of hot pancakes. But his was a feast of imagi-nation. There was nothing to eat or drink.

When Captain Best's battery opened up, it sent a projectile whistling over the blue convent, where it exploded in the trees. To Gabriel's relief, Captain Best had learned from the day before. After a few rounds, he pulled his artillery back to another position.

The mist was clearing from San Juan Hill, but all the suns Gabriel could imagine would never warm him enough.

From the left and right flank, the Spanish kept up sporadic carbine fire. Yesterday's dead, Spanish, American, and Cuban, lay where they had fall-en. Nobody crawled out to cover them.

Gabriel hoped that Roosevelt would not notice T. T. Cloud's absence. Just to make sure, he sent word for a picket to bring up the Colonel's war horse, Texas.

"Come on, Gabriel, we've been relieved," Tiffany said. They were half out of the trench when a bullet kicked up dirt. After a moment, Gabriel lifted his head until the brim of his Stetson allowed an inch of vision. Sure enough, some Tenth Cavalry boys were crawling into the end of their trench to relieve them. "Go out on the right," Tiffany urged. "To the left, they've got us."

They crawled over empty canteens, across swelling corpses. Then the trench opened out onto the rear of the hill. Gabriel tried to stand, but after days of walking in a crouch and the long night with his knees in mud, he could not.

Tiffany dropped a box of cartridges on its corner. The wood split, spilling a cascade of brass bullets. "Just in case," he said, "Load up." They loaded each other's bandoleers, then began to load the loops in their belts. Gabriel buckled his belt as tight as it would go, but the belt kept sliding over his hip bones. "You had better make new holes," Tiffany advised.

Gabriel filled a second bandoleer and slipped it over the other shoulder, Cuban style.

The heavy ammunition made him feel as though he had eaten.

There, on the edge of the hill, Gabriel saw Sergeant Eli Biddle. He turned away from Tiffany and slid into the trench beside Biddle.

"So. Still alive, huh," Biddle grinned. "The snipers are worse than the volleys. They must be better shots. You got to watch the trees and not turn your back."

When he had settled himself, Gabriel took the canteen Biddle offered him. "Thanks, Biddle," he said, handing it back. "Listen, you didn't tell me his name."

"Samuel," Biddle said, shaking the canteen to see how much water was left. "Didn't ever give a last name. Said he had his reasons and I let it go at that." Then Eli chuckled. "Plenty of us darkies had been in trouble before we enlisted. So Samuel could keep his name to himself and nobody paid mind. All that mattered out there was that a man did what he was told."

Biddle grunted. "We all worked at it, but seemed like Samuel had somethin' to prove. Volunteered for the tough assignments. Got promoted to Corporal. Captain Scriven took a cotton to him. I guess you know the rest."

"No," Gabriel said, "I just got bits and pieces from my mother."

The grizzled trooper nodded. "Tryin' to protect you, I expect. And Capt'n Scriven was careful like that too. Like he thought Samuel was a China cup, and might break."

"Tell me, Eli," Gabriel said, "what exactly did he look like?"

Biddle cocked his head in assessment. "Not big, not small. Average. Like I said not too dark, but not white either. I guess you look alike, ifn' you both were the same age. Hmmm. Come to think, a lot alike."

Gabriel felt a weight lift from his shoulders. "Tell me," he said happily, "about Montana."

"You mean when your daddy died?" Biddle said. "I didn't see it, but I heard. Captain took a squad to parley with a band of Brule Sioux. Samuel knew some Injun and was actin' as the interpreter. But something went wrong, guns went off and your daddy was gut shot."

Gabriel felt the impact of the Mauser hit his belly again and the breath went out of him.

"The squad got away," Biddle continued, looking sharply at the young bugler, "but not Samuel. They had to leave him there. And the Cap'n was never the same after that."

Gabriel imagined his father's bones bleaching on the shale of a Montana slope—as white as any man's bones had ever been.

Biddle grunted. "Listen, I meant to give you this." He opened his palm and in it lay a Jew's harp. "Borrowed it from your daddy and never gave it back."

Gabriel took the metal instrument and fingered it, feeling every edge, plucking the stiff tines with his finger. They made a sad, flat sound. Then, he clamped the Jew's harp between his teeth. Working his mouth for tone, he plucked the vibrating bar.

Biddle laughed. "I cain't believe it," he chuckled. "You sound just like him."

Gabriel stopped playing. Now he had a talisman to wear on a thong around his neck. It was better than Cloud's daguerreotype, for it was a way to make music.

*

An hour later, as Gabriel sat working out "Old Susanna" on the Jew's harp, a teamster arrived with a mule load of picks. He took off his hat, waited until Gabriel had finished, then yanked the slip knot holding the bundle and the picks clattered to the ground. "Guess y'all better dig," the teamster grinned. "Word is the Spanions might counter-attack."

The troopers passed out the picks. They just begun to spike them into the rocky soil when Gabriel saw Roosevelt, Leonard Wood, and General Wheeler trot their mounts up to where the troopers were digging.

Wheeler's face looked like drawn parchment. The little general was almost swallowed by his tan tunic as he addressed Wood in his soft, accented voice. "The question is, can we hold." He made it as a statement, not a question. Wood did not answer.

Roosevelt steadied his borrowed mount. "We must, George. I still have men I can't account for. But we'll need food. And we have little potable water. But the men have cartridges. Even if Shafter ordered it, General, I do not believe the Rough Riders would forfeit this hill. Not with men missing."

Wood chewed a grass stem. "Yet we do present a thin line. If the Spanish attack now, or shell us sharply, we'd have to fall back."

Wheeler nodded. "I agree. Takin' a ridge is one thing. Holding is quite another. Now that Cuban Colonel, Raúl García—he's going to brief us. Let's get as much information as possible. I don't want to have to withdraw unless we have to."

As they spoke, Colonel García, flanked by two body guards, galloped up the hill and threw Wheeler a salute. "As you have ordered, *General.*"

"Much obliged, Cunnel García."

"Expect to be in the trenches for some days," García said. "The *Peninsulares* have not mounted an attack in a very long time. Since the battle of Valladolid, in *España.* There, they were beaten and they are long on memory and short on imagination. We have beaten them every time they attacked us. So General Toral will wait for you to attack Santiago. He prefers to fight from a fortified position."

"Then," Wood said, "we must attack before reinforcements reach Santiago."

García looked at his hands. "I must report that they have arrived." He looked suddenly angry. "You will recall that some days ago, I practically begged General Shafter to let us intercept the relief column we knew was coming from the west. But he refused, preferring to use us in reserve at Las Guásimas and here at San Juan. But we are not assault troops. My men are the best guerrillas in the world and we can terrify and demoralize even a main force of *Peninsulares.* But," he spread his open palms, "we needed one of your cavalry units to help. And he gave us not one *Yanqui* to help us take and hold the road."

Roosevelt colored. "My boys could have done it alone," he said.

He was about to continue when General Wheeler cut him off. "That may be, but we cannot have forces runnin' amok and still expect to win. General Shafter is our commander, and it is our duty, as cavalry, even as *unmounted* cavalry, to inform him of his options."

"All right," García said. "By now the reinforcements will be coming into Santiago. But they are exhausted and will be of little use, except for morale. General Toral continues to take marines from his ships, and guns too. But that will take a few days, perhaps a week."

Wheeler scratched his beard. "Can you harass him enough to delay that action?"

Colonel García frowned. "Madrid has ordered Toral to fight to the last *peso*, to the last man. You can see by the way General del Rey held you off at El Caney. Everything in the harbor is guarded heavily. My *mambises* would not be able to do much. We are best on the move, in the countryside."

Wheeler straightened in his saddle. "Then thank you, Colonel *García*. Now I reckon we'll have to act with dispatch. We cannot afford another El Caney."

"General Wheeler," García said, "There is one more thing. I wish to be part of the negotiating team."

Roosevelt grimaced and Leonard Wood cleared his throat.

"I am sorry to inform you," Wheeler said with genuine regret, "General Shafter has decided otherwise."

García's face hardened. "Then, it is true. He has not included even one Cuban?"

"I'm sorry," General Wheeler said. "I personally asked that you be included. But Cuban participation has become a sensitive matter," he said, glancing in Roosevelt's direction, "a good many of our staff fear Cuban revenge will ruin a swift and honorable *surrenduh*. And we do not condone the beheading of prisoners."

Colonel García knew that some of his *mambises* had, against his orders, beheaded a dozen Spanish prisoners at El Caney in retribution for the atrocities and mutilations the Spanish had conducted on Cubans they had caught. As he watched the American generals ride away, García was stunned. He turned to his men and said, "It is worse than I thought. To the *Yanquis*, we are not even here!"

*

The troopers between San Juan and Kettle Hill cheered as Clara Barton's orderlies unloaded the wagons. They helped stack tarpaulins, charcoal braziers, and crates of food.

Gabriel helped haul the sacks and boxes. He read the labels off to the circle of hungry troopers. "Rice, three bags of it! Dried milk; just add water, it says, and you have a canteen of milk."

"If you can find a creek that's not full of turds," a weak but sassy Snake said.

"And tea, ladies!" another trooper jeered. "Why, we can have us a regular Temperance League meetin'."

"All we need is some fancy tea cups."

Gabriel hoisted a round, flat package. "Look boys, I can't believe it. Chocolate!"

A commotion always preceded Clara Barton. She stepped up to the pile of provisions and took mental inventory. "Doctor Hubbel," she snapped, "where are the dried fruits?"

Hubbel looked perplexed. "The Cubans stole them, ma'am."

She set her jaw. "Then we shall send those very Cubans to find fresh fruits to replace them. I understand the pineapple and banana may be found on this island. Surely we can get enough to begin. And tell the Cubans that I will not tolerate one more theft!"

Clara Barton directed the assembly of braziers, then sent volunteers for anything that would burn. She dabbed a scented handkerchief to her nose, blunting the stench that hung in the valley between the hills. "I spoke with General Shafter today, Dr. Hubbel. I told him we wished to be sent into Santiago as soon as possible. The suffering among the civilian population must be terrible. I understand that the Spanish are not more resistant to fever than our own men."

Gabriel, his arms wrapped around his middle for warmth, looked into the face of the old woman. "Do you have any quinine here?" he asked.

He felt her cool hands against his face. "Why, you are burning up! How long have you had this, young man?"

"Not long."

"Poppycock! You're jaundiced! And I imagine you are not the only one." Her mouth made a hard line. "You go to Colonel Roosevelt and send him to Siboney with directions for my staff to give him as much quinine as they can!"

Gabriel turned and started up the steep hill, which seemed to grow under his boots. He found Roosevelt scolding two Negro troopers. "You will return to your position, or I will shoot," he threatened.

"But, Colonel...," one of them protested.

Roosevelt pointed to the regimental banner of the Tenth Cavalry. "Get back there, at once!"

The two troopers exchanged glances, then started back. Halfway, they were stopped by an officer, then sent back down the hill. The officer stormed toward Roosevelt, holding his sword against his side.

Roosevelt gestured toward the two troopers. "Order those men to hold their position, Lieutenant."

Lieutenant Fleming of the Tenth Cavalry slapped his sword handle. "Colonel, don't be such an ass!" Then, before the astonished Roosevelt could recover, Fleming said, "Lieutenant Pershing just sent those men for entrenching tools!"

Roosevelt blinked. "Then I apologize. Convey my regards to Pershing."

But Fleming was not through. "The Tenth has earned this goddamned hill much as your pansy pants volunteers."

Roosevelt cocked his head. "Do I detect a New York accent?"

"You are correct, Colonel. I'm from the Bowery. "

"Ah, I thought as much. Please accept my apologies, Lieutenant. I thought..."

But Fleming was having none of it. "I know exactly what you thought, *Colonel.*"

*

As the Spanish kept up their fire, the three correspondents crouched in Gabriel's trench. Suddenly, Crane sprang up on the mound of dirt and began walking back and forth. Immediately, the Spanish fire intensified.

Richard Harding Davis, hampered by his numbed leg, tolerated Crane's display of bravado for a moment, then called out, "Get down, Stephen. You are not impressing anyone."

"Get down," Scovel added, "or you'll make a Spaniard a murderer."

Crane removed his hat calmly. "I simply wish to get a better view of the enemy."

Scovel thundered, "Then stroll over to them, or get back into the trench. You are drawing fire for no good purpose."

Just then a bullet struck near Crane's feet. He flung a defiant look toward the Spanish lines and stepped down. He soon began to cough.

"You'll end up like O'Neill, if you are not careful," Davis warned.

Crane blotted his mouth with his handkerchief. "Well," he said, "who wants to die in bed?"

"Bathos!" Scovel accused. "You've been too long with the English Romantics. You are in a war, not in Trafalgar Square."

"My Trafalgar Square friend, Joseph Conrad, is Polish," Crane corrected, "not English."

"What they yappin' about?" Snake whispered loudly.

Davis overheard him and laughed. "Why, LIT-tra-ture, son. The exquisite power of the pen!"

Snake spat in disgust.

Scovel regarded him carefully. "Had enough fighting, eh son?""

Snake pulled back his shirt, showing his bloody shoulder. "No. I just need to git even," he said.

*

The sky deepened from blue to green as lights from the city below flickered against the dark mass of the mountains. If it weren't for the groans of the wounded, Gabriel thought, cooled by a dose of quinine, this might be a beautiful sight.

"Halt! Who goes there?"

"*Que?*"

A carbine fired and a cry cut the silence that followed.

"*Tranquillo! Somos de García!*"

"Don't shoot," Gabriel commanded.

Snake swore softly.

From across the harbor, came the popping of carbine fire. Then on the hills beyond it, one blockhouse caught flame, then another. Soon, the far side of the harbor was ringed with fire. Across the reflection of flame on water they could see the dark shapes of the Spanish fleet.

CHAPTER 25

Sunday, July 3

Hammering with the butt of his pistol, Snake pulverized the coffee beans against a rock. Then a piece of the pistol handle broke off. Snake raised the gun and examined it. He snapped the hammer on an empty chamber. "It'll still fire, I reckon."

Snake raked the fractured beans into a tin cup of rain water, then stirred the mixture with his finger. He took a sip and Gabriel watched his bearded face for a reaction. There was none.

"Let me have some," Gabriel chattered. He stared at the mess, then sipped the tepid sludge. We are not an army anymore, he thought. We have become tramps the Spanish are using for target practice.

As the thunderheads blew over the Sierra Maestra the sun steamed down on the troopers. Snake fed a broken pick handle between two rocks and struck a match. A shard of ash caught the flame. "Come on, now, don't you quit on me," he coaxed. "We gonna have bacon. Gonna have biscuits. And hot coffee, yesirree! You just burn. That's it!" He nursed the flame, blew on it, then crossed the other piece of handle over it. The fire crackled to life. Gabriel poured the rain from their rusty skillet and balanced it on the stones bracketing the fire. He stripped the gauze from the white bacon. Using his bayonet, he cut thick, lardy slices. As it cooked, the fat turned transparent. Troopers licked their lips as the bacon buckled in the skillet. The smell made Gabriel's stomach growl, but his teeth would not stop chattering.

"You sound like a scairt squirrel," Snake laughed.

The bacon crackled in hot grease. They pinched pieces of soggy hardtack and dropped them into the skillet. Gabriel stirred with his bayonet.

The aroma of cooking brought Prayerful and Tiffany. The troopers crouched, not caring that their huddle made a tempting target.

Prayerful offered grace. "Lord, make us grateful for what we're about receive, amen." Then he grinned at Snake.

While the troopers ate, a pot of water steamed and the split coffee beans boiled in a brown froth.

Now Gabriel felt better. Instead of a bum's camp, this was beginning to smell more like a roundup. When the hardtack was gone and the skillet had been wiped clean, Snake doled out the coffee. The men drank it thoughtfully. From Santiago they could hear the echo of Spanish bugles.

*

Roosevelt shoved up his spectacles and focused the field glasses. Columns of black smoke rose from the harbor. The clanging ship's bells and the way the five Spanish ships were lining up were unmistakable. The Colonel's feet worked in a slow dance. "They're making a run for it, boys," he shouted, "Admiral Cervera is coming out to fight!"

"What if they beat us? We'll die here like rats!"

Roosevelt lowered his binoculars. "Who said that?"

Nobody answered.

As the Colonel peered through his field glasses, he said, "Don't worry, we've got the Spanish out-gunned, boys. It'll be like Dewey at Manila. *Iowa* is practically unsinkable. She's lined with cellulose, which swells up when wet. So even if she takes a Spanish shell, the *Iowa* will still float."

But the troopers holding the San Juan heights were not feeling as cocky as their leader. Below them, the line of great ships presented an awesome sight. Their long guns glistened in the sun, and they flew bright battle flags. The decks teemed with sailors. And the bugle work of those Spaniards, Gabriel thought, was wonderful, especially the trills at the end.

As the Spanish fleet fell into a line and steamed slowly toward the mouth of the harbor, Roosevelt read from their sterns. "The *Infanta María Teresa*," he called, watching the flagship lead the others to where the mountains and the Morro made a bottle-neck of the harbor. "And next, boys, the *Viscaya*."

The Spanish troopers had stopped firing and could be heard cheering the procession of their ships.

Roosevelt continued, ever more excited. "There goes the *Cristóbal Colón*. And The *Oquendo*. The last two must be destroyers. Aha! Yes *Plutón* and *Furor*." He swung his glasses down the harbor. "But Admiral Cervera has made his mistake. He has but one ship in reserve! The *Reina Mercedes*."

*

In the moonlight, Cloud led the mustang across the valley, forded the San Juan river, then mounted and trotted him toward the eastward. Texas was not used to being ridden without a saddle and it took him awhile to get used to Cloud's knees as a signal. But they had left the regiments behind, as Crazy Horse had briefly left the gathering of nations before the battle with Custer.

The Indian had not been alone for a long a time, and he enjoyed the silences of the open country. As he climbed, the air cooled.

As Texas followed the trail ever higher, Touch-the-Cloud realized that his tribesmen would not recognize this land. Below, lay the broad expanse of the sea, which they had never seen. A kind of prairie, shimmering in the moonlight. Instead of the howl of a badlands wolf, there came the staccato call of a tropical bird. He could smell ripening fruit but he was not hungry for it.

He followed the trail, one made by animals who always knew the easiest path. Texas, too far away now to expect army forage, plodded along, his great chest heaving, jerking his head at the slightest pressure of his knees. And the path led them up, switching back, then up again, along the twisting spine of the mountain.

By dawn they were high and above the mist. The eastern sky was the color of watery blood, and they had completely left the war. Cloud listened to the squawk of wild parrots and imagined a Caribe hunting for bright, magical feathers in the jungle. Around them was the green sinew of mountain, with wrinkled gorges falling away on either side. And then he felt Texas quicken under him and realized they must be nearing water.

They came to a clearing where the stream pooled before it fell into the valley. Cloud slid down and let Texas drink. To him, the water might as well have been stone, for his body had already begun a withdrawal from the world. Below, the stream cut through a bed of shale toward the sea. And all around it, the thick, wild growth of trees Cloud did not yet know teemed with birds and game. It seemed odd, that he had not come to hunt any of them.

Cloud tried not to stare too long into the sun, for he was not yet at the place he had heard the Mambises talk about. He needed good eyesight until he got there. He had brought only his carbine. He wore no shirt, no hat no shoes.

They continued to climb as the sun arched over them. And T. T. Cloud felt neither the heat of it nor the breezes that came up from the sea. Texas needed no guidance now. He headed higher and higher, his hooves slipping on the moss covered, stony trail, showing interest in the leafy ferns dripping with dew that lined the narrow path. Some of the trees in the thick forest were familiar—Cloud recognized pines and some that bore fruits he did not recognize. He rode with his arms at his sides.

And then, they came to the place the Cubans had told him about- a place where the ever steeper trail was flanked by huge slabs of broken stone, almost like a man-made portal. Texas stopped and snorted, unwilling to enter the space between the stones. Cloud slid down and listened. He heard the wind high in the pines, a low, moaning sound. There were many winds up hers and he began to decipher them—the soft swish, wave-like sound of warm wind. Then there was the piping call of a bird. Texas dropped his head and began to nibble at the ferns. Then, in the path above them Cloud saw a gray jay with an orange breast and feet. The bird cocked his head and sang out. His mate, who fluttered down and joined him, answered him. Then they fluttered past Cloud, nearly brushing his face, turning in the green tunnel above the path.

The Indian slipped the bit from Texas' mouth. He tied the reins in a loose hobble around the mustangs front legs.

Then Cloud climbed the steep, slippery slope of the trail, his toes gripping the moss-covered stones. Nobody had passed this way for some days. Above him, he could see the great, bare rock. Cloud finally found places where footholds had been hacked out, and he began to climb the boulder.

Above, on the great gray, lichen-covered rock that was as big as an upside-down ship, he felt the winds press against his naked chest. Off to the south lay the turquoise and cobalt sea, turned silver where the sun caught it. On his left, near a conical peak, he recognized the crescent beach of Daiquirí. Then further to the right, the wider beach at Siboney. Behind the beaches, lay the plateau where they had first fought.

He turned. To the east, north and west were more mountains and the great rock on which he stood seemed like a bony head above them all. The Indian had never been in so high or so beautiful a place. He closed his eyes. In the wind were many voices. He lay back on the rough, lichen-covered rock and spread his arms.

Cloud did not know much time had passed. The sun had moved toward the west. Thunderheads had formed and were rolling toward him, like the giant fists of white and gray lifting from the sea. And with them came a strong wind, a deep wail that seemed to come from the four corners, crossing and weaving over and under each other. Then the clouds opened and big drops flattened like bullets against the his skin and the rock. Suddenly, lightning, and seconds split the boiling cloud later, by the crack of thunder.

*

On San Juan Hill, the Rough Riders knew that the battle at sea would seal their fate. As the sound of it boomed over the mountain, the troopers tried to assign meaning to each salvo. A shell whistled over them, skipped off the surface of the harbor and exploded somewhere in the city.

"One of ours," Roosevelt beamed. "The *Brooklyn*, I'd wager. She's shooting high just now. Don't worry, boys, she'll eventually get the range."

The shelling increased. Listening made Gabriel sweat, although he was still shivering.

Roosevelt, his head cocked attentively, sat on a case of cartridges and dried his spectacles. "What I wouldn't give for Derby's balloon now," he said.

"If the Navy quits on us, " Snake said, "we'll never get home."

"We've got eleven gallant ships, twelve if you count *Vixen*. Furthermore, we've got Admiral Cervera dead to rights. Even if he escapes, Admiral Sampson can now steam into Santiago harbor, mines or no mines."

Later that afternoon, John J. Pershing stood before three depleted regiments of cavalry. At thirty-eight, he was the same age as Roosevelt and Wood. But promotions to the white officers of black regiments had been pitifully slow. But now, the Tenth Cavalry had lost eleven officers and half a dozen sergeants. His promotion would be made possible by their deaths.

He remembered the attention paid to Captain Allyn Capron and Sergeant Hamilton Fish when they died at Las Guásimas. Yet there had been almost no mention of Corporal Brown, who commanded the Hotchkiss gun that helped turn the tide of battle when the Rough Riders were still pinned down. When the Tenth rose, screamed their Comanche war cry and made the frontal assault on the stone battlements, the Spanish fell back. But Corporal Brown lay bleeding to death. But the correspondents had given the publicity to the Rough Riders. Right now though, the boys in tan britches looked pretty tired and beaten.

That Pershing had been chosen to read President McKinley's telegram was likely General Wheeler's way of thanking the Tenth Cavalry.

The men before him, both blacks and sunburned whites, were uncertain. They were smart enough to realize that their lines were thin and with supplies so scarce a counterattack by the Spanish might prove successful. He knew they needed a boost. Pershing gripped the paper, already stained with his perspiration. "President McKinley writes," he said, "The American people are proud of what you men have nobly accomplished here.' " It was a short, inconclusive message and seemed to have no effect. Especially when they could all still hear the naval guns booming in the distance.

On the San Juan heights, there were no trees to make palm thatch, so the men suffered in the boiling sun. Even talk was an effort. "What's that supposed to mean?" Snake whispered. "Are they beatin' us?"

"Shut yer trap. McKinley wouldn't say that if we were losing."

"The President cain't know what's happenin' here!"

"Hell, neither do we."

Later that afternoon, Lieutenant Hall spurred his horse up the incline and saluted Roosevelt. Without waiting for the Colonel's response he blurted, "General Shafter wishes to inform you that the Spanish fleet has been completely destroyed and that Admiral Cervera has been captured."

Roosevelt ripped off his hat. "Hear that men? I told you as much. Uncle Sam's beaten the Armada!"

Despite his aching joints, Gabriel rose to his feet.

"HIP, HIP HOORAAAAY!" Roosevelt yelled. Then raising his arms, he led cheers, repeating them until all the troopers, no matter how tired or sick they were, cheered with him.

The news reached General Calixto García as he sipped his afternoon tumbler of rum. The message bearer was jubilant, and so were the men who overheard him. They behaved as though the war was won. But the General rubbed the painful depression above his eyes. He had spent too much in the cafes of Madrid to be happy. Of course, the Americans had beaten the obsolete Spanish squadron. Admiral Cervera had begged the economically strapped Spanish War Ministry for the funds to upgrade his fleet—but he had received nothing. Cervera was a brave man—a true Spaniard. Not like Valeriano Weyler and the political zealots who had infiltrated the Spanish military.

As his men began to celebrate, General Calixto García imagined the shock of the Spanish people who would soon know that the new world they had discovered, colonized, and depended on for wealth was slipping from their grasp.

He had always been a melancholy man, and it was doubly sad, he realized, that he could not enjoy this occasion. Perhaps it was because General Shafter was clearly ignoring him.

*

That night, the remnants of the Rough Rider band formed near the captured block- house. Colonel Wood and his aides rode up the hill, followed by General Wheeler, Richard Harding Davis, Stephen Crane, a well-dressed civilian, and the unkempt Sylvester Scovel. The men of the Ninth Cavalry crowded in, waiting for the band to start up. Roosevelt approached the party and saluted Wheeler. Then he shook the civilian's hand heartily. "We are pleased to have you, Mister Hearst."

William Randolph Hearst, the flamboyant publisher, was a surprisingly young man and he was enjoying himself. "I wouldn't miss this for the world, Theodore. You know Sylvester Scovel. Although it was for a competing paper, Mr. Scovel managed to interview General Gomez in his mountain hide-out last January. And he won't let me forget it."

Roosevelt shook Scovel's hand. "Honored, sir. I remember your reportage."

"I wish Secretary Alger had bothered to read it," Scovel said, "this thing would be over by now."

Roosevelt looked surprised. "Yet, Mister Scovel, we are here."

Scovel sucked his teeth. "Yes. At the wrong end of the island. With shakes instead of surrender."

Roosevelt wanted to start the ceremony. He turned to the band.

As the band played the national anthem, "Hail Columbia," the men removed their hats. A few even sang along.

Next, the band, reading in the twilight from sheet music, struggled with an unfamiliar tune. Gabriel noticed that only Wood and Roosevelt were singing along. "What's the matter, boys?" Roosevelt said, in a hearty aside, "don't you know 'Fair Harvard' when you hear it?"

When the band had finished, Hearst turned to Roosevelt. "Well, this thing is all but won," he said. "I'm taking Davis to Puerto Rico tomorrow."

Roosevelt looked aghast. "But we have not yet taken Santiago!"

"There is bound to be surrender. Scovel can have the scoop. The Puerto Rican campaign is under way. My newspaper must follow the action."

As they left, Roosevelt muttered darkly, "Puerto Rico my eye! They are afraid of fever."

Soon, Wood and Roosevelt stood outside a tent, dispensing quinine to the line of troopers. The Fifth Army had lost one hundred forty-three killed and a thousand wounded.

Wood lifted a shivering trooper's eyelid, then as the man departed, he confided to Roosevelt.

"We can't put the fever tents up fast enough. Miss Barton's had The State of Texas bring fifteen tons of ice from Jamaica—a life saver for head wounds. Doctor Winter has given up on the abdominal surgeries. Because of lack of supplies and dressings, he's lost nearly every one he's done."

Roosevelt sputtered. "I shall wire Lodge tonight. He has the President's ear and he will inform him that Shafter's conduct is unconscionable!"

Wood cleared his throat. "I disagree. Shafter has demanded General Toral to surrender or he will bombard Santiago. That's the reason Admiral Cervera tried to break out. If Cervera had beaten us at sea it would be we who would have surrendered and Toral knows it."

"But, Leonard," Roosevelt said, "we must do something. We need food, supplies, and ammunition! This is positively intolerable!"

Brigadier General Wood poured the last of the quinine into a trooper's cup, then tossed the empty flask aside. "War itself is intolerable."

Roosevelt had a sudden thought. "Why Leonard, do you realize that tomorrow will be the Fourth of July?"

It was after midnight when Roosevelt shook Gabriel awake.

"Look," he said, "near the island." Below them the harbor reflected the bright moon. Then, as Gabriel forced his eyes open, a shaft of very bright light played against the mountains near the island.

"What is it?"

Together, they watched the lights slide. Past the narrow entrance to the harbor, where the moonlight silvered the smooth water, a great ship moved. Her smoke blocked the stars, a sfire and sparks shot from her stacks.

"My God," Roosevelt exclaimed, "It's The *Reina Mercedes*."

Heavy guns broke the silence, then silent flashes followed by the thunder of the American reply and before their eyes, The *Reina Mercedes* burst into flame. Minutes later, the mighty Spanish warship exploded and the Rough Riders began to cheer.

Captain Luna rushed up to Roosevelt. "Make them stop, Colonel. How can our men cheer while good and brave men burn to death?"

*

Texas flinched, then bolted down the trail at the boom of the distant naval guns. Touch-the-Cloud had tied a leather thong around his head and fixed the tail feather of a parrot to it. He had smeared his chest with the clay from the stream bed that had dried white against his skin. He was disappointed in his vision quest, but he reminded himself that it took time to understand such things—Crazy Horse had been disappointed too—had discounted his lightning and hail experience until it gave him power. As a result, no weapon could kill Crazy Horse, unless he was held back by one of his own tribesmen.

Touch-the-Cloud had seen too many bullets take down good men to believe himself invincible. Yet, he had been given the gift of leadership— the Tenth Cavalry troopers had sensed it. And just as Crazy Horse had held back thousands of hot-blooded braves long enough to trap Custer's command, Touch-the-Cloud had led a charge at San Juan Hill, men who screamed and fought like Indians.

Up on the rock, he had made two vows. Like Crazy Horse, he would abstain from alcohol. And he would help the Cubans in their wish to be recognized when the surrender came. These were but two small steps, and in a foreign land, but if he could make them, then it might mean that Touch-the-

Cloud had been given the power to lead his own people.

CHAPTER 26

Monday, July 4

Gabriel regarded Cloud closely. He had war paint across his face and chest. To his suspenders, Cloud had pinned cloth lieutenant's bars. The vulture feather he had worn in the band of his Stetson had been replaced by a long, iridescent green feather, tinged blue at the tip. Most of the troopers avoided him now. They didn't know what to make of T. T. Cloud.

"If I were you," Gabriel advised, "I'd take the bars off."

The Indian brushed the dust from the yellow insignia. "Colonel Roosevelt says I may keep them."

"You return his mustang?"

Cloud nodded.

"And the Colonel didn't blow up?"

The Indian shook his head. "He said something about strength coming from solitude."

Cloud no longer wore the pouch around his neck. Instead, he carried a sack of yellowish, oblong fruit. "Mangoes," Cloud explained. "They are ripe now." He took one and cut the skin, then he began to strip the stringy, yellow flesh. Spearing a piece on the point of his knife, he offered it to Gabriel.

The two friends ate, juice running down their fingers and dripping on the ground.

At the other end of the hill, a bugle sounded and the troopers saw a white flag being raised from the captured blockhouse. As the troopers watched, white cloths began to sprout in the Spanish lines. The truce had been struck!

"It's some trick," Snake accused. "You can't trust the garlics."

A hundred yards away, the Spaniards were standing too. Troopers who had been trying to kill each other for two weeks finally had a good look at each other.

Then the fleet began firing salvoes of triumph, and the guns echoed off the mountains. Bass and tenor steam whistles cut the air.

Within the hour, refugees began their exodus from Santiago along the road that ran through the Spanish lines. They labored under their loads across the road beside San Juan Hill, which was already packed with old men and haggard women, and with crying children. All staggered under bundles, afraid to meet the eyes of the *Yanquis* who held the heights.

Touch-the-Cloud, who had told Gabriel often about the forced marches of his own people, took Gabriel's arm. "They're going toward El Caney. You must tell them in their own tongue the town has been destroyed and there is no food there."

Among the refugees, Gabriel saw a young woman in a torn, yellow dress, leading a boy of six or seven. Gabriel raised his hands to show that he was not armed, then, with Cloud, approached them. The woman was fearful and tried to pull the boy back as they approached. Gabriel noticed her jewelry and fancy shoes that were now broken and muddy. The boy was not afraid of them. "*Vivan los Americanos,*" he called. The woman pulled him back.

Now some Negro troopers left their positions and began to offer the refugees hardtack.

Gabriel squatted beside the boy and gave him a mango. The boys took it and began to peel the skin away, as the woman began to cry.

Gabriel lifted the boy. He was about five and was contentedly sucking at a hole he had bitten in the skin of the mango.

"*¿Porqué,*" Gabriel asked her, "*el niño tiene hambre?*"

"There has been almost nothing to eat," the woman said.

"But there is even less at El Caney," Gabriel told her. "Turn back."

"Then," the woman said, "the old ones and the children will surely die. For Santiago will be in flames. Your general has given us twenty-four hours before he bombards us. We have been told that if you take the city, you will rape us and then kill the children." She looked at him as she said this, searching his face for some reassurance.

" Surely," Gabriel told her, "you do not believe that." He lifted the boy's chin with his finger. "*¿Dígame, muchacho, como se llama?*"

The boy looked up, the mango dripping from his chin. "*Luís.*"

And as the boy watched, Gabriel withdrew the Jews harp and twanged a few notes and the boy smiled.

But now, Lieutenant Day was calling the men back to their posts. They had been given orders not to consort with the civilian population. Yet Gabriel could not leave the young woman in the torn silk dress without knowing her name. But she would not tell him.

"Look," he told her, "we will let no harm come to you. Are you afraid of the Cubans?"

She nodded. "They will butcher us. There have been many atrocities they will repay."

Lieutenant Day yelled again. Gabriel took her hand and pressed it reassuringly. It was surprisingly smooth and soft. "Then good luck, Señora. And *buen suerte*, Luís."

"We will not go far," she told him. "I know a *finca* near Sevilla where we can stay."

Gabriel dutifully climbed the hill, but he looked back to see the woman and the boy as they walked along the road. He wanted to help them. What was the use of standing in the trenches?

*

A great *ciéba* tree grew between the two opposing armies. Lances tied with strips of white cloth stuck from its base. The tree had become the site for junior officers of the two sides to exchange dispatches from their generals. There, General Shafter's adjutant, Colonel Dorst, and Captain Luna, the translator, conferred with several smartly uniformed Spanish officers.

Up on San Juan Hill, Roosevelt paced in the heat, impatient for the parley to end. "I don't care if the Spanish have mined their harbor. Schley should send a frigate or two in anyway. We are running out of *time*. I've lost one man in four killed or wounded," he fumed. "Forty more down with fever or heat prostration! How many men must I sacrifice to pig-headed Spanish pride?"

Finally, Dorst then Luna, each carrying a truce lance, rode up the hill.

"Well?" Roosevelt asked Luna, ignoring Major Dorst altogether. Captain Luna shook his head. "General Toral will not surrender."

Roosevelt threw down his hat and scrubbed at his sweaty, sunburned neck with his kerchief. Then his head snapped up. "Then why the refugees?"

"A relief column of over three thousand has reached Santiago," Major Dorst said, "and a good many are sick. They have to be fed. My guess is that General Toral doesn't want to be bothered with civilians." Luna said. "Besides, he still believes we cannot possibly succeed."

Roosevelt's face twisted."Well if that wouldn't curdle milk!" he exclaimed. "We sink his entire fleet. And beat him in two land battles and virtually surround his capital. What does Toral want? Total annihilation?"

Dorst squinted at the Spanish lines. "General Toral has been ordered by Madrid to hold. He says he cannot surrender without their consent. He communicates with them almost hourly."

"But we cut the cables to Madrid," exclaimed Roosevelt.

"Apparently not," Captain Dorst said. He put a boot into his stirrup. "I must go. General Shafter awaits my report."

"All right, Dorst. But tell him my boys are dying up here. He should come and see for himself. We are but a mile from victory! To hesitate now is to lose."

Colonel Dorst, Shafter's representative, coolly regarded Roosevelt. "The General does not welcome advice from civilians, sir." Then he cantered down the leeward flank of the hill.

Roosevelt's teeth seemed to devour his mustache as he squinted through the waves of heat at the roofs of Santiago, a most elusive prize. Then, in a voice loud enough for all to hear, he said, "Davis me that in the north of the city, the Spanish have a slaughter house. Right next to a bull ring. Now the slaughter house you can understand. But an arena where killing is common as baseball- why that's incomprehensible!" He spread his hands to the sky. "Does The Brakeman send these blood thirsty tyrants hot lead? NO. He delivers a fluttering flag of truce! Captain Luna!"

"Sir!"

"Have Sergeant Tiffany bring up the dynamite gun."

"But the truce sir!"

"With any luck," Roosevelt snapped, "the truce will soon be over!"

*

Marcus Hammer realized his chance to get into the action at last. Church would be too busy in the operating tents to notice his absence, especially since he had feigned fever that very morning.

Besides, he had heard Fish and Tiffany talk about rowing on opposing teams- Tiffany for Princeton. In his own mind, since he rowed for Columbia with Fish, Marcus would be accepted as one of Roosevelt's "Fifth Avenue contingent." And Roosevelt's Harvard class had donated the dynamite gun.

Hammer saw that the long gun was unwieldy on its caisson. The one mule Tiffany had been allocated would not be enough to bring it forward.

Marcus helped hitch the mule to the caisson, but the animal could not quite budge the wheels from the mud. He stripped off his shirt and put his shoulder against the wheel. "Try again," he told Tiffany. Marcus imagined all those who had thwarted him. He was pushing more than iron.

The wheel moved and with a triumphant grunt, Hammer shoved it out of the rut.

Other troopers helped push it up the hill, where Tiffany blocked the wheels so the recoil would not make it roll back.

The dynamite gun had a barrel twelve feet long, the diameter of a baseball bat. This long barrel was mounted over a shorter, thicker one. Both were weighted on one end by a heavy wooden beam. Because the gun was so long and thin, it looked puny between the short, tripod-mounted Gatlings. But Roosevelt was convinced that his "secret weapon" would be the determining factor in the surrender of Santiago. The Rough Rider's own private weapon had already begun to rust in the humid Cuban climate. But Roosevelt believed the dynamite gun would give new meaning to Harvard's motto- *veritas.*

Before the battle for San Juan Hill, Tiffany had fired four shots with the gun. The first blasted a hole in a heavily reinforced wall, short of his target. After adjusting the pressure gauge, he had fired again. This time the projectile had blown the roof of a blockhouse a hundred feet into the air. But the third shell hit the limb of a tree far too close. Had the projectile gone off, it would have killed Tiffany and his gunner. The fourth shell lodged in the chamber. Tiffany had abandoned the contraption to rejoin his the regiment, which was forming up for the advance.

Now, he demonstrated to Marcus how the thing was fired. First, a blank shell was fed into the lower barrel. It would make a minor, smoky

San Juan

onation, which tripped a valve and filled the main barrel with compressed air. Tiffany then fed a long dynamite canister into the barrel and set the compressed air gauge. More pressure meant greater range. When the Sims-Dudley dynamite gun fired it sounded like the cork flying from a giant bottle of champagne. The long, silver projectile, spinning end, looked more like a gift parcel than what it was- a timed deadly dynamite charge three times more powerful than a direct hit from one of Captain Capron's field guns.

In full view of the Spaniards, Roosevelt had Tiffany aim the dynamite gun directly into enemy lines. Then he flanked it with Gatling guns, which the Spanish already feared. As they observed the guns going into place the Spanish ducked back into their trenches. Their officers ordered them out again.

Once the guns were in position, Roosevelt bellowed across the grassy valley. "General Toral," he shouted, "SURRENDER AT ONCE." He raised his gloved fist as though the leader of the Spanish forces was watching him at that very moment, "If you do not, I shall blast you to kingdom come."

On the distant hall, Spanish officers laughed and strutted back and forth, elaborately lighting their cigars and blowing the smoke toward San Juan Hill.

*

In the afternoon, a sudden storm blew Roosevelt's tent down. The Colonel got soaked to the bone and although he tried to hide it, Gabriel saw him begin to shiver. By evening, it was time to get the colonel to Doc Church. Finally, Gabriel found the cook who informed him that a medic was in the cook tent, but quite unconscious.

The little Rough Rider cook raised his shoulders in a shrug. "I think a coconut fell on him."

"Well, Colonel Roosevelt is sick and he won't go to the hospital. Can we bring him to the cook tent so that he may get dry?"

"Sure," the cook said.

Gabriel and Cloud steadied Roosevelt between them and walked him into the tent. There, on the wooden table where Pork Chop chopped bacon and cut potatoes, the medic who had been knocked out by a coconut began to regain consciousness. When he saw Colonel Roosevelt beside him, the medic leaped to his feet, suddenly recovered. He tested the Colonel's brow. "Wrap him in blankets," he snapped.

Gabriel listened to Roosevelt's feverish ramblings- a conversation, apparently with his father. "Certainly I did, sir. Yes, not giving a thought to my own safety." Then Roosevelt's eyes opened. "Men, do you hear that? The infantry is moving on our hill. Where are my glasses!

I have another pair somewhere! Scriven! Blow the charge at once. Do you hear me..."

Gabriel leaned close to his feverish Colonel's face and said, "I did, sir. And we have taken the hill."

Roosevelt fell back in a heavy sweat and closed his eyes. "Yes, of course. Good work, Scriven. Now. See to it that the boys get fed, will you? They're fighting on empty stomachs. I think. I shall take a brief rest." His voice faded to a whisper as he added, in a small boy's voice, "Good night, father."

"Yes," Gabriel lied, "good night, son."

Roosevelt's face was a mask of peace as he eased into a deep and deserved sleep.

Gabriel tumbled out of the tent. He fumbled in his pocket for a half smoked cheroot. It took him some time to light it. As he inhaled the smoke, the night birds began a sound like billiard balls rattling in a wood box.

When Surgeon Church came to the tent, he took Roosevelt's temperature. "It's almost normal," Church said. "But he shows all the signs of physical exhaustion. Let him sleep as long as he will."

As he began his long vigil beside Roosevelt, Gabriel took a pad from his pocket and began to write.

Independence Day, 1898

Dear Mother,

We have taken the last hill and now we wait for the Spanish to surrender. Colonel Roosevelt is down with exhaustion and I am keeping watch. Earlier today he commended me for saving his life. I did it with my bugle.

It is hard to imagine myself as a musician anymore. My hands are blistered from digging trenches and these army horns are as hard to play as drain pipes. Since the truce, regimental bands entertain us each evening. The Spanish boys seem to enjoy them as much as we do.

It seems like five years since I saw you. I have some interesting news. I've met a trooper who served with a Samuel Scriven in Montana. He gave me Samuel's Jew's Harp. I've been playing it. although it is much like playing a comb. You didn't tell me my father loved music. Maybe I take after him in that regard.

Peace seems to be more complicated than war. Every day, officers from both sides talk under a tree. We want the Spanish to surrender, but you can't blame them for not wanting to. They've been here since Columbus.

We've had almost no mail yet, but I know you have written. Do you know if Aura has as well? Our adjutant swears there's mail for us in one of the boats, and we're all dying to read it.

Did you know that Marcus Hammer is here? He is with the hospital corps. We have had little contact. I understand that he carried me from the field when I was wounded. Don't worry, I am fine already.

There is no time for grudges. We get swept along like straw.

I'm hoping that as soon as the Spanish surrender we'll board a big boat. When we do, I'll have the captain steam right up the Mississippi then the Missouri and we'll dock at Fort Chambers. We'll blow our whistles and you can meet Colonel Roosevelt and T. T. Cloud and Snake and all the boys So be listening for that old whistle.

Love, Gabriel Scriven,
Trumpeter, First Volunteer Cavalry

From the jungle came an almost human cry. As he folded the letter, Gabriel thought of other fatherless boys. On all sides, he knew there were already too many.

ntiago Rag

PART V *A Rag in the Dust*

CHAPTER 27

July 5
San Juan Hill

On the road below them, a woman pulled her squealing pig along by a rope. Marcus knew how the animal must feel as he paused from the letter he was struggling to write. From an old refugee's shoulder, a parrot squawked and for once, Marcus could understand the bird's frustration. He felt thick-tongued and clumsy. Writing him was even worse. During his year at Columbia he had sent his father enthusiastic letters, but they had come back, corrected in red ink.

A few troopers from what Marcus and a few other troopers called the "Nigger Ninth" went down to the refugees. He was sure they wanted to steal the pig.

The refugees were another obstacle. The sooner they were out of Santiago, the sooner the truce would end. How many dynamite canisters, Marcus had been wondering, would it take to bring down the cathedral in Santiago? He had been practicing the difficult loading procedure and he'd asked Tiffany about range. He'd had Tiffany zero in on an enemy barracks because it was, Marcus reasoned, about the same range as the cathedral—at the gun's maximum.

But today the troopers were all writing. Mail would leave by boat the next day. Marcus returned to his letter. He crossed out a word or two, swore, and then tore the letter up. He had never had much luck expressing himself on paper. Thelma Scriven said so when she had been hired to tutor him. But Judge Hammer threatened her that day, in front of Marcus, that her tenure would depend on the college-preparedness of his son.

Marcus's second attempt was little better. He started with a list of the men he had hauled to the hospital tent. He paused, wondering if he should include Gabriel Scriven, for the Judge might not even know Scriven was in Cuba. Then Marcus realized that Thelma Scriven would have spread the news all over Fort Chambers that her half-breed had become Roosevelt's chief trumpeter..

Marcus had made nothing more than a list of complaints and he knew the Judge would not tolerate them. A man was strong and never whined, his father always admonished. It mattered little whether a man had just been convicted or sentenced, or whether it was Marcus himself, caught stealing apples. The Judge was always reminding Marcus that, regrettably, he had inherited his mother's hot blood. But a man, the Judge told him, must never betray his anger in public. Rather, the Judge counseled, he should begin a cool, devastating revenge. Judge Hammer often recounted the indignities he had endured as a law clerk during the Civil War. He always ended the story, his whiskered chin held high, with how he had brought on the ruination of an incompetent captain. "But I never complained," Judge Hammer said proudly. "For complaints are the purview of women."

Marcus crushed the paper into a ball and hurled it into the brush. As he chewed his pencil he wondered what was wrong with him? He had a carbine at his side and he had faced enemy fire—something his father had never done. Yet he couldn't write the old man a simple letter!

But the Judge had taught Marcus one thing—that when obstacles were great, there must be a devious way round them. Finally, a dim idea took form. Marcus slapped his head and leaped to his feet..

*

Lieutenant Hall sat in a daze, wearing a soiled undershirt as Marcus explained his difficulty. "I can see Father reading a few lines, then tossing my letter aside."

"I doubt that," Hall said, rubbing circulation into his hands, "but perhaps I can help."

"Then," Marcus asked, "how do I begin?"

"You don't," Hall said as he began to fumble through his satchel. He looked up, a suddenly hopeful look on his haggard face. "I am a writer. And I shall wield my craft in your behalf."

Marcus had hoped Lieutenant Hall would take on this task. A letter from the Rough Rider adjutant was bound to impress even Judge Marcus B. Hammer.

Over the next half hour, Hall crafted a letter that chronicled Marcus's determination to go to Cuba despite his troop's orders to remain in Florida. Spreading it on a bit thick, Hall related how Marcus volunteered to serve in the hospital corps. While in such capacity, young Marcus had helped bury his dearest friend—the Columbia rowing captain. Then Hall added an artful paragraph of Marcus's brave action during Las Guásimas. Judge Hammer's son ignored deadly fire to carry Roosevelt's bugler to safety.

"I think we should tell him you saved Gabriel Scriven," Hall said.

But Marcus hesitated.

"Think, Marcus," Hall urged. "That you saved the life of one who wronged you shows that you have matured—grown into a man!"

As Hall finished the letter, Marcus was already imagining an afternoon tea at the Hammer home. Thelma Scriven, Doctor de Bretteville, and Aura would hear first-hand how Marcus had risked his life to save a boy who had deformed him. Marcus imagined the Judge explaining how his son had thought of the greater good and had saved Roosevelt's errand boy.

Hall ended the letter with the news that Marcus had been assigned to a special weapon under Sergeant Tiffany, the son of the famous Manhattan artisan-jeweler. The Rough Riders would soon lay siege on the enemy capital. This, Hall explained, would be no ordinary bombardment. Marcus B. Hammer, Jr., would man the special gun Roosevelt was sure would bring about the Spanish surrender.

Lieutenant Hall penned his signature, then added his title with a flourish. "I leave on the *Seneca* tomorrow, Hammer. I shall post your letter as soon as I arrive in Tampa."

As Marcus left Hall's tent, he knew that even if a sniper got him, Judge Hammer would have that letter. But it would take more than a Spanish bullet to bring him down. Say, if he were wounded! Why then, he'd return to Fort Chambers a hero. Better, by God than any sissy-pants bugler.

No matter what Gabriel Scriven did, Marcus knew the mulatto would always owe him for his life. Once they got home, Marcus would watch the bastard squirm each time he was reminded of it.

*

But Lieutenant Tom Hall had his own reasons for writing Marcus's letter. The boy's motive had been quite transparent. But Hall knew that letter could well be his last official act. He preferred to end his days as a Rough Rider on a positive note. It was fitting, he thought, that his military career end with a story. Words had always served him well. He must soon begin the real story of this regiment. And when he did, he would tell the truth.

Yesterday, Roosevelt thanked him for his help, in particular the early days at San Antonio. Roosevelt seemed interested in Hall's plans and when he mentioned getting right to work on a book about the Rough Riders, Roosevelt looked suddenly uncomfortable. He quickly announced that he was sending Hall home to recover from his fevers. The discharge would be honorable, a more or less general military order. As Roosevelt told him this, his pained look made Hall realize that the decision had been Colonel Wood's. Yet, Roosevelt shook his hand and told him he had secured a cabin on the first available transport.

Perhaps it would be good to get away from the resentful stares of the troopers, and the poisonous pen of Richard Harding Davis. But Lieutenant Hall was a professional soldier and his throat thickened when he thought leaving the boys on San Juan Hill. He vowed to say good-bye to the one trooper who knew what really happened at Las Guásimas. All that evil needs to triumph, Hall reminded himself, was for good men to remain silent.

Later that day, he found Gabriel Scriven in his trench, staring toward the Spanish lines. As Hall approached, Gabriel silenced him. "Listen," he whispered.

Hall squatted beside him. From the enemy lines came trumpet calls, interspersed by the tattoo of snare drums.

They were both artists in war, and both adjutant and bugler were appreciative and curious about the Spanish—young men who would no doubt prefer to be playing soccer or drinking on a dry afternoon in Spain to struggling in suffocating humidity of Cuba against a force of Yankees.

The Spanish trumpet trills were punctuated by tapping drums. As the music drifted over the hills, it seemed to give the war both form and purpose. Then, with a final flourish, the music stopped and the mad rasp of cicadas recorded the terrible heat.

Hall explained that he would soon be leaving.

Gabriel handed the Lieutenant a letter to his mother.

"Sure thing, Scriven," Hall said with difficulty. He composed himself and continued, "By the way, several sacks of mail have come in. I'll send them up before I leave." Then he grew silent. "Listen," he said, looking away, "it seems I'll be leaving Cuba under a cloud. Not exactly the way I'd intended." His eyes were defensive, almost like those of a man who expected to be slapped. "You saw what happened. If anybody asks you, I hope you'll stick by me."

Gabriel didn't answer.

Hall cleared his throat. "Just tell what you saw."

Gabriel nodded.

The slight motion was enough for Hall. He looked suddenly hopeful. "The Colonel thinks highly of you, Scriven. He'll listen to you. And he'll protect the good name of the Rough Riders, for he has high political ambitions. This thing may one day catapult him into high office. But when he gets back to New York, he'll have plenty of critics. The Las Guásimas 'ambush,' " Hall emphasized the word, "will be an issue. He will have to defend himself, and he'll need a scapegoat." Hall sighed. "A drunk like me."

Gabriel felt sick. "I don't think the Colonel would do that."

Lieutenant Hall got up slowly. He had lost a lot of weight, Gabriel realized. But they all had.

Gabriel accepted Hall's handshake—at first weak, but finishing with an attempt at strength. "You'll do fine, sir. Go write your own story."

Hall smiled. "I intend to," he said, "but Roosevelt is a celebrity. His book will eclipse any other. I'll be lucky if mine gets a second printing."

"Look, sir. I don't think we'll ever understand what went on here," Gabriel said. He had made Lieutenant Hall feel better, but as Gabriel heard his own words, it was as though he was listening to another man, a much older man.

CHAPTER 28

July 6

There were too many in the road to know the whereabouts of one woman and her boy. But Gabriel finally found them in a palm grove. She was trying to comb her tangled hair with her fingers. Nearby, the boy lay on her shawl. Because there were so many unburied men and horses, the flies were very bad. Now there was no lime to spread on the carcasses. The whole countryside smelled like a slaughter house.

Gabriel knelt beside the boy. *"¿Tiene infermo?* Are you sick ?"

"No, Señor," the lad replied. *"Tengo hambre.* I'm hungry.*"*

The woman sat down on the ground and buried her face in her hands. "Since the blockade, we have had only rice soup. And not much of that."

He reached into his haversack and produced a package of hardtack. "Here," he said, "suck on this."

The boy took the hard cracker, murmured his thanks, and began to nibble with his small, even teeth.

Gabriel was sorry for them, dazed and hungry now because an overfed general threatened their city.

She was looking at him with tired, angry eyes. "The *Insurrectos* have ruined everything," she accused. "Now Cubans starve along with the Spanish. In their wild uprising, they have burned the farms. Now we cannot buy even yucca root from the peasants because they are afraid of reprisals from the *Insurrectos*. In Santiago, ships brought our only food and now, no ship can reach us. The last brought rice, which was over a month ago. Dogs have begun to kill and eat each other."

She shook her head. "When you supplied guns to the *Insurrectos,*" she said, "you made everything worse. Do you know that my own brother is a rebel?" She swept her hair back with a defiant hand. "This rebellion has torn apart our families. I was born in Cuba, but because I married a Spanish officer, I am considered the enemy in my own country."

"Where is your husband now?"

At this, she shrugged.

"Look, " Gabriel said, "we have taken some prisoners. Maybe I can find him for you."

Her tired eyes flickered with hope. She assured him that her husband was well known by the Spanish soldiers. "They call him *El Rojo,* the red head.*"*

"I can't promise anything," Gabriel told her, "but Colonel Roosevelt has five children of his own. Maybe he can help." Then Gabriel remembered the officer who had nearly killed Roosevelt. "Tell me," he asked, "is your husband in the cavalry?"

She nodded.

"Then I believe he is alive," Gabriel assured her.

Now she hugged the boy and kissed him.

Gabriel was glad to give her some good news, more welcome, he realized, than food. "Your husband is wounded, but not too badly, I believe. Colonel Roosevelt let him return to the Spanish lines."

"Gracias a Dios!" she cried. And she told the boy in rapid Spanish. Then she said, "I will go to him now."

"No," Gabriel said. "We are about to bombard the city. There will be more fighting. You must stay here."

She twisted a ring from her finger. "Then," she said, "give this to one of the Spanish negotiators. In this way my husband will know that we are alive."

*

That evening, Gabriel had little appetite. The rest of the troopers slurped the beans Colonel Roosevelt had appropriated from a regiment that had been foolish enough to leave them unguarded.

Snake finished his and was eyeing Gabriel's.

"Take my duty," Gabriel told him. "I'll be back in a couple of hours."

"Sure. How about your beans?"

Gabriel grinned. "They are going to a lady." And as the troopers shot him knowing grins, he added, "and to her son."

*

Night came suddenly in the tropics. Roosevelt had been squinting at his papers and had not paid attention. He knew lighting a lantern would be dangerous. Enemy snipers were ignoring the cease fire. But he had learned to write with little or no light. His pen was relatively sure, though the lines seen in daylight might be somewhat uneven. At times, he realized, one word might slightly overlap another.

In this case, neatness was irrelevant, for an aide stood ready to deliver his message to Siboney where it would be cabled to his oldest friend, Senator Henry Cabot Lodge of Massachusetts. "Cabot" had been an early supporter of intervention against Spain and he could get the President to move. As Roosevelt wrote in the darkness, he imagined the telegrapher's finger on the key:

Lodge,

Not since Crassus against Parthians has there been more incompetent leadership. My men starving and sickening daily. Imperative you send food, ammunition, and artillery.

Ignore optimistic communiqués.
We hold San Juan Hill, but situation critical.

T.R.

CHAPTER 29

July 7

Lieutenant Hall soaped himself down, luxuriating in the Captain's bath of the rusty, crowded *Seneca*. She was the first ship being sent home and with the worst wounded. In a nearby cabin, Captain McClintock of B Troop suffered with a painful leg wound. Captain Day and Lieutenant Thomas of L Troop were similarly laid up with wounds. And in the hold, a hundred wounded troopers from different regiments gritted their teeth, and exchanged gallows humor.

The hot bath loosened more than dirt and vermin. It was a ritual for which Hall was grateful. He scrubbed hard, until his skin burned from the soap. He would grow a new one, like a molting reptile. Finally, he stepped from the bath, wrapped himself in a towel and padded onto the quarter deck. The *Seneca* swung against her anchor chain, rocking in swells that caught the moonlight and threw it against her gray hull.

Ah, illusion, Hall thought to himself. The spectacular beauty of the tropical night, the white moon above the dark mountains, and the sound of lapping waves seemed like a dream. As the night air dried him, Hall realized the bath had cooled his fever, at least for the moment.

A half mile across the bay, a string of yellow lights and a froth of silver surf defined Siboney. Hall buried his face in the towel, drying his ears, smoothing his mustache. When he looked up again, he saw that that someone had lit a bonfire on shore.

He watched as the flame blossomed, then spread from shack to shack. Then came the shouts of men across the surface of the water, exuberant shouts that sounded like boys at camp. He watched the hospital tents flare into a maw of flame and sparks spiraled high in the air.

Their shouts carried across the undulating sea and he imagined for an instant that they were the cries of the wounded below decks. Then the amber reflections of flame mingled with the cold, almost bluish moonlight. Like oil and water, he realized. And he knew he had engaged in metaphor—was again, even for an instant, thinking like a writer. He had not been able to do so for months.

Lieutenant Hall knew Siboney was being burned at Colonel Wood's order to stop the spread of yellow fever.

The fire reflected off the shallow mosquito ponds. Silhouettes of men working the flames reminded the writer of an ancient rite; one of fire, water, earth, sky. Mingled with death, life, and courage. To the mix had been added both blunder and uncertainty. That is how he would always think of the accusation that hung over him. But for another bullet, one that could have hit him, and he could be going home a wounded hero.

But no. He was being shipped home quietly, without fanfare. As an embarrassment.

As Siboney dissolved in flame, Hall's mood darkened. Roosevelt had been unusually quiet. All he could hope for now was to be spared in Roosevelt's memoirs.

Tom Hall had already decided that it was best to play the thing lightly. His own account would be an entertainment, not an accusation. It would be a humorous book—an account of this motley assemblage of men. He was sure Roosevelt's version would be self-aggrandizing.

Despite the warm night, Lieutenant Hall suddenly had a chilling thought. Hall had stored a wagon load of mail in one of the sheds at Siboney. The next morning, it was supposed to be taken up to San Juan Hill.

With a sinking heart, he realized that the burning of Siboney was not purifying at all, but the symbol of a tragedy. How would he ever live this

Hall stumbled back into the bath, stared into the mirror and saw a skeletal image. He wiped the steam away and stared into the haunted eyes of a failure.

Then he remembered the full flask of brandy the Captain had so foolishly left on his desk.

CHAPTER 30

July 8

The tattooed coxswain explained that it was twenty nautical miles down the coast to where the two Rough Riders wanted to go. A few days ago, he had taken Mister Hearst and a few newspaper men, and had gotten into plenty of trouble. The Spanish wrecks were off limits to anyone but navy personnel. But the dark lieutenant insisted, and the coxswain relented, realizing he might get into trouble if he did not fire the boiler of the steam lighter and take them.

Cloud put his arm around the sailor. "Of course you must tell nobody, for ours is a secret mission. I will make sure you are commended for a citation. But we must reach the other side of the harbor and you are our only hope."

The coxswain was not fully convinced. Gabriel decided to step in. For the occasion, he had finally sewn the chief trumpeter's chevrons to his sleeve. The three stripes with a stylized trumpet in a dark arch seemed to impress the sailor. "Look, I am Colonel Roosevelt's personal envoy," Gabriel said. "And," he added, patting his polished leather pouch, "I bear documents for a Cuban general whose headquarters are at Aserradero. You only need to put us ashore and then return. You need not wait. We will reach Santiago by other means. Lieutenant Cloud and I have our orders."

"Quickly, man," Cloud urged, "don't spare the coal. Our victory is at stake."

Mist hovered on the coast as the launch, running just beyond the breakwater, chugged westward. But in twenty minutes the mist burned off and the sun bathed the Morro Castle at the entrance to Santiago Harbor in pink light. The battlements were beautiful above the azure sea. Then the lighter crossed the narrow mouth of the harbor where Cervera's fleet had rushed out to destruction. Across the harbor, they saw the battery where Spanish guns still angled as if to blow any intruder out of the water.

The coxswain had become talkative and when they reached the rugged coast where the mountains came right down to the sea, he slowed his engine and pointed to the twisted wreck of a ship whose turrets were still bright with silver paint. "The *Plutón*," he spat, "and further down, off the starboard beam, we'll come to the *Maria Teresa*."

Gabriel stared at the twisted hulks of the ships that lay broken and smoldering. Near the lighter, the swells tossed charred life rings, scraps of wood, paper, and cloth. When they had passed the third wreck, the *Oquendo*, the coxswain shoveled more coal into the boiler and increased his speed.

The *Viscaya* had been beached in two fathoms of water. She sat on the bottom, her blackened superstructure pitted with shell holes. Her turreted guns aimed at the sky. As they came around her, Gabriel saw the a great hole blown in her bow. Just past the wreck, the coxswain turned into shore. Gabriel could make out several small huts with thatched roofs set in the coconut palms.

The sailor stared into the clear water and dropped anchor. When the lighter had swung, pulling the anchor rope taught, he lowered the dinghy over the side.

When the dinghy's bow nudged the sand, Cloud stepped over the gunwale into the surf and Gabriel followed.

The houses were deserted. As the lighter departed, Gabriel studied the steep mountains rising from the beach. Then Cloud unbuttoned his shirt, folded it so that his lieutenants' epaulets were on the outside, and they started up a steep trail. At the base of a cliff, he hid his uniform in a crevice. He reset the feather in his headband and examined his machete as Gabriel stripped off his shirt.

Then Cloud picked a rocky path and they began their climb.

Soon they were both glistening with sweat. Cloud paused. The wind blew in from the sea.

When they reached the first rise, they found themselves in a dense thicket. Cloud began to hack a path. Gabriel hoped they didn't look like *Yanqui* now, because the *mambises* might shoot them as quickly as they would a Spaniard. Gabriel couldn't much blame them, the way the American officers treated them. Gabriel had heard Wood give the order. The Cubans were to get no additional ammunition nor supplies, for most of the troopers had heard that Cubans butchered prisoners and would steal anything they got their hands on.

As Cloud swung and chopped the vines, he could not shake the image of the Bluecoats as they had herded his people from one miserable camp to another. Some of his people had stolen too. But it was not considered a bad thing to take something that someone had carelessly left behind. Now the Cubans were being treated as his own people had been. Like children, they were given ammunition and rations only when they obeyed. Now the Cubans were even being blamed for errors in judgment made by Americans.

As a stubborn vine fell to his blade, Cloud caught movement in the brush to their left. He froze and signaled Gabriel.

Then a branch was pushed back by the barrel of a rifle. Behind it, an unsmiling *mambi* stared at them.

The Cuban was a small, lean man. Once Gabriel explained in Spanish that they wanted to go to General Rabí's camp, he slowly lowered his gun.

They took a trail that cut back and forth along the ridges. Although Rabí's camp was over thirty miles on the opposite side of Santiago Bay from General García's, Gabriel knew there must be Spanish troops nearby. It would be impossible, Gabriel realized, for the Spanish to attack the Cubans in these mountains. Mountains, he realized, must be a requisite for revolution.

It was another hour before they came out of the jungle and into a palm grove where a large, discolored house was filled with wounded men. General Rabí, their guide explained, was taking his siesta. Everywhere, the wounded lay sleeping—men with clean bandages on arms, legs, and faces. Beside them were the empty half coconut shells from which they had eaten, and empty bottles that still smelled of rum.

Gabriel and Cloud found a pot of rice and helped themselves, as the

Cuban sat against a tree, took a swig or two of rum, and promptly fell asleep.

The house was set back from the cliff, overgrown with bougainvillea. On all sides of the steep hill, the jungle provided a natural barrier.

The general sipped his coffee with a bandaged hand. General Jésus Rabí had the stocky build of a Caribe. His long hair was parted in the middle and lay coarse as a horsetail over his unbuttoned white shirt. He was the most relaxed general Gabriel had ever seen. And he seemed to be quick in understanding Gabriel's Spanish.

Rabí was impressed that the two of them made the effort to find his headquarters. He recounted the meeting he had hosted nearly a month ago between General Calixto García and General Shafter. The American Admiral Sampson had come too and Rabí related his surprise again that the two Americans had argued. Jésus Rabí said that General Shafter's temper was as big as his bulk. But temper in a general was a good thing. Calixto García, he said, could use more of it. "As you see," Rabí said, "we are have made our fight and now wait for news from Santiago."

"They are still talking." Gabriel told him. "Meanwhile we have come to warn you."

General Rabí leaned forward.

"Our officers have decided to keep the Cuban forces away from the Spanish. They say your *mambises* will slaughter Spanish prisoners. Is it true?"

The Cuban General frowned. "Only the *guerrilleros,* those who do their dirty work for a few pesos." He withdrew his machete and brought it down on the wooden table, shearing the corner clean. "They get the death they deserve."

Rabí sheathed his machete. "You must remember that the *Peninsulares* believe we are savages. True, we have earned the reputation. But you do not win a war by being polite. I understand that your George Washington attacked on Christmas Day. Uncivilized, no? But very effective."

Gabriel told the general the worst news. "You are to get no more supplies. No guns, no ammunition."

General Rabí stiffened.

"The same with General García."

General Rabí stared toward the sea. "The other day, when the *Viscaya* ran aground, we went down to strip it of food. But *Yanqui* marines were already guarding the wreck. They told us, at gunpoint, to get away! They treated us like enemies, not *compañeros.*"

Rabí stood and clasped his hands behind his back. "If we are not *gringos* so we must be savages, no? Too stupid to govern ourselves!" His eyes flashed with anger. "But we are way ahead of you! Our greatest general was Antonio Maceo—a mulatto—a Negro! The *Peninsulares* were so afraid of him, they would not come out of their camps. They dug *trochas* to divide us." He spun and glared at them. "It did not work. We kept the *Peninsulares* in the cities." Rabí sighed. "We don't need your soldiers. But I would not be truthful if I did not admit we need more guns and ammunition."

"We can help," Gabriel said. "Lieutenant Cloud and I may be able to persuade..."

General Jésus Rabí interrupted him. "No. I understand completely. The *Peninsulares* and the *Yanquis* are white. Ultimately they will stick together against we who are not."

"Well, we have come to help you."

Rabí shook his head. "*Dios mio,* what arrogance! We need only weapons." He turned and gestured toward the east. "I never wanted one *Yanqui* on Cuban soil and neither did General García. Only one of our generals has been trained as a soldier—General Gomez. The rest of us," he struck his chest with his fist, "lead men because we *can.* Yet you *gringos* are convinced we can do nothing without your help. Besides, you want to bring us *civilización.*" The word made a hard sound. "To push it down our throats. First the Spanish did it and killed almost all of the Taínos and Caribes. Then they brought," he gestured toward Gabriel, "your people from Africa. And not only to slave for them, but so they could feel superior over us and give us *civilización.* And tell me, do your Indios or Negros have freedom in America?"

In the silence that followed, General Rabí's expression softened. He turned to Cloud and asked, "You are the son of a *jéfe,* no?"

"Yes," Cloud told him.

Rabí nodded, *"Bién,"* he said, "then you know what you must do."

A Rag in the

CHAPTER 31

Saturday, July 9

The water barrels had finally been hauled up from Siboney and after the white troopers had their fill, the Tenth Cavalry gathered to have their first long drink. The water was tepid but they drank long and deeply, for it was the first fresh water they had tasted in days. To Eli Biddle, it was as nourishing as mother's milk. The troopers waited on the shadeless heights of San Juan Hill, while in the valley below both sides parleyed under the *cieba* tree.

All morning long aides galloped back and forth, carrying long paper strips the troopers jokingly called the baseball edition—for they seemed to be bringing the latest score of the war.

Now the Cavalry occupied the entire San Juan heights—the Ninth on the left flank, the Rough Riders in the center, and the Tenth on the right flank. As Biddle passed between the two Negro regiments, he asked for Gabriel Scriven. Snake thought Colonel Roosevelt had sent him off on an errand. Others said they thought he and Cloud might have gone to Siboney.

Biddle had already spoken to Lieutenant Pershing about a commission for Gabriel. At Las Guásimas and at San Juan Hill, the Tenth had lost eleven officers— exactly half of the original twenty-two had been killed or wounded. Biddle and the other non-commissioned officers were doing their best to fill the gap, but is was clear that more officers were needed at once.

One or two Negros were being considered and Biddle knew this might be a chance for Gabriel to get a field commission as a regular. The boy showed pluck and resourcefulness. He'd make a good soldier. Biddle knew the Rough Riders would be disbanded soon after the surrender, and he determined to help Sam Scriven's boy toward a career. With his quick wits and light skin, Gabriel might even become an officer.

CHAPTER 32

Sunday, July 10

Because of the heat, Colonel Roosevelt shortened each man's watch to two hours.

Marcus Hammer and William Tiffany had just started down into the coconut grove when they heard a whistling sound, followed by a distant boom. Then, a shell exploded in Santiago Harbor. Soon there were other rounds exploding in the city and troopers ran back up the hill to their positions.

On the surrounding heights, the Spanish stood and watched the navy's shells lob over them. They began to shake their fists at the American lines until the Gatlings drove them to cover. When the Gatlings ceased to cool their barrels, the Spanish returned a half-hearted volley at San Juan Hill, but they seemed to be shooting high.

Sergeant William Tiffany was sorry the truce had ended. He hoped never to fire another shot. It was clear enough to him that any casualties now were wasted and he did not relish now or ever the task of shelling civilian targets. Colonel Roosevelt had given him only one directive. When the truce ended, fire as many shots into the city as possible, until General Shafter ordered a stop. Each shot fired, Roosevelt had reasoned aloud, would save Rough Riders' lives.

But Marcus Hammer did not share Tiffany's reluctance. The bull-necked trooper had never assembled and reassembled the dynamite gun, only practicing the functions necessary to fire it. Tiffany had even taught Marcus the rudiments of calculating range. But Marcus insisted that Tiffany aim the first shot, and he had, toward the barracks he knew to be empty.

Marcus eased the five pound, silver canister of nitroglycerin into the barrel and closed the breech. Tiffany watched him as he fed a blank cartridge in behind the fire wall. Then with the breech closed, he set the pressure gauge to full. Marcus looked at Tiffany and saw him nod.

He jerked the lanyard. Then came a muffled report, a puff of white smoke as the pressure chamber filled. Then the long tube popped as the canister soared high into the cloudless sky. As Marcus's pulse raced, he saw it fall into the center of the city. But there was no explosion.

But Marcus remembered where the dud had fallen. The distance was right. He had only to swing the long, brass barrel an inch to the left. Again, he loaded.

The gun popped and a canister shell soared as high as before. This time the shell exploded near the cathedral.

Hammer quickly emptied the breech, and fed another shell into the cradle. Then, as he stepped back to jerk the lanyard, Tiffany saw a Rough Rider tackle Hammer and knock him to the ground. Two troopers rolled in the dust. But with a mighty snarl, more like an animal than a man, Hammer shoved his assailant away, leaped toward the gun, and fell across the long barrel, changing its angle to almost horizontal. He did not try to correct the aim. He jerked the lanyard and the canister popped, and there was a terrific explosion in their midst.

As the debris fell and the smoke cleared, Tiffany saw Gabriel Scriven struggle to his feet. He stared at the figure on the ground. Tiffany ran over to Marcus. Both shoes had been blown off and the toes of one foot were missing.

*

The cruiser *Brooklyn* and the battleship *Indiana* shelled the Morro Castle at the entrance of the harbor for nearly an hour. This, Admiral Sampson hoped, would demonstrate to General Shafter that the Navy was doing its part to force the surrender. Sampson was still furious that the week before, at the very hour the Spanish broke out of the harbor, he had been steaming east to refuel his flagship. As a result, Rear Admiral Schley, his subordinate, had overseen the destruction of Cervera's fleet.

Yet, it had been Sampson's careful planning for months that resulted in this victory. It had been his idea to bottle up the fleet. And he had given instructions to his subordinates, including Schley, what to do if Cervera tried to run for it. They were to pursue and fire, keeping the slower Spanish vessels between themselves and the shore line. This tactic would both limit the Spanish ability to maneuver, and would quickly deplete their limited coal supply. Even though he had not been present at first, Admiral Sampson had been able to return in time to see the *Viscaya* destroyed. And to compose a message of victory to be wired to Washington. In the message, he did not mention Schley's name. There would enough glory; he joked to an aide, to go around. But Admiral Sampson did not know that Commodore Schley had already penned his own dispatch. In it, there was no mention of Sampson.

*

When Doctor Winter came around to administer morphine, Marcus made a joke about his foot, hoping Winter would reassure him. But the Doctor administered the sedative without comment.

When the doctor had left and he felt the morphine began to take effect, Marcus turned to the man in the next bed. "I'm a football player," he said. "got to have all my parts."

From somewhere in the trooper's beard came a tight-lipped reply. "Save your breath. If you're still breathin' at sundown, they give you water."

Marcus was very thirsty. The translucent canvas above him was darkened by shadow, and a hard rain drummed the tent. Wind flared the side panels and a wet breeze blew across the cots. And yet, the thirsty troopers who lay inside could only imagine the coolness of the rain.

Marcus watched sheets of it cascade down the canvas. Stalactites of condensation collected at the seams. The canvas sagged above his bed and the rain collected in a pool. If could puncture the canvas, he could drink his fill. He watched a nipple of water form in the center of the bulge. As it fell, his tongue caught it. Then, another drop began to form and he caught that too. Marcus concentrated, timing each drop. It was a game and it took his mind off his foot.

He was getting sleepy now. He must already be dreaming, for there were dark shapes all around him, going from bed to bed. "You all right, trooper?" one of them asked. Marcus opened his eyes to see a big Negro dressed in white bending over him.

"What the hell!" he exclaimed.

The trooper ignored Marcus. He tenderly wiped Marcus's face with a cool cloth, propped him up and put a cup to his lips. "You're goin' to be okay, trooper," the orderly cooed.

Marcus saw that the tent was full of them. At every bed, a Negro in a white smock attended a wounded man. "You ain't dreamin', trooper," Marcus's attendant whispered. "You ain't in heaven, with some angels you didn't figure would never make it in. This ain't heaven. No sir. But it's the next thing to it, because if you ever make it there, you'll find us guarding the gates."

"Who are you?" Marcus demanded.

The dark man smiled. "You wouldn't remember my name. We're the Twenty-Fourth Infantry. We ate lead at San Juan Hill, and took the southern end. But I expect you Roosevelt boys didn't much notice."

"If you are soldiers, what are you doing here?" Marcus demanded.

The dark orderly's nose almost touched Marcus's, as he hissed, "We volunteered, boy." Then he straightened and smiled. "Why, Massa," he mimicked, "don't you know we darkies is immune to da fever?"

Later, as Marcus eased into a drug-induced sleep, he dreamed of being guarded by black angels.

CHAPTER 33

Monday, July 11

Gabriel heard a bugle cut the mist; blowing double-time. It was a crisp blow, with new wind. He had come down to check on Isbell. He watched the column of fresh infantrymen trotting in close ranks past the hospital of tents. For a good twenty minutes they jogged past, the drums fading ahead of them.

"First Illinois," a trooper called, "from the land of Lincoln."

As the stragglers ran past, a snappy set of snares grew louder and up the road came yet another regiment of clean, beardless boys.

"Columnnnnn, HALT!"

The young men stared into the hospital tents until their officers galloped up, fell in behind Old Glory and the gold-trimmed banner that read Ninth Massachusetts Infantry.

"Faaaah-wadddd- MAAAHHHHCH."

In the distance the sky flashed. Seconds later came the sound of artillery, and the boys from the Bay State cheered.

A few weeks ago, Gabriel thought, we must have looked like this. All sass and vinegar.

A black orderly stepped up to Gabriel. "You're not a patient." he snapped. "This tent is quarantined. Get out."

"But I came to see Isbell. How's he doing?"

The orderly sized up Gabriel, "Oh, you're with Roosevelt. We've got two of your boys. One with no toes and the other an Injun shot three times."

"The Indian. How is he?"

"No worse than anybody else," the trooper said, "But we've got orders. No visitors."

*

In the column of new recruits, Gabriel found a lieutenant. "What's all the movement about, sir?"

"We just landed with General Miles," he said. "Understand you boys could use some help."

His column stretched back to the beach and seemed endless. They were kids, Gabriel thought, with no idea what war was like. With luck, before any of them found out, the fighting would be over.

CHAPTER 34

July 15

They rode single file along the road where a regiment waited. "How about a lift, old fella," a trooper called out as Gabriel rode past. He stared down at the boy, seventeen, well-fed and freshly sunburned, leaning on his ancient black-powder Springfield.

"Don't hurry," he said. "Walking's good for your circulation."

"Thanks anyway, old timer."

The artillery was quiet and a second truce had begun. Colonel Roosevelt sat with General Wood in his tent. The flaps were tied up so that the two officers had a clear view of the truce session. Roosevelt fanned himself with his ruined Stetson.

Wood was staring at the gathering of officers under the tree. "I think General Miles's arrival will convince the Spanish to surrender. And it is important that our regiment participates in the surrender ceremonies. Toward that end, you should let T.T. Cloud's battlefield promotion stick. The Tenth gave him lieutenant's bars and I see no reason for us to take them back."

Roosevelt nodded approvingly. "And Scriven, Leonard. I want to promote him to full sergeant, at once. I can see Davis's story in print now—a Sioux lieutenant and a Dakota boy who saved his colonel with his bugle. Hah!"

"I don't care about the press," Wood said. "I wish we could take the whole regiment, but we can't. We don't have a supply of clean uniforms and besides, many of your men are too sick to stand at attention. We know they deserve to be there. But it is important for our side us to look smart. The Ninth Massachusetts Infantry and the Sixth Cavalry will do nicely. I'm told the Sixth has an excellent band."

At that point, Gabriel Scriven arrived at their tent. "Private Scriven reporting, sir!"

Roosevelt frowned. "Private Scriven? Are you sure you have the right regiment? We do not have a Private Scriven, do we Leonard?"

Wood, less an actor than Roosevelt, betrayed a smile.

"Hah! Well! This is quite a dilemma!" Roosevelt feigned, stroking his mustache. He got up and walked around Gabriel. "Well, his uniform indicates he is of our regiment." He stopped in front of Gabriel and squinted through his glasses. "Weren't you once a bugler?"

Gabriel was completely taken in by Roosevelt's ruse. He though, perhaps the Colonel's fever had returned with a vengeance. "You know I am, sir."

"Well, then," Roosevelt said. "It seems we do have one position to fill. Maybe you'll do. What do you think, General Wood?"

"Trooper Scriven will do very nicely indeed."

"Then, Sergeant Gabriel Scriven, congratulations! You may sit, Sergeant. We've a bit of business to finish."

CHAPTER 39

Sunday, July 17

As the troopers, both black and white, gathered around the "surrender tree," they were grateful that there had been no sniper fire during the
night. On the hill toward Santiago, Spanish troops knelt, waiting to receive
communion from a priest who worked among them.

On Sundays there were hymns by the Cowboy Chorus, but today
most of the men were sick. As those who could walk assembled, they moved
slowly as though in a dream. Most quickly sat down. A band could not be gotten up, but the Tenth Cavalry offered a quartet of troopers who sang a slow
version of "Ezekiel Saw The Wheel," accompanied by the clapping of hands.

After leading the troopers in a prayer, the Chaplain read nine verses
from the Sermon on the Mount, finishing with, "Blessed are the peacemak-
ers, for they shall be called the Children of God."

General Wheeler donned his Stetson and cleared his throat. The men
leaned forward, for General Wheeler had a soft voice that they could barely
hear. "Gentlemen of the Second Cavalry Brigade," he said, "I am pleased to
inform you that at exactly nine twenty-five this mornin' the Spanish officially
caPITulated."

There was a weak but heartfelt cheer.

"More than any man here," Wheeler continued, "I know the difficulty of surRENduh. A vanquished army, fightin' and dying and denied victory, can only hope for dignity in its final hour. Now General Shafter intends to give that dignity to the Spanish. I reckon the rest of this Sabbath will be a ceremony of one kind or anuthuh. Durin' these, you will maintain your positions and behave like Christian gentlemen."

The little general continued with a twinkle in his eyes. "Now, boys, that means no cat-calls or spitting in the enemy's presence."

As the laughter subsided, Wheeler drew himself up. "I am right proud to have been your commanduh. Every jack one of you, whether private, officer, Nigra, white, Sioux, Jew, rebel, or even Yankee," he said, "is an American first and has fought as bravely as any men I've evuh led." General Wheeler brought his glove to his hat brim. "Ah salute you every one!"

*

At the same hour, in Santiago de Cuba, General Jose Toral saluted his flag, but with bitterness. Fate had chosen him to preside over the end of rule in the hemisphere *España* had discovered and colonized. Captain Hernán Cortez had prayed near this very spot, on his way to conquer the Aztecs with a thousand men. During her nearly four centuries of rule in Cuba, Spain had beaten off the French, the English, and until recently, the ruthless Cuban rebels. Now the Americans had come, and only their superior navy had enabled them, General Toral was convinced, to force the red and yellow flag of his beloved country to be lowered.

Beside General Toral stood Colonel Frederíco Escario, whose regiment had fought its way from Manzanillo with three thousand troops to reinforce Santiago the night after the Americans attacked San Juan heights. When the column arrived, Toral was ashamed that he had nothing to offer them except shovels to dig in. They had little food and precious little water. Colonel Escario deserved better, for he had had lost hundreds, wounded and killed as the Cuban *mambises* fired on the column as it advanced along the narrow trails. Yet Escario had succeeded to reach Santiago when the morale of Toral's troops had been at its lowest. As a result they felt a resurgence of hope and thought that they might even re-take *los altos de San Juan*.

Some of his best officers had died. General Vara del Rey, with only five hundred men and no cannon, had stopped two thousand Americans at El Caney for hours, and inflicted very heavy losses on them.

General Jose Toral and his *Peninsulares* had nothing to be ashamed of. Madrid had let them down. There had never been enough of anything—

food, ammunition, or for that matter, men. Even Admiral Cervera had been completely betrayed. How could he be expected to beat two American squadrons with obsolete ships and very little coal?

But, General Toral thought with satisfaction, he had been able to buy some time, and ultimately, the American generals knew the pride of the Spanish fighting man. The Americans were men who fought in the open and had a code of honor. Since Cervera's fleet had been destroyed, Toral had finally convinced General Shafter to transport his men back to Spain on American vessels. In return, his forces would lay down their arms, with the understanding that when they embarked, they would receive them again.

General Toral had already envisioned a welcoming parade for his men in Barcelona. They had done their best against a powerful enemy who was continuing to pour men and supplies into Cuba every day.

An aide folded the flag and handed it to the General. He lay it over his saddle horn, crossed himself and steeled himself against the difficult hours ahead. He wheeled his stallion and his officers fell in behind him.

At this same hour, Colonel Raul García finally persuaded his father to accept General Shafter's last-minute invitation to the surrender ceremonies. Only General Calixto García could adequately represent Cuba Libre, his son insisted. Only he could insist that the Cuban flag be raised over the governor's palace.

Shafter's invitation had been insultingly specific. The General was to come without his hundred man *escolta*. He could bring but one officer with him, and no firearms. General Rabí had already refused to go. He warned General García that they would be fighting the *Yanquis* next, and he had already taken his command into the mountains to prepare for that.

Calixto García had relented. He realized that to boycott the ceremony, as Rabí suggested, would gain nothing. He would take Raúl, for it was he who had become the real commander anyway.

The two Cuban officers were nearly around the hill when they were challenged by a Rough Rider private with a drawn pistol. "We are the Cuban delegation to the surrender," Colonel García snapped. "Stand aside."

But the trooper's eyes were cold. "Colonel Roosevelt said to let no Cubans pass."

Colonel García had his saber half drawn when his father lay his hand over it. "No," he said, "I can see now that we were never intended to be there. Rabí was right. Let them have their damned ceremony."

Reluctantly, the two Garcías turned their horses away from Santiago.

They rode silently for some minutes until they came to a fork in the trail. On the right, the trail led up into the mountains. Colonel Raúl García leaned over in his saddle and took the flag from his father.

"Don't be a fool, my son. They will surely shoot you."

But Raúl was not to be stopped. He leaned forward and kissed his father on the forehead, on the deep scar where the suicide bullet had exited. "Do not worry, *padre*, I will soon join you to make the fight against the *Yanquis*."

General Calixto García's shoulders seemed to slump inside his immaculate uniform. Then, he took the trail to the mountains. As he did, he heard the galloping hooves of his son's horse as it hurtled toward Santiago.

*

The view from San Juan Hill was unimpeded by trees so thousands of men could see the officers from both sides approach from opposite directions. The American's uniforms were dark against the dead grass. Off to one side, the newsmen, who General Shafter had specifically barred from entering Santiago, were lamenting their bad fortune. Frederic Remington sketched on a book-sized pad. Burr McIntosh and Richard Harding Davis set their box cameras on tripods. Stephen Crane wiped the sweat from his face. A gaunt Sylvester Scovel had found a mount and spurred his way in front of the others. He drew a tongue lashing from Davis.

Below, behind their general and several officers, a hundred Spanish cavalrymen drew up in a pale blue line. Gabriel was surprised to see that some of the officers were smiling. One of them wore his arm in a sling.

General Shafter, sitting his dray horse as straight as his three hundred pounds would allow, rode from behind the hill, followed by Generals Wheeler, Kent, and Lawton. Wheeler's mare high-stepped slightly ahead of the others.

After the officers quieted their mounts, there was a moment of awkward silence. Finally, General Shafter eased his horse forward. Something glittered in the sun as he handed General Jose Toral the sword and spurs of General Vara del Rey, the hero of El Caney.

Toral accepted with a solemn nod, then, at his command, there was the hiss of steel as his officers drew their sabers and raised them to their noses in salute.

Then another withdrawing of steel, and the four American generals returned the salute.

After he had returned his sword to its scabbard, General Toral spurred his horse next to Shafter's. The two horses shied away from each other and there was a tense moment when the two generals, who had controlled entire armies, fought to control their wary mounts.

Gabriel noticed that the Spanish officers were smiling.

Finally, General Toral offered the Spanish flag to Shafter. The General seemed reluctant to take it. For a moment, Gabriel thought he was going to hand it back.

The two officers exchanged a few words that the men could not hear, shook hands and returned to their lines. And so the surrender, which had been brought about by cannon, Gatling guns, and the screams of charging men, was accomplished in silence. This was a ceremony of soldiers, not politicians.

*

First came the American color guard, then General Shafter, followed by his officers. Brigadier General Wood and Colonel Theodore Roosevelt rode side by side, followed by Cloud who carried the regimental banner. Gabriel rode beside him, as Roosevelt had instructed, his carbine in the sheath, fully loaded. Lieutenant Pershing and Sergeant Biddle represented the Tenth Cavalry, and behind them was an officer and trooper of the Ninth.

The Sixth Cavalry Band followed, the drummers beating cadence with their sticks, and next marched the Massachusetts Ninth Infantry. Vultures soared above the double column of Americans, as they followed the Spanish through the twisted streets, at times having to break into single file as their horses clopped over boards thrown over the trenches they would have had to take in a final assault. Nests of barbed wire gleamed over fortifications of wooden barrels filled with stones.

Riding beside General Kent, General Wheeler calculated that the three lines of Spanish defense, set at right angles and inside the city at every street corner, would have cost the Americans dearly. The stench was not one of ceremony. Dead horses, many still with bridles and saddle bags, lay in plain view. The vultures had torn open shallow graves that buzzed with flies.

In the twisting streets of the ancient city, unwashed Spanish soldiers, as dirty, Gabriel reminded himself as the Rough Riders they had left behind on San Juan Hill, crowded to glimpse their conquerors. As agreed, the Spanish had already stacked their arms in the nearby Plaza Dolores. Now, the Americans filed into Plaza de Armas, the central plaza which was bracketed by the cathedral and the governor's palace. In the center, several Spanish com-

A Rag in the .

panies stood in salute to the Americans.

The second- and third-story windows of the governor's palace were crowded with people. As the sun hung directly overhead, officers barked orders in English and in Spanish.

The formations waited, the Americans facing the palace with its empty flag pole. Horses shuddered and nervously chaffed their hooves on the cobblestones.

Sylvester Scovel had somehow managed to get to the plaza. He got to a tree and shimmied up it, so that he could see the square clearly. On the roof of the palace he encountered three officers. One of them was General Shafter's son-in-law, Shafter's aide Lieutenant Miley, and General Wheeler's son. Lieutenant Miley was just preparing to raise the American flag, when he saw Scovel. He quickly called down to General Shafter, "There is a man up here, and he won't get down."

Shafter's face turned scarlet. "Then throw him down."

Beside Gabriel, Roosevelt sputtered. "My God, he may be a sniper."

Gabriel unsheathed his carbine, and ran toward the tree with Cloud close behind him. It took all his strength to climb up, but he and Cloud soon were on the flat roof. By then, Scovel had begun to climb down the tree.

Ahead, a figure in white dashed toward the flag pole. Colonel Raúl García cut the corners from the American flag and it fell to the roof. As Miley struggled with García, he called out, "For God's sake, arrest this idiot."

Gabriel pumped a round into his Krag. As he trained it on Miley the cathedral clock began to strike. Colonel García twisted away from the shocked Miley, fixed his flag to the halyard and jerked his flag up the pole. "*Viva Cuba Libre,*" he shouted.

As the twelfth bell pealed, a roar of protest rose from the Spaniards below. The confused Americans were milling about.

Then, a shot rang out.

Officers and troopers flinched, then fell over each other as they sought cover.

When they had the courage to look up, they saw the Cuban flag flying above the governor's palace.

But on the roof, Colonel Raúl García lay in a pool of blood.

The American officers hauled the Cuban flag down and after some minutes, jury-rigged the cut corners of the Stars and Stripes to the halyard. It was not a pretty sight, the flag hanging cut and limp, but as ordered, it was raised.

The Sixth Cavalry band struck up "Hail Columbia" as the uncomfortable Spanish troopers straightened their uniforms.

Cloud covered García's body with the Cuban flag and watched the blood begin to soak the white star crimson.

Gabriel had not fired.

Gabriel tossed his carbine to Cloud, and nodded toward García's body. "Don't let anybody near him," he snapped, then ran to the edge of the roof and shimmied down the tree. Once on the hard cobblestones, he trotted through the confused troopers, following the figure of Scovel. Gabriel caught up with him as the reporter reached General Shafter.

Scovel spoke to the General, and Shafter, hanging to his saddle horn, swung a fist and knocked Scovel down. The reporter leaped to his feet and yelled something as a squad of marines descended on him.

In the plaza nobody knew what to do.

Gabriel felt a hand on his arm and turned to see Roosevelt's astonished face. "My God, Scriven, " he demanded, "what did you do up there?"

The band drowned Gabriel's answer out as it struck up "Hot Time in the Old Town Tonight."

My God—no ! It seemed obscene to play this tune now.

In the din of it, the Spanish and the Americans broke ranks and began to congratulate each other.

Gabriel turned away from Roosevelt and stumbled to where General Wheeler and Brigadier General Wood had dismounted. But just as he got their attention, the artillery batteries on San Juan Hill opened up in a twenty-one gun salute. Gabriel jammed his hands against his ears, and the heavy explosions seemed to last forever.

Up on San Juan Hill, Gabriel saw the dark shapes of men almost swallowed by the white cannon smoke. They stood motionless, ragged and charred as scarecrows.

end

EPILOGUE

Gabriel Scriven received an honorable discharge after his recovery from fever at Camp Wickoff, Long Island. When Captain Pershing offered him a commission in the band of the Tenth Cavalry, he accepted. In 1906 his twelve-tone composition "Santiago Rag" was performed at Roosevelt's inaugural ball. The last movement was a cacophony of opposing national anthems of Cuba, America, and Spain. Although the piece received critical praise, it was never again performed. Scriven eventually rose to the rank of Bandmaster of the Army under General John J. Pershing. He requested front line service in France in 1917. He died during a mustard gas attack when he insisted on staying behind to blow the retreat. General Pershing awarded him a posthumous medal for bravery, the Silver Star.

Marcus Hammer returned to Fort Chambers a war hero. He married Aura de Bretteville, but had the marriage annulled when she insisted on naming their dark-skinned child Gabriella. Hammer quickly remarried and, with Judge Hammer's backing, was elected Mayor on a segregation platform. In 1919, spurred by the race riots then taking place across the country, "Dynamite" Hammer was elected to the state legislature. On his father's death, he was appointed County Judge.

Aura de Bretteville moved to Washington, D.C. where she and Gabriel Scriven raised the child, although they lived in separate residences. After Gabriel's death, Aura and General Pershing petitioned to have Gabriel buried in Arlington National Cemetery. Their requests were not granted.

Touch-the-Cloud was mustered out as a sergeant, since no Indian had yet held officer's rank. He returned to the Pine Ridge Reservation where he was first a teacher, then headmaster of the Indian School. Eventually fired for advocating classes in Lakota, he led a protest against a new rail line that would cross sacred burial grounds. He died in 1925 while sitting on the tracks to stop an oncoming locomotive. No photograph of him can be found, nor can the daguerreotype of Crazy Horse he once carried.

Snake survived Cuba and the near fatal conditions at Camp Wickoff, Long Island. Despite warnings from Colonel Roosevelt, he used his considerable gambling winnings to buy twenty acres of Nevada desert. He lived there alone until 1950, when a Las Vegas developer paid him an undisclosed amount for his land. Shortly after a 1958 radio interview, during which he praised Cuban rebel leader Fidel Castro, he disappeared with his fortune.

Theodore Roosevelt published *The Rough Riders* soon after his return to New York. He was elected Governor of New York in 1899. Despite his many efforts to obtain a Medal of Honor, Secretary Alger refused to approve it, probably because of Roosevelt's criticism of War Department logistics during the war. Roosevelt was elected Vice President during McKinley's second administration, becoming President in 1901 when McKinley was assassinated. Roosevelt was reelected in 1906. He recalled the Rough Riders for rallies and parades, but his critical comments and dishonorable discharge of Negro soldiers who defended themselves in Brownsville, Texas, cost him the black vote. In 1917, when America finally entered World War I, Roosevelt asked President Woodrow Wilson to let him raise a regiment of volunteers, but was refused. His youngest son, Quentin Roosevelt, was killed in France in 1918. In 1919, Roosevelt was again planning to run for president when he died at his home in Oyster Bay.

Although he did not live to see it, the medal Roosevelt felt he deserved was evnetually earned by his oldest son. General Theodore Roosevelt, Jr., was awarded the Medal of Honor posthumously for his part in the World War II D-Day landing.

Leonard Wood was appointed Military Governor of Santiago after the alcoholism of the first governor, General Lawton. Wood's administration was considered a model for its lasting effectiveness. While Governor, Wood seriously injured his head on a chandelier. He later served in the Philippines, where he led a massacre against 900 Muslim Moro rebels who were hiding in an extinct volcano. Roosevelt, on becoming president, appointed Wood Governor of the Philippines, where one of his aides was the young Douglas MacArthur. In 1910, Wood finally realized his lifelong dream: he became Army Chief of Staff under President Taft. He died in 1927 of a brain tumor, thought to be a result of his untreated head injury suffered while still in Santiago.

Maximillian Luna became Leonard Wood's interpreter and aide during his governorship of Oriente Province. But soon he returned to Santa Fe, where he served briefly as Speaker of the New Mexico House of Representatives. When fighting flared up with Philippine rebels, Luna enlisted in the Thirty-Fourth Volunteer Infantry as a Lieutenant. He was killed in the discharge of his duties in the Philippines on November 18, 1898. Luna's bronze bust stands in the rotunda of the State Capitol in Santa Fe, New Mexico.

John G. Pershing commanded all U.S. troops in Europe during World War I. Despite his many honors, General Pershing proudly carried the nickname given him while he commanded a troop of the Tenth Cavalry, "Blackjack" Pershing.

Hamilton Fish's younger cousin, Nathan Fish commanded the most decorated American regiment of World War I, a black regiment whose sergeant was Eli Biddle's son.

Tom Hall was given an honorable medical discharge by Colonel Roosevelt on August 1, 1898. He never fully recovered from fever, nor the accusations of cowardice made against him at Las Guásimas. Helped by Second Lieutenant Frank Hayes of L Troop, he wrote *The Fun and Fighting of the Rough Riders,* which was published in New York in 1899. As Hall predicted, Roosevelt's *Rough Riders* eclipsed his book, which never went to a second printing. Hall died of alcoholism and sunstroke in Hannibal, Missouri on August 21, 1900. Eventually, his name was added to the officer's roll on the Rough Rider monument in Arlington National Cemetery.

William Tiffany was promoted to Lieutenant, only to die of fever in Camp Wickoff, Long Island.

Ed Marshall lost one leg and the use of the other. In 1899, he published *The Story of the Rough Riders.*

Charles Johnson Post, artist and private in the New York Seventy-First, survived the fever and wrote *The Little War of Private Post.*

General Joseph Wheeler was appointed commander of Camp Wickoff, where he defended the sanitary and medical conditions that caused the death of so many quarantined veterans. He later served in the Philippines campaign. Wheeler was present for the opening of Congress in December of 1898, but was denied his old seat, since it required he resign his commission as a Brigadier General in the regular Army. Wheeler retired to his native Alabama, and died in

Brooklyn, New York January 25, 1906, at the age of 70. As his will stipulated, he was buried in his regulation blue uniform in Arlington National Cemetery, close to the former home of Robert E. Lee.

Richard Harding Davis continued as a war correspondent, novelist, and *bon vivant*. He remained critical of General Shafter and Lieutenant Hall in pronouncements and writings. His good looks made him the male escort and model for the popular Gibson Girl illustrations of Charles Dana Gibson.

Stephen Crane died of tuberculosis in 1900. His novel, *The Red Badge of Courage,* and his short stories, "The Open Boat" and "The Blue Hotel," have become literary classics.

Tom Isbell recovered from his wounds and joined Buffalo Bill's Wild West Show.

Eli Biddle saw many of his comrades in the Negro regiments sicken and die of fever, thus disproving the immunity theory. Disgusted by the treatment that black soldiers received on their return, he refused to reenlist. In 1906, President Roosevelt ordered dishonorable discharge of 167 black soldiers after a confrontation with a white mob. Eli Biddle began a protest movement about his action.

Sylvester Scovel was never prosecuted for attacking General Shafter. Along with Stephen Crane and Mark Twain, he joined the Anti-Imperialist League, a group of intellectuals who published articles against America's expansionist policies in Cuba, Puerto Rico, and the Pacific.

General Calixto García retreated with his troops into the Sierra Maestra. Broken in spirit, he resigned his command and died of a mistreatment for pneumonia in New York on December 11,

1898. The American Generals arranged a funeral parade and gave him temporary burial with full military honors, including a twenty-one gun salute, in Arlington National Cemetery, near the mast of the battleship Maine.

Colonel Raúl García's body disappeared. To this day, Cubans claim the very name Spanish-American War implies that they were not even present. The Cubans call this war their Second War of Independence, or The Spanish-Cuban-North American War.

San Juan Hill remains intact behind the Villa San Juan Hotel. In the park at the top, a half-scale blockhouse has been reconstructed. Two Remingtonesque bronze sculptures guard the summit. The bronze plaque on the stone base of the *Yanqui* sculpture has been torn off, the locals say, by vandals. A sculpture of a resolute *mambi* retains the original bronze lettering testifying to the bravery of the Cuban fighters. The forward gun turret of the Spanish *Reina Mercedes* is set at the entrance to the park. At the other end, the Sims-Dudly dynamite gun serves as a see-saw .

The Spanish have never forgotten their loss of Cuba, which to them, symbolized the end of a glorious empire. Many of the returning Spanish soldiers died of fever. Most of them are buried in a special cemetery in Barcelona. Even today in Madrid, when someone has been robbed or suffered a material loss, they shrug and say *"Perdimos mas en Cuba,"*— "We lost more in Cuba."

No Rough Rider volunteer ever received his pay.

PHOTOGRAPHS

by Al Gowan, March 1998

Front cover,
Bronze sculpture of American trooper
San Juan Hill

Back cover, page 272
The wreck of the *Viscaya*
at Playa Aserradero

Back cover, page 8
Bronze sculpture of a Cuban *mambi*
San Juan Hill

Page 98
Sierra Maestra near Daiquirí

Page 162
Gúasima tree, or Cuban Elm

Page 216
Approaching *La Gran Piedra*

COLOPHON

This book has been set in ITC Galliard
Designed by Matthew Carter in 1982

and in the display typeface Neuland
Designed by Rudolf Koch for the Klingspor
foundry in 1923

Book design by Al Gowan
using a series of ever more powerful,
smaller laptops. Each had the wonderful
quality of a book—a cover to close when finished.